# DESTINED TO LOVE

"You didn't have to come after me," Rachel said without turning.

"I wanted to come."

Her pulse picked up its pace. "Why?"

He stepped closer, his expression unreadable.

"What do you want?" She was breathless as he came closer. She glanced toward the house, but everyone else had stayed inside.

"Must I say it?" he asked. "Or shall I show you?"

"Please . . . I don't know what you want from me."

"What I want and what I must not have are one and the same."

His dark eyes glittered in the dim light. She found herself remembering the excitement of his kiss.

She swayed toward him. "Black Hawk."

He took her into his arms. He murmured something in Ojibwa, and then he kissed her. Her head spun as the world rocked beneath her feet . . . .

Books by Candace McCarthy

SWEET POSSESSION
WHITE BEAR'S WOMAN
IRISH LINEN
HEAVEN'S FIRE
SEA MISTRESS
RAPTURE'S BETRAYAL
WARRIOR'S CARESS
SMUGGLER'S WOMAN

With stories in these anthologies

AFFAIRS OF THE HEART
BABY IN A BASKET

Published by Zebra Books

# WILD INNOCENCE

## Candace McCarthy

Zebra Books
Kensington Publishing Corp.

http://www.zebrabooks.com

ZEBRA BOOKS are published by

Kensington Publishing Corp.
850 Third Avenue
New York, NY 10022

First Printing: October, 1999
10  9  8  7  6  5  4  3  2

Printed in the United States of America

To my writer friends . . .
for your friendship and support, and good humor.
*What would I do without you?*

# Prologue

*Baltimore, Maryland*
*Spring, 1838*

Organ music filled the interior of the church as Rachel Dempsey began the long walk down the aisle to the altar. Today she was marrying the man of her dreams—Jordan Jonathan Sinclair II. Finally, she'd found someone who touched her heart in a way that no other man ever had before. She'd had a lot of suitors, but they all paled in comparison to Jordan. This was the happiest day of her life.

The Methodist church was filled to overflowing with people who had come to see the young couple married. Rachel tried to see Jordan near the altar, but she was too far away to pick him out of the group of men up front. She glanced at George Bentley, her Aunt Bess's latest admirer, who had been pleased when asked if he'd give the bride away. She smiled at him briefly, before looking ahead toward the altar.

Her heart thumped harder with each step she took toward the front of the church. Again, Rachel tried to see her betrothed, but she could barely see past her happy tears.

Rachel heard murmurs from the crowd that filled the church pews.

*"She looks beautiful."*

*"Have you ever seen a lovelier bride?"*

*"Jordan is a lucky man."*

*"They make a handsome couple together."*

Rachel knew that she looked her best in the ivory and blue-sprigged satin gown, fashioned by an expert seamstress to perfectly drape her frame. Her chestnut-brown hair was pinned up, but a few curling tendrils had been left unfastened to soften the style. She wore a crown of daisies and spring blossoms. She'd wanted to be a beautiful bride for Jordan.

*Oh, Father,* Rachel thought, *how I wish you and Amelia were here so everything could be perfect.*

She wanted nothing more than to have her father and her sister present to share this special day, but John and Amelia Dempsey were several weeks' journey away, in the Wisconsin Territory, where John Dempsey had taken his physician's skills to a religious mission near Lake Superior. They had been gone for almost two years, and it had been several months since Rachel or her Aunt Bess had heard from them. The wedding plans had come about so quickly there hadn't been time to wait for her family's answer to Rachel's letter. She wished desperately that her father and sister would miraculously appear in church.

As if sensing her thoughts, George Bentley squeezed her arm with affection. Rachel smiled at the kindly gentleman, glad that she had someone as nice as him to take her father's place.

The organ music continued to resound inside the building, and Rachel blinked to clear her vision. Where was Jordan? She couldn't see him ahead.

*He must be standing off to the side, waiting for me.* As she reached the altar, the music faltered. She felt a flutter of panic. *Jordan?* Where was he?

Rachel looked toward the side vestibule at the front of the church, but there was no sign of her intended.

Suddenly, the music stopped completely, and the silence was filled with the thumping of Rachel's heart. Her steps faltered as she heard the people shuffling in their seats. She swallowed hard as several attendees turned in their pews to stare at her.

Someone coughed. A fly droned near her left ear. Rachel heard whispers from the crowd. She glanced at George, who looked startled.

The music began to play again. George patted her arm in reassurance. Drawing a deep breath, Rachel focused her gaze straight ahead as she and George continued to stand at the altar.

The organist ceased playing again. A flurry of movement behind her had her turning, and with relief, she saw Aunt Bess. Her stomach burned when she met her aunt's gaze, then noted the piece of parchment in Bess Dempsey's left hand.

"What is it?" she asked, looking at the missive as Bess arrived at her side. "Has something happened?"

Bess nodded, her expression solemn. "Come with me, child," she said softly as she took her niece's arm. Then she addressed the minister, who stood waiting patiently for the appearance of the groom. "If you will pardon us for a moment, Reverend?"

The Reverend Felcher nodded, and Bess escorted Rachel to the room off to the right side.

"What's wrong?" Rachel cried, as soon as her aunt had shut the door. "Where is Jordan?"

"My dear, there's no way to explain this gently. I am so sorry."

"Has something terrible happened to Jordan?" Rachel's chest tightened as she pictured her beloved in a carriage accident, lying bleeding and injured, and fighting for his life. She felt the blood drain from her face. "He's not . . . *dead?*"

A myriad of expressions flitted across her aunt's face as Bess touched Rachel's arm. "No, dear. Jordan is very much alive," she said with a hint of anger.

Rachel grabbed at her aunt's hand. *"What is it then?"*

"He's not coming."

She felt the room sway. "Not coming?"

Fury flashed in Bess Dempsey's blue gaze. "He sent this note."

Rachel found it suddenly difficult to breathe. "I don't understand." She felt her knees buckle, and her aunt grabbed her and set her carefully in a chair.

"I'm sorry, child," Bess said huskily, her eyes filling with tears. "This wasn't how I pictured this day to end for you."

"Aunt Bess!"

Bess bent to hug her niece tightly. "It appears, Rachel, that despite all his fancy talk and promises of undying love, your betrothed has changed his mind. He's eloped with the Widow Nanette. Apparently, the selfish, silver-tongued devil has decided to forgo marrying for love in favor of marrying for cold, hard coin."

"No!" Rachel cried. "Tell me it's not true!" She stood and started for the door, but Bess grabbed her arm. "It's a lie," Rachel insisted. "He's out there waiting for me now!" She clutched her aunt's shoulders. "Please tell me it's not true!" Teardrops overflowed to spill onto her cheeks.

"I can't tell you what you want to hear," Bess said in

a choked voice. "I'm so sorry, sweetheart." She was unable to control her tears.

Organ music once again began to play, filling the church and filtering inside the tiny room. At the sound, Rachel turned to stare blankly at the door. "Not coming," she whispered. "He's really not coming."

She slumped back onto her chair, buried her face in her hands, and began to sob uncontrollably.

# Chapter 1

"I'll be going away—far away. You have a life here with George. I don't expect you to come with me."

"Don't be ridiculous, Rachel!" Aunt Bess cried. "You can't just run off to be by yourself!"

Rachel didn't answer immediately. Seated before her vanity table, she studied her reflection with a critical eye. The young woman who gazed back at her seemed a stranger. She had Rachel's chestnut-brown hair coloring and eyes of green, but her face was paler than usual. Her eyes appeared larger, like a frightened doe's. Where once Rachel had been sure of her looks, suddenly she felt confident no longer. Her nose was too small, her lips too large and lush, and her eyes too bright. Rachel saw nothing of her own natural beauty in the mirror this day; she was conscious only of her flaws.

"Rachel!"

"I have to leave, Aunt Bess," Rachel said, her heart beating hard within her chest. "I've been humiliated before everyone. Now, I find that some of the people I considered my friends are enjoying my discomfort. It's bad enough that I had to face the crowd at the church alone.'' The memory of those embarrassing, painful moments after she'd been jilted renewed her tears. It had been days since the fiasco at the church, but the shame of it lingered.

A tinge of bitterness crept into her tone as she continued. ''Jordan is away on his honeymoon.'' Rachel closed her eyes a moment and fought the surge of pain. ''When he returns with his new bride, the talk and the rumors will only worsen. There's nothing for me in Baltimore now . . . except you, and I'll miss you terribly. But it hurts too much to live here.''

''But where will you go?'' her aunt asked with concern.

Rachel met Bess's alarmed gaze in the mirror. ''I'll join Father and Amelia at the mission.''

''But that's a terribly long way! Surely, no journey for a young woman to attempt on her own.'' She set her jaw. ''I'll go with you.''

But Rachel was determined that her aunt should stay. ''No, you will not. You have a life here. You're happy in Baltimore.'' She turned in her chair to face Bess. ''I'll hire someone to take me.''

''Who?'' Bess demanded.

''I don't know!'' Rachel exclaimed. ''But I'll not stay!'' She'd rather brave the wilderness all alone than stay and face such humiliation again.

''I know someone who can take her,'' a soft feminine voice said from the far side of the room.

The two women turned to gaze at Miranda Clark. She smiled as she approached them.

''And just who is that?'' Bess asked.

''My uncle. He travels that territory. I'm sure he'll be happy to escort Rachel.''

For the first time in two days, Rachel's eyes gleamed. "He will?"

Miranda nodded, looking pleased. "Absolutely."

"And you? Will you accompany me, Miranda?" Rachel asked. She considered Miranda Clark her one and only true friend.

Miranda looked genuinely surprised by the question. "I don't know . . ." She looked thoughtful as she considered the idea.

*"Please,* Miranda."

"I—" Her hazel eyes suddenly twinkled as she approached. "All right, I'll go. I've always enjoyed an adventure, but Rachel, don't expect me to stay out there. My family will want me to return."

"Of course they will." Rachel managed to grin. "I appreciate that you'll accompany me. We'll have a wonderful time." She feigned cheerfulness as she looked at her aunt. "There, Aunt Bess, now there is no cause for concern. Everything's all taken care of. Miranda and I will be escorted to Wisconsin by Miranda's uncle."

Aunt Bess nodded, but appeared uncertain still. "When can I meet him?"

"Uncle Rupert?" Miranda said, her voice rising suddenly. "He's not in Baltimore, I'm afraid. He lives in a small village in Pennsylvania. The only way you'd be able to make his acquaintance is if you come with us."

"Surely, it's not necessary that you meet the man, Aunt Bess," Rachel said after catching a meaningful glance from her friend. "After all, he is Miranda's kin."

Aunt Bess frowned. "I don't know—"

"Don't you trust us, Auntie?" Rachel asked.

Bess looked shocked by the question. "Of course I do!"

"Do you think Miranda and I would go with the man if Miranda didn't think he could keep us safe?"

"Well, no . . ."

"Excellent!" Rachel exclaimed. "Then it's all set. We leave for Wisconsin as soon as it can be arranged!"

Grudgingly, Rachel's aunt agreed, before she left the two young women alone in her niece's bedchamber.

Rachel wondered why Miranda didn't want Aunt Bess to meet Rupert Clark. "What's wrong with your uncle?" she asked her friend.

"Nothing really, he's a dear man, and I trust him implicitly, but—"

"But?"

"His appearance is not one to inspire confidence in your aunt. She'd take one hard look at him and promptly demand that you remain at home."

"He's that bad?"

"He looks like a woodsman," Miranda explained.

*A woodsman,* Rachel thought a week and a half later. *Miranda wasn't joking when she said that Rupert Clark looks like a woodsman,* she decided as she studied the unkempt, bearded individual whom Miranda had introduced as Uncle Rupert.

Rachel had been more than mildly shocked when she'd met him, wondering how a man this grizzly and unkempt could be even remotely related to her well-kept, pretty friend. But then she had gazed long and hard into his twinkling blue eyes, and had been reassured immediately by the kindness she saw there. They'd been traveling with Rupert for two days now, and Rachel's respect and admiration for Rupert Clark had only grown.

"Mr. Clark?"

The man turned and focused his blue gaze on her.

"How much farther is it to the Wisconsin Territory?" she asked. "Not that I mind the trip," she said, although she did. "I was just wondering."

Rupert tugged on his gray beard with tobacco-stained fingers. "Well, lass, that depends on whether or not we encounter any Injuns."

"Indians!" she gasped. "You mean we may actually see savages?"

"Better not call them that to their faces. Some take mighty exception to the term."

"Do they speak English?" Miranda asked, her eyes widening with surprise.

The old man faced his niece. "Some. Especially the ones who reside near the mission." He looked back at Rachel with a half smile. "Why did you think your father went to the mission? Just to doctor some missionaries?"

"I—ah—I guess I never gave it much thought." Rachel blushed, knowing how selfish she sounded. Her father and sister had left to live in the wilderness, and Rachel had been more interested in the impact their leaving would have on her life than in the safety and interests of her family. She'd been so caught up in her own life that she'd given no consideration to her father and sister's feelings or fears.

*I miss them,* she thought. She missed the long talks she used to have with Amelia, confiding in her sister, sharing dreams. She missed seeing the way her father's eyes would light up with pleasure whenever she walked into a room dressed up for a ball or party.

The decision to join her family was the right one. They loved her. They would understand and help soothe away the pain she'd suffered because of Jordan.

Rachel vowed to be more aware of her family's needs in the future. She felt a small smile settle on her lips at the prospect of being with those she loved. She couldn't wait to see Father and Amelia.

*          *          *

They traveled for days by carriage, by rail, by boat, then finally by wagon. Their accommodations along the way were by no means luxurious, but they were suitable, Rachel decided. They stayed at inns, hotels, and private residences of people who knew Rupert Clark. She and Miranda had suffered no ill effects from the hours of traveling, but Rachel wanted the trip to be over. Each day that saw her farther and farther from Baltimore, and the life she'd enjoyed until recently, made her heart ache. She found herself of late recalling her time with Jordan, her happiness when she'd been with him, how excited she'd been when he'd asked her to marry him.

The landscape blurred as tears filled her eyes. Why had Jordan asked her to marry him if he'd had no intention of following through?

*The widow Nanette.* Rachel had a mental image of a woman with dark curly hair, a white complexion heavy with perfumed face powder and rouge, and a large beauty mark on her chin. *An ugly mole, it is.* She felt guilty thinking it, but for only a moment. It actually felt good to feel anger instead of pain.

Rachel still couldn't believe that Jordan had chosen that woman over her. Not after he'd kissed and held her as if no other woman in the world existed for him.

*I'm a fool,* she thought. Thank goodness she'd had sense enough to keep her virginity for the marriage bed. *Something that Jordan will never have from me now. Something the widow had given up long before she'd ever met Jordan.* But now the widow had used her own experience with men to seduce and lure away Rachel's betrothed.

Pain lanced within Rachel's breast, making her stomach hurt and her head spin. She had to forget Jordan. She didn't need him. In fact, she didn't need any man. Her sister didn't have a husband or lover. She didn't need— or want—one either.

A teardrop escaped to drip onto Rachel's cheek, and she quickly dashed it away before Miranda or her uncle could see it. *I have a new life to lead. Father and Amelia will need help at the mission. I'll be happy dedicating my life to helping others.* She tried not to think of the husband she'd almost had and the children she would never conceive.

*I'll stay a virgin. The whole thing about the marriage bed sounded a little frightening anyway.*

She sighed. But she would have liked to try it, at least, just once.

As the morning wore on, Rachel's traveling party ventured into the wilderness with forests and scenery more rugged and beautiful than any they'd encountered before. As the trees thickened, and Rupert steered the wagon along a narrow path that was just large enough for the conveyance, Rachel studied her surroundings with unease.

"Is this Indian country?" she asked Rupert in a hushed voice.

"Yep," he replied without looking at her.

Rachel glanced in the back of the wagon, and was only slightly reassured by the sight of Rupert's double-barreled rifle lying behind the man's end of the seat. She wanted to ask Miranda's uncle if he knew how to use the weapon, but she knew it would be a foolish question. It was obvious that the man had to be an excellent marksman to have survived this long in this wilderness.

"Are the Indians friendly, Uncle Rupert?" Miranda asked.

"Some are, some aren't," Rupert replied.

Rachel saw that her friend wasn't concerned.

*Why can't I be like Miranda? Instead I'm nervous and*

*scared. Miranda must truly believe in her uncle's ability to keep us safe.*

"Are we in any danger?" Rachel asked.

"Life is dangerous," he said. "A lightning strike in a storm. A carriage accident on a busy street."

She sensed Miranda's gaze and turned to look at her. "Aren't you worried?"

Miranda nodded. "Of course I am. But, I also know my uncle. He's the best there is. We'll be safe enough until we reach the mission."

That night they camped out in the open for the first time. Rupert found a clearing beneath a stand of trees. There he instructed the young women to spread their sleeping pallets.

"I don't like this," Rachel muttered to Miranda as she unrolled the quilts that would serve as her bed that night. "There are wild animals out there. What if one of them comes and eats us in the night?"

Rupert hooted with laughter from a short distance away. "I don't reckon you'll sleep through it if one does!" Chuckling, the man walked back to the wagon to unload some supplies.

"Miranda, I'm scared."

"Don't worry. Uncle Rupert will watch out for us while we sleep. He'll build a fire to keep the animals away."

"But when will he sleep?" *And the Indians?* she thought. *What will keep the savages away?*

Miranda shrugged. "He'll probably nap some of the time, I suppose. But he's a very light sleeper," she quickly assured her frightened friend.

Rupert shot a rabbit for dinner. After a meal of rabbit stew, he told the girls stories as they sat around the camp-fire, while dusk turned into the darkness of night. Despite her initial fear of sleeping out in the wild, Rachel found herself caught up in Uncle Rupert's tale of the time he'd spent five days with Indians. Every once in a while, the sounds of the night invaded Rachel's sense of peace. When an owl hooted in the distance, Rupert paused in the middle of the tale to announce what the sound was, then promptly went back to his storytelling. After several such occasions, Rachel no longer started when she heard a new forest sound. She listened with rapt interest to Miranda's uncle as he related the story of one adventure after another.

"You young ladies had best turn in," Rupert said after finishing his fifth story. "We've a long day ahead of us tomorrow."

Rachel's heart thumped hard as she nodded and stood. "Good night, Mr. Clark. Thank you for sharing your stories with us."

Rupert nodded. "My pleasure, Miss Dempsey."

"Please call me Rachel. It's strange, but I suddenly feel as if I've known you a long time."

"I'm glad," he said, while Miranda beamed at the both of them. "I'd be pleased if you'd call me Uncle Rupert like my Miranda here."

Rachel smiled. "Good night, Uncle Rupert."

"Good night, Rachel. Good night, Miranda."

After the last exchange of good nights, Rachel and Miranda climbed into their bedrolls. Rupert stoked up the fire, then with his rifle across his lap, sat and kept watch.

It didn't take Rachel long to get comfortable, a fact that surprised her. She lay, staring at the lush canopy of green foliage overhead, looking for a glimpse of the stars in a break in the trees. That night the moon was bright and was nearly full. The light and Rupert's presence had a calming effect on her, and soon she closed her eyes to get some sleep.

Later, she wasn't sure what had woken her, but she felt no alarm as she opened her eyes and saw that it was still night. The sound of wood in the fire crackling and popping convinced her that Rupert was awake and at watch. Reassured, Rachel rolled over and went back to sleep without glancing at him.

A while later, she felt something in her hair—a light touch that dragged her from the depths of sleep. Believing that a breeze had begun to stir the forest, she opened her eyes, then gasped at the sight of an Indian standing above her. The savage was clad in only a loincloth with leggings. His dark eyes glinted in the darkness as he stared down at her. His hair was black and hung past his shoulders. In the moonlight, his face looked as if it had been etched from raw earth. A copper band encircled his upper right arm. Her heart stopped, then beat faster, as she saw the knife in his right hand. Terrified, unable to move or scream, she could only gaze back at the brave.

Rachel caught her breath as the Indian crouched at her side and lifted a lock of her unbound hair. The brave grunted with pleasure as he tugged on the silky strands.

She began to tremble with fear. "What do you want?" she whispered.

His gaze narrowing, the Indian rose. Rachel was afraid to look away, toward Miranda and her uncle, terrified that she might find he'd already murdered them.

She sat up slowly, carefully. "What do you want? Please, can't you just leave us alone!"

*"Gichi-mookomaanikwe."*

"I don't understand! What do you want?" She started to rise. The brave raised his knife threateningly, and she lowered herself to the ground again. He mumbled something in his strange tongue, and Rachel shook her head to tell him that she didn't understand him.

Was the brave alone? She saw no other figures in the dark.

Her gaze went quickly back to the Indian. "What do you want from us?"

His grin was a flash of white in his dark face. *"Gichimookomaanikwe."*

He bent again, and she closed her eyes in expectation of his hurting her. But all she felt was the gentlest touch on her cheek, a caress that made her shiver and nearly cry out.

When she opened her eyes again, he was gone, and she wondered if she'd actually seen the man, or if she'd simply been dreaming.

She glanced toward where her two friends had been sleeping, and was amazed to see that they continued to sleep peacefully, blissfully unaware of the Indian's visit.

She got up and grabbed Rupert's gun, telling herself that she would fire the weapon at the Indian if he returned.

Her heart thumping, her eyes wide, she lay down again. When she awoke next, the morning sun was bright in a clear, cloudless sky, and her traveling companions were eating breakfast.

"Did you sleep well?" Miranda asked upon seeing her friend rise.

"For part of the night." Rachel paused and bit her lip. "You didn't hear or sense anyone here last night?"

Miranda smiled. "Like an Indian or a wild animal?"

Rachel blinked. "Yes!"

"No." Miranda frowned. "No, of course I didn't. Why do you ask? Did you?"

Rachel glanced about, and saw that there was nothing that suggested their nighttime visitor had been real. "No, I didn't see or hear anyone."

Miranda glanced down and saw the gun near Rachel's sleeping pallet. "Isn't that my uncle's rifle?"

She felt a jolt. Her cheeks brightening, Rachel nodded. If she'd been dreaming, when did she pick up Rupert's rifle? "All right," she admitted reluctantly, "so I thought I heard something last night."

"Oh, Rachel . . ."

"I've never slept out in a forest before," she said in defense.

"I told you, Uncle Rupert will keep us safe."

"What if I said that I saw an Indian last night?"

Miranda looked skeptical. "And he just quietly left— is that it?" She smiled. "And I suppose he didn't want to wake us."

Rachel did think it seemed odd that an Indian would come and leave so quickly and quietly. She must have dreamed his visit . . . and the way he'd touched her face and hair.

As the day wore on, Rachel couldn't stop thinking about her dream. What if it had been real? What if for some strange reasons of his own, a real Indian had come into their camp, stared at them while they slept, then having been caught in the act, left because he'd had no other members of his tribe to help him take prisoners.

The image of the man was so clear in her thoughts. She couldn't control the quick little thump of her heart as she recalled his dark hair and eyes, his powerful, lithe form. *For a savage, he wasn't too terrible to look at.*

A handsome Indian? *I'm going crazy,* she thought. *I'm delirious from the journey.* Perhaps Jordan's betrayal had not only broken her heart, but robbed her of her sanity!

# Chapter 2

A mist enshrouded the domed wigwams of the Indian village as Black-Hawk-Who-Hunts-at-Dawn and his small band of Ojibwa men returned home. They had been gone for a fortnight, after journeying to the village of their Ojibwa brothers to the east. Their common enemy, the Sioux, had attacked the eastern encampment, and Black Hawk, the war chief in his tribe, had left quickly to offer aid to the community.

It was dawn, and his people were just stirring. The scent of smoke clung to the damp air as the women added fuel to their cooking fires. A dog barked from the opposite end of the village. A child began to whimper from inside one of the huts, and a mother's voice answered soothingly.

Black Hawk absorbed the sights and sounds from afar before entering the village clearing. He didn't wait for his band of men to follow him as he headed for the wigwam of the chief, Big-Cat-with-Broken-Paw. He knew his brothers were as anxious to converse with the chief as he was.

A young golden-haired girl emerged from a wigwam as Black Hawk came abreast of the structure. Her eyes lit up when she saw him. "Black Hawk! You're back!" She launched herself into the warrior's arms. "It's so good to see you!"

"It is good to see you also, Little Flower," he said, surprised by her presence. "You are growing like a weed! Are you here visiting Barking Dog alone, or did my friend Dan-yel come with you?"

The child was the niece of his white friend, Daniel Trahern. She sometimes came to stay with her friend Barking Dog and the child's grandmother, Swaying Tree.

"My family is here with me."

Black Hawk smiled with pleasure. "Tell Dan-yel that I will seek him out as soon as I meet with Big-Cat-with-Broken-Paw."

The girl nodded, then ran to another wigwam, which she entered. Black Hawk continued toward the hut of his chief.

The chief's wigwam was like the others within the village. The dome-shaped structure was constructed of bent saplings covered with birch bark. A deer hide draped the doorway. Black Hawk called out a greeting. Invited to enter, he raised the door flap and went inside. He greeted the inhabitants of the lodge.

The chief was seated on a mat near the fire. His wife was serving up a bowl of corn porridge for him. "Ah, Black Hawk," Big-Cat-with-Broken-Paw said, "you have returned. Good, good!"

Black Hawk smiled at the man's wife and sat near the fire. His expression grew solemn as he returned his attention to his leader.

"You have much to tell me," the chief said.

The warrior nodded. "Our enemy has destroyed White Fox's village. Only four of our brother warriors have survived. The attackers have taken the women and children."

The chief scowled. "The Sioux will pay for this!" he barked angrily.

"But that is not all," Black Hawk said. "They have continued their trail of destruction to the village of Red Nose just south of our brother White Fox. The women and children managed to escape, but . . ." He felt a flash of all consuming anger. "They murdered Red Nose."

"No!" Big-Cat-with-Broken-Paw cried.

"It is so," Black Hawk assured him. He felt a swish of air behind him as someone raised the door flap. His brothers Thunder Oak and Rain-from-Sky entered, followed by the chief's son, Gray Squirrel.

"Black Hawk speaks the truth," Thunder Oak said as he, too, sat by the fire. "The Sioux have murdered more of our people and kidnapped our women and children. It is time we seek out our enemy and put a stop to the killing."

"We must have a council meeting," the chief said. "This decision cannot be made quickly."

"It *must* be made quickly!" Gray Squirrel exclaimed. "Until we attack, our enemy will continue to hurt and kill our people. Red Nose did nothing to provoke the Sioux attack. His death and the deaths of his people must be avenged!"

"Gray Squirrel," Black Hawk said with patience, "I, more than you, want vengeance against the Sioux, but our chief is right. We must have a council meeting." He hated the Sioux. A band of Sioux warriors had tortured and murdered his father when he was only eight years old. It was something that he would never forget. Someday, he would find the leader of that band, who had killed his father in cold blood, and he would make him pay for all the pain and suffering and loss to his father, himself, and his people. It was often the driving force of his day.

"We shall meet in council in five days," Big-Cat-with-Broken-Paw said.

"Five days!" Gray Squirrel exclaimed.

"What matter is five days?" Thunder Oak said. "Our chief—your father—and my brother are right. We must plan to win, and such things are not easily accomplished."

"We must invite our brothers to the north and our Ottawa friends as well," Rain-from-Sky said.

All the Indians agreed. "I will send a messenger," the chief said.

"I will visit our Ottawa brother, Great Deer," Thunder Oak offered.

Big-Cat-with-Broken-Paw nodded. "Good. Rain-from-Sky, would you go to our brothers in the north?"

"I shall be honored to go there," the brave answered.

"And you, Black Hawk," the chief said, "you have some special visitors. Perhaps Dan-yel Trahern will help us as he has done before."

"I'm sure of it, Grandfather."

The meeting ended, and Black Hawk followed the others from the chief's wigwam. He headed toward the wigwam of the matron Swaying Tree, knowing instinctively that he would find Little Flower there.

"Black Hawk." Daniel Trahern's voice hailed him in Ojibwa from the direction of the forest.

Black Hawk turned and regarded his friend with delight. "You have fared well these last months, my friend."

"And you?" Daniel said. "You look well, but I hear there is much to worry you."

The brave inclined his head. "The Sioux have once again struck our people. Red Nose is dead; his village was destroyed. They have taken the women and children. Only a few braves have escaped.''

Daniel had no liking for the Sioux. They had kidnapped his wife's father. His sister had been a captive of the Sioux, although it had been white men—and not the Indians—who had attacked and raided Jane's cabin initially. Jane had lived among the Sioux for over four years. She was back with her family, residing in a small cottage not far from Daniel's house. The terrible experience had changed her and stolen her joy.

"What can I do to help?" Daniel asked.

Black Hawk grinned. "Your offer comes at the right time, my friend. We meet in council in five days. Can you stay that long?"

"We can stay."

Smiling, the Indian studied his friend. "I didn't expect to see you here so soon after your last visit."

"We came with special news." Daniel's eyes lit up like a child who'd been given a special treat. "I am to be a father. Tree-That-Will-Not-Bend is with child."

"Ayee!" Black Hawk exclaimed. "This is exciting news. Where is she?"

Daniel pointed toward a wigwam. "She rests in the lodge of Spring Blossom." Spring Blossom was Black Hawk's sister. Spring Blossom and Amelia Dempsey Trahern had become friends from their first meeting over two years ago when Daniel had brought Amelia to the village. John Dempsey had been kidnapped by the Sioux, and Amelia and Daniel had come to Black Hawk's village for assistance in rescuing Amelia's father.

"She is well?" Black Hawk asked. He had great respect for Daniel's wife. She was a strong and courageous woman. When a group of them had been captives of the Sioux, Amelia had risked her life so that the rest of them could escape.

"She is sturdy," Daniel said teasingly.

"Like a tree that will not bend," Black Hawk replied with a chuckle.

While in the village, Daniel had given Amelia the Indian name Tree-That-Will-Not-Bend, and she had rewarded him, in turn, with Man-with-Big-Head.

"Come," Black Hawk said. "We will not disturb your mate for now. She must rest for the babe. We will share a cool drink in my lodge."

He led the way to his wigwam. "Your sister Jane," he asked, "how is she?" He turned to see concern cross Daniel's face.

"She would not come. She is not happy. The kidnapping and her life with the Sioux have changed her."

"She will grow stronger. These bad memories will pass," Black Hawk said.

"It's been well over a year!" Daniel exclaimed.

Black Hawk's voice was quiet as he answered, "She has over four years of bad memories to forget. It will take time."

"I curse that scoundrel husband of hers!"

The brave nodded. Daniel's brother-in-law had been a mean bastard. A captain in the U.S. Army, he had used his authority to cause trouble for the Indians. He had organized a group of white men to attack white settlers, making it look as though Indians had done the nasty deed. He was a madman who hated the Ojibwa people, hated all the Indian people. Richard Milton had had his men raid his own cabin. Jane had been kidnapped, but his daughter Susie had managed to escape by hiding under her mother's bed. Later, Milton had held a group of them prisoner, including Amelia as well as Susie, Daniel, and Black Hawk himself.

Since the authorities had taken Richard Milton off to prison, they'd neither seen nor heard from him again.

Susie, Amelia, and the rest of Milton's prisoners had gotten over the incident, but Daniel's sister Jane was having a hard time forgetting the experience.

Black Hawk paused outside his wigwam and raised the door flap. "You have broken your fast?" he asked his friend while waving Daniel inside.

"No, actually I haven't."

"Then I shall have Spring Blossom prepare a meal for us," Black Hawk said.

"You have no woman of your own yet?" Daniel teased.

The brave shook his head, his expression solemn. "I am war chief for the Ojibwa. Until I find the Sioux who killed my father, there is no room in my heart for a wife."

"You haven't met the right one," Daniel said, as he entered the wigwam. "A man cannot help but love when the right woman steps into his path."

Black Hawk shrugged. "Perhaps my path has too many obstacles for any woman to walk it."


Rupert, Miranda, and Rachel got their first glimpse of civilization after traveling several days through the wilderness. The small settlement had a trading post, a blacksmith shop, a newly constructed inn, and a few private residences.

Rachel was never so glad to see a small hotel in her life. It had been several days since she'd last slept in a bed, and she needed to bathe and wash her garments.

The settlement was smaller than she'd hoped, but she was overjoyed at the sight of the trading post.

"How much farther is it to the mission?" she asked Rupert Clark as they headed toward the store.

"Under an hour," Rupert replied.

"Less than an hour!" Rachel exclaimed. "Why are we stopping here then?"

"For supplies," he said. "No sense going on, only to have to turn back tomorrow and head this way."

He stepped aside to allow Miranda and Rachel to precede him into the store. A bell jingled as Rupert closed the door behind them.

A man came out from the back room. "Why, hello!" He was an attractive fellow with jet-black hair and brown eyes. "What brings you to Keller's—why, Rupert Clark, you old goat, is that you?"

"In the flesh, Jack." Rupert grinned as they shook hands.

"What's brought you back to this neck of the woods?"

"Why, this little lady here, Jack." He smiled at Rachel. "Rachel, this is Jack Keller. He owns this sorry sight of a trading post. Jack, this is Rachel Dempsey. She's to be reunited with her kin."

Jack's eyes widened. "Dempsey? You're related to John Dempsey?"

Rachel nodded coolly. Jack Keller was a handsome man. Since Jordan's betrayal, she'd had no tolerance for attractive men. "He's my father."

"Then Amelia's your sister?" Jack asked.

"Apparently," she said with a touch of frost.

"Rachel!" Miranda gasped at her rudeness.

Contrite, Rachel blushed. "I'm sorry, Mr.—ah—Keller. I'm afraid I'm a bit tired from our journey." She managed to smile at him. "You know my father and sister?"

"Your sister's married to my best friend. They live in the house across the road. Daniel, her husband, is our resident blacksmith."

"You must be joking," Rachel said, shocked. "Amelia's not married. She neither wants nor needs a husband."

"Then, she must have changed her mind, 'cause she's now married to Daniel Trahern."

Rachel felt the blood drain from her face. "I don't believe it. She never wrote to tell me."

Miranda placed her hand on her friend's shoulder. "Perhaps she did, and you just didn't receive her letter."

"My father," Rachel said, "where is he?"

Jack Keller eyed her with concern. "He resides at the Whitely mission not far from here."

"Then it's true," she whispered. Amelia was married. How could she up and marry? Rachel felt betrayed again. A burning started in her stomach and spiraled outward. She was disappointed. She had convinced herself that she didn't need a man because Amelia didn't. But apparently she was wrong about her sister.

*Oh, Amelia, how could you marry without telling me?*

Rupert and Keller began to gather Rupert's list of requested supplies. Rachel turned away to stare at the wall, not seeing. She was suddenly besieged by doubts. She'd hoped that the three of them—Father, Amelia, and she—could live together happily in her father's house at the mission. But Amelia didn't need her, and Amelia had always been the one to help her father whenever he needed an assistant. Did Amelia still help her father? Or could Rachel ask to take Amelia's place?

Amelia was married! Rachel was flabbergasted. *How could you, Amelia! How could you!*

Amelia must have changed a great deal in the last two years. Rachel tried to imagine the type of man that her sister had married, and the image was a poor one.

*A blacksmith,* she thought with a shudder. She pictured the man covered with sweat and soot and smelling of horses.

Suddenly, she was nervous about seeing her family, wondering just how much they had changed since coming to live in this wilderness.

"Rachel?"

She turned at the touch on her arm. Miranda was studying her with concern. "Are you all right?" her friend asked.

Rachel bobbed her head. "Fine, fine."

"You're lying, Rachel Dempsey. I can tell when you lie. You get the strangest look on your face."

Rachel scowled. "I don't know what you mean, I'm not lying, and I most certainly don't have a strange look on my face!"

The bell on the shop door tinkled, and Rachel glanced back, wondering if she'd recognize her sister if she saw her.

Rachel knew at first glance that this wasn't Amelia. Her sister had brown hair and a shapely figure. The woman who entered had blond hair and a small, thin frame. Her blue eyes wore a haunted look.

"Jane," she heard Jack Keller say, "is something wrong?"

"Has Daniel come back yet?"

Jack shook his head. "He's due back at anytime. Is there something I can do for you?"

"No. No, I'm fine. Thank you for asking." Jane turned to leave with nothing more to say.

Rachel had watched the exchange with curiosity. "Who is she?"

Jack looked embarrassed. "Jane! Come back. There are people I'd like you to meet." He addressed Rachel quietly. "She's your brother-in-law's sister."

Looking reluctant to be introduced, Jane approached.

"Jane, this young lady is Rachel Dempsey. She's Amelia's sister."

Astonishment came and flickered in her eyes. "You're Amelia's sister?" she said as if it couldn't possibly be true.

"Yes, I am." Rachel tried to smile. "I'm sorry, but

I'm a bit taken aback about all this. I had no idea that Amelia had even married." She looked away as tears filled her eyes.

She felt overwhelmed by the events that had recently changed her life. She wanted nothing more than to be alone to deal with this new, unwelcome news. "Is there somewhere we can bathe and rest?" she asked Jack Keller.

"There's the hotel next door. Rebb Colfax's daughter from back East just opened her," Jack said.

Rachel blinked. Of course, the inn! How could she have forgotten? Because she'd been shaken by the news of Amelia's marriage, she thought. "Thank you. I'm going to get a room," she told Miranda.

"I'll go with you," Miranda said.

Rachel nodded at Jack. "Mr. Keller." She managed another smile for Jane. "Jane."

The compassion in the young woman's blue eyes surprised her. "There is no reason for you to stay at the hotel," Jane said quietly. "You're family. You can stay at Daniel's. He's not home, but—"

"No!" Rachel said, dismayed by the idea. Her tone was sharper than she'd intended; she softened it. "Really, the hotel is fine. I appreciate the offer, but I'd rather wait to see Amelia later after I've rested." She smiled tiredly. "They're not expecting me. There's been enough sudden surprises for today."

Jane murmured that she understood.

Rachel turned to Miranda's uncle. She'd grown quite fond of him during these past few weeks. "Thank you for bringing me, Uncle Rupert."

Rupert regarded her fondly. "I'll see you at the hotel later."

Rachel inclined her head, then left without saying goodbye. Miranda followed her.

Jack Keller narrowed his gaze as Amelia's sister left

the trading post. "She's not like her sister, is she," he said with a frown.

Jane looked at him with surprise. "You don't like her?"

"She certainly wasn't friendly."

"She's tired," Rupert explained.

"She's hurting," Jane said. "Why do you think a woman like that would come all the way out here to live?" she added when Jack frowned.

He shrugged. "To be with her family?"

Rupert nodded. "She does want to be with her family." He went to a side window and watched as Rachel and Miranda entered the building several yards away. "She's a good girl. Don't judge her too harshly."

"Amelia's mentioned her sister a few times," Jane said. "I wonder if she'll be glad to see her."

"I suppose you'll find out soon enough. If I'm not mistaken, that man and woman going into the house across the road is your brother and his wife."

Jane hurried toward the window. "It's them! They're back!" She spun from the opening, her face reflecting her joy.

Jack felt something soften inside him as Jane gasped out her good-byes and ran to the door.

He went to the window and watched as Jane's daughter, Susie, looked over and saw her mother.

"Momma!" she cried, running to Jane with open arms.

"Susie!" Jane hugged her daughter tightly. As mother and child pulled away from each other, they both babbled in their excitement at being reunited.

Rupert stood silently beside Jack, watching the scene. "There's a woman and a little girl who love each other something fierce." He turned to Jack as the trading post owner moved away from the window. "How come she didn't go with them?"

Something kicked in Jack's gut. "Daniel and Amelia

went to the village of an Ojibwa friend.'' The realization that it had been a long time since Rupert's last visit made him explain. ''Jane's still suffering from her captivity with the Sioux.''

''But there's more,'' Rupert said perceptively.

Anger burned at the back of Jack's throat as he thought of the cruel man Jane had married. ''Oh, yes, there is more, but it's been a while now, and I'd hoped . . .''

''You're in love with her.''

Jack stiffened. ''I am not.''

But Rupert only smiled. ''Suit yourself.'' He gestured to the counter and the growing pile of supplies they had gathered for his purchase. ''Let's finish up here. I'm kind of tired myself and anxious to sleep on one of those fancy bed mattresses.''

''Well, then you're in luck, Clark,'' Jack said teasingly, '' 'cause Rebb's little girl Maeve received a new shipment of fancy bedding for that hotel of hers just last week.''

# Chapter 3

The second-story room of the hotel was surprisingly pleasant. Rachel hadn't expected such cheerful, comfortable accommodations in the back of beyond. A large four-poster feather bed sat against one wall, a cherry washstand with white porcelain ewer and basin against another. There was a large chest of drawers with a mirror near the wall by the door.

The proprietress of the hotel, Maeve Treehorn, was a pleasant young woman with a welcoming smile. She had her husband bring up Rachel's things, then arranged for Rachel to have a bath.

Exhausted, Rachel undressed and slipped into the bathtub. It was large and an unexpected luxury. She enjoyed a long soak in the heated water, then scrubbed herself from head to toe with a delicately scented soap. When she was done, she toweled herself dry, then climbed naked between the quilts covering the feather mattress.

Her thoughts were in a whirl as she lay, staring up at

the ceiling of her hotel room. *Amelia is married.* She blinked against a mist of tears. If not for Jordan's vile betrayal, she would have been married, too.

*Oh, Jordan, how could you have done this to me? To us?*

She shouldn't have come. *But where else could I have gone?* She had no other known relatives. She didn't know her mother's people. Her father and her aunt had been secretive whenever she or her sister had asked any questions about the relatives on her mother's side.

"It's best you know little of them," Aunt Bess said once after the girls had asked about that branch of the family several times. "They disowned your mother for marrying your father. Are they anyone you'd like to meet?"

For days after that conversation, Rachel and Amelia had whispered their suspicions to each other late at night while everyone else in the house slept. The sisters had told each other romantic tales of their young physician father being summoned to some rich household, where he'd fallen in love with his female patient, their mother, Marianna Farrell. John Dempsey, they decided, had saved Marianna's life; then the two young people, smitten with each other, had eloped. They'd known that Marianna's family wouldn't approve of Marianna's marriage to a lowly doctor.

Rachel sighed and closed her eyes. What would her mother's family say if she—Marianna's daughter—suddenly appeared at their front door? That is, if she knew where her grandparents lived.

No, she'd been right to come here. She would just have to accept the fact that Amelia had married. Perhaps her father would be glad of Rachel's assistance . . . surely Amelia's marriage had changed her working relationship with Father.

It was quiet in the hotel. She was conscious of the absence of forest sounds. It was a warm, late afternoon, and the windows were shut. The only other guests at the hotel, apparently, were her friends, Miranda and Rupert Clark.

The dinner hour was fast approaching. Rachel thought that a brief nap would be just what she needed to help her face her family. She closed her eyes. She'd rest for only a few moments, until she felt well enough to go downstairs . . .

*She saw the figure standing in the forest several yards away from where she sat on a fallen tree trunk. She caught her breath as it stepped from the shadows. It was the Indian. Her Indian.*

*He stopped within a few feet, a prime specimen of a male. Her heart began to beat faster as Rachel saw the way he studied her. She scrambled to her feet as he smiled and held out his hand.*

*She hesitated. She wanted nothing more than to go to him, but she was nervous and afraid. She had no knowledge of dealing with savages, and there was something in this man's eyes that frightened her, even as it mesmerized her.*

*"Come with me, white woman," he said in a deep, accented voice. "Come and see my village."*

*Rachel felt breathless. "I don't know you."*

*"Yes, you do." He smiled. "We have seen each other before, in the forest, when you were with your friends."*

*She looked around and saw that she was alone with him. She felt a flutter inside her chest. "You shouldn't be here," she said, sensing that it was dangerous for him.*

*"I have come for you. We are destined for each other."*
*He stepped closer. "You have seen it. I have seen it. It is simply meant to be."*

*The back of her neck tingled. "Who are you?" she whispered. "Why do you follow me?"*

*"The way is clear," he said. "We share the same life path."*

*"I walk alone now," she insisted, thinking of Jordan. Rachel's heart skittered as the brave lifted his hand and caressed her cheek. His touch was light, tender. "Your journey is a lonely one," he murmured.*

*Shaken by the feelings he evoked, she shook her head. "I need no one to accompany me."*

*"It matters not," he said. "It is destined to be."*

*She bit her lip. "I am dreaming. You are not real."*

*"I am real. You hear my voice." He lifted his hand, held it out to her. "Feel my flesh."*

*She shook her head.*

*"You are afraid," he said.*

*"I don't know you.*

*"Know this," he whispered.*

*She froze as he reached out and caught her shoulders. Her heart thumped as he drew her closer. She knew she should be fighting him, but she was curious. She felt no danger, only a longing for something of which she had no current knowledge.*

*Rachel felt the male heat of him as he pressed her against his length, felt the controlled power of his muscular form. She was scared, yet fascinated by him. When he lowered his head and his mouth captured hers, she was powerless to resist him. Heat warmed her blood and quickened her pulse. His lips were warm, firm, and incited her pleasure. She gasped as desire tightened her abdomen and trickled along her spine. He trailed his lips across her cheek to her ear and back again. She arched her head back, allowing him access to her throat and neck. She moaned softly, enjoying his power over her, as his lips wrecked havoc on her skin.*

*Rachel's head felt fuzzy when the Indian raised his head to gaze down at her. She blinked to clear her vision. His face was taut. His eyes glowed hotly in the darkness.*

*"Destiny," he said softly.*

*No, she didn't need a man, she thought, shaking her head. "No," she whispered.*

*"It is so."*

*She was terrified. "No!"*

"No!" she cried as she jerked awake. It was dark in the room. Her breath rasped loudly in the silence. She closed her eyes to fight the remnants of her dream. After a few moments, she felt her sense of calm return.

Unable to go back to sleep, Rachel slipped out from under the covers and went to the window. She was surprised to see that night had fallen and it was long past the supper hour. There were no lights in the settlement. Everyone had retired for the night. She pushed open a window and stood before the opening, allowing a light breeze from the outside to caress her bare skin.

The moon cast a soft glow on the road, the blacksmithy, and the blacksmith's house across the street. Rachel gazed at the house. *That's Amelia's home,* she thought, startled. Jack Keller had said that Amelia and her husband were away. She wondered when her sister would return. Should she wait for Amelia, or continue on to the mission to see her father?

The breeze brushed her skin and teased her hair. It felt wonderful to stand there with the knowledge that everyone was asleep and no one could see her. She felt a sense of freedom in being naked. No corsets to constrict her breathing. No chemise, or pantalets, or stockings.

The warm summer air felt wonderful. Like a lover's caress might, she thought.

Rachel was suffused with a tide of heat as she recalled the Indian and her dream. First, she'd dreamt of him during the journey, that she'd seen him in the forest, when he'd spoken in his strange tongue and touched her hair.

This last dream was shocking in its detail. Why would she dream that an Indian had come and kissed her? And the Indian's kiss had been nothing like Jordan's.

Jordan's betrayal had hurt her terribly. Had the dream been a way of soothing her pain? Perhaps, a way to show herself that she was still desirable, that a stranger, even an Indian, had been attracted enough to want her? Earlier, she had gone to sleep with sad thoughts of Jordan.

Rachel shivered and hugged herself with her arms. But why would the savage tell her that destiny had linked them?

The sudden sight of movement across the street, near her sister's house, startled Rachel. She gasped and stepped away from the window, then carefully inched her head just enough past the window frame to peek outside.

She experienced a jolt of alarm as a figure detached itself from the shadows and stepped into the moonlight. He turned and looked up toward her room. She gasped. No, it couldn't be! But it was! At least, it looked like an Indian!

Her heart pounding, she quickly stepped back into the shadows. Was she dreaming still?

She pinched herself and cried out. The pain was real, which meant that the savage in the street below was real. She leaned forward, peering into the night, and frowned. The savage was gone. She waited with thrumming heart to see if the Indian would reappear, but he didn't.

*I am not crazy.* She spun from the window to search for something to put on. Ignoring a need for under-garments, she went to her clothes trunk, grabbed a gown, and dressed.

*I'll prove that I'm not crazy. If the Indian was down there, I'll find some sign of him. A footprint. Something!*

She fumbled to fasten the buttons along her bodice front, then rummaged under the bed for her kid slippers, which she put on.

Her nerves strung tightly, Rachel opened her bedchamber door and slipped silently from the room. The interior of the hotel was silent. Mrs. Treehorn had left a sconce burning to light up the hallway to the staircase. Rachel negotiated the stairs without mishap and tiptoed toward the exit.

The door squeaked as she pulled it open. She hesitated, listening. Once assured that she had disturbed no one, Rachel left the hotel and entered the night.

Her skin tingled as she clung to the side of the hotel building so the Indian, if he was still there, couldn't see her. She waited several heartbeats before venturing away from the hotel to cross the road hurriedly. She headed to the spot where she'd thought she'd seen the Indian.

There was no sign of anyone. Rachel peered into the darkness, but saw nothing. She studied the ground, but saw no footprints. She began to breathe easier. She must have been dreaming still when she thought she saw him.

Her attention went to her sister's house. *Amelia lives here,* she thought with amazement. Curiosity propelled her closer to the building. She found a window and peered in through an opening in the curtains. It was too dark inside to see, so Rachel rose up on her tiptoes to press herself against the window glass.

She growled with frustration and lifted herself higher. When she still couldn't see, she tried to open the window, but it wouldn't budge. With a sigh, she stood back to eye the cabin. She moved away, saw another window, and headed toward that opening to see if the moonlight afforded better lighting there.

Cupping the sides of her face with her hands, she pressed against the glass and peered in. She could just barely make out the outline of a dining table and two chairs.

A large hand clamped over her mouth from behind. Rachel whimpered and her eyes widened in fear. She began to struggle, but an arm encircled her, pinning her hands and body to a hard form.

She jerked her head and tried to cry out, but the figure— the man, she assumed—moved quickly, stifling her with his hand, shifting her so that she couldn't move within his hold.

Her mouth went dry, and she experienced real terror as the man began to drag her around to the side of the building, into the dark shadows, where there was no moonlight.

She stumbled as he continued to drag her along. As he tugged her upright, she kicked back at him with her foot, and was satisfied to hear him grunt with pain.

His grip tightened without mercy, and she gasped. Tears filled her eyes as she wondered if she was about to be murdered.

"If you will cease your struggling, I will release you," a dark, angry voice said.

Rachel went still.

"You will not scream if I let you go?"

He eased his grip slightly. She was able to nod.

"If you cry out, I will silence you," the voice said ominously.

She nodded again.

He slowly let go of her mouth.

Rachel drew in air to scream, but the man quickly grabbed her, cutting off her breath and stifling her cry before it was uttered.

The man tightened his grip. "I warned you, woman." Whimpering, she struggled. "If you do not cease, I will slit your throat."

He shifted, and a blade suddenly appeared, gleaming in the darkness.

She froze, her blood icing over.

He softened his grip, but didn't put away the knife. "You will not utter a sound?"

She swallowed hard and nodded. His voice was strangely accented. She wondered where the man came from and why he was here.

"Good." He released her, but kept the blade to her throat. "You may turn around slowly."

Rachel eased about carefully. She wanted to see this man who threatened her life. His face was in the shadows. She couldn't make out his features; she could barely make out his size.

"What are you doing breaking into the house of the blacksmith?" he said gruffly.

"I wasn't trying to break in!" she gasped.

"Silence!" He waved the knife; she could see the blade gleaming in the darkness.

She stiffened and jerked back. "Be careful," she exclaimed, "or you'll hurt someone!"

He grunted. "Who are you?"

"I don't have to tell you." She hesitated, then boldly asked, "Who are you?"

He tugged her out of the shadow of the building, into a shaft of moonlight, then released her. "I am Black-Hawk-Who-Hunts-at-Dawn, war chief of the *Anishinaabe.*"

Rachel gasped as she saw his long dark hair, his clothing. "You're an Indian!"

He narrowed his gaze. "And you are a white woman."

"I am Rachel Dempsey, and this is my sister's house!"

"Then why are you not inside?"

"Amelia's not here," she said. "She doesn't know I've come."

"You are sister to Tree-That-Will-Not-Bend?" He put away the knife, slipping it into the sheath in his legging strap.

"I don't know what you are talking about!"

He shifted, so that the moonlight outlined his face clearly. Rachel drew a sharp breath. "No," she whispered. "It can't be you." But it was him—the Indian in her dream.

"Why are you following me?" she asked.

He frowned. "I do not understand. I did not follow you in the forest. I have been at my village. I have come with my friend, Daniel."

She felt a jolt. "You know Daniel?"

The brave nodded. He was really quite an interesting man to look at, Rachel thought.

"Daniel Trahern," he said. "We have been friends for many winters."

"Daniel is away. Why are you here?"

"Daniel is here. I came with him."

"My sister is home?" she cried.

"She is home and asleep . . . if you do not wake her with your loud whispers. She is with child and needs her rest."

"Child?" she echoed, shocked by the news. "No . . . she can't be."

"She is with child. I have heard it from my friend." His gaze narrowed. "If you are her sister, why do you not know this?"

"I told you, she doesn't know I'm here!" *Amelia is with child!*

"How do I know that you are sister to Daniel's wife?"

"Ask me about her . . . about anything but the baby. I'll tell you whatever you want to know."

"What is the hair color of Tree-That-Will-Not-Bend?"

Rachel scowled. "What is a tree that will not bend?"

"It is the Ojibwa name for your sister."

"Then you believe that she is my sister." She was startled. Her sister had an Ojibwa name?

He stared at her hard. "I do not know this. What is her hair color?"

"She has brown hair. Not the color of mine, but softer. Her eyes are gray."

He caught her chin, held her face up to the moonlight. "You have eyes like the grass of summer." His touch burned her skin.

"I have green eyes, yes," she said, shaken by his hands on her.

"Why not you have the same eyes as Amelia?"

"We don't have to have the same hair and eyes to be siblings."

He released her. "What is 'siblings?' "

"Sisters." She was relieved when he stepped away. "Brothers. People who have the same mother and father."

An owl hooted in the near distance, startling her. "This conversation is ridiculous and pointless," she said with exasperation. "It doesn't matter whether or not you believe me. It's late, and I'm tired. I'm going across to my hotel room to get some sleep."

She started to walk away. He grabbed her.

"You are sister to Tree-That-Will-Not-Bend," he said softly.

Rachel's heart pumped hard as she looked down at his hand on her arm. She lifted her head to gaze up at him. "What convinced you?"

He withdrew his hand, but her arm retained the heated imprint of his fingers. "You are sturdy like Daniel's wife. You have hard head and courage like Tree-That-Will-Not-Bend."

She stiffened and narrowed her gaze. "Are you saying that I'm stubborn?"

He grinned in the darkness. His smile dazzled her, unnerved her. Rachel felt the hairs tingle at the back of her neck, as sensation traveled down her spine. She stared at his mouth. The memory of her dream made her blush and avert her gaze.

"You do not like to have courage?" he asked.

"Is that what I have?" she asked, glancing back, pleased by the thought.

He nodded. "I will see you in the house of your sister?"

"I suppose so." Was this Indian really Amelia's friend? *My sister has really changed,* she thought.

The brave tilted his head as he studied her. "Why have you come?" he asked.

She felt a knot form in her stomach. She wouldn't tell him about Jordan. She wasn't sure she'd tell Amelia about him. "To see my family."

"Why have you not come sooner?"

Rachel averted her gaze. "It wasn't a good time before now."

"You have come for a visit?"

"I've—ah—come to stay."

He was silent for such a long moment that Rachel shifted uncomfortably. "You are running away," he said.

"I am not!" He was too close to the truth. How could a savage even guess what she was doing here?

Black-Hawk-Who-Hunts-at-Dawn nodded his head. "Something has driven you from your home."

"Yes," she said, annoyed, "my desire to see my family."

He shrugged, calling attention to his wide, bronzed shoulders and his muscular forearms. "You go to sleep now. It is late. The morning sun will rise soon, and you will be tired."

"I'll go to bed when I'm good and ready!"

He lifted an eyebrow.

"Fortunately, I'm good and ready now," she muttered as she turned away.

She had not gone but a few feet when his voice came back to her in the darkness. "May the Great Spirit protect you while you sleep."

Startled by his words, she gazed at him. "Good night," she said softly. Then, she turned away, conscious of his continued gaze as she crossed the street and slipped inside the hotel.

# Chapter 4

"Rachel! Rachel!" A voice accompanied the heavy hammering on the bedchamber door. "Wake up! Rachel!"

Rachel sat up, feeling groggy. She blinked the sleep from her eyes, then glanced warily at the door.

"Rachel!"

"Miranda?" She finally recognized that the voice was her friend's.

"Yes! Hurry and open up!"

"Just a minute!" she called as she swung her legs to the floor. It took her a moment to get her balance. Why did she feel so tired? She had gone to bed early enough; in fact, she had missed supper. Then, she'd had this wild dream, she thought as she moved toward the door. She'd dreamed about an Indian. First, she'd dreamed she'd seen him again in the forest, then outside by the house across the road.

"Rachel, hurry! I have to tell you something," Miranda exclaimed.

"What's so important that it can't wait a few seconds!" Rachel said as she threw open the door. She stepped back to allow her friend entry.

Miranda studied her from head to toe. "You're not dressed yet! What's wrong with you, Rach? You should have had enough rest. Are you ill?"

"No, I'm not sick. I didn't sleep that well, is all."

"Well, you look peaked."

"I'm fine," Rachel said. "Really."

"Good." Miranda suddenly wore a funny grin. "I just found out something I think you'll find interesting."

"My sister is home," Rachel guessed, not really believing it. She'd dreamt it, but it couldn't be true. She turned in time to see Miranda's face fall.

"How did you know that?"

"What?"

"That Amelia came home yesterday afternoon."

Rachel stiffened. "Amelia came home yesterday afternoon?" She felt shaken. It had been a dream, hadn't it?

Miranda looked at her strangely. "You didn't know."

Rachel shook her head. "I was joking."

"Well, it's no joke that yesterday Amelia and her husband came home from wherever they were."

"I see." She turned away so Miranda couldn't see that she was upset by news of her sister's return. Why? Because Amelia was married?

"Aren't you excited?" Miranda asked. "We've come all this way for you to be reunited with your family, and now that the time is near for you to see them, you act as if you have no desire to."

Rachel spun to face her. "Of course I want to see them!" She hugged herself with her arms. "Do you think it will be easy for me to tell them that I'm a failure? Do you think it won't be hard to explain about Jordan?"

"Oh, Rachel . . ." Miranda hurried forward to hug her friend. "I'm sorry," she said softly. "I didn't think."

Rachel managed to give her a smile. "It'll be like reliving the whole incident again."

"Then don't tell them."

"Don't tell them?" Rachel echoed.

"Do they really have to know?" Miranda moved to sit on Rachel's bed. "You can tell them later, when it doesn't hurt so much."

*Would it ever stop hurting?* Rachel wondered. "I suppose I don't have to tell them."

"Right." Miranda patted the bed, testing the mattress. "You decide when you want to tell them, if you want to tell them. No sense pouring salt into the wounds."

The idea of keeping silent on the matter appealed to Rachel. She felt as if a weight had been lifted from her shoulders.

She went to the dresser and stared in the mirror. She looked bright-eyed and pale. Why did she have to tell them anything? *Because I need an excuse for why I'm here.*

"What am I going to tell them?" she asked. "They'll think it strange that I've come." She picked up a hairbrush and began to pull it through her hair. "When they left, I was enjoying the round of social engagements."

Miranda tilted her head, as if thoughtful. Her expression brightened. "I know!" She grinned. "Tell them that you had a suitor that wouldn't stop bothering you. Because of him, you felt in peril staying in Baltimore."

Rachel widened her eyes. "That might work." Surely, they'd understand that she'd wanted to escape such an ardent beau. She frowned. She didn't like lying to her family. Then, something else occurred to her. "What if Aunt Bess writes and mentions Jordan?"

Miranda gave her a funny look. "How long did you

wait for a response after writing your father and sister about the wedding? I doubt they even received that letter. And if they do happen to receive one from Aunt Bess, it will be a long time from now. By then, you would have felt comfortable enough to have told them the truth.''

The mention of the letter she'd sent her father and sister brought a nervous flutter to Rachel's stomach. "What shall I do if I find out that they received the letter I sent them? The one inviting them to the wedding?"

Her friend smiled. "All you have to say is that you found out that your intended wasn't the man you'd thought him to be. He turned out to be a jealous madman, who wouldn't allow you to even talk with another man." She got up from the bed. "Including George! That should convince them you were wise to leave Baltimore."

Rachel grinned. "I think it will work." She went to the window to stare down at her sister's house. Studying the log cabin, she searched for the courage to cross the road and knock on Amelia's door. "I hate it that I have to lie."

Miranda joined her at the window. "You don't have to," she said softly. "I'll do the talking."

"You will?" Rachel turned with a hopeful look toward her friend.

"Of course I will. You've always tried to help me. Now I have a chance to do something for you."

Rachel's gaze held surprise. "I was able to come because of you! You and your uncle made this trip possible for me."

"That's what friends are for . . . to help one another." A film of tears filled Miranda's eyes. "What am I going to do without you?" she whispered.

Rachel felt the sting of tears. "I'll miss you so much." She gave the other young woman a hug. "You will stay for a little while, won't you?"

Miranda nodded. "If I can convince Uncle Rupert. I'm not in any hurry to make that trip back."

"Not anxious to sleep in the woods again?"

Her friend chuckled as she glanced toward the window. Turning to gaze outside, Rachel stiffened as she saw the door to the cabin across the road open and a young woman step outside. It was Amelia.

"Why, there's your sister now," Miranda commented. "She looks well."

Rachel stared at Amelia and felt an overwhelming rush of love. "She looks wonderful," she said huskily. *But she doesn't look like she's with child.*

She experienced a jolt. Amelia wasn't going to have a baby. She had dreamed that the Indian had told her her sister was expecting. Their conversation hadn't been real.

"Don't you think you had better go down there and greet her?" Miranda reached to open the window. "Unless you want to call her from here—"

"No, don't!"

Miranda straightened. "Then you'd best get dressed and see your sister."

Rachel nodded.

"Are you going to wear that?" Miranda was studying a gown that was draped over the back of the chair.

Glancing toward the garment, Rachel felt the blood drain from her face. It was the garment she'd chosen to wear in her dream, when she'd confronted the Indian in the dark, near her sister's cabin.

She transferred her gaze to her clothes trunk, which looked as if it had been closed in a hurry, as the lid wasn't shut tight. A blue sleeve from one of the gowns hung over the side of the chest.

She looked around the room for the gown she'd worn yesterday. She spied it on a hook next to the bed, where she remembered hanging it when she'd undressed for her bath. A trembling invaded her body. Dear God, had it all really happened? Her meeting with the Indian? Had she really awakened in the night, gone outside, and spoken with a savage?

*No, it couldn't have happened!*

"Rachel, what's wrong? You look ill all of a sudden."

She managed to summon up a weak smile for her friend. "I'm all right. I guess I'm just feeling the effects of missing supper."

Miranda made an exclamation of sympathy. "You'd best get dressed and get something to eat then. You can see your sister later."

"Yes," Rachel replied gratefully. "That's a wonderful idea. Have you eaten?"

Miranda nodded. "Best biscuits I'd ever tasted. Mrs. Treehorn is a great cook."

Perhaps she'd be better able to face the day if she had something substantial to eat. "Would you tell her I'll be down in a few minutes for breakfast?"

"Breakfast! It's time for the midday meal!"

Rachel gasped. She had slept the entire morning away. What on earth was the matter with her?


"Amelia."

The young woman, who had opened her door a few seconds ago, looked stunned. "Rachel! My goodness, is that you?" She shook her head as if to clear it. "It can't be you." She peered at her sister more closely. *"It is you!"*

Rachel grinned, then leaned forward to hug her sister.

"I don't believe it!" Amelia gasped. "When did you come? How did you get here? Who did you come with?"

Rachel moved aside, and Miranda stepped into view.

"Miranda?" Amelia blinked.

"Hello, Amelia. You're looking well."

"I can't believe this!" Amelia cried.

"Can't believe what?" a deep male voice said from inside the cabin.

Rachel tensed as a man joined Amelia at the open door. "What's this?" he asked pleasantly.

"Oh, Daniel," Amelia gushed. "You're never going to believe this, but my sister is here! My sister Rachel and her friend."

Daniel raised his eyebrows. "Your sister?" He studied first Miranda, then Rachel, before his gaze went to Miranda. "You must be Rachel," he said to Rachel's friend.

Miranda blushed under the man's smile. "I'm afraid not. I'm her friend, and I'm pleased to meet you." She held out her hand. "Miranda Clark. You must be Daniel Trahern."

Amelia's husband took it and gallantly bent down to kiss her knuckles. "I'm pleased to meet you." He was an attractive man with blond hair and a great deal of brawn. His shoulders were broad and powerful. His chest filled out and stretched the linen of his blue shirt. The arms below his rolled-up shirtsleeves were muscular and bronzed with fine blond hairs grazing the skin. He wasn't the man Rachel had imagined. He was too good-looking, too well-mannered, to fit the picture of a wilderness blacksmith.

Daniel turned then to greet his wife's sister. "Rachel?" he asked. He narrowed his gaze.

Rachel felt the sudden frost in the air between them. "That's right," she said. She didn't offer her hand, and he didn't offer her a smile. "So you're Daniel." She was about to say more when her sister's voice drew her attention.

"I can't believe it," Amelia repeated.

Turning her gaze away from the husband, Rachel smiled at her sister. "I'm real," she said. "Can we come in so we can catch up?"

Amelia appeared flustered as she stepped aside. "Of course! Come in, come in!" With her husband looking on with indulgence, she waved the two young women in.

The interior of the cabin was a little dark, but it was cozy and comfortable, and Rachel could see her sister's attempts to brighten the inside. A large vase of wildflowers sat on the dining table on top of a crocheted table runner that Rachel recognized as Aunt Bess's work.

On the fireplace mantel was a piece of blown glass; it had belonged to Rachel and Amelia's mother, one of several pieces that had been divided equally and given to the two girls. To the right, there was a door to another room. Toward the rear of the great room, three doors led to what Rachel assumed were bedchambers. It was a big house for the married couple. Perhaps they'd built it to raise a large family?

"You have a lovely home," Rachel said.

"Surprised?" Daniel asked with a hint of sarcasm.

Amelia didn't seem to notice the mockery in her husband's tone. "We love it here," she said. "There's plenty of room for a growing family." She turned to smile at her husband.

The obvious affection between the two was painful to Rachel. "It's good to see you," Rachel said. Amelia gestured toward the sofa. The three women sat down.

"It's so wonderful to see you, too!" Amelia exclaimed. "And you, Miranda."

Miranda smiled. "Rachel has been anxious to get here. I'm afraid we didn't leave under best circumstances, I'm afraid—"

"Is Aunt Bess all right?" Amelia asked with concern.

"She's fine," Rachel assured her.

"Did you get Rachel's letter?" Miranda said, and Rachel flashed her a grateful glance.

"No, I didn't." Amelia frowned as her gaze went to her sister. "You sent a letter?"

"Some months ago," Rachel admitted.

"Then you don't know about the wedding," Miranda said.

Amelia blinked. "Did Aunt Bess finally decide to marry?"

"No, she hasn't," Miranda said. "Rachel wrote to inform you that she was betrothed."

"You did!" Amelia exclaimed. "Why, that's wonderful!" She reached across the table to grab her sister's hands. "You must be married then. Where is he? Where is your husband?"

A well of misery, Rachel stared down at their joined fingers, then gazed at her friend with a pleading look.

"Rachel called off the engagement and escaped," Miranda said quietly.

Amelia appeared confused. "I don't understand." She studied her sister. "You're not married? You didn't come with your husband."

"No." Rachel's voice sounded hoarse. "Miranda's uncle brought me."

"Her fiancé was a jealous madman," Miranda said. "Rachel learned this before it was too late. She called off the wedding, but Jordan—Jordan Sinclair—was persistent." She paused to pat Rachel's arm. "He was more than persistent. He threatened her! She feared for her own life, and Aunt Bess's." The young woman placed an arm around her friend's shoulders. "So she left . . . we left, and, well, here we are."

"Oh, Rachel," Amelia whispered. "I'm so sorry you had to go through that."

Rachel's tears were real. The mention of Jordan's name had brought back the pain.

"I'm sorry, Rach," Miranda said softly.

She nodded. "I'm all right."

"So this Jordan Sinclair fellow was bothering you," Daniel said.

Rachel looked at him. "Yes." She didn't blink. It was the truth. Jordan Sinclair bothered her still. He had stolen her heart, then trampled it to pieces when he'd run away with his widow.

Daniel continued to study her. "And your aunt?"

"Oh, Aunt Bess is fine," Rachel replied. "She has George to protect her."

Amelia smiled. "Has she married him?"

"Not yet," Rachel replied, "but soon, I think. Right before I left, I sensed that she was weakening."

"Good for George!" Seeing her husband's puzzled look, Amelia explained, "George Bentley is a kindly gentleman who is in love with my aunt. He's been trying to marry her for years. I think she loves him, but she refuses to admit it. Look how long it took before she'd allow George to court her."

"I hope she marries him soon," Rachel said. George Bentley was one of the few males left in the world that Rachel trusted. He was perfect for Aunt Bess. Rachel's experience with Jordan had made her leery of all men. She transferred her gaze to her sister's husband, who had moved to stand near his wife.

"How's Father?" Rachel asked.

"You haven't seen him?" Amelia said.

Rachel shook her head. "We arrived yesterday afternoon." She blushed and avoided Daniel's glance. "I lay down for a nap at the hotel, and I was so tired that I slept through supper."

"Father's been away," her sister told her. "Daniel will

find out for you if he's returned." She lovingly caressed her husband's shoulder. "Won't you, darling?"

His expression, which had been grim, softened as he studied his wife. "Whatever you want, love."

*He dislikes me,* Rachel thought, knowing that it was true. She decided to pretend otherwise. "I appreciate it, Daniel. You're a good brother-in-law and a true gentleman," she said with just a hint of mockery.

His blue eyes flashed with anger as he met her gaze. She nodded, smiling, then turned her attention back to her sister.

"You'll stay with us, of course," Amelia said without expecting an answer. "We have plenty of room. You can go to the mission later. I think, though, you'll find it quite comfortable here."

Rachel saw Daniel's look of dismay. "She might like it better at the mission," he said carefully.

Amelia looked at him with surprise. "You don't mean that! Rachel will like it here well enough."

"Amelia," Rachel said softly, "I don't plan to return to Baltimore. My home is here now. I can't live with you. It's not right—"

"Yes, Amelia, she—" Daniel began.

"Why not?" Amelia asked.

"No!" Daniel and Rachel said simultaneously.

"It would be awkward for Rachel," Daniel added.

Rachel softened toward her brother-in-law. "Amelia, Daniel is right," she said. "You two, well, you're married. You certainly don't need me around."

Amelia scowled at them. She narrowed her gaze at her husband. "I don't understand why you're behaving this way, Daniel. One would think you didn't like my sister."

Rachel looked at him with amusement. "Of course, he does," she said. "Don't you, Daniel?"

Her good humor faded when Daniel glared at her.

"Rachel is only thinking of the two of you, Amelia," Miranda said. "You do not need your sister living with you."

Looking relieved at the explanation, Amelia waved that notion aside. "But we would love having you."

Rachel bit her lip to keep from replying. Daniel Trahern did not want her living in the same house. Why couldn't her sister see or understand this?

"I'll stay, but only for a short time. Once Father returns, I'll go to the mission," Rachel said. "Amelia, it was only by chance that we stopped here and learned that this was your home."

"Uncle Rupert needed supplies," Miranda explained.

"Rupert?" Daniel said. "Rupert Clark?"

"Yes. He's my uncle," Miranda said. "Why? Do you know him?"

Daniel grinned. "I've met him. How is the old coot?"

"He's fine."

"You traveled with Rupert Clark?" he asked Rachel. She saw a look in his eyes that could only be disbelief.

Rachel stiffened her spine. She knew that he thought her a snob, and that she had surprised him by journeying in the woodsman's company.

She managed a smile. "Mr. Clark was extremely accommodating during our journey," she said. "I thoroughly enjoyed being with him."

Miranda grinned. "He gave her lessons in using a rifle," she joked.

It was a teasing reminder of the night she'd thought she'd seen the Indian in the forest. "Miranda," Rachel warned.

"Come, Rachel," Daniel urged. "Do you have a tale to tell? It sounds like you know an interesting story."

Rachel's jaw tightened. "There's nothing to tell."

"Daniel," his wife said, "there'll be plenty of time

for stories later.'' She rose from her chair. ''Rachel, you'll be in the second bedroom. Miranda, you can take the one to the right.''

''I can stay at the hotel,'' Miranda said, ''with my uncle.''

''I have a comfortable room there as well—'' Rachel began.

''Miranda, are you sure you won't change your mind?'' Amelia asked. She turned toward her sister. ''Rachel, you are staying here, and I want no arguments.''

''She hasn't changed, I see,'' Rachel said to Daniel without thought. ''She still likes to order people around.''

Daniel started to smile, but then it vanished as he realized that he was talking with Rachel. ''She loves you,'' he said.

Everyone rose from the table. ''Believe it or not, Daniel,'' Rachel said quietly, for Daniel's ears alone, as she came up from behind him, ''I love my sister also very much.''

He looked back at her, startled. He studied her with a frown until Amelia got his attention. Rachel had no idea how her words had affected him.

It wasn't until much later that Rachel had some time alone with her sister. Miranda had gone back to the hotel. She had been adamant about remaining there. Amelia had been equally adamant that Rachel stay at the cabin.

Daniel disappeared. Rachel wondered if he'd escaped to the smithy, but she didn't hear the sound of hammer on metal from next door. Had her father returned? Had Daniel gone to check to see if John Dempsey was at home?

The door to the right of the great room and next to the stove led to the kitchen. There was no dining area here. It was strictly a workroom with cabinets, a worktable, and a food pantry. Rachel offered to help prepare for the next meal. She and Amelia began to snap the fresh beans that Daniel had picked from a small vegetable garden earlier that day.

It had turned into a particularly warm evening. Amelia seemed to be feeling the heat, as there were tiny beads of perspiration on her forehead. Rachel felt the heat, too, but she didn't think it was too bad. She was surprised to see how much it affected her sister.

"Imagine how surprised I was to learn that you were married," Rachel said with a hint of accusation in her tone. She studied Amelia as she snapped a bean. "How long?"

Amelia looked at her. "How long have I been married?"

Rachel nodded.

"A little over a year."

"Over a year?" Rachel asked in a hoarse voice.

"I wrote Aunt Bess."

"She never got your letter." Rachel became thoughtful. "Unless . . . no," she muttered. "Why wouldn't she tell me if she'd known?" Her gaze sharpened as she studied her sister carefully. "Is he good to you?" she asked. She hesitated. "Do you love him?"

"The answer to both of your questions is yes," Amelia said with a soft smile. "He's wonderful. When we first met, we didn't see eye-to-eye on matters, but we realized later that we share the same basic ideas . . . the same hopes and dreams."

Rachel noted how radiant her sister looked whenever she spoke of her husband. She wished she could be assured that Daniel Trahern was the best thing for Amelia.

*What does it matter?* she thought. *They are already married. It's not as if Amelia has a choice any longer.*

"What kind of things did you disagree on?" Rachel asked with genuine curiosity.

"Oh, about the Ojibwa mostly."

"The Ojibwa? You mean Indians?"

"Yes. Daniel has been doing work for the Indians for years now." She broke the ends off a bean and threw it into a clay bowl. "Did you know that the U.S. government promised the services of a blacksmith to the Ojibwa Indians in their last treaty with them?"

Rachel admitted that she hadn't known.

"Daniel came here with the intention of honoring the promise to the Indians, but then he realized that the government was bent on changing them. He saw that the whites, most particularly the missionaries and the soldiers in the area, were trying to civilize the Ojibwa by trying to make them live as we whites do."

Amelia reached for a linen towel and wiped her forehead with it. She swayed a bit on her feet, which made Rachel eye her worriedly.

"Amelia—"

She waved her concern aside. "I'm fine—really." She moved the bowl aside as she reached toward the pile of vegetables.

Rachel shifted the pile closer for her sister. She studied Amelia a moment to make sure that her sister was, in fact, all right before she grabbed some of the vegetables. "You were saying something about the Ojibwa? Do you know any of them personally?"

Amelia smiled. "We just came from an Ojibwa village. Black Hawk is one of Daniel's closest friends."

*Black-Hawk-Who-Hunts-at-Dawn?* she wondered. *No, tell me I'm dreaming.*

Her gaze narrowed as she studied her sister further. "Amelia, are you with child?"

Her sister looked startled. "How did you know?"

*The Indian from my dream told me,* she thought, recalling their encounter outside her sister's home. But she couldn't tell her sister that.

"So you are expecting a babe?" Rachel asked, shaken. Perhaps it hadn't been a dream. Perhaps it had actually happened . . . her waking up in the middle of the night. Her encounter with the Indian, Black Hawk, Daniel's friend.

"Yes, I'm carrying a child," Amelia said, her voice soft. Her face lit up with pleasure. "We're very excited about it."

Rachel put down a bean and embraced her sister. "Congratulations. You'll make a wonderful mother."

The two sisters regarded each other with tears in their eyes as both of them remembered their motherless childhood. They knew they were lucky because they had Aunt Bess. Still, it would have been wonderful if they'd had more time with the woman who had given them birth.

"Are you scared?" Rachel asked as she glanced down at Amelia's belly.

"No. Well, maybe a little, but I'll have Daniel with me—and now you. And Father, of course, will be there as my physician."

Rachel thought her sister was brave. "It's just as well that I shall never have children," she said without thought.

Amelia looked at her. "What do you mean you'll never have children? How do you know this? Have you already made up your mind?"

"I cannot have children without a husband," Rachel said sadly. She was suddenly engulfed in her sister's arms.

"It must have been terribly disappointing to realize that your betrothed was not the man you thought," Amelia said.

Rachel blinked back tears. "It was," she murmured. She had certainly misjudged Jordan. She had loved and trusted him, when he hadn't deserved either her love or her trust.

"I'm sorry," Amelia said.

Rachel smiled and waved a hand. She didn't want to talk about Jordan anymore. She didn't want to think of him.

A sudden commotion in the great room had both women putting aside their kitchen work to see who had come in.

Rachel entered the great room first. She froze at the sight of one of the men. Dressed in a shirt, loincloth, and leggings, he looked as at ease in the cabin as he would in the forest.

"Black Hawk!" Amelia exclaimed. "I thought you'd left!"

"Without saying good-bye?" The Indian smiled at his friend's wife before fastening his gaze on Rachel. "Who is this woman?" he asked softly.

Rachel's gaze went to her brother-in-law.

Daniel eyed her mockingly. "What's wrong?" he asked. "Never seen an Indian before?"

"Of course she hasn't, Daniel," Amelia said sharply. "Why would you ask such a thing?"

Ignoring her brother-in-law's taunt, Rachel approached Black Hawk and extended her hand. "Hello. Are you Black-Hawk-Who-Hunts-at-Dawn?"

The warrior looked surprised but pleased as he glanced briefly toward Rachel's sister. "You have told her about me," he said accusingly.

Amelia smiled. "Only that you are our good friend."

Black Hawk's dark eyes gleamed as he regarded Rachel. "Shall I be an equally good friend to sister of Tree-That-Will-Not-Bend?"

She didn't answer. She was too stunned. *Dear God,* she thought. She *had* talked with him last night!

She caught Amelia's puzzled expression. "Rachel? How did you know his full Ojibwa name?"

Rachel shrugged nonchalantly, but inside she felt shaken. "You told me," she lied. "How else would I know?" She managed a smile for everyone in the room. "Tree-That-Will-Not-Bend?" she asked.

"My Indian name," Amelia murmured. "I'll explain later."

Daniel chuckled. His wife grinned.

Black Hawk's gaze held Rachel captive. "Will you tell her about Man-with-Big-Head?" he asked Amelia.

Daniel made a choking sound, and Rachel looked at him. Her brother-in-law was glaring at his "good" friend.

"Yes, I believe I will tell her about him," Amelia said with a soft laugh.

Daniel's gaze promised retribution. "Love, have you cooked our meal yet?"

To Rachel's great pleasure, Amelia scowled at him. "No, my dearest, I haven't." She smiled mischievously. "Have you?"

# Chapter 5

It was hard not to stare at the Indian sitting across from her. To dream of a savage was one thing, Rachel mused. To be this close to him in reality was entirely something else. He might have looked quite civilized this evening to the others in the room. But his white linen shirt, buckskin leggings, and moccasins gave him the aura of a savage. He wore a necklace of copper beads about his neck. His jet-black hair hung past his shoulders, except for two tiny braids near his face, which he'd fastened at the back of his head.

Rings made of copper hung from his ears. She wondered if the man had tattoos. Black Hawk looked up and stared. She blushed and looked away when she realized that he'd caught her interest.

There were six people at the table. Rachel studied the other diners: her sister, Daniel, Daniel's sister Jane, Jane's daughter Susie . . . and Black Hawk. It was the first time that Rachel had met Jane's little girl. Young Susie, she guessed, was about eight or nine years old.

Supper was delicious and consisted of venison stew, freshly baked bread, and for dessert, a berry pie that Jane had made fresh that morning.

Everything tasted wonderful. Rachel hadn't realized how hungry she was until she'd tasted her first mouthful and sighed with pleasure. She complimented the cooks for their contributions. Amelia looked pleased by her sister's praise. Jane smiled softly, her blue eyes warming as she met Rachel's gaze.

Daniel continued to regard his sister-in-law with veiled displeasure. Rachel didn't know what it was about her that aggravated her brother-in-law, but she was determined to ignore him. She wouldn't allow him to ruin her family reunion. She was satisfied with the knowledge that her sister, at least, was happy to see her.

When she first arrived, Susie, Jane's daughter and Daniel's niece, had eyed Rachel with curiosity from a distance. But it wasn't long before she, too, warmed to her aunt's sister, which pleased Rachel tremendously. She was grateful for the child's cheerful, friendly chatter.

Black Hawk, for the most part, remained quiet during the meal. Rachel tried to avoid looking at him. Every so often, their gazes caught and held, and she felt flustered. He spent much of the supper hour watching little Susie's antics and listening to her with a smile. There was a quiet affection between the Indian and the child. The relationship surprised Rachel and made her slightly less wary of Black Hawk.

"You seem tired, Amelia," Jane commented softly as she cut another slice of pie for her brother.

"Yes, love," Daniel said to his wife. "Why don't you go lie down? I'm sure Rachel won't mind cleaning up the supper dishes." He challenged her with a look.

"Of course not," Rachel said without hesitation. She was annoyed at her brother-in-law, but she honestly didn't mind cleaning up, as she wanted to help her sister. "You've got to think of the little one."

She caught Daniel's look of surprise at her answer, before her gaze settled briefly on Black Hawk. The brave's expression was unreadable, but she thought that maybe there was a glint of amusement in his dark eyes.

"Little one?" Jane said. "Amelia, are you . . . ?"

Amelia grinned as she nodded.

With an exclamation of joy, Jane put down the knife and rushed around the table to hug her sister-in-law. "Oh, Amelia—Daniel, I'm so happy for you."

"Momma?" Susie asked. "Why is everyone so happy?" She wore a puzzled look as she glanced from her mother to the other adults.

Jane released Amelia and held out her arm for her daughter. Susie rushed in gratefully for a hug. "Aunt Amelia is going to have a baby, Suze," her mother said as she released her.

The child studied Amelia with wide eyes. "You are?"

Amelia nodded. "I hope you'll help me take care of him."

Susie frowned. "You're having a boy?"

Her uncle chuckled. "We don't know that, Susie," Daniel said. "We won't know until the baby is born whether it's a girl or a boy."

"But you want a boy?"

"No," Amelia said. "I'd love a little girl like you, but I'd love a little boy as well. Either way I'll—Daniel and I will be happy."

Susie didn't look too pleased. "I can still come over to visit whenever I want?"

Amelia saw her husband's expression, and quickly put her hand on his arm to keep him quiet. "Yes," she said,

''you can still come over to visit anytime you want.''
She ruffled the child's hair. ''What would we do around
here without you? You know we love you very much.''

Rachel watched the child's radiant smile return, and
she thought what a complex but loving family her sister
had with Daniel's family . . . and now there would be a
new baby to warm their hearts further. Would she—
Rachel—one day feel an accepted, loving member of this
family?

She looked away from the group with the sting of tears
in her eyes. She rose and quickly began to clear up the
supper dishes, wanting only to escape for a few minutes
in order to regain her composure. Her sister had everything
that she'd always wanted. She wasn't jealous of Amelia.
Well, maybe a tiny bit. Mostly, she fought to banish the
pain left in the wake of Jordan's betrayal.

For so long, she had imagined herself as Jordan's wife,
bearing his children. It was hard still, at times, to accept
the fact that she would never have him . . . that Jordan
had chosen the widow, a woman several years his senior,
over Rachel, a woman a few years younger than he was.

She stacked up the dinner bowls and placed the eating
utensils they'd used on top of the pile. With her arms
loaded with dishes, Rachel left the great room for the
kitchen workroom. She had to blink against wetness as
she hunkered down to carefully set the stack on the worktable near the wash basin.

*I'm happy for Amelia. I really am. But I'm miserable
for myself. I won't ever love again. I won't give away
my heart only to have it broken again.* And her heart was
a long way from being healed.

Rachel heard someone come in behind her. She didn't
turn; she didn't want anyone to see her misery. The person,
whoever it was, set a small stack of pie plates on the
table directly to Rachel's right.

She knew she should acknowledge the presence, but she didn't want anyone here. She wanted to be alone.

The person didn't leave. She could sense that he or she remained. Rachel figured it was Jane, who would be concerned by Rachel's silence but wouldn't push for conversation. She kept quiet, hoping that Jane would take the hint and go.

"Thank you," Rachel managed to choke out after several long seconds.

"You are sad?"

The deep male voice surprised her, and she spun toward the sound. There, just inside the kitchen doorway, stood the Indian.

Rachel blinked and shook her head. "I'm fine." She forced a smile before she turned back to the dish basin. She had helped Amelia put a pot of water to warm on the stove in the great room earlier. She reached for a mitt, then extended her hand toward the kettle where it now sat on the worktable. She closed her eyes and prayed the Ojibwa brave would go away before she made a complete fool of herself.

She wrapped the heavy quilted cloth around the iron pot handle and started to lift it. The pot was heavy, but Rachel refused to ask for help. She had failed in her relationship with Jordan; she refused to fail in this simple chore.

As she struggled to lift the pot, Rachel no longer thought of the Indian, except to assume that he had left, having grown tired of her lack of conversation.

She managed to raise the pot a few inches in the air, before her strength gave way and the pot started to slip from her grasp. She shrieked as it started to fall and she fought to recover it. In a quick mental flash of foresight, she saw the pot hit the table edge, spill, and hot water scald her hands and her body. She cried out. Suddenly someone was there to help her, a cloth wrapped around his hand to protect it.

Black-Hawk-Who-Hunts-at-Dawn saved the pot from falling and Rachel from being burned. Unfortunately, he couldn't save Rachel the humiliation of feeling like a failure again. Rachel fought an onslaught of silent tears.

He set the pot back onto the table. Then, without a word, he set down the cloth he'd used to shield himself from the heat. He took Rachel's mitt from her shaking hands, placed it on the table next to pile of dirty dishes, and pulled softly sobbing Rachel into his strong arms.

She didn't protest. She was aware of little but her own misery. The fact of her self-pity bothered her, and it made her cry even harder.

She wasn't conscious that an Indian held her. She was aware only of the comfort of a pair of masculine muscular arms. It didn't matter whose arms they were. Just as it didn't matter whose warm, male chest supported her cheek and allowed her tears to fall and dampen sleek, smooth skin.

The strength, the power of the one who held her eased her pain, made her think of Jordan, and for a moment, it was another time when things had been better . . . when she'd looked with happiness toward the future as Jordan's bride.

Her sobs quieted. She rested peacefully, silently, within the arms. As her misery eased, her awareness of her surroundings and the man who held her increased. She grew attuned to the pleasant scent that filled her nostrils, the scent of the outdoors, of the forest . . . of fresh leaves and damp earth . . . of clear spring water, and the richness of clean, summer air intermingled with the smell of washed and freshly aired linen. She became totally aware of the texture and tautness of the muscled chest beneath her cheek. She moved her head and stiffened when she realized that she felt a male nipple pebbled against fabric, then the bare skin that was exposed by an unbuttoned linen shirt.

As her brain began to function clearly again and her senses came alive, she stood for a moment without moving . . . even as she realized who held her. She should have pulled away immediately. She moved back, but slowly and easily, not swiftly like a frightened deer.

Her heart hammered in her chest. Her pulse raced.

She eased back, waiting a heartbeat before lifting her eyes to meet his gaze. He watched her without speaking, his face unreadable. Rachel felt her heart begin to pound as she studied him. His eyes glistened under the oil lamp in the kitchen. His features appeared darker, yet softer in the golden light.

Her gaze fell on his mouth, and she wondered with strange fascination what it would be like to kiss him . . . if he'd kiss like in her dream . . . if he'd kiss as well as Jordan . . . or better.

As she shifted her attention back toward his gaze, Rachel felt warmth pool in her stomach. Then a sudden ice fill her veins as his expression changed, grew darker, harder, more frightening . . . less like a man she might want to kiss . . . more like the savage that he was.

"I—I'm sorry," she said, turning away abruptly, back to the worktable and the dishes that needed to be washed.

She gasped when he grabbed her arm and turned her to face him. His grip wasn't rough, but his expression was savage. "Why are you sorry, white woman?" He said white woman as if he wanted to remind her of their differences.

She trembled as she looked up at him. "You nearly got burned, because of me—"

He released her, took a step back. "What does it matter if a savage gets touched by fire?" he asked cruelly.

She gaped at him in shock. "Is that what you think of me?"

His smile was grim. "Perhaps you are afraid of my knife." His hand moved like lightning and there, gleaming in the lamplight, was a blade of steel.

She gasped and moved away. "It did happen! You were out there last night," she said, pointing to a window. "You grabbed me."

He slipped the knife back into his legging strap. He grinned, a flash of light in the darkness that was not sinister, but a genuine article of amusement. "It is true that you are sister to Tree-That-Will-Not-Bend. It is good to know that you did not lie to me."

Rachel relaxed as she saw his good humor. "Is that really her Indian name?"

He nodded, and the movement called attention to the play of light on his midnight dark hair. "As Little Flower is the daughter of Jane."

"And Jane? Does she have an Indian name, too?" she asked innocently.

Black Hawk's face became shuttered. "It is not one that she likes to hear."

"You won't tell me?"

He shook his head. "If Dan-yel's sister wants you to know it, she will tell you what she was called."

Annoyed by his reticence, Rachel turned away. "Thank you for your help," she said haughtily. "I had best wash these dishes."

He didn't answer her, but he didn't leave either. Rachel tried to ignore him as she looked for a bucket to fetch cold water for the washbasin. She would ladle out some of the hot water and mix it with the cold, she decided. Then, she wouldn't have to pick up the pot again, and she wouldn't have to ask for any help to move it.

From the corner of her eyes, she tried to see if Black Hawk was still there.

It was too silent in the room. She hadn't heard him leave. He must have left, she thought. But then a slight shift in the shadows against the far wall told her that he had remained.

In the corner of the room, she found a wooden bucket. She searched for an exit, realized that she'd have to go through the great room and out the front door to get water, and set the bucket down with a sigh.

As she gave the hot kettle a second study, she saw a figure bend and pick up the bucket. Then, she turned to see Black Hawk with bucket in hand disappear into the next room.

*The man is an enigma,* she thought. One minute the quiet comforter, the next the savage with danger in his eyes . . . and now the silent helper. Which one of these men was the real Black Hawk?

Weren't Indians supposed to be wild and unpredictable?

Rachel waited a long while for the Ojibwa, and still Black Hawk hadn't returned. She wondered if she had misread the Indian's intention. *Perhaps he'd taken the bucket because he had his own need for it,* she thought.

She stewed silently as she debated what to do. She couldn't stay in the kitchen area forever. In fact, she was hurt that no one had come looking for her. It justified her feelings of being inconsequential, of not belonging in this settlement . . . in this family.

"Rachel?" Amelia had slipped silently into the room while Rachel had fumed alone. "Are you all right?"

Rachel was glad that her tears had dried sometime ago. She turned with a smile. "I'm fine. I wanted to do these dishes for you, but I'm afraid I can't lift that pot!"

Amelia looked surprised. "I can't lift it by myself

either.'' She grinned when she saw her sister's face. ''Did you think I could?''

Rachel nodded.

''Well, I can't,'' Amelia admitted, ''and if I even tried, Daniel would have apoplexy.''

''He would?'' She must have stared at her sister with an odd expression, because Amelia gazed at her with concern.

Her sister frowned. ''Rachel, what on earth is the matter? You should know better than to try to pick up that kettle.''

''I—'' Rachel turned away. She was feeling weepy again. ''I don't want to be a burden,'' she mumbled.

''You're not a burden,'' Amelia exclaimed, spinning her around. ''You would never be a burden. You're my sister, and I love you. Don't you realize how happy I am that you've come?''

*She's telling the truth. She really wants me here,* Rachel thought. Her expression softened. ''I love you,'' she said as she reached for her sister. ''I know you may not believe this, but I've missed you so much.''

''Of course I believe you,'' her sister insisted. ''Why wouldn't I?''

Rachel touched Amelia's cheek. ''You're looking lovely, you know. Daniel must really agree with you.''

Amelia sighed. ''He does. I love him more than life. I never realized there would be someone like him out there for me.'' She paused, and a look of horror flickered across her features. ''I'm so sorry, Rach. The last thing you want to hear is how happy I am . . . not with your disappointment over your betrothed. What was his name? Jordan?''

Rachel nodded. ''It was better that I found out in time,'' she said.

Amelia agreed. ''There are other men out there, Rachel.

Jordan wasn't the right man for you. Somewhere, some-day, you'll find the one man whom you'd be willing to sacrifice your world for . . .'' Her voice trailed off, and her face took on a strange expression. She blinked, then smiled at her sister. ''You'll know when you've found the right one. You won't be able to think of anything but him. He'll dominate your thoughts, your every waking moment, and your dreams.''

''How will I know whether or not he loves me?'' she asked, getting to the crux of her fears. Amelia, of course, didn't know the truth, that Jordan had left her, hadn't loved her enough to stay.

''That's a bit more difficult,'' Amelia said. ''You won't know right away. He'll have to prove himself to you. If he loves you, he will.''

''And Daniel?'' she inquired out of curiosity. ''Did he prove himself to you?''

Amelia suddenly had a strange look on her face, as she undoubtedly relived some special memory. ''Yes,'' she said, ''he proved himself to me.'' She began to lead Rachel toward the doorway. ''And someday a wonderful man will do the same for you.''

''My prospects of meeting men aren't the same out here,'' Rachel said.

''I found my man here,'' Amelia replied with a smile. ''It doesn't take a lot of men to make a woman happy . . . just one . . . the right one.'' She tugged her sister into the next room. ''Now come, there is someone here I'd like you to see.''

''Another Indian friend?'' Rachel said softly.

Amelia chuckled. ''Not exactly, although some people around here think he's on the wild side.''

''Rachel?'' a familiar voice said.

''Father?'' she cried. With joy, Rachel ran into her parent's open arms.

# Chapter 6

"But Father!" Rachel pleaded. "I can assist at the infirmary. I know I can."

John Dempsey frowned as he gazed at his youngest daughter. They were in his living quarters at the mission. It was the day after he'd first learned that Rachel had come for a visit. He wasn't pleased when he'd learned that she'd come to stay. "You know nothing about medicines."

"I can learn," she said with assurance. "Amelia didn't always know what to do. She learned; you taught her."

Her father didn't look convinced. "Rachel, you belong in Baltimore, with your Aunt Bess and all those young men who always came courting you."

"I can't go back, Father. Didn't Amelia tell you?"

John narrowed his gaze. "She said something about some young persistent beau." He stood. "Frankly, I'm surprised that you left. It's not like you to run away from anyone or anything. You were always one who could handle any of your young men."

"I couldn't stay. I know you don't understand why, but believe me, my being here is for the best."

"Your sister is happy that you've come," John said. "You'd be better off staying with her and Daniel."

"Father, I'm not comfortable there. Daniel and Amelia are married. They need their privacy." She rose from the sofa in the parlor to follow him into the kitchen. "I can be useful here. I can cook for you and help with your patients."

She lifted a pitcher of water and filled a pot, which she placed on the fire. "I'm not useless, you know. Aunt Bess taught me a great deal in the past few years."

John placed two teacups on the worktable along the opposite wall. "Your aunt is a wonderful woman, but even she didn't have the stomach for assisting with my patients."

Rachel spun from the fire and approached where her father stood. "I'm not Aunt Bess."

"I realize that," he said.

"Won't you at least give me a chance? If I fail, then I'll leave here. I promise I'll not bother you again."

John's expression softened as he touched his daughter's cheek. "You're not a bother," he said quietly, "and it is good to see you." He sighed as he dropped his hand. "I could use some help here . . ."

"A month," Rachel said. "Won't you give me a month to prove myself?" She was pleased to note that her father was weakening. "Just one month," she murmured, "and if it doesn't work out, I'll find somewhere else to go."

Her father looked at her. "You'll go home to Baltimore."

Rachel knew she couldn't make that promise. "No. But I'll find somewhere to go."

"Baltimore," her father insisted. "If things don't work out here, you'll go home to your aunt."

Since she was determined that she wouldn't fail, Rachel finally agreed. "Fine, if I can't handle being your assistant, I'll go home to Baltimore." *You don't know what you're asking of me, Father.* But what else could she do but agree?

"Your sister will be disappointed if you don't at least stay a few days with her," her father pointed out.

*Amelia might be disappointed, but Daniel won't be.* "I'll stay a couple of days with her before I move my things here." Rachel viewed her surroundings with more interest. Now that she knew this was to be her home—at least for the next month or so—she was curious what the place had to offer.

She noted that it had been some time since Amelia had lived here. It was easy to tell, because the infirmary lacked a woman's touch . . . the touch of her sister that Rachel was sure had been evident before she'd married Daniel and moved out.

Rachel decided to add linens, wildflowers, and knick-knacks. "Will you show me around?" she asked softly.

John looked surprised by his youngest daughter's request. "You want to see the sickroom?"

Rachel nodded. "How many beds do you have?" she asked. "Do you get many patients at one time?"

"We have two beds in the sickroom," he told her, pleased by her interest. "We made sleeping pallets for as many as ten patients during a flu epidemic last winter."

*A flu epidemic.* "Did anyone die?" Her voice was soft as she pictured her father struggling to help a roomful of ill patients. "Where did everyone stay?"

"In every available room. And we had patients in several residences. And yes, some people died." He looked solemn. "A woman and a little girl fell victim the first week."

It was clear that the memory of that time upset him. "The rest of the family survived," he continued. "It was rough for a while, but eventually everyone else's fever broke and they all recovered. Your sister about wore herself out playing nurse. Daniel was a godsend. He fetched and carried whatever we needed. He even went to the Ojibwa people for medicines for the fever."

She thought of how tragic that time must have been. "You used Indian medicine?" she said, startled. For a moment, she had an image of the Ojibwa brave Black Hawk. She tried to picture a whole village of Ojibwa people.

John nodded. "I have tremendous respect for their knowledge of herbs and plant life. My own medicine supply had dwindled. We relied on the Ojibwa for something to help break the patients' fevers."

Rachel's lips twisted as she looked away. It was hard to imagine Daniel as anything other than the man who insulted and mocked her. He'd been ready to accept Miranda as Amelia's sister. Why did he look at her as being unworthy of being a Dempsey? She was unused to being treated so poorly by a male. Until Daniel, men had always fawned over her.

Except for Jordan, but he had still courted her . . . before he'd broken her heart by leaving.

"I promise you won't be sorry I came," she vowed to her father. "I can take care of sick patients. Why, only last year, I nursed Aunt Bess through a horrible case of the ague."

"You'll be dealing with worse cases than someone

with the ague. Out here, there are injuries to doctor. Animal bites. Wounds from battle. Sickness. Death.''

She couldn't help herself. Rachel felt a chill at the mention of death. Battle? she thought. Between the Indians and the whites? Between the different Indian tribes? ''I can handle it,'' she insisted.

''I sincerely hope so, Rachel,'' her father said. ''For I'll not put up with a spoiled little girl's tantrums. If you can't make it here as my assistant, you'll go home to Baltimore as soon as it can be arranged.''

''But I'll have a month?'' she asked. There would be things to learn; he couldn't expect her to know everything right away. She told him so.

''Yes, daughter,'' John said. ''You'll have your month. I'll teach you what I can. There are some here at the mission who can teach you more.''

''Thank you, Father.'' She gave him a hug.

''Don't thank me, daughter. By the end of the month, you may be looking forward to going home.''


Black Hawk's people were at their summer location, within a few hours' distance of the mission settlement near the great lake. They had moved their village closer to the white mission settlement during the last hot season. This land was more fertile for their corn, pumpkin, and squash crops. Here, they wouldn't have to travel a long distance to the place where they gathered wild rice in the fall. They were closer to the blacksmith and Jack Keller's trading post. The Ojibwa women liked to trade for goods at Jack's store.

''He-Who-Kills-with-Big-Stick was seen in this last Sioux attack on Red Dog's people,'' Black Hawk told Daniel. The two men were at the Ojibwa village in Black Hawk's wigwam.

Daniel raised his eyebrows. "You didn't tell me that before." He was surprised that his friend had remained silent until this time. Black Hawk had been searching for He-Who-Kills-with-Big-Stick for many years, since Black Hawk had become a man. The Ojibwa warrior had witnessed He-Who-Kills-with-Big-Stick torture and murder his father when he was eight years old. His quest for revenge had begun that terrible day when a child had learned the cruelties of evil combined with the waste of war. The child had become a man bent on vengeance, but not at all costs.

Black Hawk was a wise war chief for the Ojibwa. He did not strike his enemy unless the battle was well planned. He did not attack unless the need warranted such action. He was a good thinker, but there was a dark, painful side to him. Daniel could only hope that someday Black Hawk could find the peace, the healing, he so desperately needed. It was what the man—and the child he'd been—deserved.

Daniel trusted the man with his life. In fact, he had done so many times, and Black Hawk had always come through for him.

"I did not know of the man's presence there. It was told to me last night by White Fox." Black Hawk studied his friend closely.

Daniel looked thoughtful. "Do you know where he might have gone?"

Black Hawk inclined his head. "It is said that he has gone to the west. To the village of Runs-with-the-Wind."

He noted how Daniel tensed. This particular Sioux chief had acted honorably in the past, releasing his prisoner John Dempsey two years before after the doctor had saved his son, then later a young girl from his village. Because of the chief's actions regarding Dempsey, there was a measure of uneasy peace between this particular Sioux village and the Ojibwa.

Daniel had his own reasons for disliking the Sioux Indians, but they both agreed that it was a peace that none of them wanted broken.

"You cannot take the man in the village of Runs-with-the-Wind," Daniel said.

"I know this. I do not think he will remain in the village for long. He is an evil man. Runs-with-the-Wind will see this."

"I hope you are right."

Black Hawk hoped so, too. He would find He-Who-Kills-with-Big-Stick. He must be made to suffer as his father had suffered at the warrior's hands. The day of his father's murder was a day he would never forget. It was the driving force of his life. He would not rest unless his family was avenged and the Sioux warrior was dead.

There was a swish as Spring Blossom raised the door flap. "You are hungry?" she asked both men with a smile. She paused, as if taken aback by their grave expressions, but she didn't ask what was wrong. It wasn't her place.

Daniel made an effort to smile at Black Hawk's sister. "You have made some of that delicious porridge?"

She beamed at Daniel as, nodding, she stepped fully into the wigwam. She glanced toward Black Hawk and gave her brother a smile.

"Tree-That-Will-Not-Bend is well?" she asked Daniel softly.

Daniel's expression softened at the mention of his wife. "She is well. She grows larger with the babe every day."

"And her sister?" Spring Blossom asked, for she had been told of Rachel Dempsey.

Daniel's good humor vanished. "She is fine. She will be helping her father at the infirmary." His tone suggested he was relieved.

When Spring Blossom had left after serving both men,

Black Hawk looked at his friend. "Why do you not like your wife's sister?"

"You wish the truth?"

Black Hawk nodded.

"She is like Pamela, my late wife."

The Ojibwa narrowed his gaze. "How so?"

"She is beautiful and untrustworthy."

"You know her that well?" Black Hawk raised his eyebrows.

"I have learned much since I was married to Pamela. I have learned to recognize others like her."

"Beautiful and untrustworthy," the Indian murmured with a frown. Rachel Dempsey was certainly beautiful, he thought. If Daniel was right, then he, Black Hawk, had made the right decision to stay away from the sister to Tree-That-Will-Not-Bend. He'd thought of little else since they'd met, which bothered him, as he had work to do and no time for a female.

He-Who-Kills-with-Big-Stick had been sighted. It was the first news of the Sioux warrior for several years now. Black Hawk should be happy that the day of vengeance was within sight. He should be planning; he could not afford to make a mistake. Yet the only image in his mind lately had been of the lovely white woman with hair the color of shiny brown and copper.

"You should know a woman before you judge her, my friend," he said.

Daniel's gaze held surprise. "You think I should trust her?" he said. "Do you know that she left Baltimore so she didn't have to deal with some suitor?"

Black Hawk scowled. "Suitor?"

"Man friend."

"She has run away from a man."

"Apparently so," his friend said with a sneer.

Black Hawk shook his head. Perhaps the two sisters

were not so alike after all. He must not let his mind dwell on an untrustworthy woman.

# Chapter 7

Rachel eyed the surgery with satisfaction. She had just finished straightening her father's instruments. With a missionary's help, she had replenished the medicine cabinet with the plants and herbs necessary to prepare John Dempsey's medicines. She had met Miriam Lathom, the missionary in question, earlier that week, and been amazed by her knowledge of medicinal plants.

Rachel had moved from Amelia's house a week ago. Already, she felt a lift in her spirits. It had been difficult living near Daniel. The man brought tension into every room; Rachel had continually felt his disapproval of her. Now that she had moved in with her father, she felt a return of her confidence and self-worth.

*I can do this,* she thought. It hadn't been hard so far. During this past week, her father had treated patients for a splinter, an infected insect bite, and a broken arm. The infected bite had made Rachel slightly queasy, as it had been an ugly wound, but she'd assisted her father without flinching or turning away.

*I can handle anything if I put my mind to it.* She was pleased with how things were going. It wasn't Baltimore; she missed Aunt Bess and the social life she'd once known, but here she had her father and Amelia.

*If I have to put up with Daniel Trahern to enjoy Amelia's company, then I'll do so.* Perhaps with time Daniel would come to know, then to trust her. She didn't understand why he'd been quick to judge her. She'd done nothing wrong.

Her best friend Miranda was still in the area, but she would be leaving soon—the next day, in fact. Rachel would miss her friend terribly. They had visited each other often this past week with the knowledge that their time together was limited.

Miranda had an interest in Jack Keller, Rachel noted. But Jack's affections lay elsewhere . . . with Jane Milton, Daniel's sister. She didn't know if the others could see it, but Rachel could.

She might not get along with Daniel, but she liked his sister Jane. Jane was shy and kind. It bothered Rachel to see the sadness in her blue eyes; she wished there were something she could do for the woman.

Unlike Daniel, Jack had changed his attitude toward her. He was actually quite pleasant. Rachel didn't feel threatened in any way by him, perhaps because of his feelings for Jane. *He would be good for Jane,* she thought. But she wasn't about to interfere. She was no expert on love; she'd failed badly in her own experience with it. The pain of Jordan's betrayal still hurt bitterly. She missed what they'd had together, but she found it more difficult to picture his face these days. Was that a good thing? She wasn't sure, but she thought it might be.

With the surgery and sickroom cleaned, Rachel moved

to the living quarters. She had taken over Amelia's old room, making it her own, decorating it with her belongings. She had her own keepsakes of her mother. Among them were a piece of glassware similar to the one Amelia had displayed in her great room, and a table runner embroidered by her mother's hand. Her most prized possession sat on the dresser in her bedchamber at the infirmary: a delicate silver comb and brush set with hand mirror. Rachel had gazed into that mirror many times as a child, after Amelia or Aunt Bess had brushed and fixed her hair.

Rachel thought of her mother wistfully as she entered her father's bedchamber and saw his clothes tossed haphazardly over the back of a chair and on the bed. She smiled as she picked up John Dempsey's shirt and hung it on a wall hook. *Was he always this messy, Mother?*

The pants she left on the chair, but she smoothed the fabric so that it lay without a wrinkle.

*Were you happy together?* she wondered as she straightened his bedcovers. *Father certainly loved you. Did you love him as well?* She got misty-eyed as she picked up a cup he'd left on his bed table. *Were you sorry you married him? Did you ever doubt his love or your feelings for him?*

With a last glance around the room, Rachel took the dirty cup and brought it into the kitchen. There she eyed the remains of the breakfast dishes. She set the cup down and went about preparing to wash plates and cups.

"Hello?" A feminine voice accompanied a soft knock on the inside kitchen door trim a short while later.

Rachel turned without alarm and grinned at Miranda. "You're up early this morning," Rachel said as she continued to wash, then dried a teacup.

Miranda nodded. "Uncle Rupert wanted me to make a list of supplies for our journey home."

The women's expressions sobered at the mention of Miranda leaving.

"What am I going to do when you're gone?" Rachel asked, her throat tightening. They had been friends for so long. She would miss her.

Miranda shook her head, her eyes glistening. "You have Amelia," she whispered. "But what will I do? I'm almost tempted to stay, but my parents will be upset if I don't return soon. I've been here longer than I'd planned."

Rachel smiled through her tears. "There is a whole line of beaux waiting for you back in Baltimore."

Her friend grinned. "And you need someone there to put a stop to the rumors about you and Jordan."

The smile fell from Rachel's face. "Yes."

"Your sister has invited us for supper on our last night. You're coming, aren't you?"

"Because it's for you, I wouldn't miss it."

Miranda frowned. "Is Daniel still behaving badly?"

"Not exactly. He's civil enough to me, thanks to Amelia. But when my sister's not around, he makes no secret of his disapproval of me."

"I don't understand this. You've never had a problem getting a man to like you."

"That was before Jordan," Rachel said quietly.

Miranda hesitated, as if she didn't know what to say.

Rachel saved her friend from having to respond. "What time is supper?"

Miranda mentioned the time. "Good," Rachel said. "It'll give me some time to finish here before I go over to help her."

Her friend's eyes widened as she glanced around the room. "You're cleaning?"

Rachel smiled. "Can't you see?"

Miranda nodded. "Who would have thought . . ."

"I'm enjoying it, Randa. I never thought I would, but I do. In fact, I didn't at first."

"I'm glad for you." Miranda shivered as if the thought of such work offended her. She regarded her friend with concern. "You're sure you'll be all right here?"

Rachel's expression softened. "I'll be fine. I have Father; and as you said, I have Amelia."


Supper was an unusual affair attended by Amelia's family, Miranda and Rupert Clark, and Jack Keller and Daniel's sister and niece. Rachel had arrived earlier to see if she could in some way help her sister. To his credit, Daniel hadn't said a negative word when he'd opened the door to her, smiling instead as he'd told Rachel where she could find her sister.

Rachel had enjoyed the time spent with Amelia that afternoon as they prepared the night's feast. There were two kinds of meat, three types of vegetables, and Rachel had helped Amelia make muffins and cake to accompany the meal. Judging from the praise from the evening's guests, the sisters' efforts had been well worth it.

"Miranda, would you mind taking something back to Aunt Bess for me?" Amelia asked.

"I'd be happy to," the young woman assured her with a smile.

"I'll like you to take a note from me, too," Rachel said quietly.

Miranda nodded. "Anything for a friend."

Rachel blushed under Jack's and Daniel's curious gazes. "Thank you," she said.

The conversation at the dinner table was light and centered on the Clarks' journey back East. There was a knock on the cabin door as the guests began their dessert. Daniel rose from the table to answer the summons. Rachel heard the low murmur of male voices. Then, her brother-in-law stepped back from the doorway, and Rachel recognized Will Thornton, a young man from the mission.

Will's gaze immediately sought out John Dempsey. "Dr. Dempsey, there's a new patient at the infirmary," he said.

At the sight of Will, John had already risen from his chair. Rachel stood, ready to follow.

"What happened?" the doctor asked.

"It's Black Hawk," Daniel said, and Rachel saw what she hadn't noticed before—that her brother-in-law appeared extremely upset. "He's been attacked and shot."

"Oh, Daniel," Amelia cried, hurrying to her husband's side.

John turned to his youngest daughter. "Rachel—"

"I'm coming, Father." She quickly hugged her friend, with the knowledge that she might not see Miranda again before she departed for home. "Take care, Miranda." She touched Rupert's cheek. "Thank you, Uncle Rupert," she whispered, her eyes misting.

"I'll go with Father," Amelia offered.

"No, Rachel can handle it," John said firmly. "You've got that babe to worry about now."

Daniel looked stunned by the news of his injured friend. Rachel went to him and placed a hand on his shoulder. She knew how much the Indian meant to him. "Are you coming?" she asked softly.

He glanced at her, then nodded.

"We'll see you there," she said.

John and Rachel left for the mission, with Will Thornton and Daniel following on horseback not far behind them.

As their wagon wheels trundled along the uneven road to the mission, Rachel's thoughts turned to Black Hawk. She felt a tightening in her chest as she pictured the brave lying in bed, bruised and bleeding from a gunshot wound.

Would he be all right? She remembered the intensity of his ebony gaze, his expression when they'd locked glances.

Suddenly, she wanted to get to the mission in a hurry. She wanted to help the brave and ensure that he was safe. The thought that he might die made her blood run cold.

It seemed to take forever for them to travel to the mission. John Dempsey sprang from the wagon as soon as it stopped in front of the infirmary. Rachel followed him closely after relinquishing the reins to the horse to Will, who rode up almost immediately.

There was an uneasy quietness about the sickroom. As she entered the chamber, Rachel noticed immediately that two Indians stood along the far wall. John Dempsey was already bent over his patient. Someone had lit an oil lamp, and a golden glow fell over the room's interior and across the patient's bed.

John looked up as his daughter approached. "Hurry, Rachel," he said, "I need my forceps and a lancet."

Rachel nodded, and quickly went to the supply cabinet for the requested instruments. She returned and set the lancet, the forceps, and fabric strips to wipe away the blood on the table at her father's side.

She gasped as she studied Black Hawk. Unconscious, he lay on the bed, his pallor sickly, his face bruised and swollen. His chest was scratched, his shoulder torn open by gunpowder and shot. Blood oozed from the wound, quickly saturating the cloth that John Dempsey placed upon the injury site.

*No!* she cried silently.

Swallowing back a cry of horror, Rachel ran back to the cabinet for more bandages. Then, she filled a basin of water and set it on the work stand within her father's reach. Her pulse pounded as she worked, her thoughts with Black Hawk.

"Will he be all right?" Daniel asked as he entered the room.

John Dempsey kept his gaze on his patient, his brow furrowed with concentration. "If I have anything to say about it, he will," he said quietly.

Watching her father work, Rachel felt light-headed and slightly sick to her stomach. She glanced toward Daniel and saw the strain in his expression. "He has the best doctor there is," she told him encouragingly.

Daniel tore his gaze from his injured friend to look at his sister-in-law. "I know he has." He offered her a weak smile.

John's careful examination of Black Hawk took a long time. Besides the bullet wound, the Indian had contusions to his chest, his arms, and his legs. Rachel wondered if he had suffered any internal injuries.

She felt the tension within her grow as she waited for her father's instructions and some sign that Black Hawk would recover. "Father, will he survive?"

Ignoring her question, John Dempsey gestured toward the opposite side of the bed as he looked at his daughter. "Rachel, I need you to stand here."

"Father, will be he all right?" she asked.

"He'll live," he said, and Rachel was relieved. Heart thundering, she skirted the bed.

"Daniel, please tell Black Hawk's friends they will have to leave now," John said. "Tell them to wait in the next room."

Daniel spoke briefly to the braves in Ojibwa. One warrior seemed to argue with Daniel, until a quiet word from the second one ended the discussion. The Indians left, with one brave lingering behind briefly to gaze at Black Hawk with concern. Rachel gave him a smile of encouragement.

"Is there anything I can do?" Daniel asked when the

Indians had gone. John shook his head. ''Then I'll wait with the Ojibwa in the other room.'' The doctor didn't answer.

Rachel gave Daniel a nod to tell him that it was fine if he left. Then she returned her attention to Black Hawk.

Her stomach rolled as Rachel watched her father probe Black Hawk's open wound. ''Is it bad?'' she asked, upset by the sight of the injured man.

''Bad enough,'' John said. ''I need you to take these instruments and hold open the wound for me.''

Rachel felt the blood drain from her face. *I can do this. I will do this.*

Her father looked up when she hesitated. ''Rachel?''

''Yes, Father.'' She quickly reached for the instruments she needed.

John Dempsey instructed his daughter how to lift the edges of the wound and hold them aside. It wasn't easy. Rachel flinched when a moan escaped the Indian brave during her first attempt to touch metal to flesh. She had to be careful not to damage the surrounding bruised flesh further.

''I'm hurting him!'' she exclaimed, quickly pulling away.

''You are not hurting him, Rachel,'' her father said patiently. ''His injury is.''

''But I'm touching his wound!''

John narrowed his gaze upon his daughter's face. ''Would you like me to send for Amelia?'' he asked with a definite challenge in his tone.

Rachel shook her head. She wanted to help Black Hawk. She wanted to assist her father. ''Please show me what to do again.''

With a nod of satisfaction, John patiently explained what he wanted her to do one more time.

What followed, Rachel decided, were the most nerve-wracking, terrifying moments of her life . . . more terrifying than when Black Hawk had grabbed her from behind and held a knife to her throat. She was frightened then, it was true; but her terror had subsided soon afterward. She didn't know why, except that perhaps there had been something about the brave that had eased her fear. She'd found herself being angry with him instead of afraid.

Now, with the sight of him lying there, it wasn't anger she felt. She ached for him. She was concerned for him. If there was any kind of terror she felt, it was the fear that he wouldn't get well, that she wouldn't be able to argue with him again.

It took all of Rachel's concentration and strength to keep her hands steady while her father extracted the bullet, cleaned the wound, then stitched the opening closed.

"He can't be moved far. He'll have to stay in the other room," John Dempsey said.

Rachel nodded. "I'll check the bed." She glanced toward the door to the waiting area. "Will you talk with his friends?"

Her father inclined his head. "He'll need constant care during the next few days. Are you up to it?"

"Yes," Rachel said without hesitation. She eyed Black Hawk with concern. "What happened? Did they say?"

"There wasn't much time for conversation." John placed his hand on the doorknob. "I'll ask them now."

"Will they want to take him?"

"Probably, but I—or perhaps Daniel—will have to convince them otherwise."

"I'll wait until you're done talking with Black Hawk's friends before I check on his bed," Rachel said softly.

"Fine. I'll be right back. Call me immediately if there is any change."

Black Hawk seemed to be resting quietly. When her father left, Rachel went to the brave's side and studied him. He looked so vulnerable lying there with his battered face. His skin appeared dark next to the white bandage binding his shoulder. He was sleeping, but she could see lines of tension in his features that suggested he was in pain.

Hesitantly, she touched his brow, and was concerned by how warm he felt. The air was cool for a summer's night. Black Hawk's heat had to be related to his injury.

Had her father noticed that Black Hawk was warm to the touch? Was the brave taking a fever?

The thought of staying in the next room with him during the early hours of the morning made her skin tingle. *He'll sleep through the night. I'll not have to do much for him. He'll rest and wake up better . . . or at least until Father takes over his care.*

Her gaze wandered down the Indian's length, and Rachel felt her pulse race. He was bronzed, smooth, and muscled; she couldn't help but admire his masculine form.

Rachel flushed as her thoughts took a new direction . . . as she remembered her dream and the kiss. Flustered, she turned away and put some distance between her and the sleeping man.

She tried to summon up an image of Jordan and to recall why Jordan had appealed to her, but her thoughts remained focused on the man in the bed behind her.

*Hurry back, Father,* she thought. *I need a moment to compose myself.* The strain of assisting her father as he'd extracted the bullet from Black Hawk's shoulder had taken its toll on her. That was why she felt so rattled, she told herself. *A few moments alone will make me feel better and help me think clearly again.*

# Chapter 8

The night was silent, but for the even sound of Black Hawk's breathing. Rachel sat at the brave's bedside, checking on him frequently as she painstakingly worked on a letter to her aunt. She had gotten word to Miranda, through Daniel, that she would have the missive ready for their departure tomorrow morning. *This morning,* she thought. She turned her attention back to her letter, biting her lip as she reread some of what she'd written.

*It's much different here, Aunt Bess. There is a wild beauty about the land that is breathtaking.* She picked up her pen and continued to write . . .

*I was so shocked to learn that Amelia is married! Did you get her letter, or is this a new surprise to you, too?*

*I am living with Father. I've taken the role of his assistant. So far, it's working out well. I'm doing things I'd never imagined myself doing. In fact, we have this patient right now. He's very ill. Someone shot him today, and Father had to take out the bullet. It was a nasty,*

*jagged wound. It looked more like a tear made by a spear.
I felt queasy when I first saw it, but Father wanted me
to hold the edges of the wound open, and I did.*

*You'll be surprised to know that our patient is an Indian.
He's a friend of Amelia's husband, Daniel Trahern. (I
just realized that Amelia is no longer a Dempsey! She's
Amelia Trahern.)*

*Well, to get back to the Indian, he's an unusual fellow.
Not at all what I expected from a savage. Oh, he has
intense dark eyes, and he wears copper rings through
each of his ears and a copper armband around his upper
arm.*

Black Hawk groaned, and Rachel put down the letter
and rose to check him. He thrashed out, frightening her.
She caught his hand, and was shocked by how hot he
felt. He quieted, and she felt his forehead, then was upset
to realize that he had taken a full-blown fever.

She mustn't panic. When she'd first mentioned the
possibility to her father, he'd assured her that a fever
would most likely occur. If it did, she was to give Black
Hawk a special medicine her father had prepared for him.

Rachel tried to remember where in the surgery the
medicine was stored, and she contemplated waking her
father.

"Wake me if he worsens," John Dempsey had told
her. "If he convulses, come and get me immediately;
otherwise, give him this medicine and bathe him with
cool water."

She suddenly remembered where her father had put the
draught he'd prepared earlier for Black Hawk. Rachel
decided she wouldn't wake her father, unless she absolutely had to. She would prove to her father that she could
handle this. She didn't want him displeased with her. She
didn't want to be sent home to Baltimore.

The medicine was on the middle shelf in the hutch of

her father's cabinet. She withdrew the small glass bottle, prepared a broth as instructed earlier by the doctor, then she added the elixir to the broth.

When she returned to Black Hawk, the brave was sleeping fitfully. She stared at his swollen face and wondered how she was going to get the medicine into the patient.

As Rachel held the cup and debated what to do, Black Hawk stirred and opened his eyes. His gaze was glazed; Rachel didn't think he was aware of his surroundings. He shifted, then moaned when the movement caused him pain.

Rachel set the medicine on a table, then slipped her arm under the brave's shoulder to help him to sit. He cried out, but she managed to hold him steady. Her heart thumping wildly, Rachel grabbed the medicine cup and held it before his lips.

"Drink it, Black Hawk," she urged him. She pressed the cup to his mouth. "Please open up and drink this!"

She rubbed the cup rim over his mouth. "Open, please!" She sighed with relief when his lips parted. She quickly pressed him to drink the contents, grinning when he instinctively sipped and swallowed. He grimaced and turned his head, but Rachel held him firmly, encouraging him with soft words to finish all of the medicine. When the cup was empty, Rachel carefully laid her patient back against the pillow.

"Father said it will help your fever and your pain," she told him softly, although she knew he couldn't hear. He didn't respond. The simple act of drinking had exhausted him.

She placed a hand on his forehead, frowned, then went for a basin of cool water and some linen towels. Rachel took one of the towels, folded it into a square pad, then dipped it into the water. She squeezed the excess water out and placed the wet compress on Black Hawk's forehead.

The sight of his bruised and battered body upset her. What monster had done this? After speaking with the brave's friends, her father had learned that Black Hawk had been ambushed by white men, who'd then beaten him and shot him as he fought back.

Her insides melted with sympathy for him. *You could have been killed, Black Hawk!* Her gaze lowered past his shoulder to his stomach, and she felt herself blush as she continued to look further down. Earlier, she'd laid a blanket about his waist. In his restlessness and her attempt to get the medicine into him, the blanket had fallen. Rachel bent and retrieved it from the edge of the bed, carefully placing it over him from shoulder to feet.

Her thoughts took a strange direction as she saw not her patient, but the man who'd made her feel a wild thrill when they'd shared a meal at her sister's table.

Rachel scurried back to her seat. *I must be so tired I'm getting addled,* she thought. What else could account for this odd fascination she had for the Ojibwa brave?

With an occasional glance at Black Hawk, she tried to write again, but soon gave up the idea of finishing her aunt's letter and stared at the Indian brave.

His shoulder burned. It felt as if someone had placed a hot arrowhead against his flesh. Black Hawk grimaced as he awakened. The slightest movement caused him pain. He relaxed and lay still, hoping for the searing heat to subside, but it continued to throb and hurt him.

He couldn't think clearly. Where was he? He opened his eyes, then gasped. His face hurt; he closed his eyes. He realized then that his cheek was swollen; he had barely been able to open his right eye.

He tried to open his left eye only, but any amount of facial movement was difficult. He braced himself for more pain and leveled himself upward. He cried out with the pain in his shoulder, and suddenly there was someone there to help him. He heard a sharp feminine exclamation followed by the soft voice of concern. He felt a cool touch and detected the sweet fragrance of lilacs.

His savior laid him down again, but with pillows beneath his head to prop him up slightly. With the pain subsided and his breathing slowed, Black Hawk peeked out from beneath partially shut eyelids. And saw a white woman. Rachel Dempsey.

"Are you all right?" she asked, sounding worried. "No! Never mind, don't talk! You'll only hurt yourself."

Her concern touched him. His slight smile turned into a grimace. He bolstered himself with courage, then opened his eyes wider to study Rachel further.

"How did I get here?" he asked in a rasping whisper.

Rachel stared at him, frowning, until understanding flickered in her green eyes. "Your friends brought you. They said that some white men ambushed you."

He closed his eyes as memory returned to him. "Soldiers."

"In the U.S. Army?" She sounded outraged.

"Yes."

"Why?"

His eyes opened, and he stared at her. "I do not know."

"That's terrible!"

"Yes." There was a brief pause. "Was anyone else hurt?" he asked.

"No," she quickly assured him. "Just you."

"Your father cared for me?"

She nodded. "Yes."

He viewed her again from beneath lowered lids. "You watched over me," he guessed.

She looked away. "Just a little."

But he decided by her behavior that she'd been taking

care of him and the experience had been a new one for her.

She swung back to gaze at him with a suddenness that startled him. "Black Hawk, are you in terrible pain?"

"It is bearable." *Just,* he thought.

"My father made a special medicine for you. It's been hours since you've had some. Can you drink?"

Had he already had some of the white doctor's medicine? He didn't remember taking it. "Yes, I can drink."

Rachel looked relieved. "I'll get some for you." She turned to hurry away.

"Rach-el."

She halted and glanced back. "Thank you for your help," he said huskily.

She turned a bright becoming shade of red. Finally, she nodded. "I-I'll be right back," she mumbled; then she was gone.

Black Hawk was left alone in the room with his injuries.


"How are you feeling?" John Dempsey asked his patient.

"I am healing," Black Hawk said.

The doctor smiled. "Good."

The brave flinched as John began to cut away his shoulder bandage. Rachel noticed that Black Hawk didn't cry out when her father pulled the fabric away from the wound, although the action must have hurt him. She watched with increasing sympathy as her father removed the bandage and began to examine the site of the injury.

"It seems to be mending fine," Dr. Dempsey announced. "I'll need to prepare a salve for it; then I'll have Rachel bandage you up again."

"Me?" she asked, nervous at the prospect.

Her father smiled at her. ''The worst is over, daughter. You'll do fine.''

She nodded, then went to the Indian's side and carefully eyed Black Hawk's shoulder. ''Comfrey and wild plum?''

John Dempsey looked surprised. ''Why, yes. I didn't know you'd paid such close attention.''

Rachel glanced at her father and grinned. Then, she returned her attention back to the injury.

The doctor turned to his patient. ''As soon as we've used the poultice, Rachel will bathe you and give you clean clothes.''

Rachel tensed and looked up. ''Is it necess—''

''Thank you,'' Black Hawk said, interrupting Rachel's reply. ''I would appreciate a bath. I am tired of the smell of death.''

As he spoke, Rachel had transferred her attention from her father to Black Hawk. He looked weak and tired, and she felt a surge of compassion. She would help him in any way she could . . . *but give him a bath?* He glanced at her, and she quickly looked away.

''Rachel, can you make the poultice?'' her father asked.

''Certainly, Father.'' She was grateful for the excuse to escape.

She left without waiting to see if he would need her to do anything else. She didn't want Black Hawk to witness her embarrassment at the idea of bathing him . . . although, no doubt, he'd guess later when the time came . . . unless she managed to keep control of her composure.

The poultice had been applied and reapplied. The afternoon was late, and Rachel knew that she could no longer stall bath time. With a sigh of resignation, Rachel went to the kitchen to warm up some water. She gathered the soap, towels, and basin that she would need.

Black Hawk had his eyes closed when she entered. She had just decided that his bath could wait a little longer . . . when the Ojibwa stirred, his eyelashes fluttered open, and he looked at her. He caught sight of the bath supplies, then tried to pull himself up to sit. He winced, but managed to rise up on his pillow and lean back against the headboard.

"How are you feeling?" Rachel pretended a nonchalance she was far from feeling as she set down the basin, soap, and clean towels on the table by the bed. Her hands trembled as she fiddled with the soap and towels.

When he didn't answer her, Rachel glanced at him with concern. The brave stared at her blankly. "Black Hawk?"

He seemed to rouse himself from a stupor. "You have come to check my injury?"

She nodded. *And to give you a bath,* she thought. Why, Father? Couldn't you suspect how difficult this would be?

*Is this a test? To see if I can handle every job that is handed my way? That must be what it is,* she decided. Her father was testing her to see if she should stay. Rachel drew herself up. She would pass this test, no matter how uncomfortable she felt bathing a half-naked man. She would not give her father a reason to send her home.

"Are you hungry?" she asked Black Hawk. So far, he hadn't eaten, and Rachel was concerned. It had been two days since he'd awakened. And although he'd spent many hours sleeping while he healed, she thought that he should have an appetite.

"I can eat."

She met his gaze. "You can?"

He nodded. His facial swelling had gone down some. The swollen area near his one eye was back to normal, except for the dark discoloration left by the reduction in swelling. She could see the whole of his dark eyes now. The intensity of his gaze as he studied her made her feel fluttery inside.

"Shall I make you some broth?" she asked, suddenly glad of the reprieve from bath time.

He shook his head, and her stomach flip-flopped. "You have meat?" he asked.

She blinked. "You want meat?"

Black Hawk studied the woman before him and nodded. "I would like some meat. You have venison?" He watched her eyelashes dip and rise.

"I think so."

He smiled, and the effort didn't hurt so much now. "Good. I will have meat and *okanakosimaan.*"

"*Okanakosimaan?*"

"It is a vegetable," he said. "What you call squash?"

He enjoyed the way her expression brightened. "Oh! I'll make you some meat and squash then," she said. "We have a lot of squash." She turned to leave.

He reached out and latched onto her wrist. Then in a fluid motion, he slid his hand down her wrist and shifted his fingers to intertwine with hers. She gave a little gasp as they locked gazes; then she glanced down at their joined hands.

"You can bring food," he said, "after you give me a bath."

# Chapter 9

"Be careful," Rachel warned as she entered the room and approached Black Hawk's bed. She was inwardly trembling as she carried in a small kettle of steaming water and poured some into the basin on the bed table. She had moved the table some distance from the bed, for fear that she would accidentally spill the hot water and burn her patient in the process.

When water had filled the bottom third of the bowl, Rachel left the room to return the kettle to the kitchen. Then she fetched a bucket of cold water to lower the temperature of the bathwater.

*Please, Lord, help me through this,* she thought as she entered the room minutes later with a pail. *Let me do this without making an absolute fool of myself.*

She carefully set the pail on the floor near the bed. Knowing she could no longer stall, she grabbed a small fabric square and plunged it into the water. She gasped at the heat. She had forgotten to add the cold water. Tears stung her eyes as she mentally berated herself.

"You are hurt, Rach-el?" Black Hawk asked in his deep, dark voice.

She sighed, then faced him. "I'll be fine."

"Let me see your hand."

She shook her head.

"Rach-el."

She held out her hand, which looked slightly pink but not seriously burned. His fingers felt cool on her wrist. She was startled by the contact.

"You must be careful. Such pretty hands to be hurt so."

To her complete astonishment, he lifted her hand to his mouth and kissed the tender flesh. She felt her cheeks burn as she stared at him. He kept her hand to his mouth and held her gaze.

He released her fingers slowly, and she stared at him, entranced, reluctant to pull away.

"The water is cooling quickly," he said in accented English.

She nodded and tore her gaze away. Turning her attention back to the basin, she carefully moved the table closer to the bed. Then, after draping a towel over the edge of the mattress in case she needed it, she soaped up the linen square and began to lather and wash Black Hawk's right arm.

Bathing the brave embarrassed her. If she felt this way over washing his arm, how was she going to feel when she had to wash more . . . intimate parts of him?

Perhaps she could just wash his limbs and then hand him the soapy cloth. She chanced a peek at his expression. No, she thought, he'd tell her father, who would be upset that she couldn't perform this simple job.

So she would bathe Black Hawk . . . wherever he needed to be washed.

His arm was muscular, slightly bruised, but sleek and firm to the touch. Rachel rubbed his arm until the soap formed a rich lather, then dipped the cloth and rinsed his skin. Now that she'd done the one arm, she debated where to wash next. His chest seemed the most likely place, but she wasn't ready for that yet. She skirted the bed instead to wash the opposite arm.

Black Hawk didn't say a word as she worked, for which she was grateful. She wasn't sure how she'd handle this if he mocked her or made comments that would only add to her uneasiness.

When both arms were done, she looked at his expression, and saw that he was lying with eyes closed, with tiny lines of pain across his brow.

"Black Hawk," she whispered. "Are you all right? Shall I continue?"

He raised his eyelids, focusing his dark gaze on her. "Yes. I am well."

He wasn't well, she thought, but she wasn't going to argue with him. If nothing else, she'd learned during these last few minutes that Black Hawk might have wanted this bath, but he wasn't particularly enjoying it. His pallor, the tension on his face, suggested to Rachel that perhaps Black Hawk needed to rest more than he needed to be washed. Still, he'd said he wanted her to bathe him, so bathe him she would.

She came around to the basin again, rinsed out the washcloth, and rubbed it with soap. Eyeing him with a frown, Rachel looked at his bruised chest and shoulder wound, then began to gingerly cleanse his neck and breast area. He winced when she washed too close to the bullet wound. Murmuring an apology, she quickly withdrew the cloth and concentrated on his stomach area instead.

A blanket still covered him from the waist downward. Did he expect her to remove that bedcover and wash beneath?

He wore nothing besides the blanket. Her father had removed the brave's loincloth that first day in order to attend to contusions and injuries to his groin and upper thigh area. Rachel had been out of the room. John Dempsey had been the only one thus far who'd doctored Black Hawk's most private area.

Was there a way she could avoid that private place?

She looked at him. His eyes were still closed, but he seemed relaxed now. The sight of his ease encouraged her to continue. If she could make him feel better by giving him a bath, then why should she be nervous or embarrassed?

She lathered his stomach, and found herself fascinated with the taut muscles of his belly and his smooth skin. Here, the flesh had somehow managed to remain uninjured. Surveying the surrounding area, Rachel narrowed her gaze and silently wished a terrible pox on the men who had done this to him.

She gave no more thought to embarrassment as she carefully lowered the blanket to ease the washcloth over one hip. She kept his most private parts covered as she ran the cloth down his leg from hip to thigh to knee and to calf. He had little body hair. The lack of it surprised her, but it made him seem no less of a man. In fact, he was more masculine than any man she'd ever met . . . and that included Jordan.

She felt a moment's guilt. She had loved Jordan. She still did—didn't she?

She didn't want to think of Jordan now. She'd lost too much sleep and spent too many nights crying over the man. She was sure that Black Hawk wouldn't betray the woman he'd chosen for his wife.

Wife? Was he married? she wondered. Did the Ojibwa marry the way she understood marriage to be? Or did they spend time with one woman before finding another?

Her thoughts went wild as she moved around to the other edge of the bed, where she began to wash his opposite side.

She glanced upward, saw that his eyes were open, and froze. "Am I hurting you?" she asked him, feeling awkward.

He shook his head. Black Hawk stared at the woman before him, fascinated by the red color on her cheeks. He was tired, so tired. Her ministrations soothed him. He enjoyed her touch, the warm water, the gentle way she rubbed the cloth over him. He was sore and sensitive in certain areas, but he didn't want Rachel to stop.

"Perhaps I should leave you to sleep," she said, averting her gaze.

"I would like you to finish," he said. *"Daga.* Please."

She looked at him. He held her gaze unflinchingly. There was something that attracted him to her. He felt helpless lying here injured, but the fact of her presence made bearable his efforts to remain still.

Rachel's hair was tousled, and she had a streak of something across her right cheek. She looked tired, but lovely. He'd never wanted to touch a woman the way he wanted to touch Rachel. Since he couldn't give in to the urge to caress her, he satisfied himself with his enjoyment of her hands on him.

Unable to tear her gaze away from Black Hawk's face, Rachel rubbed a little harder than was warranted, and he grimaced. She apologized profusely and felt her cheeks turn bright red.

*I can't do this,* she thought, gazing at that bedcover. *I can't remove the blanket and wash his . . . genitals.*

She avoided that area, lifting the edge of the blanket

just enough to wash his left leg. When she was done, she went to the basin, dropped in the cloth, then with a brief glance in his direction, she began to gather the bath supplies.

To her relief, he appeared to be sleeping. He didn't open his eyes or speak as she picked up soap, damp towels, and basin, then left.

Two days later, she was not so lucky. Black Hawk was still there, and her father had decided that it was bath time again. This time the Ojibwa brave watched her the entire time she prepared for and then gave him his bath.

It was extremely disconcerting for Rachel to have Black Hawk's dark eyes studying her while she carried in the water and supplies. She flushed brightly when his onyx gaze followed her every movement as she soaped up the cloth, then turned her attention to washing her patient.

"How are you feeling?" she asked, trying conversation to banish her uneasiness.

"I am well." He shifted, and the movement called her attention to the rippling of his arm muscles as he braced himself and pushed himself to rest higher against the headboard.

"Father said you'll be able to go home soon," she replied, keeping her attention on washing his muscled arm.

He didn't respond, and she looked at him. His eyes glowed as they locked gazes. "You wish me to leave?" he asked.

"I didn't say that," she said, looking away.

She gasped when he caught her wrist. "You have cared for me a long time. You wish me to go home so you can rest."

*On the contrary,* she thought. Black Hawk made her feel restless, not tired. When she was near him, she felt more alive than she'd ever felt before.

"I am fine," she said, trying to pull away, but the brave's grip was firm. "It's important that you get well." She heard noise in the outer room, and she shifted her gaze to the door. "That will be Daniel. He came earlier to visit while you were sleeping."

Black Hawk released her wrist and slid his fingers up her bare arm. She shivered with pleasure and moved away.

"I think you're all clean now," she said brightly. She could feel the heat in her cheeks.

With a slight wince, he shifted and grabbed her arm. "I have not had a proper bath," he said softly. His eyes glowed. He gestured with the other hand toward the private area beneath the sheet.

She could feel herself flush from the neck upward as she gazed at him with horror. "Here then," she said as she slapped the wet washcloth across his chest. "You seem well enough to handle it. Wash there yourself!"

She left the room, muttering angrily under her breath when she heard his deep chuckle fill the room.


She was cleaning the surgery when she felt someone's presence. Rachel turned and gasped. A strange Indian stood inside the room not far from her. He wore an unusual headdress and was an elderly man. Her heart began to pound as she approached him.

"Can I help you?" she asked in a shaky voice.

The man muttered something in his native tongue. Rachel glanced helplessly beyond him to the door; she hadn't understood a word he said.

She shook her head. "I'm sorry but I don't know what you're trying to tell me."

The Indian repeated his words.

This time Rachel eyed the door behind her. She felt a rising panic.

Hugging herself with her arms, she looked back at him. "I wish I knew what you were saying!"

"My chief wishes to know where you are keeping me," Black Hawk's voice said from behind her.

"Black Hawk! I thought you were sleeping." Rachel spun to see the injured Ojibwa brave leaning heavily against the doorjamb. "Your chief?" she asked.

Black Hawk nodded, then stood upright, and swayed on his feet. Seeing his pallor, Rachel rushed to his side and put her arms around him to steady him. The heat of his muscled flesh enveloped her instantly. She became conscious of his scent. He smelled of the soap she'd used earlier when she'd bathed him, and another extremely pleasant scent that belonged only to Black Hawk.

"You should not be out of bed," she told him as she tightened her hold on him.

He smiled down at her before he spoke softly to his chief.

The chief answered back. Rachel thought she detected concern in the old Indian's voice.

"Come," she said to Black Hawk. "You must get back to your room. Tell your chief he may come if he'd like."

Black Hawk's dark gaze flickered with amusement as he glanced at her before addressing his chief.

Rachel waited patiently for the chief's answer. The man spoke, and Black Hawk translated. "Big-Cat-with-Broken-Paw thanks you. His only desire is to see his Ojibwa father, Black-Hawk-Who-Hunts-at-Dawn."

"His father!" She frowned as she looked at the old man and then Black Hawk. "How can that be?"

Black Hawk's onyx eyes lit up with laughter. "We do not use the word *father* as you do. I am his father and he is mine."

"I see," she said, but she didn't. She began to urge

him back into his room. "Please, Black Hawk, you must lie down before you fall on your face."

"Such a demanding woman," he whispered teasingly, but he allowed her to lead him back to bed.

Once she had made sure that Black Hawk was comfortable, she turned, then drew a sharp breath as she came nose-to-nose with Big-Cat-with-Broken-Paw.

"Tell the chief that he must not tire you," she said.

There was a moment of silence. Rachel glanced back at Black Hawk to find him studying her strangely. She flushed and turned back to the chief.

"Tell him, Black Hawk."

The chief frowned at her and said something to Black Hawk. Slowly, carefully, the recovering Ojibwa brave answered.

The elderly Indian stared at her hard.

Rachel shivered. "What did you tell him?"

Black Hawk didn't respond.

Had he fallen asleep? She glanced back. He hadn't. "Black Hawk?" She felt a chill. "What did your chief say?"

His expression was solemn as he regarded her. "He asks why the white woman with hair of brown fire keeps me prisoner."

Rachel's mouth fell open in shock. "I'm not keeping you a prisoner!"

Big-Cat-with-Broken-Paw spoke. Black Hawk answered from his bed.

"What?" Rachel said with a hint of panic, as her gaze searched for a weapon on the old man. "What did he say?"

"He asks why you treat me like *abinoojiinh*."

"*Abinoojiinh?*"

Black Hawk nodded soberly. "A child."

"I—" She felt tongue-tied. What could she say? Was

it true? Was that how it seemed to him? "Do I treat you like a child?" she asked him, meeting his gaze.

He stared at her without answering.

"Do I?"

His eyes lit with laughter. "Black Hawk, eat your food. It is good for you. Black Hawk, it is time for bed. How will you get strong if you do not get your rest?"

She could feel herself flush. Then she saw his amusement. "He didn't say that, did he. You are having fun at my expense."

Black Hawk frowned. "Do you not say these things to me? Did you not bathe me as a mother would bathe her child?"

"I—I'm trying to help you get well!" she exclaimed. Heat burned all the way down her neck.

"That is good to hear, Black Hawk. This woman cares for you to help you," Big-Cat-with-Broken-Paw said in perfect, if accented, English.

Rachel gaped at him. "You speak English!" She glanced at Black Hawk. "He—"

Black Hawk nodded. "Yes," he said. "My chief speaks your language. He has understood everything you said."

Her jaw tightened with anger. "That's a mean trick!" she exclaimed.

The chief had the good grace to look uncomfortable, but not Black Hawk. He apparently had found the previous exchange vastly entertaining.

"You should not anger the one who feeds and bathes you, Black Hawk," Big-Cat-with-Broken-Paw said.

Rachel narrowed her gaze and eyed him thoughtfully. "Your chief is right, Black Hawk. You shouldn't be mean to the one who cares for you nicely."

Black Hawk stared at the woman, uncomfortable with the look that had suddenly entered her green eyes. "Have

I not thanked you for my food? Do I not listen to you when you speak?''

She nodded, but her expression promised retribution. She spun on her heels and headed toward the door. ''Supper will be in an hour,'' she said breezily, as if their conversation and her anger had never occurred.

Watching her leave the room, Black Hawk got an uneasy feeling.

''You had best watch where you place your moccasins with that one,'' Big-Cat-with-Broken-Paw said. ''She didn't enjoy your little joke.''

''No,'' Black Hawk said. He still stared at the doorway where she'd disappeared. ''I do not think she did.''

''Ah, but she will soon forget her anger,'' the chief said.

Black Hawk looked at him with surprise. ''Why do you say this?''

The older man shrugged. ''Women soon forget these things.''

*As if Rachel Dempsey were an ordinary woman,* Black Hawk thought, *which she isn't.*

''Now,'' the chief said, ''tell me how you are feeling, and if this white woman is treating you well.''

Black Hawk glared at the older man, and laughter erupted from the chief's throat.

# Chapter 10

The Ojibwa brave was kind, and he was patient—
except with himself. Although Black Hawk was healing
remarkably well, Rachel could sense frustration in him.
She knew he was anxious to be gone. The inactivity of
his recovery bothered him. Each day her father came into
Black Hawk's room, checked the brave's injuries, and
pronounced him healing. But John Dempsey still wasn't
ready to discharge his patient.

Black Hawk was eating well again. Rachel was in the
kitchen preparing the midday meal. She thought she would
make the Ojibwa something special to cheer him up.
She'd spent part of the morning baking finger-cakes. The
mouth-watering scent of baking cake filled the entire
infirmary building. She had made sandwiches from the
bread she'd baked yesterday and some homemade jam
that Amelia had given her. She set the sandwiches and a
cup of tea along with two finger-cakes on a tray and
carried it toward Black Hawk's room.

She heard a thump followed by a groan as she approached the doorway. Concerned, she hurried inside and saw that Black Hawk had fallen beside his bed. She hastened to put down the tray so she could help him.

"Black Hawk! Are you all right?"

He was struggling to get up as she hunkered beside him and slipped her arm around his waist. Her spine tingled as her arm brushed against his skin.

"Black Hawk?" she asked when he didn't answer.

He looked at her. His breathing was labored; his effort to get up had exhausted him. "I am all right."

"What happened?"

"I tried to get up and felt weak."

"You should have called me."

"I needed to relieve myself."

She blushed. Her father had handled that matter with Black Hawk. He must have felt uncomfortable asking her for help.

"Shall I get you the chamber pot?" she queried. Warmth filled her cheeks.

"I wish to use the outhouse."

She helped him into the bed, conscious of his nearness, his weight, and his scent, and studied him. "You'll never make it. I'm sorry." She stood awkwardly, wondering what to do. "Shall I call my father?"

Scowling with frustration, he nodded.

"I'll be right back." With the sharp image of his expression firmly implanted in her mind, she escaped gratefully to find her father. She searched several places, and finally found him with Allen Whitely in the good Reverend's kitchen. After asking to speak with her father alone, she explained the situation. John Dempsey excused himself to Reverend Whitely and returned with Rachel to the infirmary.

"I'll wait in the kitchen," she said. "When you're done, I've made some sandwiches for us."

The doctor nodded and went to help his patient.

A short time later, John Dempsey appeared in the kitchen, looking for a sandwich.

"Did he eat?" Rachel asked her father.

"He was eating when I left," he said.

"He wants to go home, Father."

John frowned. "I know. I've asked him to stay for two more days."

*Two more days?* It would seem strange when Black Hawk left. He'd been with them a week. She thought she might actually miss him.

"There's cake when you're done," she said.

Her father's eyes lit up.

"I'll see if our patient wants anything else to eat," Rachel added. Then, she headed back to the room, and saw that Black Hawk had eaten and now slept. She took the empty plate and tray, and silently left the room.


She dreamt of Jordan, then woke up in the middle of the night and started to cry. It had been some time since she'd wept for him. She thought she had gotten over him completely, but then when she least expected it the memory of him would surface, making her long for him all over again.

The dream had been wonderful. It had mirrored some of their happiest times together. They had picnicked in the country, away from their family and friends, just the two of them with a basket of wonderful food, a blanket, and their love for one another. In her dream, they had eaten, and then Jordan had stretched out on the blanket with his head in her lap. Gazing up at her with hungry eyes, he had talked of their future together, the house they would live in, and the children they would have. Then, they were silent for a time, while Rachel played with Jordan's hair and listened to the hum of insects while enjoying the warm, spring sunshine. After a while, Jordan opened his eyes, looked at her, and then drew her head downward for a kiss.

Rachel's heart raced just to remember that dream and the effect of his kiss. She had been so happy . . . until she had awoken to reality.

It had taken her a while to go back to sleep after that. She had trouble rising that morning, and had to force herself from her bed to tend her patient. Fortunately, Black Hawk no longer needed all-night care. Rachel tugged on her chemise and gown, then dragged herself wearily into the kitchen to prepare breakfast.

"Good morning." John Dempsey entered the kitchen with a cheerful smile.

"Morning, Father," she murmured as she measured the ingredients for porridge.

"You look tired, daughter," he said. "Didn't you sleep well?"

Glancing at him, she shook her head. "I woke up and couldn't get back to sleep."

He didn't comment as he went to the pantry and pulled out a loaf of bread. He sliced off a large crusty piece and reached for Amelia's jam.

"Maybe you should go back to bed for a spell," her father suggested.

Rachel looked at him with surprise. "What about Black Hawk?"

John brushed her concern aside. "I'm going to release him today."

And Rachel's spirits plummeted lower.

When she carried in the Ojibwa brave's breakfast, Black Hawk was sitting up in bed. His chest was bare. The bedcover draped his lower half; the contrast of white against his darker skin drew Rachel's attention briefly to his waist. She flushed and met his gaze.

"Good morning," she said without much cheer.

*"Aaniin."*

She could feel his eyes on her as she set the tray across his lap. The warmth of him reached out to her as she adjusted the tray, then straightened.

Uncomfortable with his gaze, she began to babble. "I made porridge. I hope you like it. I tried something new. I sweetened it with Amelia's jam. And I made you tea as well. You seemed to like tea so I thought you'd enjoy it for breakfast. If there is anything else you'd rather have, just let me know and I'll be happy to get it for you—"

She paused when he touched her arm. "What is wrong?" he asked softly.

She quickly turned away to hide her tears. "Nothing."

He was silent for so long that she finally looked back. She expected to find him eating his breakfast, but he hadn't touched a bite of food. He sat, staring at her, his dark eyes narrowed thoughtfully.

Rachel wanted to escape from the room. "I have some chores to do," she said, and was relieved when he didn't try to stop her. Black Hawk affected her in a way she didn't want to be affected. Jordan had hurt her; the pain of his betrayal was still raw. The last thing she needed was to be attracted to this Indian.

She went into the surgery and began the task of checking her father's instruments. She made a list of supplies that were needed. Since Black Hawk had come to stay, her father had seen only a dozen patients, all for minor cuts, scrapes, and burns. Rachel wanted to ensure that all would be ready for the seriously injured patient like Black Hawk.

She worked hard to scrub down her father's work area. Time passed quickly as her thoughts returned to her dream. She scrubbed more briskly as she fought self-pity. Tears blurred her eyes, so that every so often she had to stop and dash them away with her hand to see.

Rachel didn't pause in her work when she heard someone enter the surgery from the back rooms. It would be her father come in to get his notes, which he would take back to their small parlor to review. There, he would jot down information about yesterday's patients. Later, after he was done, he would leave the infirmary to visit and check on some of his recovering patients.

Rachel didn't glance at her father as she continued to clean the room. John Dempsey didn't immediately go to his cabinet, as he usually did. She didn't give it any thought, for sometimes the doctor checked on the contents of his medical bag first.

She wiped down the table by the examining bed, then moved to the medicine cabinet and unlocked each compartment. As she looked into the hutch door glass, she stared at her reflection and wondered why Jordan had abandoned her for an older woman. Had it just been for the money? If so, why had Jordan pursued her so persistently in the first place?

*Why, Jordan? Why did you propose?*

She sniffed as she pulled out a new length of white linen fabric and began to cut it into approximately six-inch strips.

A hand settled on her shoulder. Rachel gasped and spun.

"Black Hawk!"

He gazed at her with obsidian eyes filled with compassion.

She blinked as she looked back at him. The warmth and concern in his expression were her undoing. With a soft sob, she flowed into his embrace and began to weep quietly against his breast. She felt his arms close and tighten around her, his hand on her hair. Then she heard his soothing voice murmuring to her in Ojibwa. And she was comforted by him.

Several minutes passed; Rachel didn't know how many. She liked being in Black Hawk's arms, but she wondered what her father would think if he saw them together. Her parent didn't know about Jordan. He would see the Indian and assume the wrong thing. She knew she should pull away from Black Hawk, but she didn't have the desire to leave him.

He seemed in no hurry to let her go either. She had spent little time in his room that morning. How had he sensed the depth of her pain?

As thoughts of Jordan left her, she became conscious of everything about the man who held her . . . the warm, smoothness of his bare, muscled chest . . . the strength of his embrace and the gentleness of his hand in her hair. He had put on his loincloth, and she was aware of the heat of his maleness against her lower abdomen.

She closed her eyes, enjoying his scent, the nearness of him. She knew she should step away, but it just felt too good to be held in this man's arms.

"Rach-el," he whispered.

She looked up, and the gleam in his eyes warmed her. "You are all right now?"

She nodded, unable to glance away. Her gaze fell to his mouth, and she had the strongest desire to kiss him. When their gazes locked, passion flared in his dark eyes, the sight of it making Rachel weak in the knees.

Black Hawk studied the woman he held in his arms, and he wanted her with an intensity that surprised him. He had come to say good-bye. The doctor had finally released him. Suddenly, he didn't want to go. He wanted to stay here with Rachel. He wanted to lie with her and show her the pleasures of the sleeping mat. His mouth went dry as he gazed at her. The look in her green eyes heated his blood, and he tightened his hold on her.

"Rach-el," he murmured, and bent his head to kiss her. To his pleasant surprise, she gave herself up to his kiss. Her lips were soft and warm and tasted sweet. He felt her hands slip to his shoulders and cling.

His heart pounded within his chest as he trailed a path of moist kisses to her ear, then back to her wonderful mouth. He released her waist to cup her face with his hands; then he deepened the kiss, delving past her lips to taste her tongue.

He heard her gasp, felt her stiffen; then she shivered with desire as her tongue ducled and mated with his own.

"Black Hawk," she moaned when he lifted his head to study her. Her eyes remained closed, her lashes forming dark feathery crescents against her smooth, white cheeks. He slid his fingers into her hair, gently cupping her behind her ears. Her eyes fluttered open, and she gazed at him with green orbs hazy with passion.

With a groan, Black Hawk kissed her again, before he released her and stepped back. "I have come to say good-bye," he said huskily.

Rachel felt a wave of pain. "My father released you." She turned away. "You must be happy that you'll be reunited with your people."

He stepped closer to her and settled his hand on her shoulder, squeezing ever so slightly. "There is no one there like you," he admitted, then silently scolded himself for those words when she spun to gaze up at him. He felt himself mesmerized by the vivid green of her eyes. He didn't want to feel anything for her, but he was helpless to fight it when she looked at him that way. "You are good with your patients," he said.

Disappointment clouded her forest-green eyes. "Yes, well, I am learning," she said, averting her gaze once again. "My sister helped Father in Baltimore. I never wanted to help."

"You must come to visit my village. You will like Spring Blossom."

"Spring Blossom?"

"My sister."

Rachel was relieved. She was afraid that Spring Blossom was Black Hawk's woman. Did he have one? she wondered. Not that it was any of her concern. They were from different cultures, and she had vowed not to have anything to do with men.

"There is no one," he said, as if reading her mind.

She released a shaky breath. "I didn't ask."

His eyes gleamed. "There is no one," he repeated. "I have no time for a mate."

Rachel blushed. "I'm sorry." What else could she say? That she was glad that he had no wife? How could she say anything without giving him the wrong idea?

*But what of that kiss? What idea have I given him by allowing him to kiss me?*

"I may have misled you with that—our—kiss," she whispered, embarrassed by the exchange.

He stared at her, his expression somber. "I understand that you were not inviting me to your sleeping mat."

She gasped. "No."

He smiled then. "You cared for me when I needed you. This has not been easy for me, but you helped to cheer me. *Miigwech.*"

She understood that he'd just thanked her. "You are welcome." She felt her throat tighten. "Good-bye, Black-Hawk-Who-Hunts-at-Dawn."

He bent and kissed her mouth. She closed her eyes and responded. *"Giga-waabamin,"* he murmured. And then he released her.

When Rachel opened her eyes, Black Hawk was gone.

# Chapter 11

The infirmary seemed empty to Rachel without Black Hawk. She missed his quiet but commanding presence whenever she entered the sickroom. That morning as she came in to clean, she gazed for a long moment at the bed where he slept. She recalled how he'd looked lying there . . . his dark hair against the pillow . . . his onyx eyes glistening as his gaze followed her about the room. He was the most intriguing individual she'd ever met.

His appearance had been much improved when he'd taken his leave of them. His gunshot wound had formed a scab, the swelling in his face had long since gone down, and the colorful bruises on his body had faded to a dull shade of purplish yellow. For someone who had been injured so badly, he had healed quickly without any serious lasting damage. Eventually, he'd have only the scar near his shoulder left as evidence of his ordeal.

Thoughts of the Ojibwa brave ultimately brought back memories of his kiss. She'd been shocked at her response to him. If she closed her eyes, she knew she could recall every single detail about him. She'd never felt this way when she and Jordan had kissed, but then Black Hawk was nothing like the suave, sophisticated man who'd once asked her to marry him. Black Hawk's looks were compelling . . . savage. And he made her heart race as Jordan never had nor ever could.

Why did Black Hawk kiss her?

*Because he was grateful, nothing more,* she told herself over and over again. Her heart began to beat faster. His gratitude certainly stirred her blood!

"Rachel."

She spun to find her father at the doorway. Fortunately, she'd brought a broom to sweep the floor, so John Dempsey wouldn't guess that she was mooning over Black Hawk.

Her father was frowning.

She was immediately concerned. "What's wrong?" she asked.

"We've a new patient. He's sliced himself and needs stitches. Would you please assist me?"

Rachel nodded and set down her broom to lean in the corner of the room.

"Is it serious?" she asked as she followed her father closely.

"I'm afraid so."

"Who is it? Anyone I know."

"Young Will Thornton."

"Oh, no," she gasped. Will Thornton was a nice young man who had been helpful to Rachel when she'd first come to the mission. He'd carried in her clothes trunk for her and helped her to rearrange the furniture in her room.

As she entered the surgery, Rachel saw Will immediately where he sat on the examining table. He looked pale as he held a cloth bandage to his injured hand. Already, blood seeped through to stain the white fabric red.

She hurried forward. "Oh, Will, what did you do to yourself?"

He looked ghastly as he glanced at her apologetically. "I was sharpening a knife for Mrs. Jenkins."

"I told him to be careful," a woman's voice said from the other side of the room.

Rachel turned and spied Freda Jenkins standing at the door to the waiting area. "I'm sure you did," Rachel said. She frowned as she centered her attention on Will again. "Will, you'd best lie down. Let me help you."

She helped him to lie back, while the doctor repositioned his supplies. When she was done, she looked at her father and asked him a silent question. At his nod, she hurriedly left the room to put water on the stove to warm. Then she rummaged through the kitchen cupboard for her father's unopened bottle of whiskey. She returned to the surgery with the whiskey bottle and placed it on the doctor's instrument table.

"What's that for?" John Dempsey asked.

Rachel was momentarily flustered. "I thought you might need it for Will."

Her father frowned. "We've got laudanum for the pain."

"I know, Father. I thought that you may need it to clean the wound."

"I'll need it after I finish with my patient," he said with a chuckle.

Will groaned at the joke, and Rachel patted his shoulder. "Don't you worry, Will. My father is only teasing me."

The young man winced as the doctor probed the area of the wound, but he managed a slight smile when John Dempsey announced that the injury wasn't as serious as he'd first thought.

"A few stitches, Will, and you'll be as good as new," the doctor said.

The patient didn't seem bothered by the prospect of being stitched up; then Rachel remembered that Will had been injured once in an Indian attack that nearly cost him his life. This cut must be nothing compared to those injuries he'd sustained at the hands of the Sioux.

Watching her father work, she shivered, recalling that her father had been kidnapped in the same Sioux attack in which Will had been hurt. If things had turned out differently, then her father would be dead or still missing. The thought of losing her father gave Rachel a chill.

There had been no talk of trouble with the Indians since she'd arrived. Did that mean that they were at peace?

Rachel frowned. What about Black Hawk? He said it was soldiers who had injured him. Why? Were there white men who hated the Indians that much?

*Of course there are, silly,* Rachel thought. *Stop being ridiculous. Remember how afraid you were of Indians before getting to know Black Hawk? Fear can drive a person to do strange things.*

As she was thinking, she automatically responded to her father's instructions. She gave Will some laudanum for the pain, and John Dempsey cleaned the cut, then closed it with neat, even little stitches. When he was done, the doctor left it to Rachel to bandage the wound.

Rachel collected the bloodstained cloth and placed it in a basin. Then she gathered fresh bandages and returned to Will.

"How does it feel?" she asked gently as she unrolled a cloth strip.

"All right," Will said.

"Does it throb much?" She held the bandage up in readiness to apply it.

"Some." He looked at her. "Your father's a good doctor."

"The best," Rachel agreed. "Now, I'll try not to hurt you."

"You won't hurt me," he said with such emphasis and confidence that Rachel stopped and stared at him. His expression made her uncomfortable. She had seen that look on the faces of many interested men.

"Will—"

"Have dinner with me this evening."

She frowned as she carefully placed the fabric over the injury. "I don't think that would be wise."

"Why not?"

She paused in what she was doing and glanced at him. "Because I'm afraid you'll take my acceptance the wrong way."

He scowled at her. "And what way is that?"

"That there could be something more than friendship between us, but there can't be."

"You're not married. Are you betrothed?"

She felt a painful pang as she carefully, gently wound the bandage about the palm of Will's hand. "No," she said. *I was.*

"Then why won't you look twice at me?"

"It's not you, Will," she said as she continued to work. "It's all men. I'm just not interested in courtship or marriage."

"You, a woman"—he mocked hurtfully—"have no interest in marriage?"

Rachel, who had just finished, paled as she stepped back. "Will, I think this conversation is over."

"Rachel—"

But Rachel was wrapped up in her own painful thoughts. She had been interested in marriage to the one she'd thought was the right man. But that man had betrayed her, proving to her that no man was trustworthy. Yes, she'd had a lot of admirers back in Baltimore, but every one of them had had their own best interests at heart. None of them, especially Jordan, had cared enough for her to worry about her happiness.

*Am I being too selfish to think this way? I would have done everything I could to make Jordan happy, too.*

"Rachel!"

Will's pleading voice finally caught her attention. She had moved to the medicine cabinet and was replacing the unused bandages. She faced him. "Yes?"

"I apologize. I didn't mean to make you cry."

*Cry?* Rachel touched her cheek and realized that it was wet. She had, in fact, shed a tear. *I've shed enough tears over Jordan Sinclair!* she thought.

"Do you see why I will not have dinner with you? You would expect more than I can give you."

"I'm sorry," he said, looking glum. "I don't want to lose your friendship. Can we forget this conversation?"

Rachel forced a bright smile. "Of course." She approached him with a small book—her father's book of notes. She flipped through pages until she found what she needed. "I'm going to give you some instructions on how to care for that cut. You'll follow them carefully?" She met his gaze. He nodded. "Good."

Rachel's attention was drawn to the waiting room doorway, through which she could see Mrs. Jenkins seated in a chair.

"Is she here to walk you home?"

"You mean you don't think I should stay?" Will teased.

She couldn't control the heat that warmed her skin. She quickly averted her glance. "I'm afraid not. Now if you'd like someone to shoot you—"

"No, thank you," he said emphatically. She looked

back and chuckled as he raised his good hand as if to ward off evil.

"William?" Freda Jenkins had moved to the open door. "Are you all right, William?"

The younger woman suddenly appeared behind Freda. "Mother told me that you'd gotten hurt," the lovely vision in blue said.

Rachel was amazed to see Will blush. "I'm fine, Ariana," he said. Ariana Jenkins was a lovely young woman with blond hair and bright blue eyes. Her blue gown complemented her coloring and fit her beautifully.

"I'll be waiting to walk you home."

"Ah, thank you."

Rachel hid her amusement as the young man gawked at Ariana Jenkins. When the two women had taken a seat again, Rachel bent closer to Will and whispered in his ear, "Perhaps Ariana will invite you to supper."

Will looked at her, then grinned. "Perhaps." His expression became solemn. "Friends again?" He hesitated, as if he wanted to offer her his good hand but good manners forbade him from doing so without a lady extending her hand first.

Rachel held out her hand. "Friends," she said.

With a smile of relief, Will captured her fingers, then left shortly afterward with the Jenkins women fussing over him.

A few moments later, John Dempsey stood at the doorway to their back rooms. Rachel was tidying up the surgery. "Rachel—"

She looked up from the instrument table, where she'd been collecting the tools that had been used. "Yes, Father?"

"I heard your conversation with young Will," he began, his brow furrowing.

She blushed. "Oh," she said, and turned away.

John entered the room and walked to where she stood and rummaged through the cabinet. "Will is a nice young man. Why don't you think you should have dinner with him? In fact, I've noticed that there have been a few men at the mission who have tried to catch your eye, but you won't have anything to do with them."

She spun to face him. "I don't want a beau, Father," she said.

"Good heavens, child, why not? You used to have lots of beaux and they seemed to make you happy."

"That was before I learned the risk of getting involved with one of them," she admitted softly.

Her father scowled with displeasure. "Just because one man made a persistent nuisance of himself is no reason to reject all men."

"I'm not ready for courtship, Father." This was a painful topic for her.

"Well, girl, husbands don't grow on trees around here, you know!"

"I'm not looking to marry," she replied stiffly. "I've decided that I am happy enough being who I am. I've done well as your assistant, haven't I?" The last was said with concern.

John's expression softened. "Of course you have." He smiled. "You've adjusted quite well. Learned faster than your sister, in fact, but don't tell her I told you so."

Rachel managed a smile. The subject of marriage was still a painful one, one she hadn't thought to consider again. Jordan was the only man who'd stirred her in any way . . . unless you counted the strange stirrings she'd experienced in Black Hawk's presence. Feelings, she thought, that had been prompted by curiosity and fear.

*Liar,* she thought. *I can't fool myself.* The feelings she felt for Black Hawk weren't rooted in fear, but in basic, elemental physical attraction.

"Father, are you in such a hurry for me to leave?" she asked.

"No!" John exclaimed. He seemed genuinely appalled that she could possibly think that way.

"Then can't you accept that I'm happy living here with you, helping you?"

"It isn't right that a beautiful young woman not find herself a young man. Look how happy your sister has been."

The comment stung. "I know she is happy," Rachel said, "but I'm not Amelia, and I don't love Daniel." *The man makes no secret of his dislike for me.*

"I just want you to be happy, too," her father grumbled.

Rachel smiled and hugged him. "I know you do. But let me decide what makes me happy."

John nodded.

She touched his cheek. "Thank you, Father." She could only hope that this particular topic for discussion was permanently closed.

# Chapter 12

A noise woke Rachel at dawn. She listened to the quiet for several seconds until the sound came again. Then she got up and slipped on her dressing gown. As she left the privacy of her bedchamber, she encountered her father pulling on his robe as he left his room.

"Father, did you hear it?" she asked softly.

John nodded. Neither one knew what it was, but they were about to find out. "The noise is coming from the surgery," he whispered. He reentered his bedchamber, and returned moments later with his flintlock pistol.

Rachel's eyes widened as she spied the gun.

Her father touched her arm as he walked past her. "In case the intruder is dangerous."

*An intruder?* Rachel wondered with mounting horror. She thought that perhaps it was an animal. What if it was a criminal or a murderer!

She followed her father closely as John Dempsey crossed to the door to the front rooms. They entered the sickroom, the chamber where Black Hawk had stayed during his recuperation, before they hesitated outside the doctor's surgery. The room housed John Dempsey's instruments and medical supplies, as well as a store of blankets, linens, and other bedding. Rachel and her father looked at each other before John pressed his ear to the door to listen inside the surgery.

A shuffling noise from the surgery filtered out into the sickroom. Rachel froze. Her father stiffened. Then, John straightened and placed one hand on the doorknob. With his other hand, he held the gun aimed and ready. He turned the knob and pushed.

"Stop!" he cried.

Rachel strained to see past him. Her father moved into the room. She gasped as she caught sight of the intruders. Indians!

She heard her father talking with them, and the strange sound of their native tongue as a warrior answered. When John Dempsey lowered the gun, Rachel sighed with relief. Ojibwa, she thought. She entered the room to get a better glimpse of the braves.

There were four Indians. One warrior stood stiffly in the center of the room. Two of the others supported the fourth, who was either injured or ill.

"Father?" She waited for her father's instructions.

"The man has been hurt," he said. "We need to get him to the examining table."

John said something to the Indians. The braves carried the injured man toward the bed.

"What's wrong with him?" Rachel asked as the warriors stretched out their friend.

"He's been shot." The doctor rolled up his sleeves.

Rachel moved to the cabinet to extract the instruments and medical supplies they would need. "Like Black Hawk?"

She looked back in time to see her father shake his head. "By another warrior," he said.

Rachel shivered. "I don't understand. One of his own kind tried to kill him?"

John lifted his gaze and locked it with his daughter's. "It was an enemy. An Ojibwa," he said with meaning.

She was confused; then understanding dawned. She noted what she hadn't before . . . the difference in these Indians' dress from Black Hawk's people . . . the furtive way they kept glancing around as if they didn't feel safe at the infirmary.

"Sioux?" she whispered as she approached with instruments to where her father stood examining his patient.

"Yes."

Her father's one-word answer chilled her. The stories she'd heard about these Indians since her arrival had been frightening. They had killed some of the missionaries here at Whitely's Mission. They had captured and held prisoner her father, her sister, her brother-in-law Daniel, and other members of his family.

*Dear God, will they kill us, too, if we're not able to save their friend?*

The Indian had a head wound. John examined the area, and looked relieved as he glanced up. "The bullet just grazed him. I'll clean it and put a bandage over the injury. This brave should be fine."

A warrior spoke rapidly and nudged the doctor. John replied slowly, carefully in the Sioux tongue.

"How did you learn their language?" Rachel asked her father when he had finished his conversation with the patient's friend.

"I learned enough to get by during my time with the Sioux, and a little more since then."

"He seemed to understand you," she said.

"I hope so."

Rachel became aware that someone was studying her. She glanced over to find one of the Sioux warriors eyeing her steadily. She shifted uncomfortably. The brave's gaze was full of masculine appreciation as he continued to leisurely examine her.

The Indian said something to her. She stared at him, unable to answer.

"I don't know what you said."

The brave spoke again. Rachel saw her father stiffen.

"Father, what did he say?" she asked.

His mouth tightened. "I believe he said that you are pretty."

Rachel nodded; she'd recognized the thought behind that gleam.

The patient appeared slightly stunned, but otherwise fine once the doctor had cleaned and bandaged the wound.

"There is no need for this man to stay here," John told her.

"Good," she whispered. "These Indians make me nervous."

Her father's wan smile told her that his thoughts mirrored her own.

Rachel cleaned up after her father, and had started toward the back rooms when the interested brave grabbed her arm. She gasped and nearly dropped the bowl she was carrying.

*"War-chah'-wash-tay,"* he said.

Her heart began to pound wildly. When she tried to pull free, the warrior released her.

*"Wee-ko'."*

"I'm sorry, but I don't understand you."

John spoke sharply to the brave. The exchange between them lasted several seconds. "He said that you are beautiful," her father told her. He looked upset by the conversation.

The brave spoke again, gesturing with his hands. Her father reluctantly translated, "His name is Clouds-at-Morning."

She blinked. "Clouds-at-Morning," she murmured. "Tell him that's a nice name."

"I don't think I should," her father said.

The warrior said something else. The Indian crossed both arms over his chest.

Her father looked shocked. "Rachel, I think perhaps that you should go to your room."

Rachel frowned, disturbed by her father's expression. "What's wrong?"

"Apparently, Clouds-at-Morning has taken a shine to you."

*"He what?"*

"The brave wants you, I'm afraid."

But she stood her ground. "Tell him I'm flattered but I don't need a man."

Her father stared at her. "I can't say that."

"Why not?" she asked.

The injured brave spoke, and suddenly all attention was turned on him. In a flurry of activity, the Sioux took their hurt friend and left.

"Why, they were in a hurry to leave!" Rachel exclaimed. Not that she wasn't glad. The last thing she wanted was a Sioux Indian brave interested in making her his woman.

"They remembered where they were. They knew they had to leave before the rest of the mission woke up and other people saw them here."

"They're worried about the Ojibwa," she said.

John nodded.

"They still fight as enemies?"

"Yes," her father said. "They have been such for many years. It has been quiet these last months, but we know that is only a matter of time before there's trouble again."

"Thank goodness they're gone! I didn't like the way Clouds-at-Morning was looking at me. Do you think they'll be back?"

"I think not, but I could be wrong."

"Let's hope not," she replied. "If it's so dangerous here for them, I don't understand why they came. The brave's injury wasn't bad, was it?"

"No, it wasn't, but perhaps they didn't know."

"Well, I'm glad they're gone." Rachel shivered and hugged herself with her arms. It was her first experience with Sioux Indians. She hoped it was her last.

A week passed with no return visit from the Sioux, and Rachel was able to relax again. She'd seen her sister twice in the last week. Amelia looked more radiant each time Rachel saw her. Although Rachel didn't particularly like her new brother-in-law, she had to admit that Daniel loved his wife. He did most everything in his power to make Amelia happy. He even acted civilly to Rachel—a woman he didn't much care for. She had to give him credit.

Amelia had invited Father and her for an early supper. Rachel had hoped to get over this afternoon to help her sister prepare for the meal, but she was kept busy with a group of missionary youngsters who had been playing a game. The children had gotten in a scuffle, and scraped their elbows and knees. Her father was out seeing a bedridden patient. There were now twenty families within the mission, and that included forty adults and seventeen children, but not the doctor and his daughter. Most of the children were older, near their teen years, but there were at least five who were under the age of ten. These girls and boys were forever injuring themselves at home or at play. This wasn't the first time that Rachel had cared for them.

Rachel enjoyed the light chatter of the boys after she'd done her best to clean and bandage their wounds. She loved to watch the girls argue with these young males. Their teasing and false exclamations of horror had her stifling smiles of amusement as each gender tried to get her to take sides.

"My knee looks more horrible than yours," one girl said.

A boy grunted. "Does not."

"Jason, Mary, why don't you wait outside until I'm done with Samuel and Elizabeth," Rachel told them after their continued argument looked as if it would become an out-and-out fight.

The two children did as they were told, but Rachel could hear them continuing their debate as they left the surgery and went outside.

Elizabeth Johnson gazed at Rachel with big round brown eyes. "Will it hurt?" she asked when she saw the salve in Rachel's hands.

"Not one bit," Rachel assured her with a smile. She spread a thin layer of salve on the child's cleaned scrape. Elizabeth had her eyes closed, until Rachel announced she was done.

"It didn't hurt!" the little girl exclaimed with surprise.

Rachel's smile grew. "I told you it wouldn't."

Elizabeth turned to her brother. "Samuel, she told the truth. She didn't hurt me."

Samuel turned a wary gaze to Rachel. "But my cut is bigger than Elizabeth's."

"Then I'll take extra care not to hurt it. All right?"

The child nodded, and Rachel went to work.

When she was done dressing Samuel's wounds and had sent the children home, Rachel straightened the surgery, then went to her bedchamber to dress. A clock on her dresser displayed the time as three o'clock. She hoped her father would return home so he could clean up and dress and they could depart for Amelia's house.

Amelia had asked them to come at three-thirty. As it stood now, they would probably be at least fifteen minutes late. Daniel would no doubt blame their tardiness on her.

She was ready at three-fifteen. Her father still hadn't arrived home, and Rachel decided that she would look for him. She found him at the first place she checked. He was at the Reverend Whitely's again, visiting with Allen Whitely, Will Thornton, and Rachel's newest good friend, Miriam Lathom.

Seeing her father through the window, Rachel knocked tentatively on Allen's front door.

"Why, Miss Dempsey! How are you today?"

"Fine, thank you, Reverend." She smiled. "I'm sorry to disturb you, Reverend Whitely, but will you please send my father home? Tell him that Amelia is expecting us at three-thirty, and we're already late."

"I'm coming, daughter." John Dempsey appeared behind the good Reverend's shoulder. "What time is it?" he asked.

"Three-twenty," she told him.

"Goodness me," he said. "It's that late already!"

She nodded. "I would have come sooner, but I was doctoring the little ones again."

Her father smiled. "What was it this time?"

"Same." Her expression softened. "Skinned knees and elbows."

"And Jason claimed to be hurt the worst?"

She chuckled. "Of course. This time he was, but I wasn't going to give him the satisfaction of hearing me say it. He says that all the time, whether it's true or not."

Rachel said good-bye to the Reverend, then left with her father's promise that he would follow her shortly.

By the time the Dempseys were on the road to the Traherns', it was three-forty-five. When they arrived at

Amelia's, Rachel guessed that they were forty-five minutes late. As they entered the house, Rachel's glance at the mantel clock confirmed it.

The scent of roasting meat filled the cabin, making Rachel's mouth water. She heard her father's soft exclamation of pleasure, and knew that he was as appreciative of the smell as she was.

"We're so sorry we're late," Rachel said as she hugged her sister. She saw that Daniel was seated on the sofa before the fireplace. Once again, she sensed his disapproval of her. *It's not my fault!*

"Oh, you're not actually late," Amelia replied with a smile. "I know Father. I said three-thirty so that you'd come by four-thirty."

Her father chuckled. "You know me so well, do you?"

"Come in and sit down," Amelia said after flashing a grin at her father.

"Can I help you in the kitchen?" Rachel asked.

"You can keep me company as I finish up and wait for our last guest."

"Oh, is Jane coming to supper?" She followed Amelia into the small work kitchen, which must have been an addition to the original cabin. In this room were the cupboards for dishes, the pantry, and a table for preparation, but the cook-stove itself was in the great room within a few feet from the dining table. Amelia opened the pantry and pulled out a loaf of bread, which she proceeded to slice evenly.

"Doesn't it bother you to fix your meals in here and then have to go out into the other room to cook it?"

Amelia smiled. "No, I'm used to it," she said. She pulled a small bowl from a cupboard and began to spoon jelly from a jar into the serving dish. "I don't mind this arrangement at all," she continued as she opened a second jar and emptied it into a separate dish. "It keeps the worst of the mess where I can't see it while I'm eating. I find I enjoy my meal more if I don't have to see what I must clean up.''

"Well, I'll clean up this evening," Rachel said. "I wanted to come over sooner, but I had some young patients." She smiled as she met her sister's gaze. "The Johnson children and friends."

Amelia chuckled. "I see." She handed Rachel a spoon of jam. "Taste this. It's a new recipe."

"Hmmm," Rachel said. "It's delicious. What is it?"

Her sister named an unfamiliar type of berry.

Watching her work, Rachel wondered how Amelia's pregnancy was affecting her. She thought her sister looked a little pale. "Are you still feeling well?" she asked.

"I feel wonderful."

"How far are you along now?"

"Three months."

"Six months to go. That will take you into what . . . March?"

"I think so."

Rachel frowned. "Does it get terribly cold here?"

"Prepare for the worst, and you might think it's only frigid."

The thought of winter gave her a chill, and Rachel hugged herself with her arms. "Amelia, I'll come weeks before the baby's birth. You'll need someone with you, and who knows how badly it will snow."

Amelia agreed that she would feel better knowing her sister was near.

"Amelia?" Daniel stood in the doorway to the great room. He barely spared Rachel a glance before he gazed lovingly at his wife. "Black Hawk is here."

"Oh, good." Amelia smiled as she pulled off her apron. "Now that everyone is here, we can visit together a while before we eat."

Rachel grabbed her sister's arm as Amelia started to leave the room. "You invited Black Hawk?"

Amelia frowned. "Yes, why? Do you have a problem with him?"

"No! No, of course not. I'm just surprised to hear he's come." Her heart had begun to pound at the mention of his name. How would she react when she entered the next room and saw him?

"I'm glad, Rachel, because Black Hawk is a good friend," Amelia said. "More like family."

Rachel's head started to buzz as she nodded, then followed Amelia from the kitchen. She spied the brave immediately, despite the fact that all three men were seated near each other on various chairs and on the sofa before the fireplace. Black Hawk stood as he spied Amelia, and watched her approach with a smile.

Rachel studied the Ojibwa brave as he gazed at her sister, and found herself remembering his time at the infirmary, her attraction to him. His sharp features looked handsome to her. She never thought she would look at an Indian that way, but then Black Hawk was no savage. This night he wore a leather vest with his loincloth leggings. His footwear was pure Ojibwa—moccasins with a puckered center seam. She noted his copper armband, beaded necklace, and bright rings through each ear. She gazed at him, intrigued as she noted every little physical detail about him.

To Rachel's surprise, Amelia and Black Hawk hugged as if they were old friends. Then Black Hawk, seeing Rachel behind her sister, greeted her politely as someone greeted a stranger. Rachel felt a keen sense of disappointment until later, when Black Hawk caught her gaze as they headed toward the dining table. She saw the admiring gleam in his dark eyes before she quickly averted her gaze.

At Amelia's instructions, everyone moved toward their set places at the dining table. As each guest found his chair, Amelia declined Rachel's offer of help and asked instead for Daniel's assistance. To Rachel's surprise, Black Hawk had been assigned the seat directly across from hers.

John Dempsey asked after Black Hawk's injuries, and the brave confirmed that he was all right. Rachel tried to avoid looking at him, which was difficult because the urge to stare at him was strong.

Amelia and Daniel returned from the kitchen area with the bread and fresh fruit; then Daniel went to the stove and removed a turkey from the oven. There was wild rice dressing to go along with it.

Daniel and Amelia good-naturedly argued over who was going to carve the turkey. Daniel insisted that Amelia do it, while Amelia pointed out that she was with child and it was a man's job.

Watching their teasing, Rachel felt a brief sadness for what she'd never have. Jordan had teased her on occasion, and she had loved every minute of it, joking with him in kind.

Rachel managed to smile as her sister and her brother-in-law continued their light bantering. She tried not to feel sad, and she was afraid that her smile appeared strained.

The sense that she was being studied drew her attention to the man who sat across the table from her. Black Hawk was watching her, not Daniel and Amelia, and she had no clue as to his thoughts. She boldly gazed back at him, but his stoic expression and lack of response made her flush and look away.

Dinner was delicious. The turkey was tender and juicy. Amelia had seasoned the dressing to perfection, and her bread was light and airy, served with jelly and jam. As they ate, the conversation centered on the infirmary and

John Dempsey's patients. Then, to her embarrassment, her father began to talk about Rachel's assistance and how proud he was of her continued efforts to help.

"She does well with patients," Black Hawk said, making Rachel's face turn a brighter shade of red.

"You mean she didn't maim or kill you?" Daniel said teasingly.

Rachel, who had been on edge since she'd first entered the house, didn't hear the teasing tone of his remark. She only heard Daniel making light of her work, disapproving of her once again.

"It's a good thing you're not a patient. Right, Daniel? I may accidentally scald you with a bowl of soup or light your bed on fire when I snuff out your bedside candle. Everyone knows how dangerous I am!

"I'm sorry, but I need some air," she murmured. She rose from her chair, despite the protests of those seated at the dining table.

"Rachel!"

But she ran toward the door, ignoring her sister's cry.

"What's wrong with her?" Daniel asked.

"She knows that you do not like her," Black Hawk said quietly. He stood. "I will talk with her."

"You'll frighten her," Daniel said.

"No," the Ojibwa brave said. "Rachel and I understand each other."

It was a clear evening. Outside, under the dusk sky, Rachel felt the tension within her ease. She knew she had overreacted, but Daniel had mocked her just one time too many.

The air temperature was cool, but she wasn't cold as she skirted the house and entered the side yard. She gazed up at the sky, feeling the light breeze that caressed her face. She closed her eyes, lifted her chin higher, and listened to the forest sounds. Such noises no longer frightened her. Neither was she afraid when she sensed that someone stood nearby watching her. She knew without opening her eyes that it was Black Hawk.

"You didn't have to come after me," she said without turning.

"I wanted to come."

Her pulse picked up its pace. "Why?"

"I have not spoken with you in a long while."

She opened her eyes then and faced him. "You want to talk?" she asked with disbelief.

He stepped closer, his expression unreadable. "I do not wish to talk with you, Rach-el."

"What do you want?" She was breathless as he came closer. She glanced toward the house, but everyone else had stayed inside.

"Must I say it?" he said. "Or shall I show you?"

She didn't know how to answer.

"Rach-el?"

"Please—I don't know what you want from me."

"What I want and what I must not have are one and the same."

His dark eyes glittered in the dim light. She noted the smoothness of his skin. Dusk had softened his sharp features. Her gaze traced his rugged jaw, before it was drawn to his mouth, and she found herself remembering the excitement of his kiss.

She swayed toward him. "Black Hawk."

He took her into his arms. He murmured something in Ojibwa, and then he kissed her. Her head spun as the world rocked beneath her feet.

# Chapter 13

*No!* she cried silently as he deepened the kiss, exploring the warm intimacy of her mouth. She made no effort to break away; she clung tightly to his shoulders . . . and moaned with pleasure as he pressed her fully against his hard length.

She tried to recall Jordan and her determination to stay away from all men, but her thoughts wouldn't cooperate. She could think only of Black Hawk and how wild and free he made her feel as he held her . . . of the rush of heightened pleasure brought by the pressure of his masculine lips against her mouth.

As his head dipped and he nuzzled beneath the collar of her gown, her world was a whirl of color. She felt the pumping of her blood through her veins, felt her lungs draw air. She heard her breath coming in sharp little pants intermingled with gasping shudders and low moans.

He wore only a vest to cover his upper torso. Rachel clutched his shoulders and ran her fingers beneath the sleeve edges to explore the warm firm flesh beneath. She wanted to feel that heated skin pressed against her own. She longed to have his lips nuzzle farther, below her bodice over her bare shoulders, down her throat to her breasts.

From somewhere deep in her mind came the thought that she should be shocked at her cravings. She had never longed for anything this badly . . . and that an Indian could incite such lust was beyond logical reasoning.

"Please," she begged.

He lifted his head and stared at her. She blinked up at him, aware only of the man and the raging desire she felt for him.

Black Hawk released her and stepped back.

"Black Hawk?"

"I did not mean to do this," he said.

"You didn't?" She experienced a pang of disappointment. He shook his dark head, and she had the strongest urge to touch his hair, to finger the silky ebony strands that fell from the crown of his head to below his shoulder.

She flexed her fingers at her side, before she raised her right hand and gave in to the desire. She trailed her fingers down his hair, over his shoulder, to where the strands ended just above his left nipple. She stared at the nipple, wanting to caress it. She bent instead and placed her lips to the bud. Black Hawk tensed, then groaned as she kissed the area, laving it with her teeth and tongue.

Finally, he grabbed her hair and lifted her face away. "Do not!"

Rachel drew back in hurt. "I'm sorry. I—I don't know what came over me. I've never done that to anyone before."

Something flashed in Black Hawk's eyes as he cradled her face with his hands. "The same thing that has come over me,'' he said huskily. "I must not give into it. I cannot!'' He released her and turned away.

She stared at his broad leather-clad back with her heart thundering in her chest. Her mouth was still moist from his kisses.

"You feel it, too?" she asked.

He didn't turn or answer.

"Black Hawk?"

"No!" He spun then, looking angry.

She swallowed and took a step back. "Don't!"

He looked stunned. "Did you think I would hit you? I do not hit females, especially you."

"You are furious with me," she said.

"I am angry with myself."

"Why?" She relaxed and tilted her head slightly.

"Because I must not take a mate."

*A mate?* Rachel thought, and felt another rush of sensation at the images provoked by his words.

"You must not remember this moment. You must not think of us. It is not a wise thing. I have much to do, and my thoughts must be on my people."

"Did I ask to be your mate?" she cried softly. "We kissed, that is all." *Liar,* she thought. "Do you think I won't forget a simple kiss? I had lots of admirers in Baltimore, lots of kisses." His rejection of her stung.

"Rach-el." He started to reach for her.

She sprang back.

"Rachel! Black Hawk!" Daniel's call accompanied the sound of footsteps across the wooden porch floor. "Is everything all right?"

At the sound of her brother-in-law's voice, she glanced toward the front corner of the house. "Yes, Daniel!" Rachel had been forced to swallow before she could speak. "We were just talking. We'll be right in."

"Amelia made rice pudding," he called back.

"Sounds wonderful," she returned calmly, while inside she felt bleak, as if she was dying. The man who had just stirred her emotions like no other man before him, had just told her that he wanted nothing more to do with her.

Rachel looked back at Black Hawk. "We'd better go inside."

"Will you be all right?" he asked with what sounded like genuine concern.

Tears stung her eyes. "I'll be fine. I'm not some simple, fragile damsel." She managed a smile for him. "I'm made of sterner stuff than that." She held out her arm. "Shall we go in?"

He gazed at her a long time before he moved to accept her arm.

He spoke softly in Ojibwa.

Rachel had no idea what he'd said, and she wasn't sure she wanted to know.

They started toward the house; then Black Hawk stopped her. "You must not be angry with Dan-yel."

She stiffened. "He hates me."

The brave's dark gaze glistened as he studied her. "He does not hate you. You remind him of someone who hurt him."

She frowned. "Who?"

"His dead wife."

"He was married before?" Rachel didn't know why she felt stunned by the news.

Black Hawk inclined his head. "It was a long time ago, before Little Flower—Sus-sie—was born."

"I didn't know," she murmured. Daniel had been married, and his wife had hurt him. How? Suddenly, she wanted to know more about her new brother-in-law.

"My friend Dan-yel is a good man. He loves your sister."

"I know," she admitted. "I can't find fault with him for that."

She stared thoughtfully at the house. "How did his wife hurt him?"

"It is not for me to say."

His answer annoyed her. "Why not? You've told me enough to arouse my curiosity. Why won't you satisfy it?"

"It was a bad time for Man-with-Big-Head."

A choked chuckle escaped Rachel's lips. "That is Daniel's Ojibwa name?"

Black Hawk's lips twitched. "Given to him by your sister, Tree-That-Will-Not-Bend."

"Good name, Amelia," she breathed softly, her eyes twinkling with amusement. The knowledge gave her something to think about. Did Amelia know the truth of Daniel's past? And would she tell her sister if she did?

Black Hawk studied the woman before him, and felt his loins tighten in response. He wanted her, but he couldn't have her. He had to protect his people, and he had to avenge his father. Until he had done both, he would not be free to take a mate.

She sighed and gestured toward the house. "Let's go inside. We've talked long enough."

Black Hawk inclined his dark head. Rachel seemed disappointed that he didn't take her arm again as they started toward the front porch of the cabin.

Amelia glanced anxiously toward the door. "Is she coming?"

"She said she was," her husband said.

"What did Black Hawk mean when he said that you didn't approve of Rachel?" she asked. "Is that true?"

Daniel looked uncomfortable. "Amelia—"

"Tell me the truth, Daniel! Do you or do you not like my sister?"

"It's not a question of whether or not I like her—" He paused when he saw his wife's raised eyebrows. "I want to like her."

Amelia jerked as if she'd been shot. "You don't like her, do you?" she cried, upset.

Her husband mumbled something beneath his breath.

"What?"

"I said I just don't approve of her!" He softened his voice. "She reminds me of Pamela."

His wife stared at him a long moment before her expression softened. "Oh, Daniel," she said. "She's not Pamela. She's Rachel, my sister, and she has a heart of gold."

"You used to tell me about all of her beaux."

She frowned. "Yes, of course. But Rachel isn't mean or deliberately cruel. She may have stolen the affections of a few of my admirers, but I should thank her for that. She didn't entice them away on purpose. They just saw her and were smitten. If she hadn't kept me from falling for a man back East, then I wouldn't have come to this territory . . . or met you." Her voice had become husky.

He looked surprised by the knowledge. "You're right. I had no right to make judgment on her when I hardly know her."

"And so?" Amelia said with a small smile. "What are you going to do about it?"

"Do I have to apologize?"

"That's entirely up to you."

"I'll have to think about it."

Amelia scowled with disappointment. "You do that."

The squeak of the front door drew the attention of everyone in the room.

Rachel entered first, looking refreshed by the night air

and quite beautiful. "Hello, everyone," she said airily as she breezed into the room.

Black Hawk followed more slowly, his expression unreadable as he rejoined the group at the dining room table.

"Did I hear something about dessert?" Rachel asked.

Amelia glanced at the Ojibwa before returning her gaze to Rachel. "Pudding," she murmured. Then, she managed a bright smile. "Are you still hungry?"

"For pudding," Rachel said. The note of cheeriness sounded false to her sister's ears. "Absolutely."

They came in the night, and Rachel didn't expect them. She heard the noise just moments before she heard her father's sharp shout of surprise. Rachel dressed quickly, then looked for a weapon. The only thing she could find was a brooch that had belonged to her aunt. She opened the backing to release the pin, and held the pin with the sharp point outward between her fingers.

She hesitated before leaving her bedchamber and listened with her ear pressed to the door. Her heart pounded so loudly, she could barely hear anything else. Her mouth had gone suddenly dry, and she had difficulty swallowing.

She pressed her fingers to the doorknob and tried to turn it without sound. Who is it? she wondered. And where is Father?

The door was torn from her grip. And she stood face to face with an Indian.

She stared at him in openmouthed horror.

"Rachel! Daughter, get back inside!"

But she couldn't. The Indian had a firm grip on the door.

"I can't," she gasped. She found sight of her father. "Who are they? What do they want?"

"They're Sioux. Clouds-at-Morning's men. They've come for you."

She inhaled sharply. "Me?" She felt a chill. "What do they want with me?"

"Clouds-at-Morning wishes to see you. They've come to bring you to their village." Her father tried to go to her, but another brave stopped him. "You mustn't go with them, Rachel!"

One warrior spoke sharply to her father, who answered. The brave raised a knife to John Dempsey's throat.

"No!" she cried. She tried to push past the Indian, who laughed and blocked her way.

One of the Indians holding her father spoke to the warrior blocking Rachel. The warrior scowled and moved aside.

Rachel eyed the brave before her, then gazed at the band of warriors in the room. One of them nodded at her, and she ran to her father.

"What shall we do?"

One of the Indians spoke up, in English. "You must come with us in peace."

"Father?"

"No, Rachel."

"If you do not come," the brave said in English, "we must kill your father!"

"No!" she cried.

"Rachel, don't listen to him! If he kills me, then they will be killing a friend of Runs-with-the-Wind."

Rachel saw the flicker in the Indian's gaze. "You are the one who saved Little Cloud?" he asked.

John Dempsey nodded, relieved that the Indian had heard of the young Sioux he had saved two years past. Because of his deed, he had earned respect within a Sioux village. It was because of this respect that the Sioux had released the surviving captives who had been taken during a raid on the mission that same summer.

"Then we will not kill you, White Medicine Man." He rubbed the dull edge of the knife against her father's throat. "We will cut you a little."

Rachel felt a wave of terror. "I'll go with you if you will release my father."

The brave nodded.

"*No!*" her father cried.

"Father, how can I stay and have them harm you!" Rachel exclaimed.

"Rachel!"

"Tell them I'll go with them."

"No," John gasped.

"Father, tell them I'll go but I want their word that I'll be released afterward. I imagine a Sioux's word is good as any man's."

She gazed at the brave who spoke English. "Please," she pleaded. "I must have your word." The man nodded.

The warriors holding John released him. The brave at the door nodded, then stepped back to allow Rachel to exit.

"Rachel!" her father cried as she preceded the Indians to the door. She paused at the opening. "Please, don't go," he added.

"I have to, Father."

"Come, white woman," the Indian said.

"You will allow my father to remain? You will leave my father alone?"

The brave nodded, then spoke to his men. The Indians grabbed John, then tied him to a chair.

"No!" Rachel cried. "Don't hurt him!" Why had she trusted the word of savages?

"The white doctor will remain unharmed. We cannot

let him run for help. Soon, your friends will find and free him.''

Rachel saw that the Sioux had indeed tied him up and were leaving him.

''Come,'' the brave said.

''I will be back, Father,'' she told him. ''Won't I?''

The warrior's dark eyes gleamed as he pushed her through the doorway. He never gave her an answer.

# Chapter 14

"I wish for you to come live with me," the Indian said. "I will be your hus-band. You will be my wife."

Rachel tried to hide her horror as she stared at Clouds-at-Morning. "I am flattered, but I cannot marry you."

"Why cannot?" he asked.

She thought quickly for a good excuse. "I must care for my father. He needs my help."

"Father can come live here."

She shook her head. "He will not come. He has his work at the mission. He is a good medicine man, and his people need him."

They were in the Sioux's teepee. Before Clouds-at-Morning could answer her, another warrior entered the structure, speaking directly to Clouds-at-Morning. Clouds, who had been sitting cross-legged on a mat, rose. As the two Indians conversed, Rachel studied Clouds, trying to judge his reaction. If she continued to reject him, would he become

angry enough to kill her? Would he force her to marry him
. . . or her father to come?

She was thankful that he could speak English. He had
given no clue that he spoke the language when he'd come
to the infirmary to get help for his friend. To make her
feelings known would have been much more difficult if
their conversations needed a third person to translate. At
the mission, she'd had no other choice but to trust the
English-speaking brave.

The Indians and Rachel had traveled to the Sioux
encampment through the night. They had reached their
destination while it was still dark. As day broke, Rachel
decided that this was a temporary village of sorts, for
there were only a dozen or so teepees with few women
and small children. And they hadn't traveled far enough
from Ojibwa territory. Her father had once told her that
the Sioux lived where the land was flat and open with
little trees. Here, they were in the forest . . . which gave
Rachel the hope that she would be rescued soon, provided
that someone found her father fast.

To stifle her nervousness, Rachel turned her attention
to cataloguing the appearance of Clouds. He wore a
breechclout that fell to mid-thigh in the front and was
longer in the back. She had seen him and the other Sioux
braves wear fringed leggings, but this morning Clouds
wore none, giving her a good view of an indecent amount
of bare thigh and leg. He wore no shirt as well, and it
embarrassed Rachel as they had talked, because each time
she looked at him, his size brought an expansive amount
of naked chest to Rachel's eye level. He wore a bear-
claw necklace; his dark hair had been braided into two
long, below-the-shoulder plaits. Heavy earrings of some
indefinable origin dangled from the Indian's earlobes.

To a Sioux woman, Clouds-at-Morning would probably
seem like a good husband. He wasn't ugly, and he was

muscular, and he would probably make a good provider for the right woman. But that woman wasn't Rachel. She had no desire to become the Indian's wife ... or any other man's, for that matter.

The other brave, having finished whatever business he had, left, and Clouds-at-Morning sat and faced her again.

He regarded her thoughtfully for a long moment. Rachel shifted uncomfortably, wishing he'd let her go. "I will give you time to think of this," he said, much to her surprise.

"I can go home?" she asked, hardly able to believe her ears. They were keeping their word! Since she had come in the night, she had been treated fairly and kindly.

The brave nodded. "I will give you until the moon rises big in the night sky. Then, I will send for you."

Rachel was at a momentary loss for words. "Thank you," she finally said.

"Two Foxes!" he called, and immediately the other Indian entered.

Had he been waiting outside all the while? she wondered.

"Go," Clouds-at-Morning said. "Two Foxes will take you to your people." Two Foxes was the one who spoke English.

She scrambled to her feet. "Thank you." She had almost said *miigwech,* the Ojibwa word for thanks, until she remembered she was speaking to a Sioux. She started for the door, but the Indian grabbed her arm, stopping her.

"Rachel," he said. He released her arm to caress her cheek. She forced herself not to shrink away from his touch. "I will speak with you again."

She nodded. The last thing she wanted to do was anger him. When he finally released her, she hurried from the teepee, anxious to get home to be with her father again.

* * *

"What are we going to do!" Amelia cried. "Someone has to rescue her! What if they hurt her?" With a harsh sob, she started to cry.

Daniel pulled her into his embrace, then glanced over his wife's head at his father-in-law. "Are you all right?"

Only hours before, John Dempsey had been discovered in the infirmary, bound to a chair. The missionary Miriam Lathom had found him. She had come to the infirmary with a supply of newly harvested herbs for the doctor's medicine cabinet. She had knocked, then entered as usual, calling out Rachel's and the doctor's names as she headed toward the surgery to put away the herbs. When she received no response, she'd gone into the sickroom, then into the rear living quarters, where she'd found John Dempsey bound to a chair and unconscious. She'd thought that he was dead at first. Horrified, she'd gone to untie his hands and feet, and the doctor, who was only asleep, had awakened. Then, Will had taken the doctor to his son-in-law's.

"I'll have a word with Black Hawk. Perhaps he can help us," Daniel said.

Amelia pulled from her husband's arms. She sniffed back tears. "Yes, Black Hawk will help us."

Daniel lifted her chin to dry her tears. "We'll find her, sweetheart." She nodded. "Please try not to worry. You need your strength. Remember our babe."

"But my sister—"

"He's right, Amelia," her father said. "With Black Hawk's help, we'll find Rachel. Clouds-at-Morning wants her for his wife. He won't harm her."

"I hope you're right."

"He's right," Rachel said from the doorway.

"Rachel!" her family cried simultaneously. Rachel was suddenly being hugged from all sides.

"I'm fine!" she assured them, but she hugged them back, even Daniel. "Really, I'm fine," she said when everyone pulled away. "He treated me quite well . . . only he still wants to marry me."

"Out of the question!" Daniel said.

Rachel narrowed her gaze. "You think I'll say yes?" she challenged.

"No," he said quietly. "But he is a Sioux, and the Sioux are dangerous. Ask your father and sister. Ask Black Hawk."

Black Hawk, Rachel thought. Her stomach fluttered as she got a clear mental image of the Ojibwa warrior.

"I'm sorry," she said, knowing that she'd overreacted once again to her sister's husband.

He gazed at her with concern. "Are you all right?"

She nodded. "Just a bit shaken. I'm not accustomed to being kidnapped, proposed to, then freed by Indians."

"He released you?" Amelia said, sounding surprised.

"To give me time to think about being his wife." Her gaze lovingly examined her father. "You're unhurt?"

"Yes. Miriam found me this morning." His voice was tight. He was clearly upset with her. "You shouldn't have gone with them."

"And have them kill you?" she cried. "Father, he held a knife to your throat!"

Amelia started. "You didn't tell us that!" she said to her father.

Daniel frowned.

John Dempsey looked away. "It didn't matter. She shouldn't have gone."

"Father," Rachel said, "I'd go again if it meant saving your life."

He looked at her with tears welling in his eyes. "I didn't know if I'd see you again."

With a sob, she rushed into her father's arms and embraced him. "I'm all right, Father. Please don't cry. I'm back, and they didn't hurt me."

"But the man expects to see you again," Daniel said.

Rachel glanced at her brother-in-law as she released her father. "Yes, he says he'll come for me when there's a full moon."

"No!" Amelia protested.

Daniel patted his wife's arm. "We'll think of a way to protect Rachel," he said.

"Is there anything I can do?" Amelia asked her sister.

Rachel nodded. "Yes. Take care of yourself and that babe you're carrying." Then she smiled ruefully. "And do you have anything to eat? I'm starved."

Everyone laughed then, and the seriousness of the situation was put aside for the moment.


"... and apparently the man has promised to return for her."

Black Hawk listened with a stoic expression as his friend Daniel told him about the kidnapping by the Sioux and the return of Rachel Dempsey. Inside, he experienced a mounting horror.

"She is not safe," he said. "We must protect her."

Daniel nodded. "But how?"

"We will bring her here. She will be safe in my village, hidden among my people. Clouds-at-Morning will not come to this village. If he does, we will be ready for him." He would bring her here if he had to kidnap her himself, Black Hawk thought. It was for her protection. He wouldn't allow anything to happen to her.

"It sounds like a good plan," his friend said, "but how are we going to convince my sister-in-law?"

"I will talk with her," Black Hawk said calmly. "She will listen to me."

They came for her when she was alone in the infirmary. It was dusk. Her father had gone to visit patients. Miriam had left a short while ago. Rachel had no one to help her when the savages came for her.

She tried to fight them. She had the satisfaction of seeing one brave's surprised reaction before he subdued her, gagged and bound her, and carried her off. Her heart thundered wildly with fear as she saw the band of warriors waiting for her kidnappers. There were a dozen braves at least, none of them familiar to her. *Clouds-at-Morning's men,* she thought.

Rachel whimpered behind her gag. What was going to happen to her? The brave had given her little time to consider his proposal. Had he decided to marry her whether she was willing or not?

The Sioux had taken off her ankle ropes and urged her to walk. When they left her mouth gag in place, she'd glared at them angrily. If thoughts could kill, she mused, these Indians would be dead. *I'll tell Clouds-at-Morning about your behavior! He'll punish you for your harsh treatment of me!*

*As if he would,* an inner voice taunted. *As if he'd listen to you, a mere female. As if he really cares what you think . . .* Still, he had released her once, hadn't he? And she certainly hadn't expected that.

It was dark when the Indian band and their captive broke from the woods into a village clearing. Rachel had no idea how long she'd been with them. To her, the nightmare of her capture had seemed an eternity. Rachel tensed and her eyes widened. Her chest constricted with fear.

*This isn't the Sioux encampment!*

This was an Indian village of some other tribe. There were no teepees scattered about the clearing. These structures were dome-shaped, with tree-bark covering the roof and sides and animal hides draping the doorways.

*Who are these people? And why did they kidnap me?*

A brave halted her and carefully removed her mouth gag and then her wrist ropes. He smiled at her, and she felt the strongest urge to smack his grinning face.

"Welcome. I am Rain-from-Sky," he said, as if he and his friends hadn't brought her here by force.

"Why am I here? Why have you kidnapped me?"

"You must not be afraid. We will not harm you. We will protect you."

"Protect me!" she cried, feeling a rising panic. "You should have left me alone. My father must be frantic."

But the brave simply shook his head. "Come. There is someone who wants to see you."

"Who?" she demanded, digging in her heels.

Rain-from-Sky nodded to someone behind her. "Come," he said. And he took one arm, while another Indian took the other. Together the two carried her, struggling and crying out, toward a domed wigwam.

"No!" she cried, jerking away. "No, I won't go in there!"

But her strength was no match for the Indians.

One brave lifted the door flap and thrust her inside. She fell into the wigwam, screaming unladylike words at her captors when she landed on her hands and knees. As she scrambled to her feet, she lifted her gaze.

"You!" she exclaimed.

Black Hawk eyed the woman before him with concern.

He moved to help her to her feet, but her expression stopped him. "You are all right?" he asked huskily.

"No thanks to you and your friends!" she spat back.

He frowned. "I will talk with Rain-from-Sky. He should have been gentle with you."

For some reason, his words seemed only to incense her more. "I'm no weak female to be coddled!" she cried. Then she blushed, perhaps remembering how she'd fallen only seconds before.

He stifled a smile. How was he to calm her anger and gain her cooperation so he could successfully protect her?

Black Hawk gazed at her with regret in his dark eyes. "I am sorry that my friends have hurt you."

Rachel humphed. "You should be."

"How can I make things better?" he asked.

"You can tell me why I've been kidnapped!"

"We did not kidnap you."

"I didn't come willingly!" she exclaimed. "What else would you call it?"

Disheveled, she looked beautiful, Black Hawk thought. Her green eyes glittered with anger. Her lovely chestnut-brown hair was tousled, and her pink lips were a temptation to any man. Studying her sweet mouth, he felt a tightening beneath his breechclout.

"You have come for protection."

"From whom!" Rachel cried, disturbed by the look in his eyes. "The only one I seem to need protection from at this moment is *you!*" She was startled to see a hurt look enter his expression. She softened her voice. "Don't you realize that you've worried my father?"

"John Dempsey knows you are here."

"*What?*" Had she heard him correctly? Rachel felt a gut-wrenching dread in the pit of her stomach. "And my sister?"

He nodded, and she closed her eyes in an effort to hide the hurt.

"Why?" she whispered.

"Clouds-at-Morning," he said.

Her family was worried about the Sioux brave, Rachel realized. If they had wanted her to go to Black Hawk's village, why hadn't they just asked her? She glared at him, believing that he had convinced her father to remain silent.

"They did not think you would come," Black Hawk said as if he'd read her thoughts.

Rachel tried to consider it reasonably. "I don't know if I would have come willingly or not." She narrowed her gaze. "I was never given the chance."

Emotion flickered in his dark eyes and was gone. He gestured toward a woven mat on the dirt floor. *"Namadabi,"* he said. "Please sit."

She regarded him warily. She had just begun to trust him when he'd done this awful deed in conjunction with her family. Why did Black Hawk's betrayal hurt more?

She thought about refusing to sit, but then she realized that her refusal would seem childish. Black Hawk had asked nicely. Wasn't that what she'd been complaining about—that no one had thought to ask her?

Rachel did as the brave requested and sat down on the mat, arranging her skirts carefully about her knees. She saw Black Hawk's approving look as she did, and felt a niggling of reluctant pleasure that she'd pleased him.

*This is ridiculous!* she thought. *This man had me kidnapped! Why should I care whether or not he is happy with me?*

"I want to go home," she said.

He peered at her from beneath lowered lashes. "You cannot. You must stay here until the danger from the Sioux is past."

"Who says I'm in danger?" Her tone was defiant. "Clouds-at-Morning treated me only with kindness. *He* let me go!"

She saw a muscle twitch along Black Hawk's jaw. "The Sioux are dangerous. If the warrior comes for you again, he will not let you go. If you do not agree to marry him, he will make you his prisoner." He paused. "His slave."

Rachel shook her head. "No, he wouldn't," she whispered.

Black Hawk's expression hardened. "I know the way of the Sioux. They tortured and killed my father. They have killed many of my people. They will not be kind to you."

She shivered at his words, but did not want him to see her fear. "You're just saying that because you want me to stay."

"It is true that I want you to stay. It is for your safety that we have brought you to our village. Here you will be treated kindly. You will stay with Spring Blossom, my sister. She will feed you and care for your needs."

"You want me to stay with your sister?" she asked, surprised.

"Yes, Spring Blossom." Black Hawk tried to judge what Rachel was thinking, but he had difficulty. She was an unusual woman. She never reacted as he expected.

She was thoughtful as she continued to gaze at him. "How long will I have to stay?"

A flash of elation centered in his gut. "Until we learn where this Sioux brave is located . . . until we know that it is safe for your return."

"All right."

He blinked. "You will stay in my village, where I— we—can protect you? You will do as we say in all things?"

"I will stay, but as for doing everything you say . . ." She smiled suddenly, and the sight of her good humor made his blood pump hard and fast. "I will have to judge each request on its own merit." Her tone challenged him.

He had not expected her to capitulate so quickly or so easily. Perhaps he should be wary, he thought. He stared at her hard, but he could find nothing in her expression that told him she was being deceitful or insincere. "Good."

"Daniel," she said bitterly. "This was his idea, wasn't it."

Black Hawk shook his head. "The idea was mine," he said, noting her shocked, then angry expression, "and mine alone."

# Chapter 15

The crunch of dead leaves and dry brush alerted Black Hawk to someone's presence. He waited in the darkness for the person to reveal himself.

"Black Hawk?" came a harsh whisper.

The brave stepped from behind a tree. "Dan-yel, my friend."

"How did it go?" Daniel asked. "Is she all right?"

Black Hawk nodded. "She was angry, but she will stay."

"Good." Daniel looked relieved. "Thank you. Perhaps Amelia will be able to rest easier now."

The warrior acknowledged his friend's gratitude with a nod. "John Dempsey," he said. "What will you do with him?"

"He will work at the mission during the day. At night, he'll stay with us."

Black Hawk frowned. "Do you think this is wise?" He waved the other man toward his village. Daniel fell into step beside him. "What if our enemy returns when the sun lights up the day's sky?"

Daniel's brow furrowed. "Do you think this is likely?"

"We cannot take chances."

"My father-in-law will not hide out until the danger is past. He'll want to continue his work," Daniel said.

"Cannot the people send word to him when they need him?"

"I'll talk with him about it."

Black Hawk nodded. "This is good."

They were within sight of the Ojibwa village. The light from a large cookfire cast a golden glow over the nearest wigwam and the two men.

Daniel halted, reluctant to go farther. "I will not enter, my friend. It's best if my sister-in-law does not see me just yet."

A glint of amusement lit up Black Hawk's dark eyes. "You do not wish to suffer her anger."

Daniel's mouth curved. "That is part of it, yes, but I fear that she will see me and latch onto me to escape." He saw awareness in the Ojibwa's expression.

"Then it is wise that you go," Black Hawk said. "Will you be safe?"

Daniel knew what his friend was asking. Who was to protect those at the trading post? In their anger, the Sioux could attack anyone. "I've asked for help from the Army." He saw his friend tense and understood why. How could he trust the U.S. Army? There'd been trouble with soldiers twice before. The first time a band of men, led by Daniel's evil brother-in-law, Captain Richard Milton, had kidnapped and attacked villages and homes. Milton's men had not been acting on orders from U.S. Army officials, but on Milton's command. The second most recent time was when Black Hawk had been ambushed, shot, and left for dead.

"Don't worry, Black Hawk. I've sent word to our friend Cameron Walters. He'll see that we have soldiers we can trust. Your people will not be harmed. Cameron has already caught the men who attacked you. They were deserters—a group of cowards looking for a lone man."

"I hope you speak the truth, my friend," Black Hawk said, his expression somber. "We have one enemy; we do not need two."

"No! Leave me alone! Touch me again, and I'll hit you!"

Black Hawk heard the woman's shrieks as he neared his sister's wigwam. He raised the flap and entered. His eyes widened as he caught sight of Rachel Dempsey with her back against the wall, clutching her gown to her strangely clad body. Spring Blossom and two other Ojibwa women were trying to coax her to give up her garments.

He spoke to his sister in Ojibwa. The sound of his voice silenced all the women, except Rachel, who spied him as the next target of her anger.

"Black Hawk! I'll not give up my clothes!" she exclaimed. "Tell them to get away from me!"

Spring Blossom spoke rapidly to her brother. The other two women joined in the conversation, until the wigwam was filled with the frustrated tones of the Ojibwa females.

Black Hawk grunted, then nodded. All the women left, except for Rachel Dempsey and Spring Blossom.

"Rach-el, you cannot wear your garments in our village. If we are to protect you, you must appear as one of us."

Eyeing him warily, she pressed her gown higher. "I don't want to go about half-naked." Rachel was mortified at the thought that they expected her to dress as they did.

Many of the women went around bare-breasted, with only kilts to shield them from the weather and the others' attention. She'd kill first before she'd abandon her practice of being fully clothed.

She watched as surprise, then understanding flittered across Black Hawk's face. His mouth twitched. Was he amused? she wondered with increasing outrage.

"This is not funny!" she cried.

His features sobered.

"Rach-el," Spring Blossom enunciated carefully. "You not have to wear kilt. Wear tunic. Like this." She held up a lovely, full-length deerskin dress. "It better for village life. You not be happy in your—thing," she said, pointing toward Rachel's corset.

Rachel could feel her cheeks heat. She felt exposed in her chemise, corset, and pantalets. The Ojibwa women had nearly torn off her gown in their efforts to undress her. But she had gotten ahold of it and wasn't about to relinquish it. She held it out to inspect it, saw that it was damaged, and clutched it back to her breasts.

Then, she became aware of Black Hawk's interest in her underclothing. Embarrassed, she backed up another step, and cried out as she bumped the back of her head against the ceiling where the dome curved down to meet the wall.

Black Hawk started forward. "Are you all right?"

"Stop!" she cried. "Stay where you are!"

He froze, looking hurt.

Her heart thumped wildly within her chest as she eyed Black Hawk and his sister. Without her own clothes, she'd feel naked, vulnerable, as if she'd abandoned every last part of herself.

Then, she recalled the bright colors in the clothing of some of the Indian women and men. They wore garments made from calico and other fabrics traded from the white men. Why couldn't she? She mentioned it to the Ojibwa brother and sister.

Black Hawk shook his head. "Our people look Ojibwa in white men's dress. You, Rach-el Dempsey, would look too much like white woman."

"Please," she whispered. She gripped her gown tighter. "Let me go home. I want to go home."

"Rach-el," Black Hawk began, seeing her fear. He was deeply wounded by her behavior. He had kissed this woman, and she had trusted him enough to respond to his touch. What had happened to that trust? Had his bringing her here killed it?

"All right," she whispered. Her expression caused his stomach to contract. "You and your sister go outside, and I will put on your Ojibwa dress."

Black Hawk and Spring Blossom exchanged glances.

"I will wait outside," Spring Blossom said. She handed the dress to her brother before she stepped out into the night.

"Here." Black Hawk held out the doeskin gown to her. He expected her to come and get it. He wanted her to reach for it.

"Toss it over here."

He narrowed his gaze. "No."

Her eyes widened. "You expect me to approach you?" At his nod, she exclaimed, "But the way I'm dressed, it's not proper!"

The brave sighed. "Rach-el, this is not a village of white people. We are the *Anishinaabe*. We do things differently."

"I can see that!" she cried.

He didn't relent, but held the tunic out to her. If she wanted it, she would have to cross the wigwam and take it out of his hand.

She eyed the dress and seemed to contemplate the distance between them. Her face reddened as she began to move a few inches at a time across the dirt floor.

"I hate you," she said.

"You do not hate me, Rach-el. I have done nothing to harm you. Be angry with Clouds-at-Morning. Be angry with the Sioux, but do not be angry with me—your friend."

She had continued to move slowly toward him. She kept her gown against her body to protect herself from his gaze, but it didn't matter to him. He had a good imagination, and Black Hawk used it now as he speculated what was under those ridiculous undergarments.

"Why do white women wear so many clothes?" he asked.

She halted. "We don't!" She shut her mouth abruptly as if she suddenly realized that they did, in fact, wear many garments. She appeared to give serious thought to the matter. "To look good, I suppose."

"You do not need ugly garments to look beautiful," he said huskily. His skin began to warm as she started forward again.

She kept her gaze on the doeskin dress as she stopped within inches of him and reached for the garment. Black Hawk raised it back, out of her range.

Her startled eyes shot to his.

"You do not trust me," he said, making no effort to hide his dismay.

She blinked. "Black Hawk—"

"Here," he said, and tossed her the doeskin tunic. "If it pleases you, I will stay away from you." He turned and lifted the door flap.

"No!" she cried.

He hesitated, dropped the flap, and looked back.

She appeared upset. "I'm sorry, but this whole situation takes some getting used to."

He looked at her a long moment, then gave a nod. "The Sioux are our enemy," he said angrily.

Rachel was stunned by his tone. "You hate them enough to kill?" The savage she'd first encountered was back . . . and he was real. How could she have forgotten him?

Black Hawk's features looked fierce. "They have killed my people. I will kill before I will allow them to hurt another of the *Anishinaabe.*"

*And her?* Would he kill because of her? She shivered.

His features softened with concern. "You are cold. Put on tunic. I will send Spring Blossom in to help you." He eyed her corset as if it were an unknown dangerous animal.

"No," she said, "it's not necessary. I will call her if I need her."

He gazed at her for several long seconds. The air seemed to vibrate and quiver between them. Rachel looked away, then back again. "We will do what we can to make your stay here happy," he said.

*"Miigwech,"* she said softly, thanking him in Ojibwa. She saw his eyes widen, and he smiled.

Then he raised the door flap and was gone.

*"He what?"* Amelia glared at her husband. "Tell me he didn't."

"I'm sorry, my love," Daniel said, looking sheepish. "Black Hawk was convinced it was the only way to get Rachel to his village."

"So you allowed him to kidnap her!"

"She's all right," he assured her. "Black Hawk spoke to her, and she's agreed to stay."

Amelia looked skeptical. "She'll hate it there. Rachel isn't used to that simple life."

Daniel narrowed his gaze. "Some people find their simple life rewarding."

His wife had the good grace to blush. "I want to see her."

"I don't think that's wise, Amelia," he said. "We wanted Black Hawk to help us, didn't we?"

She nodded.

"Then we have to trust Black Hawk to do what's best. He'll see that she's well treated."

"I know she'll be well treated," she said softly. "I've stayed with the Ojibwa. I know how kind they are."

"Then, will you please relax and just worry about our baby?"

The mention of their baby put a smile on Amelia's face. "I love you," she said. She embraced him.

Daniel's expression softened as he put his arms around her and kissed the top of her head. "I love you, too, my sweet."

Then he thought of Rachel and frowned.


Her stomach felt queasy as Rachel stared at the deer hide. "I will show you how to fix skin," Spring Blossom told her.

"Fix?" Rachel echoed, her nausea increasing. "You have to do something to it?"

Spring Blossom nodded. "Must know how to fix hide. Use for tunic. Use for blank-it. Make smooth. Make nice."

Rachel nodded. *How did one take a horrible, deceased animal and turn it into one of these lovely skins?*

Her stomach roiled as she watched Spring Blossom pick up the knife and begin to scrape off the red matter on the inside of the fur. The smell from the decaying meat made Rachel gag and look away.

"Here, you take," the Ojibwa maiden said, extending the knife.

Rachel turned and realized with horror that Spring Blossom expected her to take over the chore. She took one look at the remaining layer of deer entrails and fought the urge to vomit. "No, not yet. Let me watch a little longer."

Spring Blossom gazed at her white face, then nodded. "I will show you how to use knife on fur."

Relieved, that she didn't have to scrape the inside, Rachel inclined her head.

As she waited for Spring Blossom to finish the one side, Rachel smacked at a mosquito on her arm. Her poor white skin had become a mass of red welts. For some reason, it seemed as if the bloodthirsty insects had chosen her—and only her—to feast on. She started to scratch the area, and suddenly her other bug bites began to itch.

Spring Blossom finished the one side of the deer. She frowned when she saw Rachel scratching. "You put on grease?" she asked.

Rachel shook her head. The salve that Spring Blossom referred to was a smelly greasy concoction made with ingredients unknown to Rachel. She had considered using it when Black Hawk's sister had first given it to her, but she had quickly decided against it. She'd thought the smell would make her sick. And she worried what the grease would do to her smooth skin.

"Rach-el use bear grease. Keep bugs from biting. Bugs will eat many bites if white woman does not use."

*Grease from a bear?* She was beginning to see the benefits of using the grease. Rachel decided that the smell couldn't be as bad as this deer hide. She would use the bear grease at the earliest opportunity, which she hoped was soon, as there were more mosquitoes vying for her flesh.

"Rach-el." Black Hawk's deep voice caught Rachel by surprise. Since their discussion the night before, she'd seen him in the village, but only from a distance. What magic did this man have that caused her heart to race whenever he came near?

She turned slowly, so as not to appear anxious to speak to him. He was frowning when she met his gaze. Her spirits fell.

She nearly flinched when he reached out to touch her cheek. She realized what he was doing when he touched a red welt. He spoke rapidly to his sister. Spring Blossom answered.

"Don't blame Spring Blossom," Rachel said quietly. "I was too stupid to use the grease."

He looked at her with surprise.

"I'll use it as soon as we're done," she promised.

"You will use it now," he said sternly.

She stiffened. "Spring Blossom needs my help."

Rachel and Black Hawk both turned to the brave's sister.

"This can wait, Rach-el," she said. "Go and use grease. I will be here when you get back."

Still angry with Black Hawk, she nodded stiffly, then headed toward the wigwam. To her dismay, Black Hawk fell into step behind her.

She halted and faced him. "You don't have to follow me. I already said that I'd use the grease."

He nodded, but when she continued on, he was right behind her.

She stifled annoyance as she reached Spring Blossom's wigwam, lifted the door flap, and went inside. She gasped when Black Hawk followed her in.

"What are you doing in here?" she cried. Her heart gave a lurch as she stared at him. She didn't want to notice how attractive he was, but she couldn't help it.

His commanding presence seemed to fill the interior of the wigwam.

Without answering her, Black Hawk reached beneath a platform in his sister's home and withdrew a container of bear grease. She saw his intent in his eyes. She held out her hand.

"Thank you," she said, hoping he'd take the hint, give her the grease, and then leave.

But her efforts to get him to leave were futile. She could see the determination in his glistening ebony gaze, and knew that he intended to oversee her use of the bear grease.

"I told you I'd put it on," she said, "and I will."

He nodded without a word.

"Then give me the salve and leave me!" she cried. The air between them had become thick with a strange tension that increased when Black Hawk's gaze slid down her scantily clad length. She became conscious of how little the doeskin tunic concealed. Since putting it on last evening, she had come to enjoy the freedom of movement the garment afforded her. Today, with so many women with fewer clothes than she had, she had forgotten her unease until now . . . under Black Hawk's continued stare.

"What?" she asked. *"What is it?"*

Something flashed in his eyes, and she felt her body tingle in response. The strange sensation didn't go away as Black Hawk turned his attention to opening the container.

He approached her with the grease and a look that made her flush right down to her toes. Rachel jerked when desire hit her hard. Her physical attraction toward him disturbed her.

The memory of his kiss made her lips quiver. When he touched her arm to smooth a layer of bear grease, she swallowed against a suddenly dry throat.

She met Black Hawk's gaze as he spread the grease

over her shoulder. His touch was caressing, and she nearly moaned aloud at the pleasure. She bit her lip, then gasped when the action drew his attention to her mouth.

She licked her dry lips. Desire flashed in his dark eyes, and she responded to it. She wanted him to kiss her. She wanted it so much that it physically hurt.

"Black Hawk," she gasped.

He dipped his finger in the bear grease and smoothed it above the scooped collar of her doeskin tunic. She jerked at his touch, then trembled as her skin tingled and burned.

Black Hawk seemed fascinated by the way the grease coated her white skin as he took more of the salve and spread it up her throat and down, lingering a long time at the throbbing pulse point near its base.

"Black Hawk," she whispered achingly.

He stopped and gazed into her eyes. Something wild and savage flashed in his obsidian eyes as their gazes locked and her feelings were openly displayed for him to see.

"Please," she gasped, unable to help herself. She swayed toward him. *"Please."*

With a harsh groan, Black Hawk dropped the container of grease and jerked her into his arms.

# Chapter 16

His kiss made her head spin, and she clutched him tightly as her legs threatened to buckle. His mouth savagely demanded that she respond, and Rachel did, happily, gloriously, moaning softly when it seemed as if he couldn't get enough of her.

The exchange was a fusion of hot mouths desperate for contact. Rachel never knew a kiss could be so stirring, so hungry . . . so wild.

She heard a groan. Had it come from her? Or him? Her thoughts were muddled. Her nerve endings hummed with life. Her heated blood rushed through her veins, arousing every inch of her to a fever pitch.

Black Hawk framed her face with his hands as he continued to devour her with his kisses. Rachel knew she should be shocked. But she felt no sense of impropriety . . . only pleasure and the desire for it to continue on and on.

As abruptly as the kiss had started, it ended the same

way when Black Hawk released her and turned away. Rachel stared at the Ojibwa brave's back while her breath labored from her chest. She could still feel the imprint from his touch, his heat. And she wanted more. The warmth of his nearness enveloped her and made her tingle.

"Black Hawk."

He faced her, almost reluctantly, and she gazed into his glistening onyx eyes. She saw desire, perhaps confusion, and some other emotion she couldn't read. She knew she felt some of what he was feeling and more. She knew that at this moment she wanted Black Hawk as she'd never wanted another man.

He bent and picked up the container. "You must put this on now," he said. His dark gaze looked troubled. He spun as if to leave.

"Wait!" she gasped. He was just going to go away as if nothing had happened between them? As if their passion didn't exist?

He froze, but didn't look back. That was when she knew that he had been affected as deeply as she'd been. And that the knowledge disturbed him.

"Black Hawk," she whispered. "Please."

He turned as if reluctant to face her. "I will not come near you again. This man shouldn't have kissed you. I am sorry."

Not come near her again! she thought. No! She didn't want that. He made her feel alive. She didn't want him avoiding her.

Rachel shook her head. "Please," she said. "Don't be sorry."

Pain flashed across his features. "You are under my protection. This will not happen again."

"Black Hawk," she cried. *"Black Hawk!"*

But he didn't stop.

Rachel stared at the moving door flap after Black Hawk

had left the wigwam. "It will happen again if I have anything to say about it!" she murmured. She couldn't deny that they were attracted to each other, that she had enjoyed Black Hawk's kisses and wanted them again.

She frowned as she began to smear the bear grease over every inch of exposed skin. "It can't be love I feel for him," she whispered. "I love Jordan."

If Jordan came for her and claimed that he'd made a mistake, she'd forgive him and return with him willingly. *Wouldn't she?*

"I don't know," she said beneath her breath. "I never expected to feel this way about Black Hawk. About any man." She still didn't understand what she was feeling, but she had the sense to realize that this feeling for the attractive brave was powerful. Was it just physical?

She shivered and hugged herself with her arms. *I think not!*


Big-Cat-with-Broken-Paw had sent scouts out to find Clouds-at-Morning and the Sioux. They had been gone three days when a brave returned with news.

"I have seen our enemy. They sleep in the forest where two waters meet," the Indian said. "There is a great one with them. I have watched him practice with bow and arrow. I have seen guns. They have many horses."

The chief turned to Black Hawk with a look of concern. He had assembled his most trusted men before him to share in the news. Black Hawk was his war chief and he valued the brave's opinion greatly. Even when it seemed that Black Hawk would act one way because the situation was personal, the war chief did not. He acted only with wisdom and courage and skill.

"What is your wish?" the chief asked the brave.

"Let us go and see who these Sioux are," Black Hawk said.

Big-Cat-with-Broken-Paw nodded. "This is wise. It may be true that a certain old warrior may ride with them. You may find the one you seek for vengeance rides among those who kidnapped the white doctor's daughter."

Black Hawk nodded. "We will go and see. We will not waste life needlessly."

"Go then, Black Hawk. Choose your warriors and may *Gicho-Manidoo* watch over your path."

Within the hour, Black Hawk and his small band of chosen Ojibwa men left to find these Sioux. Black Hawk did not try to see Rachel before he left. He thought it best that he keep away from her. She stirred a fire in his blood that made it difficult for him to breathe.

Before he left, he spoke to his friends to ensure that she'd be well protected during his absence. Then, he slipped out into the night to find his enemy.


Rachel was upset when she learned that Black Hawk had left the village without a word to her. She became frantic when she found out where he'd gone. She alternately cursed him and prayed for his safe return.

"Just wait until he comes back," she grumbled beneath her breath as she went to the river for water. "I'll give him a piece of my mind that he won't soon forget!"

*If he comes back,* she thought with chilling horror.

She closed her eyes and began to pray. "Please return safely, Black-Hawk-Who-Hunts-at-Dawn."

After a week, Rachel had begun to enjoy life in the Ojibwa village. She no longer cringed when she helped Spring Blossom tan animal skins. The first time she'd nearly sickened while she watched the Indian maiden rub the scraped fur with the animal's brain matter. Whatever the animal's size, there was just enough matter to cover and preserve the whole hide, Spring Blossom explained. Rachel had difficulty not turning away as she watched the skin turn supple under Spring Blossom's hands.

During her stay, Rachel had learned much about Ojibwa life. She learned how they prepared their food, built their wigwams, and made their clothing. Since first coming to the village, she even looked more like an Indian. Besides the fact that she'd taken well to wearing deerskin clothing, she used a dye given to her by the Ojibwa to darken her skin and a salve to protect her from sunburn. With her naturally dark, unbound hair and her darker skin, she could easily pass as an Ojibwa maiden. As long as one didn't look too closely at her green eyes, she thought, or the color of her hair. In direct sunlight, one could see a reddish tint in her long tresses.

Black Hawk had been gone for three days. She missed him. She wondered if he was all right, what he was doing. Had he found his father's murderer? Or Clouds-at-Morning?

What did he plan to do once he found either one? Kill him? She experienced a chill. What if he got killed first?

She didn't want to imagine him hurt or injured. Seeing him vulnerable once had been enough. She didn't want to see him that way ever again.

And she couldn't imagine him as a murderer.

It had been a while since she'd seen her father and sister. Were they all right? She missed them. If only she could see them, even if it was just for a short visit. Black Hawk had said her family knew where she was. Why hadn't they come to see her?

She mentioned this to Spring Blossom and one of the Ojibwa matrons, Woman-with-Hair-of-Fox.

"They think you angry with them," Spring Blossom

said. The maiden looked a lot like her brother. Being with her caused Rachel to continually long for Black Hawk.

Rachel frowned. "I'm not angry with them." She was over her anger. She realized that her family was concerned for her safety.

The matron spoke up. "It may be too dangerous for them to come."

"Dangerous?" Rachel felt a flicker of alarm. "Because of me?"

Woman-with-Hair-of-Fox inclined her head.

"How can I find out if this is true?"

"Our chief would know this."

"I'd like to speak with him," Rachel said.

Spring Blossom looked startled. "You wish to talk with Big-Cat-with-Broken-Paw?"

Rachel nodded. "If he is the one who can tell me what I need to know."

The Indian women exchanged glances.

"I will ask my husband, He-Who-Comes-from-Far-Away," Woman-with-Hair-of-Fox said.

Rachel smiled. *"Miigwech."*

It was the next morning when Woman-with-Hair-of-Fox came to her. "My husband has spoken with Big-Cat-with-Broken-Paw. The chief said that your father and sister may visit."

Rachel, glad of the news, wasn't bothered by the fact that she hadn't spoken with the chief personally.

"Who will let them know?" she asked.

Woman-with-Hair-of-Fox told her that Rain-from-Sky had been sent to the trading post to inform her sister.

Her eyes sparkling with unshed tears, Rachel put a hand on the woman's shoulder. "Thank you."

\* \* \*

The Sioux encampment had packed up and moved. Black Hawk stared at the vacated clearing with an angry scowl.

"You must return to our village," he told the others. "I will follow their trail for a time before I, too, return."

"I will go with you," Thunder Oak said.

"I want to go, too," Gray Squirrel said. He was the Ojibwa chief's son.

One by one, all six men in Black Hawk's band agreed that they would accompany Black Hawk as he followed the Sioux's trail.

"They head to the south, toward the trading post," Black Hawk said.

Thunder Oak nodded. "We will find our enemy before they can harm us."

"Let us go then now!" the chief's son said. "We must not waste time."

Black Hawk nodded while he regarded Gray Squirrel thoughtfully. It would be wise if he kept a close eye on this young son of Big-Cat-with-Broken-Paw. *He wants war, but doesn't know how terrible it can be. He reacts before he thinks. He wants to fight, and I will have to stop him before he does something that may harm our people.*

It was night as the Ojibwa band led by Black Hawk left the forest clearing in search of their Sioux enemy. Black Hawk was tired. He wanted to return, but he wouldn't until he learned whether or not Clouds-at-Morning traveled with these Sioux men. And although he knew he shouldn't, he longed to see Rachel again.

And there was still He-Who-Kills-with-Big-Stick. Black Hawk hadn't forgotten that the warrior had been spied among the Sioux who'd attacked and murdered Red Dog's people. Perhaps these Sioux they followed would know the whereabouts of the man.

The day of reckoning was near between Black Hawk and He-Who-Kills-with-Big-Stick. Until that day had come, Black Hawk would never truly be free. Until then, he could not think of Rachel Dempsey and this powerful passion he had for her.

*Baltimore, Maryland*
*September, 1838*

"Jordan!" Bess Dempsey stared at the young man standing on her doorstep.

"Aunt Bess," he said softly. His gray eyes regarded her warmly. "May I come in?"

Frowning, she hesitated. She was not happy to see him.

"Please?" he begged. "I must see Rachel."

Bess waved the young man inside. After she closed the door, she faced him. "Rachel isn't here."

He looked impatient. "When will she be back?"

"She's not coming back," Bess said coldly.

Jordan flinched as if struck. "What do you mean she isn't coming back?"

She was almost tempted to feel sorry for him. *Almost, but not quite.* "Rachel left Baltimore. She's no longer in Maryland; she's in Wisconsin with her father."

"But she couldn't have gone!"

Bess's jaw snapped. "I can assure you, young man, that she did, in fact, leave. Now, you too must leave. You've taken too much of my time, young man." She opened the door in a not-too-subtle hint for him to depart.

"Wait," he cried. "I have to see her. I love her!"

She scowled at him. "You picked a fine way to show her," she said. "Leaving her at the altar." She narrowed her gaze at him. "That girl thought the world of you, Jordan Sinclair, and what did she get for her trouble? A broken heart, that's what!"

She grabbed his arm and steered him toward the open doorway. "A broken heart and a great deal of humiliation in front of this whole community!"

"I was trapped," he exclaimed. "The widow Nanette is dead, Aunt Bess. She married me knowing that she had only a little while left to live. I married her for our future—Rachel's and mine."

His gray eyes pleaded for her understanding. "My late wife left me her property. All of it! The house, the money, every last bit. I want to share it with Rachel. To marry her."

"You expect her to marry you after what you've done?" Bess shook her head and made a *tsk* sound with her tongue. "Good luck convincing her, boy, if you think to try. You're going to have a devil of a time getting that child to look twice at you after all the pain you've caused her."

The young man looked miserable. "I'm sorry, so terribly sorry. I love Rachel. I honestly do."

Bess didn't want to soften toward him, but his misery was so evidently heartfelt. "It's not me you need to be apologizing to. It's my niece."

"Tell me how to find her," he begged. "How did she get there? Where exactly did she go?"

The woman eyed her niece's former beau and fiancé; then she sighed heavily. "A man named Rupert Clark took her."

"Clark," Jordan echoed, his mind obviously trying to place the name. His eyes brightened. "Clark as in Miranda Clark?"

Bess nodded. "As in Miranda's Uncle Rupert."

"Thank you!" he cried, and hugged her.

She pulled back, feeling flustered. "Don't you be thanking me until after you've seen Rachel. You may be cursing me into the grave before it's all over.''

*Or else Rachel will be,* she thought.

The Sioux came to the infirmary at night. John Dempsey was at the mission. He'd finally convinced his daughter Amelia that he'd be safe there alone. This was his second night at the infirmary. As he worked to set up his medical instruments for the next day, he heard a noise and turned to face Sioux Indians.

"Where is Rach-el?" Clouds-at-Morning asked. He must have decided to come for John's daughter himself. The Sioux warrior stood straight and tall as he gazed at John Dempsey. He looked disappointed that she wasn't in the room.

Eyeing the armed men, John trembled as he struggled to hide his fear. "She's gone."

"Where she go?" her persistent suitor asked.

"She left a week ago to visit friends. She hasn't returned yet."

Clouds-at-Morning's face darkened with anger. "What mean you she left to visit?"

"Actually, someone came for her, so she had little choice but to go. I think she's safe, but I don't know when she'll return."

"I want to see her now!"

"I'm sorry, but that's impossible."

"Then I make it possible." He barked an order in his native tongue to his friends. The men moved, and suddenly John was surrounded, imprisoned by strong warrior arms. "You come with me then. You stay until daughter returns and comes to Clouds-at-Morning."

"But I don't know when that will be!" John exclaimed.

"No matter. White Medicine Man will stay as long as it takes. As long as Rachel not here to be my wife."

"But she cannot marry you!"

The brave snorted and brushed that notion aside with his hand. "She says she need to care for you, but you not need her. She is not here, and you are fine."

"Because she hasn't been gone too long. I do need her here. She's my daughter. I need her."

"You do not need her," the brave insisted.

John nodded. "Yes, I do."

The Sioux warrior smiled. "I need Rachel more." He turned and barked a command to his men. With a wave of his hand, John Dempsey was suddenly surrounded and being led from the surgery to the waiting area.

"You will come to village until Rachel returns. I will talk with Rachel soon."

The Indians dragged the doctor from the building. More braves with horses waited for them beyond the mission, in the forest.

The Sioux Indians were kidnapping him to get to his daughter, and John Dempsey was powerless to stop them.

# Chapter 17

Rain-from-Sky gazed at his friend Daniel across the dining table. He'd arrived at the Trahern cabin only moments before, and already he'd been urged to sit and share the family meal. The brave was happy at the invitation, as he loved Amelia Trahern's cooking, especially her dessert cakes.

"Rachel wants you to visit her. She misses her family," he told Daniel when his wife was out of the room.

Daniel frowned. "I don't know."

"She is no longer angry, my friend," Rain-from-Sky assured him. "She has adjusted to our life. She enjoys our village."

The white man raised his eyebrows. "That doesn't sound like my sister-in-law."

"She has changed."

"She must have," he muttered.

Amelia entered the room, and Daniel tensed and grew silent.

She must have seen them talking. "What are you two discussing so earnestly?" she asked with a smile.

Daniel didn't immediately answer, and the Ojibwa brave saw the indecision in his expression. "Rain-from-Sky comes with news of your sister," Daniel said.

Alarm sharpened Amelia's features. "Is something wrong?" Her gaze shifted back and forth between the two men, before settling on her husband.

"Rachel is fine," Daniel said softly. "She misses you. She wants you to visit her."

Gladness flickered in her expression. "Can we do that? Visit?"

It was clear that Daniel had had no idea how much his wife had wanted to see her sister. It made him feel guilty for promptly dismissing Rachel from his mind once he'd known she was safe.

"She wants to see her father, too," Rain-from-Sky said. He grinned up at Amelia when she set a plate of finger-cakes before him.

"Of course, Father will want to go," she said. "Only . . ."

"What is it?" Daniel asked. "What's wrong?"

"Father will never believe us if we go to him now and tell him that Rachel wants to see us. After only two nights there, he'll think it's a new excuse to convince him to return home here. I don't like him staying at the mission, but he insisted. If I tell him he has to leave now, even if it's to visit Rachel, he'll think I don't trust his ability to protect himself."

"I'm in the middle of a job that I have to finish," Daniel said. "It'll take two more days to complete. If we leave after that, your father won't become suspicious or angry."

Rain-from-Sky agreed as he looked at husband and wife. "I can visit the mission, talk with John Dempsey."

Amelia's expression brightened. "Would you?"

The brave nodded.

"I don't think that's a good idea," Daniel said, making his wife frown. He addressed Rain-from-Sky, who had just taken a bite from the food that had been placed before him. "My father-in-law knows that you have a weakness for Amelia's cooking."

The Indian lowered the remaining cake from his full mouth. He could only nod as he finished chewing.

"I'll speak with your father when it's time to leave," Daniel told his wife. "I'm sure he'll have no trouble leaving when he sees that we are ready to go ourselves."

Amelia smiled. "All right." Then she beamed at Rain-from-Sky for bringing the news from Rachel. "Another cake, Rain-from-Sky?" she asked, extending a full platter toward him.

The Ojibwa warrior grinned as he reached toward the plate. *"Miigwech."*


Black Hawk and his band of men gave up the Sioux trail after two days. "We cannot catch up to them. Not with their horses. They do not stop to rest, or we would have seen signs of a fire."

Thunder Oak nodded. "We must return to our village and hope there is word from our Ottawa friends."

Gray Squirrel didn't agree. "You give up too easily, Black-Hawk-Who-Hunts-at-Dawn. We will find and kill our enemy."

Black Hawk fought to control a flicker of anger. "Have you forgotten our peace with the people of Runs-with-the-Wind? We will not kill needlessly. Certainly not to please an inexperienced boy!"

The young brave flushed with fury. "I will speak to my father!"

"Do this and you will be unhappy," another brave said. "Your father will listen to Black Hawk. Black Hawk is our war chief. We know and respect his skills."

But the hotheaded young Indian refused to listen to reason.

As they came within sight of his village, Black Hawk had never felt so tired. He had been gone for six days, and he hadn't accomplished anything. He hadn't found Clouds-at-Morning, and there was no sign of He-Who-Kills-with-Big-Stick. To his surprise, he found that his failure to find Clouds-at-Morning disturbed him most. He'd been searching for his father's killer for many years; he wasn't surprised by his lack of success in finding He-Who-Kills-with-Big-Stick.

During the last hours of his journey, his thoughts had turned to Rachel. Although he knew he shouldn't, he looked forward to seeing her again. As the first wigwam within his village came into view, he found himself hoping for a glimpse of her.

It was early afternoon when his people greeted the returning men.

"Black Hawk!" Spring Blossom appeared delighted to see her brother. She hugged him, then stepped back as their chief, Big-Cat-with-Broken-Paw, commanded his attention.

"I am sorry, but the Sioux escaped us," Black Hawk said.

The chief was not upset. "You have returned to us safely. It is as it should be."

Rain-from-Sky grinned at his brothers, Black Hawk and Thunder Oak. "You look as if you have not slept, my fathers."

Thunder Oak scowled. "We have come a long way. We did not sleep during the last darkness."

The two brothers shared a teasing exchange. Black

Hawk, unaware of what his siblings were saying, searched for Rachel. He was disappointed when he didn't see her.

Spring Blossom grabbed his arm and began to urge him to walk with her. "You are hungry?" she asked.

Food was not at the root of his current hunger. "No." He craned his neck to better see who stood among a group of women across the yard.

"She is down by the river," his sister said quietly.

Black Hawk frowned when he looked at her.

"Rach-el," Spring Blossom said with a smile. "You search for her. You will find her in the tiny clearing where we go to be alone."

"She is all right?" he asked. "Nothing has harmed her?"

"She is well. She longs to see her family. Rain-from-Sky has spoken with Daniel. Daniel and Amelia will bring John Dempsey to see her soon."

Black Hawk felt guilty for having kept her from her loved ones. He loved his family and couldn't imagine being forcibly separated from them for any great length of time. His father and mother were dead, but he had two brothers and his sister, Spring Blossom, as well as his father's and mother's sisters and brothers.

"You need sleep, Black Hawk," Spring Blossom said.

Black Hawk nodded, but his attention had turned to the path that led down to the river . . . and Rachel.

"Go," his sister said. "Go to her. I will see that no one looks for either of you."

He grinned. *"Miigwech."*

He saw Rachel immediately as he entered the small clearing. Her chestnut-brown hair glistened under the sun. Her skin, he was surprised to note, looked darker, but no less smooth or beautiful.

His gaze dropped to the hem of her tunic and the lovely length of bare leg that was exposed. She had taken off her moccasins and had waded into the river. She stood, staring out over the water. She looked preoccupied, lost in some deep thoughts.

She was so caught in her musings that he approached without her knowledge. He stopped a few yards from her and drank his fill of her beauty. Desire kicked in his gut as he realized that ever since he'd left the village, he'd waited anxiously for the moment when he would return and see her again.

A fish jumped in the water. Rachel gasped at the sound, then chuckled when she realized what it was. It was a lovely afternoon. She had finished her daily chores and so she'd come here to be alone and dream . . . and think wistfully of Black Hawk.

It had been too long since he'd left the village, and she was frightened that something dreadful had happened to him.

She tried not to think of what the Sioux might have done to him, but terrible, torturous images kept popping up in her mind. She'd lost the last couple of nights' sleep over concern for Black Hawk.

*He can take care of himself,* she thought.

*Can he?* an inner voice taunted her.

*Yes! I have to believe it.*

But the mocking voice wouldn't go away. *What would you do if you knew that he was all right, that he'd come back alive?*

"I'd kiss him breathless," she whispered. "I'd kiss him and touch him until I was certain he was all right."

*Why?*

"Why?" she whispered. "Because I care for him, that's why." *I love him.*

*How can you love him?* the voice continued. *You don't*

*know what love is. You thought love was Jordan, but you
were wrong. Can you trust your own feelings? Can you
be sure that you really love Black Hawk?*

Rachel blinked back tears. "I think so," she murmured.

*It doesn't matter. He's an Indian. You could never have
a future together.*

She released a soft sob. *I know.*

"Rach-el?"

She spun, shocked by the sight of Black Hawk. Joy
slammed into her heart that he was here, gladness followed
quickly by pain as her previous thoughts returned to dull
her happiness.

"You're back," she said quietly.

He nodded. "I am here."

"Was your journey a successful one?" Even while she
was happy to see him, she felt a flicker of annoyance that
he'd left without telling her.

Black Hawk shook his head as he approached. He
looked wonderful in a leather vest, loincloth, and leggings.
Rachel remained in the water, wondering if he would
enter the river or stay on its shore.

"You look tired," she said with concern.

He untied and removed his leggings. Next, he took off
his moccasins and waded into the water until he stood
beside her. "You are beaut-i-ful."

She drew a sharp breath as her gaze lovingly traced
every inch of his rugged face, then looked deep into his
glittering obsidian eyes. "Black Hawk—"

"I have missed you."

"You've only been gone six days." It seemed like
longer to her.

He ran a finger down her bare arm. "I have missed
touching you."

She trembled and shook her head. She shouldn't respond
to him. There could never be anything permanent between

them. Why wouldn't her heart stop thundering in her chest? Why couldn't she turn off her feelings when it came to this magical man?

He continued to run his finger up and down her arm. She shivered with pleasure, then stepped back to break the enchantment.

Black Hawk followed her. He didn't touch her again, and Rachel found herself disappointed that he'd given up so easily. *It must be my imagination that he feels desire for me.*

He gestured toward some point down the river and across the water. "See that tree?" he asked her.

She squinted and tried to follow the direction of his hand. "I think so." It was hard to tell for it was in an area in the far distance.

When he didn't immediately say anything, she turned to him with curiosity, and found him staring not across the water but at her . . . and with a strange look in his eyes.

"Is something wrong?" she asked, alarmed.

After a moment, he shook his head, as he seemed to come out of a trance.

"That tree?" she reminded him. "What did you want to tell me about it?"

He smiled then. "There is a place there, a pretty place where two people can be alone." He gestured down the riverbank toward an Ojibwa birch-bark canoe. He then held out his hand to her. "Come with me," he invited.

Rachel's heart began to thump harder. "Now?"

"The sun is still up. I have not been to this place in a long time. It would be best if we go now."

She watched him as he spoke, and knew that she would go wherever he chose to lead her. She was drawn to this kind man; she couldn't refuse him if she wanted to— which she didn't.

"All right," she said.

His smile was like a fresh burst of sunshine on a spring day. "Good." He grabbed her hand and pulled her through the water toward the canoe.

"Our moccasins!" she exclaimed. *And your clothes.*

He shook his head. "We will return for them."

"But Spring Blossom," Rachel said. "She will wonder where I am!" It wasn't the pace he set for them that had her struggling for air. It was the depth of her longing for him.

"My sister will not search for you," he said. "She knows I am home. She knows that you are with me."

"Oh." Rachel felt butterflies in her stomach. She didn't know how she felt about that bit of knowledge. What did Spring Blossom think she and Black Hawk were doing? Had Spring Blossom guessed of Rachel's desire for her brother? Did Black Hawk suspect?

They reached the canoe, and Black Hawk assisted her into the craft. Then, he climbed in himself, picked up a paddle, and began to row down the river. The canoe slipped easily through the water for a short distance before Black Hawk stirred the craft toward the opposite shore.

It was peaceful on the river. There was only a light breeze, and the ripples created by the air currents were quite lovely. The breeze transformed the water, rustled the forest treetops, and teased Rachel's unbound hair. Black Hawk handled the canoe easily, expertly. Rachel closed her eyes to better enjoy the physical sensations and the sounds of day's ride. The breeze felt wonderful on her skin. The warmth of the sun caressed her face. Birdsong filled the air from a treetop, and nearby she heard the buzz of an insect.

Black Hawk was silent, as if he, too, was enjoying the moment of peace. The only sound he made was that of the canoe paddle being dipped into the water. And Rachel imagined she could hear the rhythmic sound of Black Hawk's breathing.

All too soon the end of the canoe bumped slightly against the shore, then slid farther upland. Rachel opened her eyes, and her peace was shattered as she watched Black Hawk pull the canoe until the bulk of the craft was on dry land. Then, he held out his hand to assist her.

As his fingers surrounded hers, Rachel's hand tingled. He pulled her up into the forest and released her. Despite the coolness of the shade, with Black Hawk so close, Rachel felt a searing heat.

She glanced at him briefly to see if he had sensed her strong reaction to him, but he had already turned away.

"Come," he said, and urged her to follow him a short distance.

Glad to have something to do, Rachel fell into step behind him. Her curiosity was piqued as he stopped before a thick grove of small trees. He parted branches for her and gestured for her to walk through.

As she entered the secluded clearing, Rachel felt as if she'd stepped into a private fairyland. The place was lush and quiet but for the sound of water that she couldn't see. A beam of sunlight shot through a hole in the leafy canopy above, lighting up the clearing and the wildflowers that added a splash of color. Struck by the beauty, Rachel faced Black Hawk with the intention of thanking him for bringing her here.

But once again, he was not studying his surroundings. He looked at her with an intensity that brought Rachel a hot shaft of pleasure tinged with a tingle of nervous excitement.

"Come," he said, offering her his hand.

She didn't hesitate in placing her fingers within his grasp. She felt it—his desire for her. Since she felt desire, too, she couldn't deny that she was glad he had brought her here.

He chose a spot in the sunlight for them to sit. Rachel sat down beside him and then studied the clearing, conscious of the fact that she was more interested in the man beside her.

"You are quiet, Rach-el," he said softly.

She nodded. "It's lovely here." Her skin tingled with anticipation.

"*Ina.* Yes."

"You said it's been a long time since you've been here." How many women had he brought here before her? she wondered.

"I used to come here to think of serious village matters. As war chief, I have decisions to make, decisions that affect the welfare of my people. I do not take this responsibility lightly."

Rachel was not only surprised by his answer, but also pleased. There had been no other women with him here, she decided. Then it dawned on her what he'd just told her. That he came here to this secret place when he was troubled . . . that he cared a lot for his people and wished to do nothing that would jeopardize their lives. He was not a savage who killed ruthlessly, but a man who, unless provoked, thought carefully about what he was doing before he did it.

Which meant that he'd thought about it before deciding to bring her here. She was flattered.

"This is a good place to think," she said.

"It is a good place for many things. I have not done what I want to do most."

Curious, she looked at him. "Oh? What is that?"

His dark eyes burned as he caught her shoulders and turned her to face him. His gaze fell to her mouth, and she inhaled sharply, with pleasure, as he lowered his head and placed his mouth on her lips.

Fire shot through her body. She moaned softly beneath his kiss, opening her mouth in an invitation to further the intimacy between them.

She wove her fingers into his silky hair, holding him to her firmly, arching her neck and groaning with pleasure when he trailed his mouth down her chin to her throat. When his tongue touched the soft swell of her breast where the lace ties of her tunic had loosened, Rachel gasped and shuddered. She didn't object when he pressed her back to the soft earth. She clutched at his shoulders, then ran her hands beneath his leather vest.

Black Hawk raised up and removed his vest, and Rachel murmured her approval, sighing with pleasure, when he lowered himself against her length. Only her tunic and his loincloth separated the increasing heat of their desire.

Black Hawk cupped her head and nibbled on her lips, then raised on his hands to gaze into her eyes.

"Black Hawk . . ."

"You are bright like the sun and soft as the gentle rain," he murmured. "You are warmth like fire, yet as smooth as ice."

"And you are strong as the earth yet gentle as a summer's breeze," she replied.

"Let me touch you."

Holding his gaze, she nodded. "If you want to."

"I want," he said huskily. He rolled off her and reached for her tunic's hem.

She gasped as he began to raise the bottom edge of her doeskin dress. She felt the breeze caress her knees and thighs. She experienced a flutter of alarm as the tunic was lifted higher until she was bare below the waist. She closed her eyes.

*"Gaawiin,* Rach-el. You are beautiful. Please look at me."

She opened her eyes and saw something in his gaze that stirred her beyond fear to desire, beyond desire to something more.

"I've never . . ." she began.

He nodded. "Do not be afraid. I will not hurt you."

She blinked. "You do not frighten me."

She trembled when his hand moved to touch her. When his fingers settled on her stomach, her belly quivered under his touch.

"You are smooth, Rach-el."

She gazed at him, mesmerized by his look and caresses.

"You are white here. Here, my hand looks dark against you."

She nodded.

"If I raise your tunic, will you be pale there, too?"

Rachel swallowed hard. Her heart pounded with anticipation. "Yes."

He smiled. "Let me see."

She sat up, no longer afraid of what she was feeling. She wanted more of his attention, of his touch. She started to struggle free of her tunic.

"No," he said, stopping her.

Her startled gaze moved to gauge his reaction. She flushed a bright red. She felt like a wanton. Had she misread his desire?

"Lie back," he told her. "I want to kiss you."

Her alarm passed, and she offered him a slow smile.

He bent his head, and she cried out in shock as his mouth settled not on her lips but on her belly, where he began to explore the smoothness of her white skin.

"Black Hawk!" she cried when his head dipped lower.

But he continued on relentlessly until Rachel was lost in a whirlwind of mindless pleasure.

# Chapter 18

She was so lovely. He hadn't expected her to be so breathtakingly beautiful in her passion. Black Hawk rose up to look into Rachel's glistening green eyes. His gaze fell to her mouth, and the urge to possess those sweet pink lips was strong. He bent his head, touched his tongue to her lips, and felt a jolt in his loins when she opened for him. She met him tongue-thrust for tongue-thrust, clutching his head as they devoured each other.

He was laboring for breath when he raised his head. He looked down at her quivering white belly, and had to touch there again.

"Black Hawk," she whispered.

He lifted his hand from her stomach to caress her cheek. The scent of her was intoxicating, a mixture of wildflowers and a fragrance that was hers alone. He buried his face in her neck to absorb the smell, enjoying the silky texture of her hair on his cheek and chin.

He wanted to make love to her. To bury himself deep

inside and hear her wild cry echo about the isolated forest glen, but he held back. She was an innocent. He had tasted it on her lips, felt it in her reaction to his touch. She was wild innocence, and she was everything and more than he'd ever wanted in a mate.

But she couldn't be his mate, he thought. He couldn't take a mate. He had a quest to find his father's killer, and now he was equally determined to find Clouds-at-Morning.

Black Hawk knew he should leave Rachel alone, but he was unable to keep from touching her, kissing her, enjoying the passion that brought a flush to her skin and a glazed brightness to her green eyes.

When her hands started to move over him, he groaned aloud and fell victim to her caresses. Her tentative touch grew bolder, sliding over his shoulders and across his back, then circling to his chest, where she rubbed his nipples until they hardened and peaked.

He caught her hands to stop her, and instead of releasing her, he drew her fingers to his lips. He heard her sharp intake of breath, and smiled.

She smiled back at him, then closed her eyes and moaned softly when he placed her hands above her head, then kissed a path down each arm until he could turn his attention to her face . . . her neck.

Rachel gasped as Black Hawk worked pure magic on her senses. Her nipples pebbled beneath her tunic, and she wanted suddenly to be free of the garment. He released her hands, and she waited with anticipation to see what he would do next. She hoped that he would touch her breasts, which were tingling with life in their longing for him.

He kissed her mouth, so sweetly, so gently, that Rachel felt tears well in her eyes.

"I love you." The admission burst out of her as he trailed a path of kisses down her throat toward her breasts.

He froze, and she caught his head, encouraging him to continue his journey of pleasure.

Still, he didn't remove her tunic. In a wild burst of longing, Rachel sat up and the tunic hem fell to cover her as she worked to untie the garment's strings. Black Hawk's fingers settled on her hand, stopping her.

"Rach-el."

She looked at him, pleased at his expression of intense longing. But something in his eyes shifted, alerting her to a change in Black Hawk's mood. "Touch me," she urged him.

He glanced down toward her breasts where her nipples strained against the tunic.

"Please," she whispered.

She cried out with joy as he placed his hand in the opening of her garment, cupped a breast, and lifted it free.

He rubbed his thumb across her nipple, making her whimper and gasp. "Beautiful," he said huskily.

"Kiss me," she pleaded.

And he took her into his mouth, sucking the nipple until she had to hold on to him for balance.

The attention he paid to her breast seemed to go on and on, bringing her more pleasure, until her abdomen ached and she felt the desire to be fully possessed by him.

Just when she thought she would slump, feeling weak, to the ground, he replaced her breast inside the tunic, then reached for its twin. The pleasure started anew, building and building, until Rachel thought she'd surely faint from it.

She wasn't quite sure how it happened, but somehow in the midst of their passion, they'd removed their clothes.

She vaguely remembered reaching to help him with hers, then caressing his chest while he untied and removed his loincloth.

When his last garment was gone, Rachel gazed lovingly at Black Hawk; then her eyes widened as she looked down.

"Oh, my!" she gasped. For he was glorious, big and male, and she was a virgin who wondered if she could take him.

He pressed her to the ground, and she rejoiced in his weight, in the burning heat of his skin. She was startled to feel him stir between her legs, but it felt good. She opened to accommodate him.

Black Hawk was driven beyond pleasure to the point of pain. Suddenly, who he was and the past didn't matter. The only memory, the only thought, was the woman beneath him and in his arms.

When she opened her legs and arched her back in invitation, he gritted his teeth and waited. He wanted to see her soar alone, before they flew together high into the heavens.

He reached down to stir her pleasure, and felt a wondrous satisfaction when he saw the shock on her face before she cried out with joy. It had never felt like this before, he realized. This was power, possession, and passion. This was strength, feeling, and . . . love.

"No!" he growled even as he felt his body acting on its own, thrusting deep to further possess and love. "No!"

She cried out and stiffened. Then she was kissing him, his face, his neck. She drew her legs about his waist and offered up her innocence.

Pleased by the gift, Black Hawk groaned as pure physical sensation took over. Rachel cried out in ecstasy. Black Hawk roared his pleasure to the sky as he sank deeply into her softness one last earth-shattering time.

When it was over, Rachel lay with his weight heavy upon her, but she loved it. She enjoyed the closeness, caressing his back and shoulders, running her fingers through his long hair. He hadn't made a sound since it had happened, but she didn't mind. She had heard his cry of release, felt his body straining to join fully in glorious wonder. *I love him,* she thought. How could she have imagined a future without him? She'd been a virgin, but she didn't regret that at all.

She recalled her dream, the one in which Black Hawk had appeared, claiming to share her destiny. Had he had similar dreams? She knew that the Indians put great stock in the power of dreams. Visions, they called them.

She had loved Jordan, but this feeling she had for Black Hawk was different. It was more intense; it consumed her every waking and sleeping moment. Every minute he wasn't with her, he was in her thoughts, teasing her memory, stirring up fantasies in her mind.

Did he feel the same way? He'd said he had much to do for his people. He'd told her that he could not take a wife while there was much in his life that held his attention.

But couldn't she help him? Make him see that some things weren't as important as one sometimes thought?

Then she recalled what she'd learned about his childhood, the terrible things that he'd seen. How horrible for a child to see his father murdered! She shivered and hugged him tightly. She wished she could do something to soften the memory. She'd wished she'd been there for the little boy.

Black Hawk stirred and rolled to her side. She stifled a cry of disappointment, as she didn't want him to leave her. She turned to him, hoping he'd take her into his arms again, to snuggle. But he lay on his back, without touching her, his arm across his eyes, as his breathing became steadier.

As she watched the rise and fall of his magnificent naked chest, she recalled the sound of his heartbeat after they'd made love.

Her fingers itched to touch him again, but she resisted the urge. "Black Hawk?"

He shifted, raising his arm a little to peer at her. She felt a sudden chill when he didn't smile or speak.

Unable to help herself, she touched his arm, trailing her fingers to his chest, down farther to his stomach. He was still naked, and his manhood was slightly swollen, nestled within its bed of dark curls. She felt a rich surge of lust as her gaze lingered. His shaft started to harden, and fire shot through her, dampening her once again.

She lifted her glance to find that he'd dropped his arm to stare at her.

"Rach-el." He reached out a hand to catch her head and bring it down so he could kiss her.

Despite his growing desire, he was gentle with her mouth. His gentleness only increased her passion, until she was pressed against him, driving her tongue between his lips.

They kissed hotly, and Rachel moved against him, wanting him to love her once again, but Black Hawk ended the kiss. With a light caress on her cheek, he stood and began to dress.

"Black Hawk?" She was hurt that he didn't want to make love with her again.

"We must get back. My people will be looking for me."

"But I thought you said that Spring Blossom . . ."

"We have been gone a long time," he told her.

"Oh," she said weakly, averting her gaze. "I see." Suddenly she felt ashamed of her nakedness. She rose and dressed quickly, anxious to shield herself from his gaze. Apparently, the experience they'd just shared was not new for him, nor was it as meaningful to him as it was to her.

She had slipped on her tunic, and was fumbling with the ties when Black Hawk's fingers touched her hands. His expression was grave. "Let me help," he said.

Shaking her head, she turned away. *No,* she thought. *I don't need any help! Men aren't to be trusted. I shouldn't have forgotten, but I did.*

She wanted him to be different. But the way he'd used her, then cast her aside, hurt. It pained her more than Jordan's betrayal. *For I gave you, Black Hawk, more than I've given any man.* She blinked against tears. Well, she was the foolish one, wasn't she? Black Hawk had warned her, but she had fallen in love with him anyway.

*I'll not make the same mistake!* she thought. *I'll not allow myself to be hurt this way again.*

Then, she heard it . . . the sound of someone calling them in the distance.

She glanced in Black Hawk's direction and saw that he'd heard it, too. He looked concerned; in fact, he looked worried.

"What is it?" she asked, anxiety temporarily misplacing the pain. "What's wrong?"

He shook his head. "We must go."

He waited only a second to ensure that she followed him. Within minutes they were back in the canoe and heading toward the village.

*"Black Hawk!"*

As the canoe glided across the water and closer to the the village lay, Black Hawk identified the cry. It was Spring Blossom's. He frowned and increased his paddle strokes.

When Daniel Trahern's voice rose to join Black Hawk's

sister in the search, Black Hawk tensed. He knew instinctively then that something was terribly wrong.

"No!"

Black Hawk saw Rachel's face whiten as she heard the news. The Sioux had kidnapped her father.

"It's all my fault!" she cried, swaying on her feet.

"It is not your fault, Rachel," Daniel said quietly. "You did nothing to encourage this man's interest."

"He's taken Father because of me," she insisted. "If I hadn't come, Clouds-at-Morning would never have seen me. He wouldn't have kidnapped Father!"

"Rachel," Amelia said, looking shaken and pale. "Please don't blame yourself. We know what these Sioux are like. We can only hope and pray that Runs-with-the-Wind, one of their own kind, will help us."

But Rachel was too upset to listen to reason. She had been feeling particularly vulnerable as she and Black Hawk had taken the canoe down and across the river. The memory of their joining lingered on her mind. The passion. The heady power. The hot, searing fire of Black Hawk's kiss. Then, there had been his reluctance to love her a second time, and the pain of being rejected by him.

The news of her father's kidnapping, compounded by her vulnerability with Black Hawk, had done her in.

"I have to go to him. They'll let him go if I do what they say."

"No!" It was Black Hawk who objected.

"Yes!" she cried. "Don't you see that it's the only way to save his life!"

"You will not save his life," he told her. "They will not release him because you want it. They will keep him as they will keep you. Then you both will be prisoners of the Sioux."

Rachel shook her head, not wanting to believe it. "No," she whispered.

"Rachel, Black Hawk is right," Daniel said. He spoke more softly than he'd ever spoken to her before. "I love John like my own father, but I agree that sacrificing yourself won't accomplish what you think."

"Then what can I do?"

Black Hawk touched her arm, and she nearly bolted from the sensation of warmth. "We will rescue your father. We will think of a plan."

She looked at him, then at Daniel with hope. "You will?" She decided she'd go to the Sioux if it proved the only way.

Daniel nodded. "We'll have help. Lots of it. We'll let you know what we decide."

"But you will go soon?" Rachel said. "You won't wait too long?" She was frightened that something dreadful would happen to her father. She had expected Clouds-at-Morning to come for her. She hadn't suspected that he would use her father to ensure that she consented to be his wife.

"Clouds knows I've been hiding from him," Rachel said miserably.

"You haven't been hiding!" Amelia exclaimed.

Rachel could only point out how much she looked like an Ojibwa, an Indian. "If this isn't hiding, then what would you call it?"

"I'd call it being smart," Daniel said. "Staying protected."

"Well, it worked just fine for me, didn't it?" she cried. "But it didn't do much for my father!"

She began to cry for her father, for the emotional upheaval she'd suffered at Jordan's and now Black Hawk's hands. Her involvement with Black Hawk hurt her more than had the end of her relationship with Jordan.

Amelia fought back tears as she looked helplessly at her sister and then her husband. "Daniel, I can't believe he's been taken again."

Daniel nodded and pulled her into his arms.

"Did the Sioux brave say anything more?" Black Hawk asked. Daniel had been the one to receive the message that John Dempsey had been kidnapped and Clouds-at-Morning wanted Rachel in exchange for John's life.

"No more than I've told you," Daniel said.

Black Hawk's features hardened. "We will find this man and rescue John Dempsey. No more will the Sioux hurt one of our people or yours."

Amelia pulled from her husband's arms to go to her sister. "Come, Rachel. Let's lie down in the wigwam."

"I can't sleep!" she cried. "Not while Father is missing!"

"Well, I need to rest," Amelia said. "For the babe. Father would want me to, and I prefer not to be alone."

As the two women left the men, Black Hawk's scowl deepened. He clenched his fists. His jaw clamped tight, and his dark eyes gleamed with fury.

"Clouds-at-Morning will not live until the next season of the summer sun."

Daniel felt the same anger his friend was feeling, but he knew that Black Hawk had much more reason to hate. He hoped that hate wouldn't destroy the Ojibwa brave in the end.

"What should we do first?" he asked.

Black Hawk blinked, and the glaze of fury cleared from his obsidian eyes. "We call a council meeting, and we find horses. We will reach the Sioux only if we can travel as they do."

"I can help with the horses," Daniel said. "I can borrow them."

"Soldiers?"

Daniel nodded. "And men I've done work for."

"We must not allow Rachel to leave this village," Black Hawk said with vehemence.

Daniel nodded. He was beginning to respect his sister-in-law. She had courage and wasn't selfish, as he'd first imagined. But if she was anything like her sister, then he feared Rachel was stubborn as well. Her determination to free her father could complicate the situation if she decided to leave the village and face the Sioux alone.

"Rachel must be kept in the village for her own good," he said. "I fear she is much like Tree-That-Will-Not-Bend." He glanced toward the wigwam where the two women had disappeared. "Perhaps Amelia should remain in the village also."

Black Hawk nodded his head. "Yes. And Jane and Little Flower," he replied.

# Chapter 19

The soldiers pulled their horses before the trading post. A sergeant climbed down off his horse, secured the mount, and entered Keller's store.

"Can you tell me where Daniel Trahern is?" the young man asked Jack Keller.

Jack narrowed his gaze. "Who's asking?" He noted the uniform hat, dark blue jacket, and light blue trousers.

The man took off his hat and cradled it under his left arm. "Cameron Walters of the United States Army," he said, extending his right hand.

"Walters?" Jack hesitated before accepting the handshake. "I've heard the name."

Walters smiled. "I've been here before, about a year and a half ago."

Jack's eyes widened. "You're the young man who helped Daniel and Jane escape!" He grinned. "I knew I'd heard that name! It's nice to meet you, Private Walters."

"It's Sergeant Walters now," he said.

"Did that have anything to do with your bringing in Richard Milton?"

The sergeant nodded. "It did."

"Congratulations."

Walters thanked him as he looked around. "The place hasn't changed much, I see. You've added to your stock."

Jack nodded. "Always looking to add new things for my customers."

"Was that a hotel I saw coming in?" Walters asked.

"Sure is," Jack said. "Run by Maeve Treehorn and her husband Samuel."

"Good. I'm sure the men are tired of sleeping outside. A hotel room would be a nice change for them."

"Men?" Jack inquired. "How many men?"

"Fifteen, with more on the way. Daniel asked us to come. Seems there's been some trouble with the Sioux."

"They captured John Dempsey," Jack said. "Been after his daughter."

"Amelia? They're after Amelia?" Walters had befriended Amelia Dempsey when he was a private and she had worked at her father's infirmary. They'd met when he'd come for medical assistance from John Dempsey.

"No. They're after Rachel, his youngest," Jack said.

"So Amelia has a sister . . ." He frowned as he thought of the good doctor. *Poor Amelia.* He didn't know her sister, but felt bad for her as well. He wished he'd arrived in time to prevent John Dempsey's kidnapping. "Where is Miss Dempsey?"

Jack hesitated before answering. "She's with the Ojibwa."

"Black Hawk's people," Walters murmured.

"That's right."

"Daniel wasn't home when I knocked. Any chance you know where he went?"

"To the village. He's due back any time now."

The door behind the soldier opened and shut. Both men turned to see who'd entered.

"Jane," Jack said.

Jane Milton looked alarmed as she approached. "What's happening? Why are all those soldiers outside ..." Her voice trailed off as she spied the sergeant. "Cameron?" she said. "Cameron Walters?"

Walters blinked, then smiled as he recognized one of the people he'd help rescue. "Mrs. Milton, it's wonderful to see you. How are you and your little girl?"

Jane frowned at the way he'd addressed her. Walters, realizing the "Mrs." must have brought back bad memories, apologized. "I didn't want to take the liberty of calling you Jane," he explained.

She smiled. "Please. Call me Jane. I don't mind at all." She turned her attention to Jack. "Jack, Daniel's just come back. He wants me and Susie to go to Black Hawk's village."

"Daniel's back?" Walters asked.

Jane nodded, and the sergeant excused himself with his intention of visiting Jane's brother. Jack and Jane were now alone.

"I think it's wise of you to go, Jane," Jack said. His expression was soft as he gazed at her. "After what happened to John, I don't think it's safe here for you and Susie."

"I know," Jane said. She seemed upset by the thought of leaving her home. "That's what Daniel said, but ..."

"The Ojibwa aren't the Sioux, Jane," he said. "They'll treat you kindly. Remember, Rachel has been there for some time now, and apparently she is content."

"Content?" Jane said with a rise in tone. "How can she be content knowing that her father was kidnapped?"

Seeing the sudden panic in her eyes, Jack placed his hands on her shoulders. "I'm sure she's upset now. But it's not because she's with the Ojibwa. Do you understand what I'm saying?''

"I don't want to go."

He released one shoulder to touch her chin. "It will be all right." He had loved this woman since she'd first entered his life after she'd been rescued from the Sioux and brought here to live near her brother. Jane was so sweet, so fragile. He wanted nothing more than to take her into his arms and kiss her breathlessly, to cherish and keep her safe forever. Her and her little girl. But Jane still suffered from the horror of the past and a husband who had been a vicious monster. Until she healed, he must keep his distance. There were times, like this moment, when Jack had a helluva time guarding his heart and keeping his hands off her.

"Jack, what if the Sioux come again?" Jane asked. "What if something happens to Susie?"

He brushed his knuckle against her cheek. "It won't. Daniel has enlisted the help of a lot of people. With aid of the soldiers and the Ojibwa and Ottawa people, we'll get John Dempsey back and drive away the Sioux for good."

"We?" Her eyes flew to his in alarm.

"I'll not stay home while John Dempsey is out there and needs our help."

"Oh, Jack . . ."

"I'll be all right," he said with a soft smile. "We'll all be just fine."

"I hope so." Tears pooled in her beautiful blue eyes. "I don't want anything to happen to you, too."

"Jane," he said with a groan. "Don't cry, darlin'." Unable to resist, Jack pulled her into his arms and held her. He was ecstatic when she didn't fight him or try to pull away.

*Progress,* he thought with a flicker of joy. He closed his eyes. *Praise God.*

"Cameron and some of his men will be going with us," Daniel explained to his wife and sister-in-law. "Jane and Susie will stay with you. Black Hawk has contacted other villages. The Ottawa have promised to help as well."

"How do you expect us to stay behind and just wait!" Rachel exclaimed. "I'll go mad!"

Daniel scowled at her. "Rachel, I thought we discussed this already. You must stay here. We can't leave and do what we have to do if we have to worry about your safety!"

"How can you say nothing?" Rachel demanded of her sister.

"Because, unlike you, she's been through this before," Daniel said with a gentle look at his wife. "She's learned that it's best to have the right people handle the matter."

"He's right, Rachel," Amelia said with tears in her eyes. "Because of me, those I love almost got killed. I'll not interfere in such things again."

"Don't you see it's for the best?" Daniel said to Rachel. He drew his wife to his side and hugged her.

"Whose best?" Rachel challenged.

"Your father's," Black Hawk said quietly, speaking for the first time.

The Ojibwa's soft voice did strange things to Rachel's insides. "Black Hawk," she whispered, her green gaze filling with tears.

His expression held compassion. "Come, Rach-el," he said. "Walk with me."

Conscious of the presence of Cameron Walters's soldiers, Rachel flashed a brief glance at her sister and brother-in-law, then fell into step with Black Hawk.

The Ojibwa warrior stopped when they had left the others behind. She studied their surroundings. They were alone in the forest.

"Rach-el," Black Hawk said, turning her to face him. "We will bring back your father." He placed his hand on her jaw.

Her heart melted as she closed her eyes. "I don't want anything bad to happen to you," she said. She lifted her lashes to study him. The sight of him never failed to stir her emotions. He wore face paint, which she'd never seen on him before. With his long, unbound dark hair, copper earrings, and Ojibwa clothing, he looked more the savage than ever before. But there was gentleness in his eyes that pulled at her heartstrings. She knew the power of his touch and experienced the kindness of his heart. She loved him, more than she had ever loved Jordan.

"Rach-el." Something flickered in Black Hawk's expression as they locked gazes. Then, he startled her by kissing her deeply. His mouth clung, delved, and captured hers completely. Her world tilted, then righted itself as he pulled slightly away.

"I will return," he said. "Nothing will happen to me."

"I've already seen what can happen to you!" she cried. She was frightened for his safety. Her memory of his gunshot wound was painfully vivid. She couldn't stop loving him just because he didn't return her love.

"I was alone then," he said. "I will not be alone this time."

She grabbed the edges of his leather vest. "Promise me," she gasped, her eyes filling with tears. She pulled him closer. "Promise you'll return, that you'll all return without injury."

"I cannot promise that there will not be bloodshed."

"And while knowing this you expect me to stay?"

He touched her hair, fingering the silky strands that

fell across her shoulder. "I care for you. I hope you will stay because I ask you."

"Black Hawk—"

"Say it, Rach-el," he demanded. "Tell me you will stay."

She felt as if she were drowning in his dark gaze. Her eyes fell once again to that sensual mouth. She knew at that moment that she was powerless to resist him.

She nodded.

"Say it, Rach-el."

"I'll stay."

His smile warmed her. "Good."

"But Black Hawk," she said as he captured her fingers. He led her back toward the village with her hand in his. "—I shall kill you myself if you don't come home safely."

He grinned. "You? A doctor's daughter would harm this man?"

She closed her eyes and shuddered. "Just bring back my father and the others safely . . . and *please* don't let anything happen to you."

Desire flared in his expression. He kissed her again until she clung to him, moaning. "*Giga-waabamin.* I will return to you, Rach-el Dempsey."


The Sioux village was quiet. It was the dead of night and only a few warriors were posted as guards. The evening was clear, without a breeze to carry scents and sounds or to hide them. Black Hawk and his men, along with Daniel and the soldiers, had slipped into the area and surrounded the encampment. They kept their distance as they waited for Black Hawk to initiate the signal to attack.

Black Hawk's heart thundered as he narrowed his gaze and studied the Sioux village. As he thought of this enemy, he tightened his grip on the handle of his knife. John Dempsey was inside a teepee. Which one?

The Ojibwa war chief didn't move. During the hunt, he could sit for hours patiently, alertly, waiting for the right moment to move in for the kill. He was trained equally well to meet his enemy. He would sit outside this village all night without movement if necessary. He would not attack unless he was certain that it was time.

Black Hawk thought of Clouds-at-Morning, the Sioux brave who wanted Rachel. *Rachel!* Anger made him clench his jaw. The Sioux warrior would never have Rachel! Not as long as he, Black Hawk, lived and breathed and could protect her!

He had promised to rescue her father. He'd told her he'd return to her when it was done. But Black Hawk knew that he'd do whatever it took to free John Dempsey, even fight to the death. He would do that for Rachel.

Black Hawk stared at the village, and his vision blurred as the past returned with stark mental images of blood and death. He could hear the gut-wrenching cries of his father, Bear Tooth, and the other dying brave, Water Turtle. He could hear the *thunk* of wood and metal meeting bare flesh, the adult screams that followed . . . and the wild laughter of the savage warrior who enjoyed inflicting pain. *He-Who-Kills-with-Big-Stick.*

Black Hawk was suddenly a little boy again, witnessing cruelty and death . . . his father's murder.

Tears filled his eyes as he relived the agony . . . the pain. He'd been unable to act to save his father. He'd felt helpless . . . powerless . . . saddened and enraged.

He heard the slightest stir of movement, and was suddenly forced back to the present. He exchanged glances with his friend Daniel, and realized that this day things were different. He had the power to strike back. Before him were the enemy. He would think carefully and outsmart them. He would win, not by senseless killing, but by making them feel helpless, powerless, enraged.

Black Hawk lifted a hand at Daniel's questioning gaze in a silent message that said, "Soon, but not yet."

He felt the strength inside him build as he saw his friend's nod of agreement. He was Black-Hawk-Who-Hunts-at-Dawn, a seasoned warrior, an experienced war chief. He was not the child who had watched the senseless torture and death of his beloved father.

Black Hawk shifted his gaze back to the village and felt instinctively that the right time had come. Cupping his hands to his mouth, he hooted like a night owl. A distant call came as if answered by the owl's mate.

Then, within seconds, the rescue party shrieked wild war cries as they rose from their hiding places to attack.

# Chapter 20

*He will return to me. Me!* Rachel thought. Had she read too much into his words? She hoped not. She wanted Black Hawk to return to her.

This morning she worked to make a rush mat. Weaving was just one of the many things that Spring Blossom had taught her. Standing in the warm sun, Rachel looked at her sister's frame and smiled at Amelia's awkward attempts to weave. Her gaze went to Daniel's sister, who sat on the ground. Jane obviously knew what she was doing as her fingers moved quickly to weave a colorful shoulder sash.

"Where is Susie?" Rachel asked. She hadn't seen the child since the men had left yesterday morning. She knew that Susie had come; she was surprised that the little girl didn't cling more closely to her mother.

Spring Blossom and two Ojibwa matrons worked near the white women. "Little Flower is with Barking Dog," Spring Blossom said. "They are at the rice marsh with Swaying Tree."

It was the time of year when the Ojibwa took their birch-bark canoes into the waterways to harvest *manoo-min,* which was wild rice. The Ojibwa used the rice in many dishes. Rachel had tasted several of them, and she had found the meals very palatable.

"Is it safe there?" Jane asked. She'd appeared nervous when she'd first come. She seemed more relaxed now, as if she finally understood that the Ojibwa were a kind people, who were no threat to any of them.

"Swaying Tree will watch over Little Flower," Spring Blossom said. "Tomorrow, when the sun rises, I will show you how to harvest the rice. Rach-el can go with Woman-with-Hair-of-Fox. Jane can come with me."

"I don't know." Jane was hesitant about going.

"Why not, Jane?" Amelia said. "It sounds like fun." She patted her belly. "I'd love to go myself, but I'm not my best in the morning." She suffered from morning sickness these days, although she felt well by the after-noon.

"Tree-That-Will-Not-Bend, you can go with Swaying Tree later. Barking Dog's grandmother will show you what to do."

Amelia's expression brightened. *"Miigwech.* I'd like that."

"Wild rice gathering!" Rachel exclaimed. "I don't want to gather rice!" She looked accusingly at Amelia. "How can you think of harvesting while Father remains a Sioux captive!"

Her sister looked hurt. "Rachel, you must have faith in Black Hawk," Amelia said.

"I do," Rachel whispered, her eyes suddenly filling with tears. She felt a dull throbbing at the back of her neck. Contrite, she touched Amelia's arm. "I'm sorry, Amelia. I just can't stop worrying about them. What if the Sioux are stronger? What if they ambush our men first?''

''They won't attack first,'' Jane said, speaking of the matter for the first time. Rachel knew that Jane was as worried as the rest of them, for her brother and Jack Keller were in the rescue party. ''Black Hawk knows what he is doing.''

''I hope you're right,'' Rachel said. ''Yes, I know you're right, but . . .''

Later, while the others had gone to harvest the wild rice, Rachel stayed behind with a headache. Spring Blossom gave her a broth made from herbs for the pain; then Rachel went to the wigwam and lay down. Soon, her headache went away. Her concern for Black Hawk and the other men got her up and wandering aimlessly about the village.

She fretted about her father's kidnapping, and she worried about her new feelings for Black Hawk.

She loved Black Hawk and wanted to know more about him. But whom could she ask? Who would tell her about his boyhood and his father's murder?

Would she ever fully understand the man?

*Black Hawk wants me,* she thought. *At least, he does in the physical sense.* Would he ever feel more? Could he ever love her?

He was consumed with finding his father's killer. How could there be room for love with revenge in his heart?

Rachel spied Woman-with-Hair-of-Fox near the edge of the village yard. Would the matron answer her questions about Black Hawk? The woman had been kind and patient with her, and she spoke perfect English. Woman-with-Hair-of-Fox had been born white, and then she'd been captured by the Ottawa Indians when she was eleven years old. Her life with the Ojibwa had come later after the Ottawa had traded her to the village of Big-Cat-with-Broken-Paw.

Rachel hailed Woman-with-Hair-of-Fox as the matron handed a water sack to a young boy. The woman shooed the child toward a wigwam, then waited with a smile for Rachel to join her.

"I have something to ask you," Rachel said, "but I don't know if you want to answer my question."

"What is your question?" The matron looked curious.

"Will you tell me about Black Hawk's father?" Rachel asked her. Her first thought had been to ask Spring Blossom, but then she remembered that the man had been the maiden's father, too. Any questions about him would only bring up bad memories for her.

Woman-with-Hair-of-Fox gazed at Rachel for a long moment without answering. "Come," she said. "Let us walk."

Rachel nodded and followed the woman's lead. "I'm sorry if I seem curious, but I just had to know."

The matron gave her a soft smile. "You love him."

"Why do you say that?" Rachel said with alarm. She looked away.

"I have seen it in your eyes when you watch him."

"Oh, no!"

Woman-with-Hair-of-Fox patted her shoulder. "Do not be upset, Rachel. I see what others do not see. I see your love for Black Hawk, and Jane Milton's feelings for Jack Keller."

"Jane cares for Jack?"

"Yes." The matron gestured toward a path through the forest. "I saw this, just as I saw your sister's love for Man-with-Big-Head."

Rachel changed direction, following the new trail. At the mention of Daniel's Indian name, she grinned.

"I will tell you what you want to know," Woman-with-Hair of-Fox said.

They followed the river to the edge of a great lake. It was a cloudy day, but the water was no less beautiful. Here, Rachel could enjoy the clean air. She felt the breeze blowing in from off the water. She closed her eyes to savor the moment.

"Let us sit," Woman-with-Hair-of-Fox suggested. They found a rock large enough for two. The matron was quiet for a time before she began to speak.

"He was a little boy, only eight years old, when he went on his first hunt with his father, Bear Tooth," she began.

"The Ojibwa hunt so young?" Rachel asked.

"Sometimes, yes. Sometimes, no. Bear Tooth felt that his son was ready. Black Hawk was a good boy. He was very wise for eight summers. He had a sharp eye and could kill a bird in flight with a single arrow."

Rachel smiled, trying to imagine him as a child. "I would like to have known him then."

Woman-with-Hair-of-Fox smiled knowingly. "His father was proud of him. We were all proud of Black Hawk. The young warrior was pleased and excited when he learned that his father was to take him on his first big hunt."

A shadow fell across the matron's expression, dulling her light eyes. "They left early when the sun was not yet up in the day's sky. Four warriors went with young Black Hawk. Bear Tooth taught his son how to track deer and other big animals, just as he'd shown him how to shoot a bird in flight. By the time the sun was high in the sky, the hunting party had two deer and one bear between the five hunters. Black Hawk's prize had been the biggest— a large black bear. The warriors were pleased. There would be food for everyone in the village. Two of our braves, Silver Wolf and Laughing Lake, went back to the village with the deer. Bear Tooth, Water Turtle, and Black Hawk stayed behind with the bear to prepare the animal and offer thanksgiving to the Bear Spirit. A bear is sacred to the *Anishinaabe*. A special offering to *Gichi-Manidoo* is made after a brave kills a bear.''

Tears filled the matron's eyes as she paused before continuing. ''Black Hawk had left the clearing to find firewood. Bear Tooth and Water Turtle were there with the bear when the Sioux warriors came.''

Rachel felt a sudden chill and hugged herself with her arms. ''What happened?'' She wasn't sure she wanted to hear the tale, but she wanted to know . . . because of Black Hawk.

''There were many enemy warriors and only two of our braves. The enemy surrounded Bear Tooth and Water Turtle; then they began to taunt and beat them. They cut them with their knifes and stabbed them with their spears. Black Hawk was returning to the campsite when he heard the enemy's laughter . . . his father's screams.''

The matron's voice thickened. ''The boy crept closer. Such a wise child not to run ahead and let his whereabouts be known.''

Rachel felt a burning in her stomach as she pictured the scene in her mind.

''Black Hawk waited,'' the matron said. ''He wanted to save his father and Water Turtle, but he didn't know how.''

Woman-with-Hair-of-Fox rose from the rock and moved to the edge of the water.

Rachel stood silently and joined her. Her throat felt so tight that she could barely swallow. She'd be forever haunted by the image of a frightened young Indian boy.

''What happened?'' she said so softly her voice might not have been heard.

But the matron's sigh told Rachel that she had heard her. "There was a Sioux warrior. His name was He-Who-Kills-with-Big Stick. He was a cruel man. He enjoyed giving pain, even to one of his own people.

"This warrior began to poke and prod, first at Water Turtle and then at Black Hawk's father. He had *bagamaa-gan,* a big stick with a blade at one end. Many of the People have such weapons."

"War clubs," Rachel said.

The matron nodded. "Yes, war clubs." She continued her story with a solemn expression. "He-Who-Kills-with-Big-Stick liked to use his war club more than most braves."

Her imagination took over before Woman-with-Hair-of-Fox finished telling the tale. Rachel's stomach churned as tears filled her eyes so that she couldn't see. As the matron went on with the story, Rachel's imagination proved accurate. She heard about the awful horror that the two Ojibwa adult males endured that day. The horror consisted of torture, tormenting, sticks, and fire. Bear Tooth tried bravely, but futilely, not to cry out with pain, as Black Hawk watched, with tears trailing down his cheeks, as the Sioux tortured and murdered his father.

"There was a time during the ordeal when Black Hawk could no longer stay still. He started to go to his father's aid; but as if sensing his son's intention, Bear Tooth caught his son's gaze. It was said that the warrior sent his son a message with his eyes to save himself. Black Hawk was almost captured as he gazed at his father. A Sioux warrior heard his movement and looked to the forest where the boy was hidden. To keep his son from discovery, Bear Tooth began to taunt the Sioux and further enrage them. He brought their attention away from Black Hawk and back to himself. Bear Tooth suffered, but was glad he had saved his son.

"When the Sioux were done, there wasn't much left of our warriors. Black Hawk stayed hidden while his father and friend were killed, and then longer still while the Sioux braves feasted on Black Hawk's bear. When the Sioux left, they left the rest of the bear behind. Black Hawk ran to his father and Water Turtle. Then, with tears on his face and his weapons drawn, he watched over the bodies to protect them from predators."

"Poor Black Hawk," Rachel whispered, her throat aching.

Woman-with-Hair-of-Fox nodded. "When the warriors and Black Hawk didn't return to the village, Silver Fox and Laughing Lake came back to look for them. They found the little warrior Black Hawk sitting rigidly in a tiny clearing, his expression blank, his weapons still raised for protection. Horrified and grieving, the warriors brought the bodies back to the village for the funeral ceremony.

"Black Hawk was quiet for a long time after that. There was such sadness in his eyes, it hurt to look at him. The people in the village called him a great hunter because he had killed the bear. They were sad and angry at the death of their own, but they saw the greatness in Black Hawk. Time had passed since Bear Tooth's passing; they wanted to celebrate his son. But Black Hawk didn't want to celebrate. He didn't want to be a great hunter. He only wanted his father back."

"Oh, Black Hawk," Rachel whispered.

"Then one day, Black Hawk spoke," the matron said. "He vowed vengeance on He-Who-Kills-with-Big-Stick and the Sioux who had done this. He said no more about the killings after that. He lived among us as any young brave. He had proved a mighty warrior when he killed his first bear. Despite having seen his father's death, Black

Hawk was a wise warrior. Big-Cat-with-Broken-Paw made him war chief. Black Hawk is a good war chief.''

"But his desire for revenge hasn't made him"—Rachel thought hard for the right word—"reckless?"

The matron shook her head. "He fights when it is time to fight. He has waited many years to find He-Who-Kills-with-Big Stick. Only when his father's death is avenged will Black Hawk be healed."

They returned in the bright light of day. Rachel heard the joyful cries of the villagers. Hurrying from the wigwam, where she'd been spreading fresh scented pine boughs on the floor, she saw the group of men. She cried out with gladness and rushed to meet them.

"Father!"

John Dempsey, looking weary but well, smiled as he saw his youngest daughter. Amelia had already joined the group and was hugging her husband Daniel. After embracing her father, Rachel searched for Black Hawk, but didn't see him. Her heart started to pound with fear. Where was Black Hawk? Had he been hurt . . . or killed? She studied her brother-in-law. Surely, Daniel would have told her immediately.

"Black Hawk is in the wigwam of Big-Cat-with-Broken-Paw," Daniel said as he approached her. His smile for her reached his blue eyes. "We made it back—all of us. We're all fine."

Rachel felt dizzy as she closed her eyes. "Thank God," she said. Her lashes fluttered open, and she grinned at her brother-in-law. "Thank you, Daniel." She wanted to hug him, but wasn't sure he'd appreciate the affectionate display.

He opened his arms to her, and she felt his embrace for the first time. It felt like a gentle bear hug. When he released her, Rachel saw her sister grinning at the two of them.

"You've got a fine husband, Amelia," she admitted, feeling warmth for Daniel Trahern.

"I know," she said. "Man-with-Big-Head can be charming when he wants to be."

Rachel chuckled. "I'm sorry," she apologized, grinning, "but that name—it makes me laugh."

Daniel wasn't offended as he shot a rueful smile at his pregnant wife. "Your sister's idea, I'm afraid," he said.


The chief stared at their Sioux prisoner. "You will speak to us, Clouds-at-Morning," he said. "You have done a terrible thing to take our friend John Dempsey. We do not like this. Runs-with-the-Wind will not like this."

Black Hawk stared at the Sioux warrior with hard eyes. "You have knowledge of a certain brave. We wish to know where he is."

Clouds-at-Morning stiffened. "I do not have to tell you anything."

"His name is He-Who-Kills-with-Big-Stick," Black Hawk continued, as if the Sioux had not spoken. "He killed my father. I must know where he is."

"I do not know him."

But a flicker of emotion in the man's dark eyes told Black Hawk that the brave did. "You can tell us now or tell us as you die. It makes no difference to us."

The Sioux brave looked alarmed. "He is a cruel warrior."

Black Hawk nodded. "He kills because he enjoys it."

"If I tell you where he last was, will you release me? Release my people?"

The rescue party had taken five braves prisoner to

ensure John Dempsey's safe release. The U.S. soldiers had stayed behind to guard the remaining villagers and to make sure that Black Hawk and his men weren't followed or ambushed.

"We will release you and your people on one condition," Big-Cat-with-Broken-Paw said. "You must not bother John Dempsey or his daughters again."

A spark of anger lit Clouds-at-Morning's gaze. "I have given the daughter Rachel the right to choose me as husband."

"Rachel does not want to marry you," Daniel Trahern said as he entered the wigwam. "She has told me so. You frighten her." He scowled. "And apparently she's had good reason to be frightened."

"You will not come near Rachel Dempsey again," Black Hawk warned. "If you do, we will hunt down you and your people, and we will kill every one of them."

"I will stay away from Rachel Dempsey," the Sioux brave murmured. But there was anger, not fear, in his dark eyes.

Daniel's smile was grim. "Good."

"About He-Who-Kills-with-Big-Stick," Black Hawk said.

The Sioux shivered. "I will tell you what I know, but he must not learn who told you."

Black Hawk felt a trickle of excitement. "He will not know."

"He was last seen in the village of Great Buffalo. He does not stay too long in any one place. Our people respect him, but many fear him. He comes for a time, then leaves to visit the next village."

"Great Buffalo," Black Hawk murmured. "Where is this village?"

Clouds-at-Morning turned defiant. "I should not tell

you. How do I know you will not attack and kill my people?''

"Did you attack the village of Red Dog?" Black Hawk asked, and was relieved when the Sioux brave shook his head. "I do not want your people. I want only He-Who-Kills-with-Big-Stick. I give you my word that we will release your people. They will not be harmed.''

Clouds stared at Black Hawk a long time before responding. "The village is where we meet for council, where the buffalo follow the big mountain." He went to describe how to get to this place and how long it had been since He-Who-Kills-with-Big-Stick had left Clouds-at-Morning's village.

Big-Cat-with-Broken-Paw waved to the warrior guarding the doorway. "Take Clouds-at-Morning to the wigwam of Sleeping Bird. See that he is fed and rested." He then addressed the Sioux brave. "Tomorrow we will talk one last time.''

"You said you would let me go!" the brave cried as he was led from the wigwam.

"So I did," the chief said. "And so you shall be." He glanced at Black Hawk. "Are you sure this is the right thing to do?''

Black Hawk's look was steady as he gazed at his chief and then at his friend Daniel. "I want the warrior He-Who-Kills-with-Big-Stick.''

"Then you shall have him," the chief said.

When the Sioux was taken away, Daniel turned to Black Hawk. "Can you trust him?''

"I do not know," Black Hawk said, "but we will honor our word." He had waited a long time for his father's murderer.

*Soon,* he thought. *Soon, He-Who-Kills-with-Big-Stick will meet Black-Hawk-Who-Hunts-at-Dawn. And I, Black Hawk, will avenge my father's death!*

# Chapter 21

*Black Hawk is back!* Rachel thought. She was anxious to see him. Would he be glad to see her?

She was disappointed that he hadn't immediately sought her out. What had happened? How did they get her father away so easily? Where was Clouds-at-Morning?

*Father is safe,* Rachel thought. *Black Hawk is safe!* There was still much to learn about the rescue, but Daniel had promised to tell the story later, after they'd eaten the evening meal. Rachel hadn't argued with her sister's husband. She was happy with the turn of events and her new friendship with Daniel. She sensed a change in her brother-in-law's attitude toward her; she couldn't be more pleased.

Black Hawk was with the Ojibwa chief, Big-Cat-with-Broken-Paw. Rachel longed to see him again, but she knew he would be with his leader for a long while. She headed back to Spring Blossom's wigwam, where she'd been staying with the Indian maiden, Amelia, and Jane.

There was to be a feast this night in celebration of the rice harvest. The meal would include Ojibwa and white man's food. Daniel had gone to the cabin to fetch the necessary ingredients for dessert cakes, Amelia's contribution to the meal.

Rachel decided to make *mashkodesimin,* an Ojibwa soup made from beans. It was just one of many dishes that she'd learned to cook during her stay at the village.

As she searched for a clay bowl and cooking utensils, Rachel's thoughts lingered on Black Hawk. Now that her father was back and the threat of invading Sioux was gone, the time had come for her to return to the mission. She didn't want to leave him. She wanted to stay and spend more time with Black Hawk. What if she went away and never saw him again?

*Oh, Black Hawk, come to me.*

She longed to speak with him and find out how he felt about her. He'd said he'd return to her. *Her,* she thought. What did he mean? That he loved her enough to come back?

They'd been lovers. Was it love that had driven him to take her? Or desire?

*And he does desire me. I've seen the way he looks at me. I've felt his kisses and his touch. He's not indifferent.*

She unearthed the basket of beans and dumped them in the clay pot for cooking. *But desire isn't love,* she thought as she added herbs for seasoning. On impulse, she threw in a handful of dried corn kernels and a few other ingredients of her own.

*Is he so driven by revenge for his father's murder that he'll never be able to love a woman?*

Rachel stirred the contents of the pot, then set it to simmer over the fire. As she added other ingredients to the dish, she recalled herself and Black Hawk in a secluded forest glen . . . two bodies cleaving together in the most special act of love that two people could share. She felt a shiver of pleasure at the memory.

Whatever happened, she thought, she wouldn't regret giving herself to Black Hawk. Her lips curved in a slow feminine smile as she remembered her initial fear of the marriage act. Loving Black Hawk had been so wonderful. It seemed silly to her now that she'd ever felt afraid.

Her smile vanished as she realized that if Black Hawk didn't love her, she would never experience the joy again. *No wonder love makes children,* she thought. *Children!* Dear Lord, what if they had produced a child!

Rachel cradled her belly as if the tiny life had already sprouted inside her. Black Hawk's child, she thought. An Ojibwa baby.

Her expression softened. *Black Hawk would be a good father.* She loved the idea of having his babe. Rachel knew it was unusual to feel that way, considering that she was unwed and the notion would be scandalous back in Baltimore.

*But this isn't Baltimore.* And she wanted to have Black Hawk's child.

*There will be those here who will not accept the babe. They will look upon him as a "breed," hurting him with their nasty words, striking out whenever the mood takes them.*

"And I will fight to protect this child of love," she vowed. "I will want him. He was conceived in love, my love for the babe's father."

*This is ridiculous!* she thought. *It's too soon. You don't even know whether or not you're with child!*

She thought she heard Black Hawk's voice among the villagers who had gathered in the clearing. Heart pounding, she remained in the wigwam and calmly, carefully, stirred the contents of the cooking pot. Outside, dogs barked, and the Indians shared laughter. She heard a young boy call to his friend, and a mother scold her daughter.

"Rach-el."

She spun toward the doorway. Black Hawk had lifted the deerskin door flap and stepped inside. Rachel took one long look at him and felt emotion well up and tighten her throat. He looked wonderful. He had bathed recently; his dark hair was shiny and damp, and his skin looked scrubbed clean.

"Black Hawk," she whispered.

"I came back," he said.

She nodded.

"We brought your father."

She swallowed. "Yes, I saw him." She felt emotionally fragile. She was afraid that at any moment she would start to cry. "Thank you." She blinked back tears.

"Come," he said, and opened his arms.

With a wild cry, she went to him and held onto him tightly. "I was so afraid for you."

He had thought of her as they'd approached the Sioux village. Black Hawk had worried about failing her, but the Sioux had been careless. The attackers had slipped into the village after surrounding it on all sides. The fighting had been over before it'd begun.

"I was never in any danger," he assured her. "There were many of us and so few of them. We circled their village, then we went in while they slept and took prisoners."

Rachel pulled away. "You have prisoners?"

He nodded. "Clouds-at-Morning and some of his men," he said. He saw a question in her green gaze. "No, he has not been harmed. No one has been killed." He didn't tell her of the guard that had attacked one of the soldiers and had been shot by another. The brave had been severely wounded, but he was alive.

Black Hawk gazed into her eyes, saw her sweetness, and groaned as he bent his head to kiss her. Her mouth was moist and warm and all that he'd remembered. He wanted to continue kissing her forever, but he forced himself to stop. Soon, he'd have to leave, and she would be gone.

"Rach-el," he murmured. Holding her gaze, he stroked her hair. "Soon, you must return to the mission, and I must leave my village."

She stiffened. "You're leaving? *Why?*"

"I go to find my father's murderer. I will come back after I find the one called He-Who-Kills-with-Big-Stick."

"But that's crazy!" she cried. She grabbed onto his arms. "What if you get killed?"

Black Hawk's smile was grim. "I must go. Only when the man is dead, will I find peace in my heart."

*And love?* she wanted to ask him. *Will you find it in your heart to love?*

"You're not a murderer," she said, believing it to be true. "How will killing him bring back your father?"

His gaze hardened. "You do not understand our ways," he said. "This is necessary. I kill when I must."

"No," she gasped. Couldn't he see that she was frightened for him? He couldn't go. He mustn't! Her eyes filled with tears. "Black Hawk, I don't want you to go."

He scowled and freed himself from her hold. "You do not have the right to tell me what to do."

Pain tightened her chest, making it difficult to breathe. "I know that." The truth cut her deeply.

"I will leave when this night of feasting is over," he said. He was like a cold, dark stranger as he spoke without kindness or love. "When I get back, you will be gone. Be happy that you have your father."

Desperate to make him understand, she reached for him. "I am! I—"

"Clouds-at-Morning should not bother you again." He brushed her hands aside. "If he does, there will be men who will kill him."

Rachel stared at the man she loved and saw the dark savage in him. *How could I've thought he had feelings for me?* Men weren't to be trusted. They used women as it suited them, then tossed them away when it was no longer convenient.

*A convenience. Was that all she was to Black Hawk? A convenient, willing female? Someone to slake his lust?* She remembered his kindness and his caring. She wouldn't, couldn't believe it! He had to feel something more.

"You care for me," she whispered. "I know you do."

He narrowed his gaze. "You are a foolish woman."

"Are you saying that you felt nothing when we made love?"

His jaw hardened. "It does not take love to make *niinag* rise," he said crudely.

She blanched. She didn't need an interpreter to understand the Ojibwa term. "That's all I was to you? A woman?"

He shrugged, as if he didn't sense her pain.

She became blinded by a red haze of fury and pain. "Get out," she spat. "Get out before I do something I'll regret!"

If she'd ever thought she'd felt worse pain, she'd been mistaken. This hurt her worse than when Jordan had left her at the altar.

Black Hawk looked at her without emotion, then raised his eyebrows as if he thought of her as nothing more than a silly female. Rachel suffered a slow, painful inner death.

"Please leave," she said, averting her gaze. She refused to look at him. The man she loved had just slashed her heart in two.

"Thank you for rescuing my father," she said, "but I want you to leave me now."

He hesitated.

"Go!" she cried, turning to face him. "Leave me!" She'd lost the battle to keep her pain hidden.

"Rach-el Dempsey." He'd said it so softly that she wasn't sure she'd heard him.

Heart pounding, she looked at him, but saw only a swinging door flap. Black-Hawk-Who-Hunts-at-Dawn had gone.

She knew the remainder of the evening would be horrible. While everyone else within the village celebrated, Rachel pretended to enjoy herself, but felt miserable inside.

The celebration began with a ceremony using the wild rice. Each family brought a small covered container of cooked rice to the village ceremonial house.

"Rice must be taken to big house for special blessing," Spring Blossom explained. "We close lid tightly to protect rice from evil spirits."

Rachel watched without enthusiasm as the Indian maiden prepared the rice. Then she followed Spring Blossom, Amelia, and Jane to the big house.

Inside, all the Ojibwa had gathered for the blessing of the harvest. Spring Blossom placed her rice pot on a small table with the others. After uncovering the pot, she joined Rachel and her other guests off to one side.

When everyone had placed their offering of rice, an Ojibwa man stepped from the gathering and approached the table. He was elaborately dressed in a deerskin breechclout and leggings. His shirt was white fabric— a white man's shirt—but he had a long fringed sash, embroidered in a brightly colored diamond pattern and adorned with porcupine quills. His loincloth was fringed and highly decorated as well. On his head, he wore a feathered headdress.

The medicine man lit a pipe and blew tobacco smoke in four different directions.

Woman-with-Hair-of-Fox had come to stand near the two Dempsey sisters. "White Shirt is our medicine man," Rachel heard her explain to Amelia. "He blows pipe in the direction of the four winds. It is an offering to the spirits."

Rachel glanced toward the matron and saw that both she and Amelia were engrossed in the ceremonial proceedings. A voice spoke, and she turned her attention back to the center of the room.

Another older Indian had come forward. His tone rose and fell as he chanted in Ojibwa.

"That's He-Who-Comes-from-Far-Away," Amelia told her sister softly. "He's Woman-with-Hair-of-Fox's husband."

Rachel nodded. She knew who he was; she'd met him during her stay. "What is he saying?" Despite herself, she was intrigued.

"He is praying to the spirits," Woman-with-Hair-of-Fox said. "He gives thanks that our people have lived to enjoy another harvest of the rice."

Rachel watched as the medicine man took a small amount of rice from one pot and ate it. The owner of the pot stepped forward and ate his own small share. The medicine man then went to another pot, and the same procedure occurred for that pot and all the others on the table. As a container was eaten from, the rice, or *manoomin*, inside was considered blessed or consecrated. The remaining rice was then carried outside for feasting.

The villagers had prepared a feast, the likes of which Rachel had never seen before. There was roast venison, bear meat, and fresh fish . . . vegetable dishes and cakes made from corn, and sweets from maple sugar along with Amelia's dessert cakes. Once again, Amelia's cakes proved to be a favorite among the Indian men and now the children, who'd received their first taste.

And there was music. Wherever she went in the village, Rachel could hear the rhythmic shake of birch-bark rattles and the accompanying beat of the Ojibwa water drums.

There was much laughter and gaiety as everyone took their share of food. Rachel found a seat on the ground next to Amelia. Daniel came to sit on his wife's opposite side.

Although she felt separate from the gaiety of the celebration, Rachel pretended to be happy as she smiled frequently at her family and the Ojibwa participants.

Of Black Hawk, there was no sign. Rachel told herself she was grateful. She managed to convince herself that she didn't want to see him. Seeing him would be too painful for her, she reasoned.

Yet she looked for him, hoping . . . wishing that their last meeting had never occurred . . . that she'd dreamed the whole encounter and that Black Hawk wasn't going to leave.

But she knew that it had happened. Black Hawk's absence from this group of friends only confirmed that things were not as they should be. Amelia apparently thought so, too.

"Where is Black Hawk?" she asked Daniel.

Daniel shrugged as he continued to eat. "This soup is delicious," he said.

Rachel felt a lightening of her spirits. "Thank you."

He looked at her with surprise. "You made this?" She nodded. "It's good."

"Are you shocked?" she asked without anger.

He smiled. "No, not at all. I may have underestimated you before, but not now."

Rachel allowed her lips to curve. "That means a lot to me."

"Daniel," Amelia said, "you still haven't told me where Black Hawk is. I heard something about him leaving soon. Is that true?"

"Where did you hear that?" Rachel asked, her heart thumping hard. Had someone heard her conversation with Black Hawk?

"Susie told me. Apparently, Conner overheard his grandmother."

"And Conner knows so much?" Daniel teased.

Amelia looked at him. The way he said it told her that it was in fact true. "He is leaving, isn't he?" she said quietly. Her questioning glance went to Rachel.

"It's true," Rachel said.

Amelia turned back to her husband. "What is it?" She frowned. "Does this have something to do with his father?"

Daniel looked uncomfortable. "What do you mean?"

"Yes," Rachel said, and husband and wife looked at her.

"He told you," Daniel murmured.

"Yes, he told me."

Her brother-in-law looked at her thoughtfully. "I didn't know if he would."

"Told her what?" Amelia asked.

"That Black Hawk is leaving to avenge his father's death," Rachel said with bitterness.

Daniel frowned. "He has to go, you know."

"What Black Hawk does means little to me," Rachel said stiffly.

Amelia regarded her sister, then her husband curiously. "Rachel, I thought Black Hawk and you were friends."

"We were—are."

"Then how can you be so unconcerned?" Amelia asked.

Rachel stood with her bowl. "I'm not indifferent. It's just none of my business," she said as she started to walk away.

"But, Rachel—"

"Leave her be, love," Daniel said.

Amelia looked at him and saw a frown settle on his brow as he continued to study her sister. As if sensing Amelia's regard, he turned and smiled at her. She didn't return his smile.

"Is it possible that she's in love with him?" she asked.

"I hope not," Daniel answered.

"Why would you say that? He's your friend."

"I say it because Rachel doesn't have a chance, and I don't want her to be hurt. Black Hawk has only one thing on his mind right now and that is finding his father's murderer."

"You don't think she . . . they . . ." The thought of intimacy between Black Hawk and Rachel under the circumstances deeply disturbed Amelia.

"No." Daniel shook his head. "No, definitely not. Black Hawk wouldn't." He finished eating and put aside his bowl. He reached for his wife's dish, and she handed it to him.

"And Rachel *would* . . . lie with him?" she challenged, upset. Did he think that Rachel was a wanton?

"No!" he said. "I don't mean any offense."

She raised her eyebrows when he looked at her. "What do you mean?"

He touched her cheek, then ran his fingers down to her neck. Cupping her throat, he kissed her. She closed her eyes and gave in to the kiss.

"That," he said softly as he released her. "I have only to touch you and you're mine."

"But that's different. I love you and . . ." Her eyes widened with understanding.

He smiled. "And if your sister loved Black Hawk?"

"She'd give herself to him without thought," Amelia answered.


Feeling guilty for leaving them so abruptly, Rachel returned to find Daniel and Amelia kissing. Startled, she hung back until they parted. As she approached, she overheard their conversation. Her jaw tightened. They'd been talking about her and Black Hawk.

"That's my point," she heard Daniel say to her sister. "But not to worry. Black Hawk's an honorable man. He wouldn't touch her."

Amelia smiled with relief. "Of course, you're right," she said. "Black Hawk would never touch her."

*Wrong, dear family,* Rachel thought. She hurried away before her family could see her. *He already has.*

# Chapter 22

She couldn't sleep. Rachel rose from her sleeping pallet and left the wigwam. There were still other villagers about the clearing. A matron moved silently from one wigwam to another. The scent of tobacco smoke drew Rachel's attention toward the edge of the clearing and a group of men in quiet conversation, sharing a pipe.

Embers glowed from the communal fire. Rachel headed toward its warmth and was surprised to see her father. John Dempsey sat near the fire, staring into the flames. She approached and hunkered beside him.

"Father," she said softly, drawing his gaze, "what are you doing up?"

"I couldn't sleep."

She studied him with concern. "Are you all right?"

He nodded. "Couldn't sleep either?"

"No," she admitted. "No, I couldn't." She slipped her hand beneath his arm and shifted closer to him, snuggling against his side. "I'm glad you're safe. I was so worried."

He gave her a slight smile before his gaze returned to the fire. "I was fine. They never harmed me."

"But they could have."

"Yes," he said, "they could have." He reached toward a pile of sticks and added a few to the fire. Flames sprang to life, and the wood crackled as it burned. John stared, as if mesmerized, at the orange sparks that floated toward the sky.

Rachel frowned as she studied her father. "What's bothering you?" she asked softly.

He looked at her. "I shouldn't have brought you here. You or your sister."

"You didn't bring me," she pointed out. "I came on my own."

"Still, you shouldn't be here. It's not safe. I'd convinced myself the first time that it wouldn't happen again, but it did."

He was referring to the first occasion when there'd been trouble with the Indians, she realized. She captured his hand and cradled it within her fingers. His hands were soft, without calluses, a doctor's hands. "Amelia and I are here because we want to be."

He stared for a moment at their joined hands. "You belong in Baltimore, with all your young men."

She cringed. *All of my young men?* Had she had that many? She only remembered Jordan, the one man she'd wanted back then. Her other beaux had paled in comparison to Jordan. Their attention and flattery seemed a distant memory to her. "I like it here. I don't want to go back to Baltimore."

"You had a life there. Parties. Balls. What do you have here? Nothing. Just an old fool for a father."

Rachel gazed at him with alarm. "You are not an old fool," she said. She gave his hand an affectionate squeeze. "You're a fine man and a wonderful father."

"You should go home to Baltimore."

She tensed. "No. I like it here." Hadn't she been a good assistant? She asked him.

"Of course, you have." He glanced back at the fire.

"Then, please, no more talk of my life in Baltimore."

"But Rachel, you're a beautiful woman. You had many beaux there. What do you have here but an old man?"

"I resent your calling my pa an old man," she said. She was pleased to see his lips curve.

"Your annoying young man must certainly be over you by now. Surely, it's safe for your return."

*Oh, he's gotten over me by now,* she thought. "It's not what you think, Father."

"Good for you to be with people your own age," he murmured, ". . . beaux . . . husband."

Rachel frowned. *He isn't making any sense.* She sighed heavily and closed her eyes. Perhaps it was time to tell her family the truth. "Father, about Jordan—"

"Rach-el."

She froze, then glanced up to find Black Hawk a few yards away, gazing at her, looking tense. His dark eyes glistened in the firelight.

"Black Hawk." She felt suddenly breathless.

"John Dempsey," he said to her father. "I would speak with your daughter."

John looked at the two of them and pulled his hand from Rachel's grasp. Rachel glanced at her father. "Go on, daughter," he urged her.

Black Hawk was there to help her up as she scrambled to her feet. The warmth of his fingers made her stomach flutter. He released her hand as soon as she was standing.

"Come," he said.

Rachel glanced at her father to see his reaction, but John Dempsey stared at the fire again, consumed with his own thoughts.

"Where are we going?" she asked. Her voice sounded weak and shaky to her own ears.

"Not far."

She followed Black Hawk's lead into the forest. They continued until the village and the glow from the fire were out of sight. This night there was enough light to see. Black Hawk touched her arm, then gestured toward a fallen tree trunk. Rachel sat and Black Hawk positioned himself beside her.

Her heart thundered within her chest. She hadn't expected to see him. With his decision to leave the next day, she would have thought he'd be in his wigwam sleeping, so he'd be well rested for his journey. But here it was late and he was awake. Had he changed his mind?

Neither spoke, and the tension for Rachel became unbearable. She shifted on her seat, then started to rise.

He grabbed her arm. "Don't go."

She tensed, then sat again. "Why have you brought me here?"

"You go back to the mission tomorrow."

She didn't reply. Yes, she was going back tomorrow, she thought. Did he think she needed a reminder?

"I did not want you to go without this man's apology."

She flashed him a startled glance. "You want to apologize?" she said. When he nodded, she asked, "For what?"

"It is not true what I said before. You are not a foolish woman. This man does care for you."

*This man,* she thought blankly. Was he truly speaking of himself? "You care for me," she said quietly. She was afraid to hope.

"Yes."

Her heart rejoiced. "Then—"

"It changes nothing," he said. "Tomorrow I leave my village, and you return to the mission."

"Why tell me this then?" she cried, rising to her feet. "I know you're leaving. Why apologize now?"

"I would not have you think bad of me." He stood. "We are friends."

She closed her eyes as she sat again. It was a fight not to feel wounded. She didn't want to be friends with Black Hawk; she wanted more. "We are friends," she repeated. "So that's it."

When she looked at him again, he hadn't moved. He studied her without expression.

What had happened to the warm, passionate man who had brought her pleasure? The man before her was the Ojibwa war chief. He gave no clue to his thoughts. There was no affection in his gaze.

Rachel felt a sudden burning in her belly. "You don't expect to come home, do you?"

He didn't answer right away. "I cannot promise I will return."

"You're going to get yourself killed!" She jumped up, grabbed his arm.

"I go to find He-Who-Kills-with-Big-Stick." He stared briefly at the hand that held him.

"Your father's killer," she said.

"Yes." He seemed uncomfortable with the subject. He glanced away, staring off into the night. He pulled from her grasp, moving to put distance between them.

"Tomorrow, Sleeping Bird and Gray Squirrel will take you and your family back to the mission," he said. "We will release the Sioux. Dan-yel will need help bringing you home."

Rachel studied him. "Do you think he will come after me? Clouds-at-Morning?"

Black Hawk didn't turn. "I think it wise that we do not take chances. Sleeping Bird and Gray Squirrel will follow Cameron Walters and his men. They will keep watch behind you."

"You do expect the Sioux to attack!" she accused.

"I do not know this." Black Hawk gazed at the woman before him, and felt an ache in his chest. He didn't know when he'd be back. If he was successful, then perhaps they would have a chance at a future together. Would she be happy in his village? She seemed to have adjusted well during her stay.

He mustn't think of that now. He couldn't allow her to believe that there was anything more than friendship between them. If he was killed, she needed to go on and live her life.

She'd been innocent when he'd taken her. She could easily have confused pleasure for love. How could he know if she truly loved him?

"We must return," he said. He started to head back. He heard Rachel follow him, and he waited for her to join him.

They walked in silence until they reached the village clearing. The men sharing the pipe were gone. How long had they been gone? Rachel wondered.

This would be the last time she'd spend with Black Hawk. She halted, touched his arm. "Black Hawk," she said with longing as she faced him.

She saw him blink. She wanted to hug him, but his expression forestalled her.

"You wish to say something?" he asked.

She gazed at him, striving for the courage to speak her mind. "No," she murmured, looking away. "Nothing."

They entered the village and paused before heading to their wigwams. If she didn't say it now, she would never again have the chance.

"Yes," she told him. "I do have something to say."

He seemed patient as he waited for her to speak.

"I love you, Black Hawk. I know you don't love me, but I had to say it again." She reached out and touched his cheek with shaking fingers. He felt warm and very much alive. She trembled with the depth of her feelings for him. "I love you."

She caressed his jaw, then released him. There was no tenderness in his gaze, no passion . . . nothing.

"That's all I had to say," she said. A lump rose to block her throat. "Good night," she whispered hoarsely.

He didn't stop her. He didn't speak. She refused to look back as she raised the door flap of Spring Blossom's wigwam and stepped inside.

Black Hawk stood for a long time staring at the wigwam that Rachel had entered. He left when his vision blurred and he realized that she would not reappear.


Feeling listless and groggy, Rachel rose from her sleeping pallet the next morning. She'd had a terrible night. During the brief intermittent periods she'd actually dozed, she'd dreamt of Black Hawk and relived the happiness and then the pain of loving him. He was gone, and she might never see him again. She agonized about his leaving and about the journey ahead of him. *Please, God, keep him safe.*

*Today we are going home,* she thought. This would be the last time she ate with the Ojibwa, the last time she'd share the Ojibwa women's daily bathing ritual in the river.

*The last occasion to wear Indian dress.* Someone, most probably Spring Blossom, had laid out her old gown and undergarments. With regret, Rachel slipped off her doeskin tunic and laid it on her sleeping pallet. Then, she put on the chemise and pantalets. To her surprise, someone had repaired the torn sleeves of her gown.

Eyeing the tunic longingly, Rachel decided that she

didn't care if others thought her a loose woman, she would not wear her corset again. She had enjoyed the freedom of Ojibwa dress too long to want to return to such a restricting garment. Her leather shoes were nowhere in sight. She was apparently to keep the moccasins. She was glad, because they were more comfortable for her feet than her other footwear.

*It's not as if there's anyone here who cares about proper social attire,* Rachel thought. Here she didn't have to worry about impressing the society matrons and any beaux. Here she wasn't a wanton just because she enjoyed wearing fewer clothes. She would please herself and wear what she wanted.

The other women were already gone from the wigwam. When Rachel stepped outside, she saw that the Indians were busy at work, roasting and drying their rice harvest. She looked for her sister and father and didn't see them.

Then, she saw her father talking to the soldier, Cameron Walters. There were ten soldiers on horses, all impressive figures in navy and light blue.

Daniel appeared from the wigwam of the chief. He glanced over, saw her, and waved. Rachel lifted a hand in response.

"Rachel!" She turned to find her sister coming up the path from the river. Amelia's damp hair and skin said that her sister had already had her bath. "Good morning."

"Did you see Father?" Amelia asked.

Rachel gestured toward the group of men. "He's over talking with Sergeant Walters."

Her sister smiled, then started past her toward the wigwam. Amelia paused and turned back. "All ready to go?"

Rachel nodded. "Are you?"

Amelia shrugged. "It's nice and peaceful here, isn't it? I'm going to miss it."

"Me, too," Rachel murmured softly as Amelia continued on her way.

"Rach-el."

She spun. "Black Hawk! I thought you'd left." Her pulse raced at the sight of him.

"I will go to the mission with you before I leave."

Rachel eyed him closely, startled by his decision to escort them. "Why?"

"Because I wish to see my friend home safely."

"I see." She didn't really, but she was glad of the extra time with him . . . even if she had to share it with her family and a group of men.

Daniel, seeing them, approached. "Are you ready to go?" he asked.

"I'm ready," Rachel said. "I don't know if Jane and Susie are. I haven't seen them."

"They've been ready since first light," Daniel said with a smile. "They've gone for a walk with Jack." He frowned as he noted her attire. "Do you want to ride?"

"I'd prefer to walk, thank you."

Her brother-in-law shrugged. "Suit yourself. Your sister wants to ride. I'd better help her onto her mount, before she has ten other volunteers for the job." He grinned. "I prefer to assist my wife." He left then, leaving Black Hawk and Rachel standing alone again.

"Thank you for letting me stay here," Rachel said. "I know it's been an imposition. Your sister has been generous—"

"You are welcome in my village at any time," he replied.

She felt a tingle of pleasure. "Thank you." He acted as if they were polite strangers and had never been lovers. It had been only one time, but Rachel would carry the special memory with her always.

Rachel sought out Spring Blossom to thank her and

say good-bye. Then she searched for each villager who'd been kind to her during her stay. She knew that she would miss all of the Ojibwa people. They'd been patient in teaching her their ways. They'd protected her when she'd needed protection. She'd always remember them with gratitude and fondness.

"Rachel!"

"Coming, Father!" she called. She hugged Woman-with-Hair-of-Fox. *"Miigwech,"* she said softly. "Thank you for everything."

The woman smiled sadly. "Do not give up hope, Rachel Dempsey. You will find your way home soon."

Puzzled, Rachel only had time to nod, wave, and then hurry toward the group.

By the time the traveling party left the village, it was mid-morning. Five of Walter's men rode up front to scout the trail before them. They had brought two extra horses. Amelia rode in front of her husband on one. John Dempsey and little Susie rode on the second mount. Jane and Jack, who had wanted to walk, positioned themselves between the Traherns' and John Dempsey's mounts to be near Susie if she needed anything.

Rachel had had difficulty convincing her father to ride, but she'd finally managed it. She'd used Susie as an excuse, telling him that the child wanted to be held. She'd meant it when she told Daniel that she wanted to walk home. She needed the exercise to clear her mind, to put her thoughts and feelings for Black Hawk into perspective. It wasn't an easy task as Black Hawk had chosen to walk beside her. Rachel did her best to ignore the Ojibwa brave, but she was conscious of his movements. *How can I ignore the man I love?*

It wasn't a long journey home from the late summer camp of the Ojibwa. They would reach the mission by late afternoon. Rachel hoped the trip would remain an uneventful one. With three Indian braves, ten soldiers, her father, and brother-in-law, she certainly felt safe. She didn't imagine the Sioux would dare to bother them.

They stopped once to rest and eat, and then they were back on the trail quickly. Later, they had to stop again for Amelia, who was embarrassed that she had to relieve herself. Rachel had noticed that her sister had felt the need more often as her pregnancy advanced.

It wasn't long before they were back traveling again. They came to an area of the path that was narrow, just big enough for a single horse or two men walking next to each other. There were gaps in the group as the trail wound back and forth through the wooded terrain. For a time, it seemed as if Rachel and Black Hawk journeyed alone. The horses before them had ventured far ahead.

Black Hawk didn't seem concerned with the distance between them, Rachel noted, so she wasn't going to worry either. The soldiers behind them had kept their distance deliberately as they, with the two Ojibwa warriors, scouted the area carefully and watched for followers.

She wondered if Black Hawk's silence meant that he was alert, looking for signs of danger. She gave a quick glance and saw that he seemed thoughtful, not attuned as he usually was to the things around him. She frowned while looking straight ahead. He was an enigma, this man. Why had he come? Because he believed they were really at risk from Sioux attack?

Her heart skipped a beat. Or because he hadn't been ready to leave her?

Rachel wanted to ask him, but didn't. She gazed surreptitiously at him instead, trying to gauge his mood. Her inattention to her path had her stumbling, but Black Hawk's arm shot out and he saved her from falling.

*"Miigwech,"* she said, feeling her cheeks flush. Apparently, he was more alert than she'd thought. She felt the

warm flush of heat deepen. Had he noticed her studying him?

He looked at her, really studied her for the first time since they'd left the village. "You have been quiet," he murmured, his dark gaze roaming her face.

"So have you."

He inclined his head in agreement.

"Is something wrong?" she asked. It seemed that she was always asking that question, she thought.

*"Gaawiin."* No.

The two became silent again as they spotted Amelia and Daniel's horse.

Feeling awkward suddenly, Rachel picked up her pace to reach her sister, until she felt Black Hawk's hand on her arm, slowing her. She glanced at him, expecting him to warn her against tripping along the trail. Instead, she saw his gleaming gaze, his sensual smile. Her skin tingled.

Rachel halted and stared at him with her pulse racing. She saw his expression change as if he fought his inner thoughts.

"Rach-el, I—" With a groan, he grabbed and kissed her. Rachel's heart floated free as she responded. His kiss was better than she'd remembered. She embraced him, leaned into him, and a whimper came from deep in the back of her throat as he explored her mouth.

His breathing was labored as he set her away. She felt dizzy, wonderfully dizzy, as everything female within her pulsated to life.

"I am sorry," he said.

She blinked to clear the haze. "No," she protested, "don't say that. Don't apologize." She was on the verge of tears. *He cares for you. Don't do this to yourself,* she thought.

With a hand at her spine, he urged her to walk. She was surprised by his touch, confused by his mixed signals.

She gazed ahead while she walked, wondering what he was thinking, conscious of the heat of his continued touch. She felt a glimmer of hope when he didn't remove his hand.

The trail widened, the terrain becoming easier to negotiate, but still she could feel Black Hawk's fingers at her back.

Amelia hailed her from ahead. Now seated sideways on the saddle, she waved at her sister from within her husband's arms. "Are you tired?" she asked.

Still, Black Hawk stayed close to Rachel.

"No!" Rachel called back. "I'm fine!" And at the moment, she felt more than fine. Black Hawk had kissed her, then instead of withdrawing, as she'd expected, he seemed content to remain close.

She was disappointed a short time later when Black Hawk released her. She saw that the soldiers to the rear had caught up to them, and she wondered if it was their presence that had prompted him to step away.

Rachel realized that she'd thought wrong when suddenly Black Hawk captured her fingers as he took a firm grip of her hand. She caught his gaze and smiled at him.

The barest hint of a grin touched his lips, but the look in his onyx eyes spoke volumes. She felt lighthearted as she beamed a smile at him.

All too soon, they reached the mission. Rachel felt the change in Black Hawk as they approached. He released her hand, and pulled away.

She mourned the loss of the sun, for an inner darkness had descended as he withdrew. She dared to look at him and touch his arm.

He gazed at her with a look of pain that stole her breath. *He doesn't think he's coming back!* she thought as they entered the mission yard. She opened her mouth to tell him that she'd wait for him, but she was startled to silence by a male voice from her past.

"Rachel! Rachel Dempsey!"

Rachel froze and stared in disbelief at her former fiancé as he left the church. "Jordan?"

Jordan Sinclair hurried toward her, a boyish grin on his handsome features. Halting before her, he gazed into her eyes. "Hello, darling. I've been searching for you everywhere."

"Jordan!" she exclaimed; then she was suddenly swept up in the man's embrace. "What are you doing here?"

# Chapter 23

Jordan's kiss transported Rachel back in time to those pleasant days when they were an engaged couple. The scent and embrace of the man who held her were all too familiar. *Familiar perhaps,* she thought, *and pleasant, but not as exciting as Black Hawk's kiss.* She pushed him away.

Jordan released her and studied her. "You look radiant, Rachel! Wonderful!" Anxiety transformed his features, darkening his blue eyes. "I thought I'd never see you again! I was frantic when I heard what happened!"

Rachel's head was in a whirl. The sudden appearance of her former fiancé had shaken her; she could barely think straight.

*Black Hawk,* she thought, and started to turn, but Jordan caught her shoulders.

"Rachel!" he gasped; then he kissed her and stole her air, and she was powerless to break free. "Oh, Rachel," he said when he lifted his head. "You don't know how long I've been wanting to kiss you.'' He started to lean toward her again; she put out her hand and stopped him.

"Don't, Jordan!" she demanded. Then she looked back for Black Hawk, and felt a jolt of pain when she didn't see him.

"Rachel, I can explain," Jordan began.

She narrowed her gaze. "Where's your wife?" she said, and was surprised at how bitter she sounded. She had, after all, gotten over the man, hadn't she?

She was relieved to see her father approaching. She felt grateful when she saw Amelia and Daniel following him. Her family eyed her and Jordan quizzically.

Jordan hadn't answered her last query. She tore her gaze from her family to the man she'd considered spending her life with. "Nanette's dead," he said sadly.

Rachel was startled by the news. "I'm sorry," was all she could think of to say. The implication of his presence dawned on her, renewing her anger.

"So your wife is dead," she said evenly, "and you thought you could come to me and I would take you back."

A guilty look entered his expression. He was so handsome, she thought. His golden brown hair had been cut in the latest style. His eyes, a deep shade of blue, had the power to seduce and capture many a young lady's heart. He had the classic features of a Greek god, like the ones recreated in statues and paintings. As she studied him, she understood why she'd fallen for him with his good looks and easy charm. What she didn't understand was why she didn't see through to the basic selfish core of him.

"It was always you I loved, Rachel. Always," he said vehemently.

"Yet you married another, a woman almost twice my age! And not only did you marry her, you didn't have the bullocks to tell me before our wedding. No, you had to leave me at the church!''

The gasps she'd heard alerted her to her family's presence. So now they knew the truth, she thought. They knew that she had lied about her reasons for leaving Baltimore. They understood now what a failure as a woman and a fiancé she'd been.

The silence that followed her outburst seemed louder than any noise.

''Rachel,'' her sister murmured; then Rachel felt the love of her family surround her, just when she needed it the most. Black Hawk was gone, and Jordan Sinclair stood before her, ready to take her back. But she didn't want him to take her back. *No,* she thought, *I want Black Hawk.*

But would she ever see Black Hawk again? Did he love her and would they ever have a chance?

Rachel closed her eyes, summoning the image of Black Hawk's face those moments after his last kiss. She recalled the intensity in his dark eyes. The emotion. He felt something for her, she decided. *But love?* But whether or not he'd return safely and successful was a different story. And if he returned successful, would he tell her of his feelings?

There had never been talk of marriage between them, of anything but friendship. But she couldn't deny that he was physically attracted to her . . . and more. He would have left before she'd awakened that morning if he hadn't cared for her.

She was aroused from her thoughts by her father's voice.

''Young man, are you bothering my daughter?''

''Daughter!'' Jordan exclaimed. ''You're Dr. Dempsey?'' At John's nod, he said, ''Sir, I love your daughter.''

John frowned. ''She doesn't seem to be too happy to see you—''

"Father—" Rachel began.

"Rachel." Daniel stepped forward. "If you'd like me to get rid of this scalawag, just say the word and I'll be happy to—"

"Daniel!" her sister cried. "You'll not be fighting, do you hear? Why don't you ask Rachel exactly what she wants?" Amelia said to her father and husband.

"If I can get a word in edgewise," Rachel said, "I'll be happy to introduce Jordan."

The three members of her family glanced at her with anticipation.

"Father, Daniel, Amelia, this is Jordan Jonathan Sinclair II. He and I were . . . friends . . . back in Baltimore." She sensed Jordan's annoyance at the explanation of their relationship.

John Dempsey's gaze narrowed on the young man. "Is this the young rascal who's been an annoyance?" he said.

Apparently, she'd been wrong, Rachel thought. Her father couldn't have heard her and Jordan's exchange.

"Not exactly," she said.

"Has someone been bothering you?" Jordan asked, looking ready to do battle for Rachel's honor. "Because if someone is, I'll—"

The sudden humor of the situation struck Rachel, and she began to laugh loudly, half hysterically, until the murmurs of concern from her family made her stop.

"No, I'm all right," she said in answer to her sister's query. "Just give me a minute."

They all stared at her. "Please," she said, "I'll talk with the rest of you later. Apparently there are a few things that Jordan would like to discuss with me."

"Are you sure?" Amelia said. She eyed her sister with concern.

Rachel gave her a genuine smile. "Yes, I'm sure." Her

gaze went to Daniel. "You'll stay at the mission awhile?" she asked him.

He nodded his blond head. "I'd hoped for a meal."

"I'm sure we'll be able to find something to eat." Rachel addressed her father. "I'm all right, Father, really," she said. He looked worried. He'd had enough worries and regrets since the first appearance of Clouds-at-Morning. She felt the need to reassure him more than anyone else.

Reluctantly, her family left, and she and Jordan were alone.

"Rachel, I can explain about Nanette," he said, his expression pleading for understanding.

"There had better be a good explanation, Jordan," she said firmly. "I still can't believe that you're here."


Black Hawk had stood in the forest and watched Rachel with the white man. He'd known instantly that the man had once been important to her, that Jordan was the reason she'd left her Baltimore home.

When the couple had embraced, the shaft of pain he'd felt had nearly paralyzed him. *This is the man she loves,* he'd thought.

He'd been wrong to kiss her again. He'd fought the urge, but his departure and the knowledge that he might never see her again hung heavy in his heart.

Rachel had forgotten his existence from the moment the white man had called her name. Black Hawk had waited for a second for her to turn around; and when she didn't, he'd slipped away unnoticed . . . aching from his loss of her.

*Be happy, Rachel,* he thought. *Be happy with your Jordan.*

Then, without waiting for his friends, Black Hawk left the mission, leaving his heart behind him.

* * *

Rachel and Jordan walked to the stream beyond the mission church. There, Rachel turned to her former fiancé and studied him.

"Well? You said you wanted to explain." As she gazed at the man before her, she compared him unfavorably to Black Hawk. She thought Black Hawk's sharp, rugged features much more attractive than Jordan's smooth handsome face.

*Black Hawk,* she thought, longing for him. How far had he gone? Was he all right? Would he find his killer? Would he return safely? She was continually plagued by concern for him.

Jordan drew her attention back to him when he caught her hands and held them tightly. His expression was earnest as he gazed into her eyes. "First, I want to say that I love you. I've never stopped loving you, not even for a second."

"You already said that—"

He raised her one hand to his lips and kissed the knuckles as he'd often done in the past. Unmoved, she stared at him while she waited for him to continue.

"You're angry," he said. He gave her a boyish smile meant to charm. He caressed the back of her hand.

Annoyed, she tugged her fingers from his grip. "And I shouldn't be?"

"Well, yes, I suppose so."

"Explain, Jordan. I don't have that much time. I'm anxious to get back to my family."

His eyes flickered. "Your aunt said you'd be hard to convince. I guess she was right."

"Aunt Bess?" Rachel gave him her full attention. "You saw her?"

Pleased by her interest, he nodded. "How do you think I knew where to look for you?"

"Aunt Bess told you where I'd gone?" She was startled by the news. She hadn't thought her father's sister would give away her whereabouts.

"She tried to discourage me, but I was persistent."

She narrowed her gaze. "Yes, I suppose you were." When she thought back, she realized that Jordan Sinclair never gave up until he'd gotten what he wanted.

"It wasn't easy coming here, you know."

"I've been on the journey," she said. "I know what it's like." She had little sympathy for a man who would leave his fiancée to face the humiliation of being jilted.

"I found that Rupert fellow. Miranda's uncle?" Jordan scowled. "Not a pleasant sort at all. He wouldn't bring me. I had to hire someone else."

Rachel stifled a smile. "I found Rupert quite pleasant."

Jordan stared at her as if she'd gone mad. "You've changed," he said.

"Really?" she said with scorn. "Well, if I have, it's because you've changed me."

He leaned to pull her into his arms. She resisted, stiffening. He caught hold of her shoulders and bent his head as if to kiss her.

"No!" she said firmly, jerking away.

He pouted like a petulant little boy. "I told you I was sorry."

She sighed. "Jordan, if you think that a simple apology is going to make the past go away, you're wrong. I'll not allow myself to believe your fancy lies again."

He blanched, as if wounded by her words. "I meant what I said, back then and now."

"Meant what? That you wanted to marry me? Or what you'd said in your note . . . that you'd decided the widow would make a better wife!" The pain of his note that day returned to further anger her. "You had your chance with me, Jordan. You had it and you ruined it."

"No," he cried, trying to draw her into his arms again. "Don't say that! I love you. I must have another chance! Do you think I'd come all this way if I didn't love you?"

His statement aroused her curiosity. "Why did you come?" she asked. He wasn't capable of love, she thought.

"My wife——" He blushed as if he'd just realized to whom he was speaking. "She left me everything. I married her for that, don't you see? She promised to give me her estate if I'd marry her and care for her during her illness. She knew she was sick, Rachel. She married me because she needed someone she could trust, and I was the only one she trusted."

Rachel gazed at him with disbelief. "You married her for her money?"

"For us, Rachel! For us!" Jordan stepped back to pace. "We needed money for our future! With Nanette's estate, we'll have everything. Our love, a mansion . . . and lots of money! Think what we can do for our children with the money."

"How much money?" she asked. She wanted to know how much money it had taken to destroy their love.

He named a figure that made her gasp.

He smiled. "And that's not all," he said proudly. "There's the rent on the land and the investments in the mercantile."

"Oh, and I suppose there is a great deal of land?"

He nodded, looking pleased.

"And you married for us," she said. "You and me."

"Yes." He smiled. "I knew you'd understand."

"For her money."

"For our future," he insisted.

"I see," she said. She touched her chin as she studied him. "I understand perfectly. You married a sick widow for her money, thinking that eventually you'd be free to marry me."

"Yes, yes, that's right."

"That's despicable."

The good humor fell from his face. "What?"

"I can't believe you'd think I'd marry you after what you've done."

Jordan's cheeks turned a bright shade of red. "But—"

"You didn't even have the decency to tell me to my face. You sent a note! I'd never been so humiliated in all my life!"

"Rachel, I'm sorry."

She glared at him. "Well, I'm sorry, too, Jordan. I loved you. We could have had a wonderful life together, but now I don't love you anymore."

His face lost color. "You don't mean that."

Her smile was grim. "Yes, yes, I do."

"I came all the way out here for you!" he exclaimed.

"I didn't ask you to come!" she shouted.

He grabbed her then, forced her to accept his kiss. "I can make you want me."

She eyed him coldly. "No, you can't." She didn't slap him. She just didn't care enough to do anything but stare.

"I thought you were different," he said. He narrowed his gaze as he studied her. "You look different." His eyes widened with sudden understanding. "There is someone new."

"That, dear Jordan, is none of your business."

"Who is it?"

She stiffened. "I didn't say there was anyone." She felt a flicker of pain as she thought of Black Hawk.

"Does he know what a prude he's getting?" Jordan said cruelly.

Rachel struck him then, a good hard resounding slap across his cheek.

His handsome face lost all remnants of charm. He was angry, and his blue eyes burned in his fury. Frightened of something in his expression she'd never seen before, Rachel stepped back and hugged herself with her arms.

"Bitch!" he spat as he reached for her.

She gasped and began to run. She sped toward the church building and pounded on the door. Jordan caught up with her, roughly spinning her around. How could she have ever thought herself in love with this man? she wondered. He was a consummate actor, she thought. A suave, deceitful, attractive fiend.

He shook her and called her nasty names. When the door behind her opened, she stumbled and fell right into the steadying arms of Will Thornton.

Will, sizing up the situation quickly, thrust Rachel behind him and raised his fists ready to hit Rachel's attacker.

Upon seeing the young man's fighting stance, Sinclair stepped backward and raised his hands in surrender. "My argument's not with you, fellow," he said.

Hands clenching at his sides, Will looked livid. "No, it's with Rachel, isn't it? A woman. Do you always pick on those less able to defend themselves?"

"Will," Rachel said, touching his arm. "It's all right." She flashed Jordan a look of warning. "Jordan is leaving the mission now. He understands that his stay here is done. He's going to leave peaceably. Aren't you, Jordan."

A muscle twitched along Jordan's jaw. "I'm going."

Rachel felt herself slump against Will with relief. "Good-bye, Mr. Sinclair," she said.

"We're two of a kind, Rachel," he said. "You're a fool to pass up my offer."

"I don't want you or your tainted proposal, Jordan."

Jordan gazed at Will Thornton, and his face took on a look of scorn. "Is it him?"

Rachel shook her head.

To her disgust, Jordan looked satisfied. "I didn't think so. You need a man, Rachel. Not a boy."

She saw Will ball up his fists in anger. "It's all right, Will," she assured him. "Jordan Sinclair doesn't know what a real man is, for you see, he's just a boy. A spoiled, little rich boy."

"You'll be sorry, Rachel," Jordan said as he walked away. "You'll be sorry you didn't marry me!"

"I doubt it," she replied. "Although I must say I have something to thank you for, Jordan."

The man paused as if anxious to hear what she had to say. "Leaving me at the altar was the nicest thing you could have done for me."

With a growl, Jordan spun and stomped away. Only when he was out of sight, did Rachel breathe a sigh of relief. She became aware that Will was staring at her. "Thanks, Will," she said, her tone gentle.

He nodded. "You were going to marry him?"

Rachel shuddered and rubbed her arms. " 'Fraid so. I guess it was worth the humiliation to have escaped him. Dear God," she breathed, "when I think what my life would been like if I'd married that fool."

"Hell," Will said.

"I think you're right, Will." With that knowledge, she felt a lightening in her heart that was dimmed only by her concern for Black Hawk.

How could she have ever considered Black Hawk a

savage? He was the kindest man alive besides her father. And Daniel, she thought with a smile.

*Oh, Black Hawk,* she thought, *keep safe and return. I'd rather live without you with the knowledge that you're alive and well . . . then have your love and see you hurt or killed.*

# Chapter 24

"And so I told Aunt Bess that I wanted to come here," Rachel said.

Her family sat around her, listening to the story of her disastrous wedding day. Amelia, shocked that Rachel had never said anything about the suffering she'd endured, gazed at her sister through a film of tears.

"You should have let me knock him flat," Daniel said.

"You!" her father exclaimed. "I'd like a go at him myself."

"Well, it's over and done with it, isn't it," Rachel said. "There's no need for a fight. Jordan is gone and he won't be back."

"Thank goodness!" Amelia said, touching her sister's arm. Rachel smiled at her sister and impulsively gave her a hug.

"Why didn't you tell us?" Daniel asked.

Her father and sister seemed to hold their breath as they waited for her answer. "I felt like a failure," Rachel admitted. "I thought I had done something wrong. Something to drive Jordan away and make him stop loving me."

She scowled as she recalled the last confrontation between herself and her former fiancé. "I realize now that the problem wasn't me. It was Jordan. He's a vain, selfish fool who thinks only of money. Apparently, he thought I wanted to be rich as much as he did. I never knew how much money he had or didn't have. I never cared about such things. Back in Baltimore, I only cared about our love. And I thought he felt the same."

She became lost in a distant memory. "We used to talk about the future. It was never a fancy house I wanted, although now that I think of it, he did talk about one. It was the children I looked forward to, the cozy evenings we'd spend together." *The nights we'd make love.*

"Well, you're better off without him, I say," Amelia said firmly.

Rachel smiled. "That's what I told him. In fact, I thanked him for jilting me. Said it was the nicest thing he could have done for me."

Daniel chuckled. "And what did he say?"

She looked amused. "Let's just say that he wasn't happy with me at the time. Not happy at all."

The sound of the Sioux ceremonial drums floated on the evening air, reaching Black Hawk, who sat hidden on a cliff above. Down below, the Sioux people had gathered for a council meeting, their number greater than the Ojibwa brave had anticipated.

Black Hawk stared at the scene below him, but was not put off by the difficulty ahead. He had been here for two nights; he would wait two more if needed. The days of the Sioux were filled with games and activities, the nights with ceremonial dances and feasting.

He was here to find his father's killer. He had waited years for this moment; a few hours or days more wouldn't bother him. At present, the Sioux warriors were pitting their strength against each other in mock fighting games.

Black Hawk frowned. There were many warriors with many weapons. He wasn't bothered. No matter the danger, he wouldn't abandon the quest now. If the consequences meant his death, then he would die knowing that his father had been honored, and justice had been done. He shifted on the rocky outcropping as he gauged his next move.

The Sioux were camped in a valley. Black Hawk saw teepees as far as his eyes could see. Which one housed He-Who-Kills-with-Big-Stick?

Black Hawk refused to die before he had vengeance. To be captured and die when he'd come this far would be a terrible thing.

Thoughts of Rachel kept invading his mind, disturbing him at a time when he could ill afford the distraction. He recalled her and Jordan's kiss, and used anger to shove her from his mind. It worked for a time, and then her image was back.

He should not have lain with her, he thought. Once he'd had her, how could he expect to forget the smooth softness of her satiny skin . . . the silky texture of her hair. Her breasts were ripe and full, perfect for kissing. He was plagued by images of her flat belly, her white curves . . . her wild cries as he took her and felt her reach her pinnacle of pleasure.

Movement down in the valley below had him sliding back from the edge. He tried to force Rachel from his mind, but her image returned. The echo of her words taunted him.

*"You're no murderer! If you do this, you'll be just like him!"*

*"Do you want to get yourself killed!"*

He didn't want to die. But he was prepared to die to honor his father, just as he'd lay down his life for Rachel.

Black Hawk waited until darkness fell completely with only the Indians' fires to light his way. He knew there would be guards, but he wondered if they'd be careless. The size of their gathering might have made the Sioux more confident that no one would attack them.

But then they did not know that he, Black-Hawk-Who-Hunts-at-Dawn, waited to enter their encampment to find a man whom he would kill that night. And if things went his way, they wouldn't know of his presence until after he had killed his father's murderer and gone.

Judging the time right, he began the climb down the mountain. He'd watched for hours as the Sioux performed a dance ritual, waiting to make his next move.

The Sioux Indians broke from the gathering and headed toward their teepees.

He was surprised when he caught sight of Clouds-at-Morning among the group. Black Hawk noted the location of the brave's teepee. It would be best to head there first to learn the whereabouts of his father's killer, he decided.

Black Hawk's plans changed when he recognized He-Who-Kills-with-Big-Stick lingering outside another teepee to share a smoke with a friend. He would never forget the man's face. It would always be etched clearly in his memory.

He was startled to realize that the brave wasn't as old as he'd thought. He-Who-Kills-with-Big-Stick was a warrior in his prime. The Sioux must have been a young man when he'd murdered Black Hawk's father. Convinced that the spirits were with him, Black Hawk slipped into the encampment under the cover of darkness. He crept toward the teepee of He-Who-Kills-with-Big-Stick.

He did not get far. A Sioux guard spied him lurking behind a teepee.

Black Hawk knew the spirit of death had found him when the warrior prodded him with his rifle. He had no choice but to move toward the large teepee that loomed ahead.


"Rachel."

"Daniel!" Rachel was surprised to see him at the infirmary. The family had eaten supper together the previous evening, their time together more precious to them after all that had occurred in the last months. She would have thought Daniel too busy at his blacksmith shop to afford the time away.

She felt a cold dread as she studied his face. "Is it Amelia?" Had something happened to her sister? Or the babe?

He softened his expression. "Amelia is fine."

She closed her eyes, her relief evident in her sigh. When she looked at him again, she smiled at him. "What can I do for you, then?" She searched for injury. "You didn't burn yourself at the forge, did you?"

Daniel shook his head. His sister-in-law hadn't ceased to amaze him yet. She was a kind and giving woman. How could he have thought otherwise?

*Because of Pamela,* he thought. Which didn't make him feel less guilty for his earlier treatment of Rachel. He'd been fortunate to have Amelia's love for the better part of two years. Pamela should have been a distant memory, one that didn't hurt him anymore. Because of Amelia and her sister Rachel, he felt that he had finally gotten over the pain of his late wife's duplicity.

"If you're looking for Father, he's not here," she said. "But I've just baked a pie, if you'd like a piece."

He smiled. "Pie sounds good," he admitted. "But don't tell your sister. She'd scold me for destroying my appetite before dinner."

Rachel looked at the size of the man and wondered how any amount of food could destroy his appetite.

His knowing grin said that he'd read her thoughts and agreed.

"She judges me by her own eating habits," he said as he followed her into the kitchen.

"I see," she replied. She sliced a piece of pie and placed it on a plate, which she handed him. "There are forks in the drawer," she told him, gesturing with her free hand.

She cut herself a slice and joined Daniel at the dining table. She took a bite and watched as Daniel enjoyed her culinary efforts.

"Actually, Rachel, I've come hoping to have a word with you."

"Me?" Surprise had her pausing with her fork in mid-air. "About what?"

"Black Hawk."

He watched emotion charge her expression, before a shutter lowered over her features and her guard was in place. "Black Hawk? Is he back? Have you heard from him?"

She said it casually as if it was just a topic for conversation, but Daniel knew differently. He could tell that she was anxious for news of him. He wished he had news to give her, but he didn't.

"As far as I know, Black Hawk hasn't returned yet."

"Oh." She seemed upset by the news.

Daniel watched her as she forced her mood to brighten. She smiled. "What about Black Hawk?"

He decided to be blunt. "Are you in love with him?"

She seemed to reel under the impact of a blow. "What makes you ask?"

He could tell she was trying to sound casual, but he could also tell she was shaken. "Just a feeling I've had when I've watched the two of you together," he said.

Tears filled Rachel's eyes as she gazed at him. "All right, I admit it, I love him," she said. "Is that a crime?"

He felt compassion for her. "No, of course it's not."

"Then why are you questioning me?" she asked, her voice sharpening, as if the intrusion into her heart bothered her.

"You've been unhappy," he said. "You're back to work and doing wonderfully, but you seem different. And I can't help wondering why."

Startled by how easily he could read her, Rachel looked away. "I love him, but he doesn't love me. I'm trying to go on with my life."

Daniel stared at her. "Did he touch you?"

She gasped. "I don't have to answer that!"

"Because if he has, I'll—"

"You'll what?" she asked, her expression softening. "Defend my honor by fighting him?"

He shrugged his shoulders as if he wasn't sure what he'd do. Black Hawk was one of his closest friends and fighting him seemed unthinkable, but Rachel was his sister-in-law and his family. He would do whatever it took to defend her honor.

"I—yes, I would."

To his surprise, she chuckled. "No, you won't," she said, "because I won't let you touch a single hair on Black Hawk's head."

Daniel wasn't amused. He set down his fork. "So he did touch you!" he snarled.

"He did nothing I didn't want or need. Everything I did I did willingly."

"Rachel—"

"Daniel," she interrupted, her tone firm. "I appreciate your concern and caring"—she smiled—"but this is my life and I'll live it."

"But—"

"No buts. This is my business, and Black Hawk's. And I'll thank you to keep this conversation a secret. You're not to tell a soul. Not your wife or Father."

Daniel looked unhappy with the situation.

"Please?" she asked softly.

He stared into her eyes and when she smiled and batted her eyelashes, he couldn't help grinning. He knew he'd have to respect her wishes; he cared for her too much not to. "I won't tell a soul."

"Good," she said, pleased. Rachel scooped up a forkful of pie and placed it between her lips. When he hesitated in eating, she flashed him a look that had him placing a forkful in his mouth. "More pie, Daniel?" she asked, then grinned.

He stared at his empty plate. "Yes, please."

Her green eyes twinkled. "It's my pleasure to serve you," Rachel said. She smiled, knowing that her brother-in-law was an honorable man and that her secret would be safe and sound with him.

The Sioux warriors surrounded him, staring, and spoke rapidly in their own tongue. Black Hawk understood a little of what they said as he stood before the council of Sioux chiefs and awaited his fate.

There was no one he recognized in the teepee. The brave who had captured him had left, and the only warriors who had joined the council were strangers. Not that he had encountered every Sioux by any means.

The door to the teepee opened. To Black Hawk's surprise, he recognized Runs-with-the-Wind as he entered and joined the Sioux council. Black Hawk and the warrior had shared an easy peace for almost two years . . . since the Sioux had learned that Black Hawk and the white doctor, John Dempsey, were friends. Indebted to the doctor for saving his son's life, Runs-with-the-Wind had assisted in the release of Sioux prisoners. The deed had formed a friendship between warriors who had been enemies, a friendship that had lasted until now.

The warrior didn't appear to recognize him. Or he didn't want the others to know he and Black Hawk were old friends, Black Hawk thought. Runs-with-the-Wind joined in the discussion between the tribal chiefs.

Moments later, Black Hawk's heart went still as another warrior entered the teepee. It was Clouds-at-Morning, a brave angered by Black Hawk's threat to kill him if he didn't leave Rachel Dempsey alone. Even now, while his own life hung in the balance, Black Hawk didn't regret the threat. It had been the only way to protect the woman he loved.

Clouds-at-Morning narrowed his gaze as he caught sight of Black Hawk, before he sat next to Runs-with-the-Wind. He looked angry, as did the other Indians within the teepee.

Black Hawk stood with his wrists and his ankles tied with sinew. A Sioux guard stood behind Black Hawk, ready to strike the Ojibwa if he attempted to escape. At a nod from a tribal chief, the guard shoved his captive, and Black Hawk fell to his knees.

Black Hawk faced them stoically. He didn't cry out or beg for mercy. He just stared at his captors with an empty expression, silently cursing his failure to find and kill He-Who-Kills-with-Big-Stick.

Runs-with-the-Wind said something to the chiefs, drawing everyone's attention. A man nodded and the rest agreed.

Runs-with-the-Wind then focused his gaze on Black Hawk. "My chief wants to know why you have come into our camp with your weapon drawn," he said, referring to the fact that Black Hawk had his knife ready when he'd been captured.

"I'm not a threat to your people. There is only one brave whom I seek."

The warrior looked surprised. "Who is this man? Or it is a woman?"

"It is the warrior He-Who-Kills-with-Big-Stick," Black Hawk said.

"Why do you seek this man?"

Black Hawk drew in a sharp breath. "He killed my father. I have searched many years for him. I seek vengeance on the brave who took the life of a man I loved."

Runs-with-the-Wind spoke to the chiefs, and there was much discussion among the men. Black Hawk sensed Clouds-at-Morning's intense regard, but he didn't acknowledge that he knew the Sioux, not by a look or a smile.

"How did you know where to come for the warrior?" Runs-with-the-Wind asked.

"I heard a tale from the village of my brother Red Dog." He controlled his fury as he recalled the Sioux attack. "He was last seen by my people there."

The volume of conversion rose among the council. The men quieted and one of the chiefs spoke. "Runs-with-the-Wind says that he knows you. He said you are a friend, yet you come into our midst seeking to kill one of us."

"It is my father's honor!" Black Hawk exclaimed.

The chief nodded. "This warrior—did he kill in battle?"

"He did not," Black Hawk said. "We were on a hunt. My father was about to make an offering to the spirits for the meat we'd received."

"You were there?"

"Yes. I was eight summers. He-Who-Kills-with-Big-Stick did not see me, but I saw him."

Clouds-at-Morning spoke to the chief in the Sioux tongue. Then the chief addressed Black Hawk again.

"Clouds-at-Morning says he has knowledge of your honor. That you do not kill needlessly. You kill only to defend or protect. Is this true?"

"It is not protection I seek when I came to this place," Black Hawk said. "It is the blood of He-Who-Kills-with-Big-Stick."

All the Sioux leaders began to talk at once. One, who appeared older than the rest, held up his hand to silence the council. Finally their conversation ended and this man, who Black Hawk later learned was Wise-Man-with-Gun, addressed Black Hawk. "We have decided on this matter, and you shall be allowed to fight this warrior."

Another chief spoke, and Black Hawk, who knew enough Sioux to communicate if the words were spoken slowly and carefully, was able to make out what was being said.

The eldest chief seemed to agree with his peer, then gazed at Black Hawk. "You will fight He-Who-Kills-with-Big Stick," he said. "It will be a fight to the death."

Black Hawk smiled grimly. *A fight to the death.* The thought should have chilled him, but it didn't. This was the reason he had come.

# Chapter 25

The fight between the Ojibwa brave and the Sioux warrior began the next day at sunrise. The Sioux people gathered in a circle, in a clearing between teepees. The crowd was large around the two men.

He-Who-Kills-with-Big-Stick was not the old warrior Black Hawk had expected. The Sioux warrior must have been a young man when he'd tortured and killed the two Ojibwa men. Staring into the Sioux's eyes, Black Hawk recalled the man's cruelty and his laughter.

The warriors had stripped to only their breechclouts and moccasins. Their faces were painted with vermilion and black stripes. Black Hawk stared at his opponent and saw mocking laughter in the brave's eyes. Hate formed a ball of constriction in his breast as he clutched his knife. He wasn't surprised that He-Who-Kills-with-Big-Stick's chosen weapon was the war club.

Black Hawk stared at the club, then held up his hand

to address the gathering. "I could use a war club," he said. "Is there one among you who would give his weapon?"

A warrior stepped forward. Runs-with-the-Wind. "You may use my war club," he said.

Black Hawk thanked him with a nod and took the club. In return, he handed the Sioux brave his knife.

"If I die, this knife is yours," he said.

The Ojibwa brave examined the war club. The *baga-maagan* was a fine weapon with steel spikes, highly decorated with brightly colored paints. It was a club used for ceremonial purposes. He doubted it had ever been raised to an enemy that wasn't imaginary or symbolic. This day it would wound and kill another human being. It would kill He-Who-Kills-with-Big-Stick.

With his hand fisted about the long club, Black Hawk faced his enemy.

"You will die this day, Ojibwa," his father's killer said.

Black Hawk laughed. "You will be the one who reaches the end of his path, dogface! Today I seek justice for the wrong done to my father and my father's friend. It is you who will suffer, He-Who-Kills-with-Big-Stick. You will die by your own weapon. You will scream for mercy before the earth ceases to exist for you!"

The men stood at each end of the circle's diameter, waiting for the signal from the eldest chief, Wise-Man-with-Gun, to begin.

The crowd jeered at Black Hawk and shouted encouragement at He-Who-Kills-with-Big-Stick.

Black Hawk stared at his enemy, his dark gaze burning with hate, his fingers flexing around the weapon's handle.

The signal was given, and the braves began to circle one another with clubs raised to defend.

He-Who-Kills-with-Big-Stick struck out first. Black Hawk was quick at the defense, deflecting the warrior's

blow with an equally powerful swing. The Sioux brave
grunted and stepped back, snarling. Black Hawk grinned
and muttered insults to his opponent to incense the man.

The land was dry and dust filled the air as the braves
fought. Black Hawk, seeing an advantage, swung toward
the man's shoulder, cutting him with his weapon's spike.

He-Who-Kills-with-Big-Stick howled with rage and
charged, swinging wildly. Black Hawk ducked and evaded,
taking a blow to his arm but only with the Sioux's club
handle.

The Sioux gathering grew quiet as the warriors pitted
themselves against each other. Sweat dripped down Black
Hawk's forehead, and he swiped it away from his eyes,
leaving a streak of dirt mixed with war paint.

The spectators began to chant. Black Hawk ignored the
sound, concentrating instead on his enemy. He gazed
steadily into the man's eyes as he crouched and circled.
He stared at the brave and laughed.

"You are a coward," Black Hawk said, using his
knowledge of the Sioux language.

He-Who-Kills-with-Big-Stick bellowed with rage. Black
Hawk had planned a long time for this day. There was
much he had to say to his father's murderer before the man
died.

"You cannot win," He-Who-Kills-with-Big-Stick said.
"I am more powerful than you. You are nothing!"

Black Hawk snarled. "You kill only those who are
defenseless, like women and children and men you can
take by surprise. *You* are nothing!"

He watched the Sioux brave carefully, noting his weak-
nesses, using the man's anger to his advantage. A man
blinded by anger was a man at risk.

"Come, Big Stick!" he said. "Come and get Bear
Tooth's son. See if you can kill the son as you killed the
father!"

"I can kill you with my hands tied!" Big Stick spat as he lunged and swung his weapon. Black Hawk crouched, and the club went over his head. He laughed, and the fight grew in fury.

The Sioux people were taking sides. Some of the spectators taunted Black Hawk, who wasn't bothered. Others jeered insults at Big Stick, who got angrier by the minute. So enraged was he by the taunts of his people and Black Hawk's deadly calm, Big Stick became careless in his attacks. He swung his war club wildly, missing Black Hawk after suffering a glancing blow to his side.

Blood welled to the surface of Black Hawk's skin where the Sioux's weapon had nicked him. Unaffected, Black Hawk remained steady and calm, determined to bring down his father's killer.

*"You are not a murderer."* Rachel's word's appeared in his thoughts, startling him. *"Why start now?"*

*I will not give up this moment,* he thought. *I will finish what I've begun!*

Although his attention remained on Big Stick, it seemed as if Rachel were there, watching. *You're going to get yourself killed!* she cried.

*Does it matter?* he thought. *You are gone, Rachel. What do I have but this moment of vengeance!*

Big Stick's club struck the side of Hawk's face. Black Hawk moved, but not quick enough, and the blow to the head made him dizzy. He-Who-Kills-with-Big-Stick's laughter egged him on. He blinked to clear his vision; and focusing on his opponent, swung and struck Big Stick's chest. The man screamed.

Black Hawk was satisfied by the move, until he imagined Rachel's voice again. *No, Black Hawk. I love you. Don't do this.*

*Go away!* he thought. Angered by the tricks his mind had begun to play on him, Black Hawk focused again and swung at Big Stick's war club, sending the weapon flying out of the man's hands.

Throwing down his own club, Black Hawk lunged at his opponent, pinning him to the ground. The two fought in the dirt with sweat and dust streaking their muscled bodies, blood seeping from open wounds.

"I will kill you now, Black Hawk!" Big Stick cried as they struggled.

"You will die by my hand!" Black Hawk growled.

Big Stick shoved Black Hawk to the ground. Black Hawk rolled, then rose to a defensive crouch. He saw Big Stick's gaze go to his war club, and Black Hawk attacked the man before he had a chance to retrieve it.

With the Sioux's attention elsewhere for that fraction of a second, Black Hawk had won. With his arm across Big Stick's throat, Black Hawk pinned the Sioux to the ground. He saw the man's war club, grabbed it, and raised it to strike.

Rachel's words continually invaded his thoughts.

*You're no murderer, Black Hawk. Will your father return because you killed this man? I love you. Love you. Love you.*

Black Hawk stared at the man he'd hated for so long. The Sioux could barely breathe as he gasped for air, his throat constricted by Hawk's arm.

*Your father will not return because you killed this man.* Her soft voice continued in his mind. *Don't do this, Black Hawk.*

Fear had entered Big Stick's expression as Black Hawk glared at him. The Sioux warrior couldn't move. The end of his life had come.

His chest heaving with the exertion of the fight, Black Hawk came to a decision quickly. He glanced up from his victim to search for the chief.

"I take this brave's life to avenge the death of my

father,'' he announced. "I take it and give it back to you,
Wise-Man-with-Gun, for your keeping. Do with him what
you wish.''

In so speaking, he released He-Who-Kills-with-Big
Stick and stood. He had spared Big Stick's life. His
father's murderer would go free, but Black Hawk felt
relief. He could have taken Big Stick easily, but had
chosen a different path.

The Sioux chief respected the act of honor. Black Hawk
had won without taking a life. The people applauded him.

Black Hawk bent to retrieve Runs-with-the-Wind's
weapon. Catching sight of the man, he gave him both
war clubs. "You have given me the chance to free and
honor my father's spirit,'' he told the Sioux brave. "You
are a friend.''

Runs-with-the-Wind nodded as he returned Black
Hawk's hunting knife. The peace between their villages
would remain unbroken, Black Hawk thought, pleased.

Clouds-at-Morning called out to Black Hawk, and the
Ojibwa turned to the brave with a smile. As he approached,
he heard someone cry out. A shot rang in the air. Big
Stick fell to the ground, wounded.

Big Stick had grabbed a knife from another brave and
had been ready to attack Black Hawk.

All eyes went to the young Sioux warrior holding the
trade gun.

The brave, who was still a boy, addressed his people.
"This man deserves to die,'' he said. "He has acted
dishonorably. He has hurt our young braves.''

Black Hawk saw the flash of pain on the young warrior's face. "He has hurt *me,*'' the boy said.

Everyone in the crowd began talking at once until the
old chief silenced his people.

Wise-Man-with-Gun's expression was angry as he studied the boy who had shot Big Stick. "You have been hurt by this man?"

The brave nodded. "I have."

"As have I!" A younger boy stepped from the crowd.

"And I!" another child shouted.

The chief looked shocked. "What is this? Why has no one told this?"

"He threatened to kill me," the brave with the rifle said. "I was a little child when he hurt me. And he said he'd kill me if I told."

There were gasps and murmurs from among the people.

"Let him die!" one mother cried.

"Kill him!" another shouted.

Black-Hawk-Who-Hunts-at-Dawn left the Sioux gathering without killing his father's murderer, but he had had his revenge.

With the new revelations about his actions, He-Who-Kills-with-Big-Stick was a dead man.


Three days after her return home, Rachel was back to work at the mission. Miriam Lathom had taken over the work at the infirmary in the Dempseys' absence. The missionary had been happy to see Rachel and the doctor safe. She'd given them a list of patients with notations about their ailments, before she'd left with the promise to return to assist them anytime they needed her.

"I have chores to do," Miriam had said, "but I will help you again if you need me."

This early autumn morning, Rachel walked through the infirmary and saw that everything was as it should be. She had prepared the surgery for the day's work yesterday. There wasn't anything else for her to do, so she wandered into the waiting area. The room was spotless. With no patients in sight, Rachel headed toward the kitchen to wash the breakfast dishes.

"Any tea left?" her father asked as he entered the room.

She smiled at him, glad that they were together again. "I can make another pot."

"That's all right. I'll be heading over to Freda Jenkins's house. Seems the woman had a slight accident with a kitchen knife, the same knife that Will Thornton got cut on. Miriam bandaged and cleaned the wound. She didn't think it needed stitching, but I want to take a look at it."

Rachel had known about the accident and understood her father's desire to check on his patients, although she was sure that Miriam would have sewn the cut if she'd thought it'd needed it.

"Will you be gone long?" she asked him.

"No, I'll be back shortly. After our absence, I don't want our patients to think we've abandoned them."

"All right, Father." Rachel smiled.

As she worked to clean up the kitchen after the morning meal, Rachel wondered where Black Hawk was. Was he all right? Had he found his killer?

She paused in drying a dish and closed her eyes. "Black Hawk, please don't get yourself killed."

She had never said good-bye. He'd left so quickly. Her heart gave a lurch. He must have seen Jordan. Is that why he hadn't stayed?

*No,* she thought, *he probably slipped away because he was in a hurry to leave. He's waited a long time to find the Sioux brave, He-Who-Kills-with-Big-Stick.* He would have been anxious to depart, before the Sioux warrior moved on.

Wondering about Black Hawk, worrying that he was all right, was pure agony for Rachel. *I can't stop loving him just because he didn't stay.*

This morning when she'd awoken, she'd learned that she'd gotten her womanly courses. She was unhappy that she wasn't to have Black Hawk's child. It was probably for the best under the circumstances, but knowing that didn't make her feel better. She wanted to have Black Hawk's baby. She wanted the baby as much as she wanted the child's father.

But it wasn't to be. There would be no babe and no Black Hawk in her life. *Lord, please, keep him safe.*

A noise out in the front rooms attracted Rachel's attention as she was finishing up in the kitchen. She left the back rooms and headed toward the surgery. For a brief moment, she experienced a moment's fear as memories returned. She was reminded of their Sioux visitors, of her father's kidnapping and the events that had followed . . . and all because of an Indian brave's attraction to her.

Clouds-at-Morning had been released. While she applauded Black Hawk's honor in keeping his word, she wondered whether or not the Sioux had such honor. Would he stay away from her as he'd promised Black Hawk?

She hesitated outside the sickroom, waiting until she garnered enough courage to go in.

*This is ridiculous! You can't be afraid all your life!* She'd told her father that she liked it in the Wisconsin Territory. He'd never believe her if she didn't stop jumping at shadows or gasping at every sound.

Drawing a sharp breath, she opened the surgery door and stepped inside . . . and saw nothing. Then, she heard the noise again and realized that it had come from the waiting room. She scolded herself for being silly. A Sioux warrior intent on kidnapping wouldn't remain in the waiting room until she came out.

She moved toward the open doorway and saw a young man in one of the chairs. "May I help you?"

He looked up and stood. He seemed surprised to see

her. "I'm sorry, I thought that I'd find Miss Lathom here. Has she gone?" He seemed uncomfortable as he glanced away.

"Miriam is still at the mission," she told him. "Are you hurt?"

Meeting her gaze, he nodded. "Just a scratch really, but Miriam—I mean, Miss Lathom said it's best to be careful about such things." He wore a white linen shirt and pale blue pants.

Rachel recognized his clothing as U.S. Army-issued when she spied the navy blue jacket on the seat next to him. "You're a soldier?" she asked.

He nodded.

"Would you like me to take a look at your wound?" she asked. "Then, if you'd like, I can tell you where to find Miriam."

The man looked pleased. "I don't wish to be an imposition."

She shook her head as she extended her arm to lead him inside. "It's no trouble. And Miriam is right—the smallest cut can fester and become a problem. It could even kill." She glanced upward and noted by the angle of her neck that he was very tall. "My name is Rachel Dempsey. My father is the doctor here."

"Robert Barning," he said. "Private." He bowed slightly. "It's nice to meet you, Miss Dempsey." His smile was genuine.

If her heart hadn't been otherwise engaged, she might have found this soldier attractive. But interestingly enough, despite his good looks and pleasant manners, Rachel realized that she wasn't interested.

She gestured toward the examining table and waited patiently while he hopped up.

"Now where is this cut?" she asked.

He rolled up his shirtsleeve and held out his arm. A red scratch about two inches long marred the white flesh.

"Well, now, that doesn't look too bad," she said. "But, it's a good thing you came. It's starting to swell. I'll clean the scratch, then put some salve on it."

"Thank you."

She smiled at him. "You're welcome."

She had just finished applying the salve on Robert's arm when her father entered the surgery. Rachel explained about the man's injury and what she'd done for it. John Dempsey checked the wound, pronounced Rachel's choice of treatment correct, then with a beaming smile for his daughter, he discharged the patient.

"You'll find Miriam in the building two doors down from the church," Rachel told the young man. Watching him leave, she bit her lip, wondering if she'd done the right thing in telling him where Miriam was. What if Miriam didn't want to see him? She mentioned this to her father.

"Not to worry, daughter," he said. "Miriam will get rid of the fellow if he's a nuisance." Then he looked at her oddly. "Are you all right? No tears? No crying over Jordan Sinclair?"

"I told you. I'm finished with him," she said, meaning it. "If I'd wanted him back, I wouldn't have sent him away."

*If only I could dismiss my feelings for Black Hawk as easily.*

"If you're certain you're fine . . ."

"Yes, Father, I'm fine," she said. At least she would be once she knew whether or not Black Hawk was well.

As if her prayers had been answered, Rachel finally heard news of Black Hawk a few days later. It came in the form of his sister when Spring Blossom came to trade with the missionaries.

At the Indian maiden's request, Miriam Lathom brought her to the infirmary to see Rachel.

"Spring Blossom!" Rachel cried when the young woman entered the building. She hurried forward to greet her. "How are you? Are you ill?"

Had she come to the infirmary for medical treatment?

"She's fine," Miriam said. "She's not here for treatment, Rachel. She came for a silver cross." She smiled at the maiden, who grinned back. "Spring Blossom asked where you were, and I told her I'd bring her."

Rachel saw the lovely silver cross hanging from a chain about Spring Blossom's neck. "It's beautiful," Rachel said sincerely.

"I'll leave you two alone to talk," Miriam said, and departed.

Pleased to see her friend, Rachel invited Spring Blossom into the kitchen at the back of the infirmary building.

"Would you like something to eat and drink?"

Spring Blossom shook her head. "I tasted a cake at Miss Miriam's house." She smiled as if the memory was a pleasant one. "It was good."

"I have some cakes that you can take back to the village," Rachel offered.

*"Miigwech,"* the maiden said. "I'd like that."

Seeing Black Hawk's sister again made her memory of Black Hawk sharp. She couldn't stop thinking of him, worrying about him. Should she—dare she—ask?

"Spring Blossom, about Black Hawk—"

"Ah, it is good, yes?"

"What's good?" Rachel asked. Her heart started to pound.

"That Black Hawk has returned."

"Black Hawk's back?" Rachel said.

Spring Blossom frowned. "You did not know this?"

Rachel shook her head. How could she have known?

"I thought Dan-yel—"

"Daniel?" Rachel's tone sharpened. "Daniel knows Black Hawk is back?" She had seen her brother-in-law only yesterday. Daniel knew how she felt about Black Hawk. Why didn't he tell her that the Ojibwa brave had returned safely?

Calming herself, Rachel realized that she might have jumped to conclusions about Daniel. Daniel did know of her feeling for Black Hawk. With their new relationship based on trust, how could she be so quick to judge?

"Is your brother well?" she asked.

Spring Blossom nodded. "He was hurt in the fight, but not bad."

Rachel felt her stomach burn when she heard he was hurt. Then she realized that Spring Blossom had said he was fine. She felt lighthearted all of a sudden. "I'm glad."

"You come soon to visit our village?" Spring Blossom asked.

"I'd like to, but I don't know when I can leave here."

She continued to rejoice over Black Hawk's safe return. *Thank God.* She felt as if her whole body had released several weeks' worth of tension.

"I must go," Spring Blossom said. "Thunder Oak is waiting for me."

"Thunder Oak is here?" She would like to see the brave. She'd like to see all of her Ojibwa friends.

"Thunder Oak went to Keller's," the Indian maiden said. "He'll be here soon."

Rachel nodded. "Let me wrap some cake for you." She cut a huge chunk of cake and placed it in the center of a clean linen towel. "Here you are. The next time you come to the mission, stop in and I'll give you some cookies."

Spring Blossom looked puzzled. "Cookies?"

"They are treats like cake, but smaller. Hard, but sweet. Good to eat."

"Ah," the maiden said. "Good to eat."

"Yes, that's right." Rachel grinned. Her smile vanished as she gazed at her friend. "I miss you," she said.

"Miss?"

"It is not the same when I don't see you."

Spring Blossom was nodding her head. "Yes, miss. It is not the same with you gone."

Rachel hugged her, and Spring Blossom hugged back. "Good-bye, Spring Blossom."

*"Giga-waabamin."*

*I'll see you, too,* Rachel thought when Spring Blossom had left. Tears filled her eyes as she thought of Black Hawk. *Please give my love to your brother.*

# Chapter 26

Rachel started to fret when days went by and there was no sign of Black Hawk. Why did he not visit her? Had he stayed away because he wanted her to get over her love for him?

Closing her eyes, she fought a wave of pain. Surely, he knew how worried she'd been while he was gone.

*Why hasn't he come?*

She had made every effort to get on with her life by putting her energy into her mission work. Besides her work at the infirmary, she helped Miriam make the silver crosses that Spring Blossom and the Indians liked so much.

Amelia had been after her to visit, but Rachel hadn't wanted to leave the mission. What if Black Hawk came and she wasn't there? She refused to go far. She wanted to be here for Black Hawk.

Another week passed without an appearance from Black Hawk. Rachel realized that she'd never be able to forget

Black Hawk without seeing him one last time. With the idea implanted in her mind, she accepted a dinner invitation from her sister. She needed to speak privately with her brother-in-law. She had to convince Daniel to take her to Black Hawk.

Rachel pretended cheerfulness during her visit with the Traherns. She knew Amelia was concerned about her. With her advanced pregnancy, her sister didn't need to worry, so Rachel laughed and smiled as she ate her meal.

Because she had a new plan of action, Rachel found enjoying herself easier than she'd thought. She was glad she had come. It had been worth the effort to see the pleasure on her family's faces.

*But I can't fool Daniel,* she realized. He acted as if all was well, until she caught sight of him studying her thoughtfully. Twice, she'd met his gaze and raised her eyebrows comically to lighten his mood. Both times, he chuckled, apparently convinced, until the next time she'd found him staring.

Through the late afternoon and early evening, Rachel waited for an opportunity to talk with Daniel alone. It seemed as if she'd never have a chance without arousing the rest of the family's suspicions. Then, Daniel mentioned a project in his smithy, one he wanted to show Rachel.

"A project?" Amelia asked with a puzzled look. "What kind of project?"

Daniel smiled at her. "Sorry, my sweet, but you're not to peek. It's a gift for you. You don't want to spoil the surprise, do you?"

"No," she replied with a frown. "Of course not."

John Dempsey remained silent. Either he wasn't interested or had seen it, or perhaps he suspected that Rachel and Daniel needed to speak alone.

The inside of the shop was dim, until Daniel fired up

the forge fire from the embers that had been left from his workday.

Rachel was silent as she watched him add fuel to the fire, then blow air into the flames with the forge's bellows. As the flames grew, Rachel turned her attention to her surroundings.

As she wandered around the forge area, she wondered how she was going to broach the subject of Black Hawk to Daniel. Would her brother-in-law take her to the village? Or would he try to convince her to stay home and forget his Ojibwa friend?

"You don't really have anything to show me, do you?" Rachel said.

"I do, but it's not the reason I asked you here," he admitted. "I wanted to talk with you."

She'd thought so. "I wanted to talk with you, too."

He smiled as he leaned back against his work block. "I could tell."

She regarded him with skepticism. "How?"

"Just a feeling."

Rachel was alarmed. "My sister doesn't share that feeling, does she?"

Daniel shrugged. "I doubt it. You've given a brilliant performance all day. If I didn't know about your secret, I probably wouldn't have noticed anything amiss either."

Blushing, she turned away. "I see." She sensed his approach.

"Rachel—"

She spun to face him. "I have to see him, Daniel," she said before he could argue. "I know you won't think it wise, but I have to know. I have to see with my own eyes that he's all right."

Daniel opened his mouth to object. "I don't know if that's a good idea."

"Please," She pleaded. "I have to see him. *I need to*

*see him.* And I'd like to visit Spring Blossom and the Ojibwa.'' She gave him a soft smile. ''I miss them.''

He looked surprised. ''You do?''

She nodded. ''Life is simple there, but I learned things that are important. And I felt good making and doing things.''

''And if Black Hawk is there, and he isn't interested?'' He rubbed the back of his neck as if he was troubled. ''What will you do then?''

Rachel suffered a fresh wave of pain. ''Then I'll leave. I'll go home to the mission and go on with my life without him,'' she murmured. ''Without Black Hawk.''

''You love him a lot,'' he said.

She swallowed against a lump in her throat. ''Yes, I do.''

She touched his arm. ''Please, Daniel,'' she whispered.

Daniel looked torn. ''If I take you, Amelia will want to go, too.''

''No,'' Rachel said. ''I don't want her there. I don't want her to come. I love her, but she's liable to see the truth . . . and then she'll try to interfere.''

''She cares for you.''

''I know,'' she said. ''And her love means a lot to me, but Daniel, I have to do this on my own.''

A strange look entered her brother-in-law's expression. ''. . . something,'' he muttered.

''What?'' she said.

''You're an amazing woman, Rachel Dempsey.''

She grinned. ''I am?''

He smiled. ''I hope Black Hawk sees the truth, that you're the right one for him. I hope he wants you as much as you want him.''

''I hope so, too,'' she choked out, her eyes filling with tears.

A sudden thought occurred to her. ''Will Amelia be

all right at home? I hate to take you away from her. I could ask Jack Keller to take me."

"Amelia will be fine," he said. "I won't be gone long. It's not that far to the village." He frowned. "Unless the Ojibwa have left for their winter camp."

Her heart gave a lurch. "Do you think it's possible? Spring Blossom was just here."

"They're probably still here then. It's early in the season yet, and the Ojibwa like to fish there in autumn." He scowled. "There's bound to be one problem we'll have to contend with—Susie."

"Susie?" How could Daniel's young niece be a problem?

"She'll want to go with us. She'll be extremely upset if she can't. She misses her friend Conner."

"Barking Dog," Rachel said.

"Yes."

"I don't mind if she comes along, if you don't."

"You don't?"

She smiled. "No."

He looked relieved. "Good." He gave her a grin.

"Daniel, won't Amelia wonder what's going on if we don't go back to the house soon?"

Daniel seemed startled. "You're right. First, come look at this." He gestured her toward the corner of the room, where a woolen blanket covered a large object.

"What is it?" Rachel asked, intrigued.

"The surprise." He tugged off the blanket. "A cradle. For the baby."

Rachel took one look at the expertly crafted baby cradle and her heart melted. "Oh, Daniel, it's beautiful. You do all that engraving work yourself?" He was a blacksmith, she thought, but here he had created something magnificent from wood.

Flushing, he nodded.

Impulsively, she gave him a hug. "She's going to love it," she said as she pulled away.

"Love what?" Amelia said from the shop door.

Rachel gasped and spun. She tried to hide the piece of furniture with her body. "Amelia, get out!"

Her sister looked hurt.

"Please, Amelia," she said more softly. "It's a surprise, a wonderful, beautiful surprise."

Amelia hesitated as she studied her husband and sister. The look in her eyes said that she felt left out.

"It's all right, sweetheart," Daniel said. "You can come in and see it. It's finished."

His wife brightened as she stepped farther into the room. "What's finished?" she asked curiously.

Rachel stepped aside. "This."

Amelia gazed at the cradle and tears filled her eyes, making them glisten. "Oh, Daniel," she breathed. She looked at her husband with love.

"My time to leave," Rachel murmured as she saw the way the two stared at each other. She felt a jolt. She wanted Black Hawk to gaze at her the way Daniel looked at her sister.

Rachel heard another "Oh, Daniel!" as she hurried to the door.

"I love you, Amelia," Daniel said huskily.

There was silence after that, but Rachel didn't look back as she left the blacksmith shop. She figured some moments were private, and this one belonged to her sister and brother-in-law.


Jordan Sinclair had been traveling for days when he'd stopped at an inn. Upset at what had happened between him and Rachel, he drank and sulked, and felt sorry for himself.

*You loved me, Rachel,* he thought, sniffling. *And I can make you love me again.*

He stared into his glass, seeing her image, wanting her more than ever.

*I can make you love me.*

He stiffened and put down his glass. "I can shtill make her love me again," he muttered drunkenly. He had handled the situation badly. He could woo her, make her his betrothed a second time.

He winced as he recalled some of the things that had been said between them. It would take all his powers of persuasion, but he could do it. She was angry with him, and she had every right, he thought. He shouldn't have left her.

He had been too forward. He should have been more patient with her.

Smiling stupidly, Jordan got up from the table, then swallowed the remainder of his glass before stumbling toward his room.

*I'm coming back, Rachel. I'll be gentler, more understanding. I'll patiently court you until you fall in love with me all over again.*

Drunk, he shuffled on unsteady legs up the stairs and down the hall until he reached his door. He fumbled with the key until he opened his lock. He shut the door, leaned heavily against it, then with a grin on his face, lurched toward his bed.

He tripped against the edge of the bed. Then, he fell on his back on the mattress and closed his eyes.

"I'ms comin', my sweet Rachel," he slurred. "I'ms comin' to get you."

Amelia wanted to go to the village, and no one, it seemed, could convince her to stay. Adamant, she faced her sister and husband, winning the argument before it had begun.

"I'm going," she insisted. "I'm perfectly healthy. Susie and Jane will want to go, too. So will Father."

Rachel groaned inwardly as she exchanged looks with Daniel. "Amelia, wouldn't it be better for the babe if you stayed and rested? And what about Father? What about his patients? Who will help him while we're gone?"

"Miriam Lathom can help him if he doesn't want to go," her sister said.

"Amelia," Daniel began.

She flashed him a smile. "Yes, love?" Amelia slipped a hand beneath her husband's arm and leaned close to kiss his neck.

Rachel watched her brother-in-law melt beneath her sister's smile. *Coward!* she thought.

"If you're sure you'll be fine," he said to his wife, "then you can go."

Rachel scowled at him, and Daniel gave her a sheepish smile.

"I still don't think it's a good idea," Rachel said.

"I'm going."

"She's going."

Amelia and Daniel had spoken simultaneously. And so it was decided, but not by Rachel. Her sister would go with them to Black Hawk's village.

The weather when they left on their journey was pleasant. The scenery was delightful, and Rachel, anxious to see Black Hawk, was glad her sister had come.

John Dempsey stayed behind to work at the infirmary. Miriam Lathom consented to assist him, for which Rachel was relieved.

Little Susie Milton was a happy child, excited about visiting her Ojibwa friend again. During the journey, she pleaded with her mother to allow Conner return with them for a short stay.

Jane looked hesitant. "I don't know, Susie."

"I'm sure you have nothing to worry about, Jane," Jack Keller said. He too had elected to come. "Conner is a good boy. It will be fun for Susie to have him come."

When Rachel had first seen the number of people in her traveling party, she'd rolled her eyes, wondering how the Indians would react to so many uninvited guests.

And how was she to get in a private word with Black Hawk? Her family would be there, watching her, following her every move. Would she be able to find time alone with him?

As she watched Daniel and Amelia, Rachel knew she wouldn't have to worry about them. They'd enjoy this special time together, two people in love expecting their first child.

Jane Milton and Jack Keller's friendship was growing, Rachel noted. She was glad for both of their sakes. Jane needed a man like Jack, and Jack loved and needed Jane, a pretty blond woman with sad blue eyes.

Susie would be with Conner and his grandmother. Rachel doubted she'd see much of Daniel's niece.

Her thoughts went ahead to the village. She imagined seeing Black Hawk again. Her stomach fluttered and her blood warmed as she remembered his touch.

*Oh, Black Hawk, please be happy to see me,* she thought. And what if he wasn't? Then, she'd pretend to be cheerful, and then leave the village as soon as possible.

She knew she was putting her heart at risk by going to Black Hawk, when it was he who should have been coming to see her . . . if he cared enough.

What if he still wanted only friendship? The thought made her quiet and reflective as they traveled along the forest trail.

Jack Keller cried out that he saw smoke up ahead. Heart thumping, Rachel became more aware of her surroundings.

*We're here,* she thought.

"There's Conner!" Susie cried, and Rachel's heart started to thrum.

Barking Dog, Susie's little Indian friend, ran forward to greet them. With a cry of gladness, he murmured greetings to the adults, before he captured Susie's hand and the two children ran off.

Jane, watching her daughter run away with the young Indian, inhaled sharply.

"It's all right, Jane," Jack said softly. He wrapped his arm about her shoulders. "Susie will be fine. The village is like a second home to her."

Jane looked up at Jack trustingly. Jack caught his breath as he gazed into her liquid blue eyes.

"Yes, you're right," Jane said. "I'm sorry to be so silly."

"You're not silly, love," he said, giving her shoulders a little squeeze.

Jane's eyes widened and she stared at him. Rachel, watching the exchange, smiled with understanding as embarrassment colored Jack's expression a bright red.

*Jane doesn't seem to mind that you called her love, Jack,* Rachel thought. Jack must have realized it, too, because suddenly he grinned.

"Rach-el!" a soft feminine voice called, drawing her attention from the couple.

Rachel turned to find Spring Blossom on the edge of the village clearing, waving to her.

"Spring Blossom!" she exclaimed, and rushed forward to hug the girl. "It's good to see you."

"You have come to stay?" the Indian maiden asked.

Rachel shook her head, although she wished that she

could. "I've come for a visit ... to see you and your people ... and Black Hawk."

Spring Blossom frowned. "Black Hawk is not here."

"He's not?" Rachel felt a sharp flutter of disappointment. "Where is he?"

"He has gone on the hunt with Thunder Oak and Rain-from-Sky."

The two women entered the village. "Will he be back soon?" Rachel asked. She studied her surroundings with a smile. She had missed this place. She had missed its people.

"Black Hawk will be home as soon as he gathers meat for our village." Spring Blossom smiled at her friend. "You will wait to see him?"

Rachel searched for sight of her brother-in-law. "If I can." But the decision wasn't hers. It was Daniel's.

"Dan-yel will stay, so Rach-el can stay, too," Spring Blossom said as if she'd read Rachel's mind. "We will make him and Tree-That-Will-Not-Bend feel welcome. Man-with-Big-Head will be happy to stay."

Catching sight of their guests, the Ojibwa people greeted them with smiles, hand waves, and laughter.

Watching her sister and Daniel, Rachel realized that the couple was comfortable in the village. They even had Ojibwa names. She'd stayed at the village for weeks. Why didn't she have an Ojibwa name? She found Spring Blossom studying her strangely. "What is wrong, Rachel?"

Rachel felt silly. "Nothing ... it's just that Amelia and Daniel ... and even Susie have Ojibwa names. But I don't. Why not?"

"You wish Ojibwa name?" Spring Blossom asked, looking pleased.

"Yes," Rachel said. "I think it would be wonderful."

The maiden smiled. "We will give you Ojibwa name.

I will ask chief. Ask matrons. Maybe ask Woman-with-Hair-of-Fox.''

''I'd like that,'' Rachel said. ''Thank you.''

Grinning, Spring Blossom raised the door flap and motioned Rachel inside her wigwam.

# Chapter 27

Black Hawk thought he imagined her. She was a vision of loveliness in a blue silk gown. He blinked to clear the image, but Rachel was still there before him with her eyes glowing and her expression soft.

"Rach-el," he said.

She smiled and approached until she was within inches of him. "Black Hawk." Her voice was husky. "It's been too long since I've seen you. Why did you leave without saying good-bye?"

His heart hammering in his chest, he reached out, touched her smooth cheek. "I had to go," he said as he caressed her skin. She felt warm beneath his fingers. He gazed at her tenderly. A burning heat invaded his midsection. He had wanted her for so long. Now she was here . . . and his.

"Why did you have to go?" Her green eyes regarded him curiously. "I wanted to introduce you to Jordan."

"Jordan." He felt a sharp shaft of pain as he withdrew his touch. "The man you will marry."

She nodded. "Yes, the man I will marry." She smiled and captured his hand. "You're a good friend, Black Hawk. I wanted you to meet him."

"Friend," he murmured. She wasn't his. She belonged to a white man named Jordan. He was responsible for this, Black Hawk thought. He'd offered her friendship when he'd wanted more.

"Was your journey successful?" she asked conversationally.

He frowned. "I found my father's killer."

She inhaled sharply. "You didn't . . . kill him?"

No, he hadn't killed the man . . . for her, because he hadn't been able to forget her words. "When I left his village, He-Who-Kills-with-Big-Stick was alive."

"Good." She looked satisfied. Her voice seemed to soften. "I am glad you are well, Black Hawk."

He nodded, trying to read her thoughts. "Why have you come?" Why had she sought him out if she was to leave to marry the white man Jordan?

"I heard you were back, and I wanted to say good-bye."

His fingers itched to touch her again. He clenched his hands into fists at his sides. "You are leaving the mission."

"Yes." She smiled and caressed his jaw. "Jordan and I are returning to Baltimore." She released him and stepped back. "I will miss you, Black Hawk."

"You will be happy with your Jordan." He suffered a pang of pain when she didn't deny it.

"Thank you for protecting me from the Sioux. I will always be grateful."

"Go in safety," he said. He wanted to stop her, to ask her to stay with him in the village, but she was obviously

*happy that Jordan had come to her. Black Hawk scowled.*
*He didn't like this Jordan. He had never met him, but*
*the man was a fool. He had allowed Rachel to get away*
*from him once. Would he treat her more kindly this second*
*time?*

*"Well," she said, looking as if she found the moment*
*awkward. "I'd better go. Good-bye, Black Hawk."*

*He nodded and fought the urge to pull her into his*
*arms and kiss her. He loved her. He didn't want to make*
*her angry. "Good-bye, Rachel Dempsey."*

*She waved as she walked away.*

*Black Hawk stared as Jordan appeared from behind a*
*stand of trees, embracing Rachel as she joined him. He*
*watched with a rapidly beating heart as the two kissed*
*passionately. The kiss seemed to go on forever. Black*
*Hawk wanted to look away but couldn't.*

*No! he cried silently. Don't leave. This man cares for*
*you!*

*As if the couple had heard him, they turned to him as*
*one and smirked at him.*

*"Rach-el!" Black Hawk called.*

*"It is too late, Black Hawk," Rachel replied. "You*
*wanted your father's murderer, and now I have Jordan."*

*"No! Come back!"*

He woke up in the dark, gasping. Black Hawk sat up
and looked around, and reclaimed an awareness of his
surroundings. He and his brothers were in their hunting
lodge. He was not in the village. He had not seen Rachel.

He sighed as he rose to his feet, then slipped out of
the wigwam. Behind him, Thunder Oak and Rain-from-
Sky slept on, undisturbed. The sound of their breathing
was loud in the silence.

Outside, a gentle rain fell, a fine mist covering the land.
Black Hawk stood for a moment with his face turned
toward the sky, allowing the rain to cleanse him.

They'd had a good hunt. Black Hawk moved toward a tree to check on the game they'd killed. They had shot two deer and snared five rabbits. Before seeking their sleeping pallets, they had hung the deer high in the tree to keep other animals from eating it. They had gutted and cooked one rabbit; the others they'd stored inside the hunting lodge.

After he was satisfied that the ropes holding the deer would hold, Black Hawk stood on the edge of their camp clearing, staring into the night.

Soon, it would be dawn, he thought. When the sun climbed in the autumn sky, he and his brothers would head back to the village, bringing their game.

Yesterday, after they'd shot and killed the first deer, they had given thanks to the deer's spirit. They had lit an offering of tobacco and sang to the deer spirit and *Gicho-Manidoo.* They had made an offering each time they'd made a kill.

The forest seemed quieter than usual. The mist continued, soaking Black Hawk, but he didn't seek shelter. He stood in the rain, his thoughts wandering to another place ... to Rachel Dempsey. His dream vision returned to him, saddening him, making him wish that his time with Rachel could be recaptured.

*Rachel,* he thought. She was gone. Why couldn't he forget her?

The mist clung to his hair, coated his skin, and formed droplets on his eyelashes before dripping down his face.

*I love Rachel,* he thought. But it was too late. As he'd seen in his dream vision, Rachel had left Ojibwa land to return to Baltimore with the white man named Jordan.

Rachel, his Rachel, was gone.

\*     \*     \*

*"O-dah-ing'-um,"* Spring Blossom said. "This name we have chosen for you, Rach-el. It means 'ripple on the water.' "

"Ripple-on-the-Water," Rachel murmured, enjoying the title. "Why did you choose that name?"

The Indian maiden smiled. "It was Woman-with-Hair-of-Fox who said it. She said that a calm lake was a pretty thing to see, but a ripple on the water made the lake a breathtaking sight."

If she hadn't liked the name before, Rachel thought, she would have after hearing the explanation.

She smiled. "I like it. *O-da* . . ." She frowned, unable to recall the whole phrase.

*"O-dah-ing'-um,"* Spring Blossom repeated.

Rachel said the name, her mouth finding the pronunciation a bit awkward. "I won't know when to answer," she admitted with a laugh.

"We will call you Ripple-on-the-Water," Black Hawk's sister said, "and you will know that it is your name."

The white woman grinned. "Thank you."

Spring Blossom had found Rachel in the forest, gathering fresh pine boughs to line the floor of the wigwam. Rachel bent to lift some branches from her newly acquired pile. Spring Blossom helped her by picking up the remainder of the boughs.

"Gray Squirrel, He-Who-Comes-from-Far-Away, and some of our warriors have returned with deer and beaver. Black Hawk still hasn't come," Spring Blossom said.

Rachel had been present when Gray Squirrel and his hunting band had returned last evening. Her heart had leapt when she'd heard the Ojibwa people's welcoming cries, until she'd learned that Black Hawk and his brother were not among the returning hunters.

"Do you think they've been hurt?" she asked.

"*Gaawiin.*" Spring Blossom smiled. "I think they are well and will come soon."

*How soon?* Rachel wondered. It had already been three days since her arrival. They'd been gone for a week before that. How much longer would her family wait?

If the hunting party didn't return soon, then she would have to leave without seeing Black Hawk.

*Come home, Black Hawk,* she thought. *Please come home soon.*

Daniel came to her later that afternoon. He seemed troubled as he approached her. "Rachel, we have to go home. Your sister isn't feeling well."

"Is she all right?" Rachel was instantly concerned. "What's wrong?"

"I don't know. She said her stomach has been hurting her. I know she probably shouldn't travel, but I'd like your father to take a look at her."

Rachel knew she couldn't be selfish. "When do you want to leave?"

"Tomorrow morning?"

She nodded. "I'll be ready. Is there anything I can do?"

"Will you talk with her? She says she's fine, but she seems frightened. She's in our wigwam."

Daniel and Amelia had been given a wigwam of their own. The lodge belonged to an Ojibwa woman who had gone to visit clan members in another village.

"Of course I will," Rachel said, and she hurried to see her sister.


"I'm sorry, Rachel," Amelia said.

Rachel studied her sister with concern. Amelia looked pale as she sat on her sleeping pallet. "You have nothing to apologize for, Amelia. We've been here long enough. You need to see Father. You must take care of your babe.

"But what about Black Hawk?" she whispered miserably. "I know you want to see him."

She should have known she couldn't fool Amelia. "You know, don't you? You know why I came."

"Of course, Rachel. I know you. You're my sister." She gestured for Rachel to sit. "You care for Black Hawk."

Rachel blushed. "Is it that obvious?"

Amelia gave her a gentle smile. "No. Only to those who know and love you." She extended her hand toward her sister.

Rachel grabbed her sister's fingers and sat down on the pallet beside her. "I love him, Amelia," she said. "I love him so much it hurts inside."

Tears filled her eyes as a sad smile touched her lips. "Can you believe it?" Rachel said. "Me, the one who became horrified if I wasn't dressed properly for a party? I'm in love with an Ojibwa war chief, and my one thought in coming here was to see him one more time."

"How does he feel about you?" Amelia asked.

Rachel dashed away tears. "I don't know," she admitted. "Sometimes it seems as if he loves me, while other times . . ."

Amelia squeezed her hand, and Rachel smiled through her tears.

"He wanted to find his father's murderer," Rachel said. "It's all he's thought about since he was a boy." She released her sister's hand and stood. "Well, he found him, and he's back. I wanted to see for myself that he was all right."

She wiped her eyes. "Black Hawk is back, but he hasn't come to see me. Why not, Amelia? Why didn't he come?"

"What did he say before he left?" Amelia asked. She rubbed her stomach as if the area pained her.

"He didn't say anything," Rachel said. "We didn't get to talk. Jordan was there and . . ." She frowned as she noticed her sister rubbing her pregnant belly. "We never said good-bye to each other. He just left when . . ."

"He saw you with Jordan Sinclair." Amelia smiled.

"Yes," Rachel said. She recalled Jordan's enthusiastic greeting and her less-than-happy response. Had Black Hawk seen her push Jordan away?

"But what if he didn't?" she murmured.

"Didn't what?" Amelia asked.

"What if Black Hawk saw Jordan kissing me, but he didn't see me push him away?" Rachel looked at her sister with a glimmer of hope. "What if he became angry? Or hurt?"

Amelia continued to rub her stomach. "You've got to wait for him, Rachel."

"No. Tomorrow, we leave for home—all of us," Rachel said firmly. "You're not feeling well, and I'm going with you. You're my sister and I love you. You've always been there for me when I needed you. It's my turn to be there for you."

"But—"

Rachel narrowed her gaze. "No buts, Amelia. It's home tomorrow to see Father. I told Black Hawk once that I loved him. Perhaps he needs time to think about it, to understand that I know how I feel. How he feels."

The next morning, the Traherns, Rachel, Jane, Jack, and little Susie Milton headed toward home. Black Hawk and his brothers had not returned to the village. As they'd left, Rachel had looked longingly at the village one last time, then forced her thoughts to new concerns . . . her sister's health and how she was going to get through life without the man she loved.

* * *

John Dempsey frowned as he examined his eldest daughter. "How long have you had this pain, Amelia?"

"A little while," she said in a weak voice.

"How little?" Rachel asked.

Amelia looked sheepish. "About a week."

"A week!" Daniel exclaimed.

"Well, the pain was barely a twinge at first. I thought it was nothing."

"Oh, Amelia," Rachel said. "And you went to the village with us . . ." She studied her brother-in-law with sympathy. He was rightfully upset. When she glanced toward Amelia, her sympathy went to her sister. Amelia looked more than upset. She looked alarmed and guilty, and ill.

"Now, don't get excited," John said. "I'm sure Amelia and the baby will be just fine."

Amelia brightened. "You are?"

He nodded. "That is, if you follow my instructions carefully."

"What instructions, John?" Daniel asked.

"She needs to rest," the doctor said. "No lifting, bending, working, cooking."

"No cooking!" Amelia cried. "Am I to be an invalid for four months!"

Her father scowled at her. "If you would let me finish . . ."

Blushing, she apologized.

"Go on, Father," Rachel urged. "Amelia is understandably anxious." She sensed tension between husband and wife, and felt bad for them. She could imagine how much Daniel's anger upset Amelia.

John Dempsey's expression softened. "I know." He helped his daughter to sit up on the examining table.

"Amelia, you know I wouldn't ask this of you if I didn't think it important."

"I know," she said, tears gathering in her brown eyes. "It's my fault, isn't it?"

"It's no one's fault but nature's, daughter," he said.

"Father, how long does Amelia need to rest?"

"We'll try it for a few weeks first. See if her resting will alleviate the pain. If it does, then she can begin to move around a bit more. I may even allow her to cook, as long as she continues to avoid lifting."

"But I'll be useless!" Amelia wailed.

"Useless?" John said in a voice that scolded slightly. "Amelia, your job right now is to see that your baby gets into this world healthy and safe. Believe me, you'll be busy enough after he's born. Then, you'll wish for a few minutes' peace . . ."

"What will we do? Daniel has so much to do at the shop—" She halted as she began to cry. Daniel was there beside her immediately, putting his arms around her. He crooned to her that they would manage, that everything would be all right.

Rachel grabbed hold of her father's arm and drew him aside to speak privately. "Father, you've managed well enough without me these last days, haven't you?"

"Why, yes, daughter, of course. Although I did miss you," he added with a smile.

"I'd like to go to Amelia's for as long as she needs me."

"That's a very generous offer, Rachel," her father began.

"I can cook and clean and do whatever needs to be done," she said. "And if you'd like, I can come here for a couple of hours a week to straighten the infirmary."

John regarded his youngest with a gentle smile. "You've grown up to be quite a wonderful woman, Rachel Dempsey." His eyes glistened with emotion.

Rachel hugged him. "I love you, too, Father." She blinked against tears as well. "Now we just have to convince Daniel."

"Let me handle it," her father said. His eyes twinkled.

"Daniel," he said. "Rachel would like to come stay with you to help out."

"Yes, Daniel. I know you think I'm incapable . . ."

Daniel looked taken aback. "Rachel, I never thought that."

"You didn't?" she said, pleased. She knew they had reached past the stage of friendship to becoming family, but she hadn't known how he felt about her abilities.

He nodded. "I may have misjudged you when you first came. Rachel, I've seen how hard you've worked at the mission and at the village. And you've come to our house and helped Amelia many times."

"Then you feel I can handle things?"

He frowned. "It's not a question of whether I feel you can handle the work. I know you can. But it's not fair to you . . . or to your father."

"I've agreed to it, Daniel." John Dempsey said.

"I'll make Amelia rest," she reasoned. She flashed her sister a mischievous grin. "I've always wanted to be the one in control."

"Rachel!" Amelia's gasp of outrage made everyone chuckle.

"Done!" Daniel said.

"Excellent!" Rachel and John said simultaneously. "Don't I have any say in the matter?" Amelia complained.

"Absolutely none!" the three other occupants of the room chorused.

Amelia smiled. "Good." And they all stared at her.

Rachel smiled knowingly. Her sister was a wise, subtle, and persuasive woman who knew how to get just what she wanted.

# Chapter 28

The Ojibwa hunters returned to the village, and there was a celebration of thanksgiving for a successful hunt. Black Hawk stood on the fringe of the gathering and watched Big-Cat-with-Broken-Paw address his people. The *Midewiwin*, the society of medicine men of the tribe, waited behind their leader in their special ceremonial dress. When the chief was done, the *Midewiwin* would sing their sacred songs, heal the sick, and tell stories of the *Anishinaabe*.

Soon, the Ojibwa would leave this place and venture to their winter village. Black Hawk wasn't ready to leave this place. He wanted to stay. His memories of this village were good, but he knew he would have to move on.

The weather had turned cool, and everyone had dressed warmly in buckskins, furs, and woolen clothing. Black Hawk tugged up the woolen blanket about his shoulders and gazed at the gathering from a distance.

"I thought you might be hungry," Spring Blossom said as she approached with a plate.

Black Hawk smiled as he accepted the meal. *"Miig-wech."*

His sister gestured for him to sit, and the two found a rush mat on the ground and sat next to each other.

"You are not hungry?" Black Hawk asked. He readjusted his blanket before he took a bite of food.

"I will eat later," she said. "I would like to talk with you first."

Her tone bothered him. He glanced at her with concern. "Is something wrong, my sister?"

"Dan-yel was here in our village."

Black Hawk stopped eating. "Dan-yel?"

Spring Blossom nodded. "And Little Flower and Tree-That-Will-Not-Bend."

"They did not stay to see me." His brow furrowed.

"They went home. Tree-That-Will-Not-Bend did not feel well." Her expression was troubled. "It was the babe."

Black Hawk frowned. "When did they leave?" He wondered if Amelia and the baby were all right. He felt concern for his friend's family.

"They left yesterday. We have heard nothing, but it is too soon. Still, I worry that something terrible has happened." Tree-That-Will-Not-Bend had become a good friend to her, as had her sister Rachel, Ripple-on-the-Water.

"No one has gone to the trading post to find out?" he asked.

Spring Blossom shook her dark head. "There has not been time. Our people have been busy preparing to leave our summer village. I thought that you could go."

Black Hawk felt a burning in his stomach as he studied his sister. "When do we leave this place?"

"Big-Cat-with-Broken-Paw wishes to leave when the sun rises twice more to brighten the day sky."

"Two days," Black Hawk murmured. "I shall go to Dan-yel tomorrow. If I do not return before our people leave, I will meet you in the forest of our winters."

Spring Blossom nodded. "Black Hawk?" she said when he started to leave. "Rachel Dempsey was here, in our village, with them."

"Sit down, Amelia," Rachel scolded as she carried in a basket of wet laundry. She proceeded to hang clothes over a rope strung across the width of the room near the heat of the stove. "You're not to do anything, Amelia. Why is that so hard for you to understand?"

Amelia sighed with frustration and sat on the sofa in the great room. "I hate this!" She looked longingly at Rachel as her sister draped a wet shirt over the clothesline. "I'm not used to being idle."

"Well, get used to it," Rachel said. "It's for your own good—you and your baby." She bent and pulled a pair of pantalets from the basket.

"You're enjoying this, aren't you?" Amelia regarded her with a scowl.

"Actually, I enjoy helping you. I'm not enjoying your surly mood."

"Surly!" Amelia exclaimed.

Rachel nodded, then laughed. "Surly," she repeated. "Surly. Bossy. Rude and irascible." There was a teasing twinkle in her eyes as she spoke.

A reluctant grin warmed Amelia's expression. "Oh, you!"

"How does it feel to be the little sister?" Rachel said.

Amelia frowned. "Is that how I make you feel . . . incapable?"

Rachel regarded her sister with alarm. "Amelia, surely you don't feel that way! You may be surly, but you are not incapable and ineffectual."

She set down a wet shirt and approached. "You're going to be a mother, Amelia. Think about it! A mother!" She sat down beside her sister and took her hand. "You have a tiny baby growing inside of you. It's so magical! You've created a little life, and now you're taking care of it."

Rachel's eyes glistened as she stood and went back to the clothes. "You've made life, Amelia. How can you feel useless?" Her voice softened. "You've made a baby!"

Amelia was silent, but Rachel didn't look at her as she hung clothes. She wanted a child, but without Black Hawk she'd never have one. She'd never love or marry another.

"I'm sorry," Amelia said huskily. "I know I've been unreasonable—"

Rachel draped the last garment over the line, then faced her sister. "You're not unreasonable, Amelia," she said seriously. "You're surly." She grinned as she headed toward the kitchen.

"Oh, you!" Amelia laughed.

"Ready for dinner?"

"Yes, of course!" her sister called back.

Rachel stuck her head through the doorway. "You are enjoying one thing." When her sister looked at her questioningly, she said, "Eating for two." She ducked out as a pillow came flying in her direction.

Amelia had a soft smile on her face as she stared into the fireplace. It was good for her to have Rachel here. She suspected that it was good for Rachel, too. Her sister hadn't been happy since leaving the village after her lengthy stay, and Amelia knew it was because of Black Hawk.

"Sandwiches all right?" Rachel shouted from the other room.

"Fine!" Amelia called back. She felt a twinge in her stomach. Frowning, she rubbed the area of the pain.

A shriek from the kitchen had her rising to her feet. "Rachel?" she yelled. "What's wrong?"

Seconds later, Rachel came out from the back room, her face white, one hand holding a towel wrapped around the other one. Blood seeped through the cloth, making a red stain.

"Rachel!" Amelia cried as she rushed to her sister's side. "What happened? What did you do to your hand?"

Rachel gave her a wan smile. "I cut it while I was slicing bread," she said weakly. "The knife slipped." She swayed on her feet, looking ill.

"You need to see Father," Amelia said.

"I'll be all right."

But then her pallor worsened, and Amelia helped her to sit at the dining table. "You stay still, and I'll tell Daniel."

Rachel had tears in her eyes when she looked up. "I'm sorry," she said, looking miserable. "I'm supposed to be taking care of you."

Amelia smiled as she touched her sister's cheek. "Relax, Rachel." Her smile vanished as she noted her sister's pallor.

"You'd better lie down before you fall down," she said. She offered to help her sister up, but Rachel, conscious of the reason for her stay, refused Amelia's help.

"I can walk," she said, stumbling but managing to right herself.

Watching her, Amelia bit her lip. She stayed in the room until she saw with relief that Rachel had reached the sofa without mishap. "I'll be right back," Amelia then told her.

Rachel nodded silently.

Her heart pounding with fear, Amelia hurried to find her husband at his smithy next door.

Miriam heard the door to the infirmary waiting room open and shut. She was in the surgery. "Hello," she called. "Can I help you?" She wandered toward the front room.

"Hello," a deep male voice answered. A man came to the doorway. "I'm looking for Rachel Dempsey," he said. "Is she here?"

Startled by his good looks, Miriam smiled. "I'm sorry, but no. She's not here. She's at her sister's." She frowned. "Are you a friend of hers?"

"Yes, I am." Jordan smiled pleasantly. "She's expecting me. I've come all the way from Baltimore to see her."

She frowned. "You might like to wait here for her . . . unless you'd like to go to her sister's. Dr. Dempsey has just been summoned to the Traherns. Rachel cut herself with a kitchen knife."

The man turned white. "Good God," he said. "Will you tell me how to get there?"

Miriam nodded and gave him directions. "Tell her I was asking about her," she told him.

Jordan Sinclair nodded and left the infirmary. Within minutes, he was heading toward the trading post in a wagon he'd borrowed from a mission resident.

Black Hawk arrived at the infirmary by mid-afternoon. He hesitated before entering the waiting area. He frowned. Where was everyone? Where were Dr. Dempsey and Rachel?

"Hel-lo!" he called. "Is anyone here?"

"May I help you?" A young woman came out of the sickroom. Her eyes brightened when she saw him. "Black Hawk!"

"*Aaniin,* Miriam. I have come to see Tree-That-Will-Not-Bend."

"Amelia is not here, Black Hawk. Dr. Dempsey and Rachel aren't here either. They're all at the Traherns. It seems Rachel's had an accident."

"An accident?" His blood froze.

"She's hurt herself with a kitchen knife. Daniel came for the doctor a little while ago."

"Rach-el is hurt?"

"I'm afraid so," she said. "I don't know how badly, but Daniel seemed upset. You may want to go there."

"*Miigwech,*" he said.

As Black Hawk ran down the road that led to the trading post, his thoughts raced with concern for Rachel. She was still here. Where was Jordan?

*I must see her,* he thought. He wanted to see Daniel's wife, and he needed to see Rachel.

He'd tried without success to forget her. His dreams, his thoughts, were filled with her image. He had to see her now that he knew she was here. Why had she come to his village?

Black Hawk came upon a white man stopped along the road. With the recent rain, the land was wet and muddy. He had run his wagon off the road, and was struggling to get the wheels unstuck from the mud.

He halted when he recognized the man who'd been kissing Rachel when Black Hawk had seen her last.

"You!" Jordan called. "Can you help me?"

Black Hawk hurried over to help. "I will push and you pull," he suggested.

Jordan eyed Black Hawk up and down as if he were

someone beneath him. "I thought I'd sit on the wagon and steer."

The Ojibwá brave narrowed his gaze. "I will push and you pull," he repeated.

It looked as if Jordan was going to argue. Black Hawk stared at him. "Pull," the brave said.

With a heavy sigh of resignation, Jordan went to the horse's head. Grabbing the reins, he urged the animal to pull. The wheels of the wagon spun, sending mud flying.

Jordan released the reins and glared at Black Hawk. "This isn't working. Can't you think of anything better? I'm in a hurry."

"Pull," Black Hawk said.

Jordan picked up the reins, and Black Hawk pushed, anger at the man giving him added strength. The wheels spun, but slowly the vehicle started to move.

"It's moving!" Jordan cried.

Black Hawk pushed. "Pull," he ordered.

The wagon rocked, and then was finally free. Jordan had trouble, but finally was able to control the horse.

Jordan stared at Black Hawk with a scowl. "What are you doing on this road?"

"You are Rach-el's friend?"

"You're the second one to ask me that question," Jordan complained. "Yes, yes, I'm her friend. I'm more than her friend."

"How is she?" Black Hawk demanded. "How bad was she hurt?"

The white man narrowed his gaze. "Who are you to ask after Rachel?"

"I, too, am Rachel's friend. My name is Black-Hawk-Who-Hunts-at-Dawn. I am here to see Rachel."

"There's no need for you to see her, Mr. Black Hawk," Jordan said. "I'll see to Rachel." He paused. "She and I are to be married."

Black Hawk tensed. Rachel was going to marry this man. It didn't matter, he thought. He still wanted to see her. "I will see her. I will see her sister."

"Amelia?" Jordan asked, as if he knew Rachel's sister well.

"Yes, Amelia."

"Oh," he said. "You want to see both sisters. Well, I suppose I can't stop you from going. But I must insist you stay outside until I'm sure Rachel is well enough to see you."

The man gestured toward the wagon. "Climb on, Mr. Hawk. You helped me get this horrible conveyance unstuck from the mud. You might as well ride in it."

A muscle twitched along Black Hawk's jaw, but he climbed up in the vehicle, anxious to get to Rachel.

The man chattered annoyingly during the short trip to the trading post. Black Hawk hopped off the vehicle before it had stopped.

"Wait," Jordan said. "I said I will see her first!"

Although he wanted to ignore the man and go inside, he waited while Jordan climbed the porch steps and then disappeared inside the cabin.

The door to the smithy next door opened and his friend Daniel came out of the building. "Black Hawk!" He regarded the brave with a thin veil of hostility.

Puzzled by his friend's behavior, Black Hawk approached. "How is Rach-el? How is Tree-That-Will-Not-Bend?" he asked.

"Amelia is fine. The babe will be fine if my wife rests like she should. Rachel was doing Amelia's chores, but she's injured herself."

Black Hawk stared at the house, waiting for some sign that he could enter and see the woman he loved. "How bad is Rachel hurt?"

"Her father is with her now. She has a nasty cut, but I'm sure she'll be fine. John stitched the wound."

Black Hawk closed his eyes as relief made him weak. "This is good."

"Why are you here, Black Hawk?"

The brave looked at his friend. "What is wrong? Why are you angry?"

"Why am I angry? I'll tell you why in one word. Rachel."

Black Hawk stared at his good friend. "Rach-el."

Daniel nodded. "You've hurt her," he snarled. "You touched her!"

"I love her," Black Hawk said softly.

"You should've—" Daniel halted. *"You what?"*

"I love her."

"You love her," Daniel echoed. He looked confused. "I see." He scowled. "No, I don't see, Black Hawk! Tell me again why you're here."

"I love her. I must see her."

"And if she doesn't want to see you?" Daniel asked.

"Then I will leave here. I will not bother her again."

Daniel saw his friend's pain and responded. "Black Hawk—"

A loud shuffling sound from the direction of the cabin porch drew both men's attention.

"I told you to get out!" a feminine voice cried.

"Hold on here!" a male voice answered. "I just want to talk with her."

Black Hawk's eyes widened as he saw Amelia Trahern dragging the white man out of the house with a firm grip on his ear.

"Get out, Jordan Sinclair!" she scolded. "Go away and don't come back. Rachel doesn't love you. She loves—"

Amelia stopped and turned suddenly to stare at the Ojibwa brave. "Black Hawk!" she whispered.

Jordan jerked free. "Just let me talk with her," he pleaded. "I made a mistake and I'm sorry. I must tell her I'm sorry. She loves me. I know she does. Just let me talk to her."

Hearing the commotion from inside the house, Rachel rose from the sofa, where she'd been resting.

She heard Jordan and Amelia arguing as she crossed the great room. Her father had stitched her wound, and her hand throbbed with pain.

Rachel had almost reached the door when she heard Jordan's pathetic appeal to speak to her. *Go away, Jordan! Amelia's right. I don't love you. Go away!*

She felt weak and dizzy as she grabbed the door frame and clung. "Jordan!" she gasped.

The young man looked up with relief. "Rachel! Please, I need to talk with you. Please tell your sister to let me inside."

"Go away," Rachel said. She closed her eyes and clutched wood and her mind reeled. "I don't want to see you again. I don't want to hear your voice. I want you to leave me alone."

Jordan placed a foot on the bottom porch step. "I know I behaved badly."

She issued a short bark of laughter. "Badly?" she said. "That's an understatement, Jordan. You were a cad, and I hate cads. So, please just leave me alone." Her knuckles whitened as she held on.

"I apologized, didn't I?" he whined. "Why won't you forgive me?"

She raised her eyebrows. "You want my forgiveness."

He nodded.

"Fine," she said. "I forgive you." She sighed. "Now go away." Feeling sick, she started to turn.

"Rachel!"

"I don't love you Jordan," she said without looking

back. "I love Black Hawk." She started back across the room toward the sofa.

"An Indian!" he cried as he climbed the porch steps.

Rachel spun back to him in her fury and nearly fell. She caught the edge of the dining table to steady herself.

"He's more of a man than you'll ever be!" she cried.

Stunned by the scene that was rapidly taking place, Black Hawk started toward the house. A hand stopped him on his arm.

"Wait, Black Hawk," Daniel said softly.

Black Hawk gazed at his friend, then glared at Jordan. His muscles coiled, ready to strike, as the things Jordan was saying increasingly angered him.

As he stared at the house, he saw Rachel at the door, ordering Jordan to back away. The white man stepped back, but only as far as the top porch step.

Jordan got ugly then, abusing Rachel with words, and Black Hawk sprang forward to attack.

"No, Black Hawk," Daniel said, grabbing the brave's arm. "He's mine!"

Before Black Hawk could react, Daniel was at the man's side, dragging Jordan down the porch steps.

"Daniel, be careful!" Amelia cried as Daniel raised his fist and took the first swing.

Jordan stepped back and threw up his hands. He attempted to hit back, but Daniel caught hold of his wrists and stopped him.

Suddenly, John Dempsey appeared from the trading post across the street. "Let me!" he cried, and he hurried to reach his daughter's former fiancé.

Daniel, seeing his father-in-law, stepped back and allowed John to grab Jordan by the collar and give him a lecture while he shook the man silly.

Jordan was disheveled, dirty—and bruised where Daniel had managed to get in one good punch.

It wasn't long before John released Jordan, who scurried away, cursing. He'd admitted he had no hope of getting Rachel back.

John Dempsey and Daniel looked at each other and exchanged grins.

Black Hawk stared at the house, searching for a glimpse of Rachel. He'd wanted to fight Jordan, but the doctor and Daniel had had things well under control.

While the two men congratulated themselves for ridding Rachel of a problem, Amelia spied Black Hawk and waved him inside.

Black Hawk hesitated before climbing to the porch and entering the house. He looked at Amelia. Rachel's sister gave him an encouraging smile.

"You heard her say it," she said. "She loves you. Isn't it time you told her the same?"

He nodded. Rachel loved him, he thought. He grinned at Amelia and stepped inside.

The interior of the cabin seemed dark after the bright outside light. Black Hawk waited a moment for his eyes to adjust before he searched for Rachel. He didn't see her at first. Then, he saw movement and spied her lying on the sofa across the room, her lovely chestnut hair spread about the seat cushions, her face pale. He stared for a moment at her bandaged hand, until his concern for her pulled him forward. She had her eyes closed, but he was sure she was not asleep.

"Rach-el," he said in a quiet voice.

He thought he heard her gasp before she sat up and looked back.

His heart started to pound. He saw surprise . . . love . . . and gladness, until she quickly masked her expression to protect her private thoughts.

He clung to the memory of her loving look. Encouraged,

Black Hawk approached the sofa and crouched near Rachel's side. He looked up to meet her gaze.

"I thought you had gone," he said. "I thought you had gone with Jordan."

"You did?" Her mouth suddenly went dry as Rachel stared at the man she loved. She could hear the wild pounding of her heart.

"I thought you had married him. I thought you had gone back to Baltimore." He seemed to hesitate before he spoke again. "You do not love him," he said, his eyes burning brightly.

Her senses began to hum as the blood began to flow hotly through her veins. "Jordan?" At his nod, she shook her head. "No, I don't love Jordan." *I love you.*

"I am glad." Black Hawk smiled and rose. He held out his hand, and she took it. He gazed at her with a smile as he gently helped her to stand. "I love you, Rachel Dempsey. If you can forgive this man, I would be most honored to take you as wife."

Rachel had to swallow against a lump. "You love me?" Her eyes filled with tears when he nodded. "You want to marry me?"

"Yes."

Rachel couldn't believe it. Black Hawk was here, and he loved her!

"I want to marry you." He caressed her cheek. "I wish to give you children."

Her tears escaped to trickle down her cheeks. "Oh, Black Hawk," she sobbed.

He frowned. "Why do you cry? You do not want me for husband?"

She closed her eyes. "Yes, yes, of course I do." She sniffed. "I am crying because I'm happy."

His features brightened. "Then you forgive this man?"

She opened her eyes. "Forgive you?" she asked. "For what?"

"For leaving when I should have stayed." He wore a scowl as he released her. Then he pulled her into his arms. "For putting vengeance before love."

She drew back to cradle his face with her hands. "You didn't kill He-Who-Kills-with-Big-Stick," she said. Rachel smiled. "Spring Blossom told me," she explained when he looked surprised.

"I wanted you more than vengeance," he said. "I want you more than anything on this earth."

"Oh, Black Hawk . . ." She felt weepy as she leaned forward and kissed him.

She withdrew and gazed into his eyes. He seemed troubled. "What's wrong?" she asked, afraid.

"Even now, this man has anger."

She felt a jolt. With her? she wondered. With his father's murderer? Would he ever be free of his pain? "I see."

"No," he said as he cupped her shoulders with his hands. "My anger is not with you or He-Who-Kills-with-Big-Stick." His smile was grim. "It is with the white man Jordan. I did not hit him, and I wish to strike him for hurting you."

Rachel's eyes widened. She saw the amused resignation in his expression as he looked longingly in the direction Jordan had gone. She grinned. He was all she wanted and more.

"Too much anger to love?" she whispered.

His eyes twinkled. "My anger is not in my heart. There is only love in my heart, Rach-el . . . my love for you."

"Oh, Black Hawk . . ."

He pulled her into his arms. When he kissed her, Rachel's world spun, then leveled itself.

"You will be happy in my village?" he asked with concern.

She raised on her toes to initiate another kiss. "Oh, yes," she gasped before she kissed him a second time.

Rachel pulled back to compose herself. "Yes, Black Hawk," she said, "I will be happy in your village . . . I'll be happy anywhere . . . as long as you're there by my side."

# Epilogue

The sound of a baby's wail broke the stillness of the forest. Cries of joy resounded about the Ojibwa village. Ripple-on-the-Water had given birth to a son.

John Dempsey left the wigwam where Rachel and the babe rested. "Black Hawk, you may go in now." He smiled. "Mother and babe are doing fine." The doctor appeared happy with his new grandchild as he joined his friends and family, including his visiting sister Bess, where they waited in the village clearing.

Trembling, Black Hawk entered the wigwam. He was anxious to see his wife and child. His gaze fastened on Rachel first. His heart gave a jolt. She lay on her sleeping pallet with her eyes closed, looking tired and pale, but so beautiful that she stole his breath.

As if sensing his presence, she opened her eyes. "Black Hawk," she whispered, and held out her hand to him.

He went to her without hesitation. "Have you seen our

son?'' she asked as she captured his hand. She kissed his fingers.

He shook his head. She smiled and gestured toward a cradle that sat on the other side of her bed. Black Hawk skirted the sleeping platform to view his son.

The child was pink, perfect, and had a smattering of dark hair. Black Hawk reached to lift the infant. "He is a fine son," he said in a choked voice.

"I love you," Rachel said softly. There was a smile on her lips and love in her eyes for him and their newborn son. "I love you, Black Hawk, and I love our baby."

He didn't answer her as he returned his son to the cradle. Then he sat on the edge of Rachel's sleeping pallet.

"I love you, Ripple-on-the-Water," he said. His voice was husky with emotion as he'd seen her tears. Overwhelmed with love for this woman, Black Hawk bent and kissed her.

*"Kisakeen,"* he whispered. *"I love you."*

And she smiled.

And life was perfect for them.

# ABOUT THE AUTHOR

Candace McCarthy lives in Delaware with her family. She is the author of several Zebra historical romances, including *White Bear's Woman, Irish Linen,* and *Heaven's Fire.* Her last book, *Sweet Possession,* is the tale of other characters in *Wild Innocence,* Rachel Dempsey's sister Amelia and Daniel Trahern.

Candace enjoys hearing from her readers. You may write to her at P.O. Box 58, Magnolia, Delaware 19962. She also has a Web site on the Internet:

http://members.aol.com/candacelmc/index.htm

# <u>BOOK YOUR PLACE ON OUR WEBSITE</u><br><u>AND MAKE THE</u><br><u>READING CONNECTION!</u>

We've created a customized website just for our very special readers, where you can get the inside scoop on everything that's going on with Zebra, Pinnacle and Kensington books.

When you come online, you'll have the exciting opportunity to:

- View covers of upcoming books
- Read sample chapters
- Learn about our future publishing schedule (listed by publication month *and author*)
- Find out when your favorite authors will be visiting a city near you
- Search for and order backlist books from our online catalog
- Check out author bios and background information
- Send e-mail to your favorite authors
- Meet the Kensington staff online
- Join us in weekly chats with authors, readers and other guests
- Get writing guidelines
- AND MUCH MORE!

**Visit our website at<br>http://www.zebrabooks.com**

# Put a Little Romance in Your Life With
# Janelle Taylor

# Enjoy *Savage Destiny*
## A Romantic Series from
# Rosanne Bittner

__#1: **Sweet Prairie Passion**         $5.99US/$6.99CAN
      0-8217-5342-8

__#2: **Ride the Free Wind Passion**   $5.99US/$6.99CAN
      0-8217-5343-6

__#3: **River of Love**                $5.99US/$6.99CAN
      0-8217-5344-4

__#4: **Embrace the Wild Land**        $5.99US/$7.50CAN
      0-8217-5413-0

__#7: **Eagle's Song**                 $5.99US/$6.99CAN
      0-8217-5326-6

---

Call toll free **1-888-345-BOOK** to order by phone or use this coupon to order by mail.

Name _____

Address _____

City _____ State _____ Zip _____

Please send me the books I have checked above.

| | |
|---|---|
| I am enclosing | $_____ |
| Plus postage and handling* | $_____ |
| Sales tax (in New York and Tennessee) | $_____ |
| Total amount enclosed | $_____ |

*Add $2.50 for the first book and $.50 for each additional book.

Send check or money order (no cash or CODs) to:

**Kensington Publishing Corp., 850 Third Avenue, New York, NY 10022**

Prices and Numbers subject to change without notice.

All orders subject to availability.

Check out our website at **www.kensingtonbooks.com**